THE FAMILY

Mario Puzo

The Family

COMPLETED BY CAROL GINO

arrow books

Published in the United Kingdom in 2003 by Arrow Books

7 9 10 8 6

Copyright © 2001 by The Estate of Mario Puzo and Carol Gino
Map by Jackie Aher

Carol Gino has asserted her right under the Copyright, Designs
and Patents Act, 1988 to be identified as the co-author of this work

First published in the United Kingdom by William Heinemann
First published in the USA by HarperCollins Inc., 2001

Arrow Books
The Random House Group Limited
20 Vauxhall Bridge Road, London SW1V 2SA

Random House Australia (Pty) Limited
20 Alfred Street, Milsons Point, Sydney
New South Wales 2061, Australia

Random House New Zealand Limited
18 Poland Road, Glenfield
Auckland 10, New Zealand

Random House (Pty) Limited
Endulini, 5a Jubilee Road, Parktown 2193, South Africa

The Random House Group Limited Reg. No. 954009

www.randomhouse.co.uk

A CIP catalogue record for this book
is available from the British Library

Papers used by Random House are natural, recyclable
products made from wood grown in sustainable forests.
The manufacturing processes conform to the environmental
regulations of the country of origin

ISBN 0 09 946474 8

Printed and bound in Great Britain by
Cox & Wyman Ltd, Reading, Berkshire

Let me be vile and base, only let me kiss the hem of the veil in which my God is shrouded. Though I may be following the devil, I am Thy son, O Lord, and I love Thee, and I feel the joy without which the world cannot stand.

—FYODOR DOSTOYEVSKY,
The Brothers Karamazov

FOR BERT FIELDS

WHO SNATCHED VICTORY
FROM THE JAWS OF DEFEAT
AND WHO COULD BE
THE GREATEST CONSIGLIERE
OF THEM ALL

WITH ADMIRATION
MARIO PUZO

For Bert Fields

Who snatched victory
from the jaws of defeat.
And who could be the
greatest Consaghire of
them all
            with admiration
            Mario Puzo

ITALY
IN THE
15TH CENTURY

Adriatic Sea

PO

Bologna
Imola
ROMAGNA

Faenza
Forlì
Cesena
Pesaro

Pisa

ARNO

Urbino
Senigallia

Florence

THE MARCHES

Siena

Camerino

Perugia
Fermo

Capodimonte
Orvieto
UMBRIA

Bassanello

Soriano

SABINA

Tolfa Nepi
Bracciano

APULIA

PATRIMONY OF ST. PETER

Rome

Ostia

LATIUM

CAMPAGNA

Tyrrhenian Sea

```
0        25        50 miles
0              50 kilometers
```

 THE PAPAL STATES

Mediterranean Sea

PROLOGUE

As the black death swept through Europe, devastating half the population, many citizens in desperation turned their eyes from the Heavens to Earth. There, in order to master the physical world, the more philosophically inclined tried to uncover the secrets of existence and to unravel Life's great mysteries, while the poor hoped only to overcome their suffering.

And so it was that God fell to Earth as Man, and the rigid religious doctrine of the Middle Ages lost its power and was replaced by the study of the great ancient civilizations of Rome, Greece, and Egypt. As the thirst for the Crusades began to fade, Olympian heroes were reborn and Olympian battles were fought anew. Man pitted his mind against the heart of God, and Reason reigned.

This was the time of great accomplishments in philosophy, the arts, medicine, and music. Culture flourished with great pomp and ceremony. But not without cost. Old laws were broken before new ones were created. The shift from the strict adherence to the word of God and the belief in eternal salvation to the honor of Man and reward in the material world called *humanism* was, in truth, a difficult transition.

Then, Rome was not the Holy City; it was a lawless place. In the streets, citizens were robbed, houses were plundered, prostitution was rampant, and hundreds of people were murdered each week.

Moreover, the country we now know as Italy did not yet exist. Instead, there were five great powers: Venice, Milan,

Florence, Naples, and Rome. Within the boundaries of the "boot," there were many independent city-states ruled by old families led by local kings, feudal lords, dukes, or bishops. Inside the country, neighbor fought neighbor for territory. And those who conquered were always on guard—for the next conquest was close at hand.

From outside the country, there came the threat of invasion by foreign powers who wished to expand their empires. The rulers of France and Spain vied for territory, and the "barbarian" Turks, who were not Christians, were moving in on the Papal States.

Church and state wrestled for sovereignty. After the travesty of the Great Schism—when there were two Popes in two cities with divided power and reduced revenue—the formation of the new seat of the throne in Rome, with only one Pope, gave the princes of the church new hope. Emerging even stronger than before, the spiritual leaders of the church had only to fight the temporal power of the kings, queens, and dukes of the small cities and fiefdoms.

Still, the Holy Roman Catholic Church was in turmoil, for the lawless behavior was not limited to citizens only. Cardinals sent their servants armed with stones and crossbows into the streets to fight with Roman youths; men of high position in the church—forbidden to marry—visited courtesans and kept many mistresses; bribes were offered and taken; and official clergy at the highest levels were ready to accept money to deliver dispensations from the laws and write up sacred papal bulls to pardon the most terrible crimes.

It was said by many a disillusioned citizen that everything in Rome was for sale. Enough money could buy churches, priests, pardons, and even the forgiveness of God.

With very few exceptions, men who became priests entered the church because they were second sons—trained from birth for professions in the church. They had no true religious calling, but because the church still held the power to declare a king a king, and to bestow great blessings on earth, every aristocratic Italian family offered gifts and bribes to get its sons named to the college of cardinals.

This was the Renaissance; the time of Cardinal Rodrigo Borgia and his family.

I

1

The golden rays of the summer sun warmed the cobblestone streets of Rome as Cardinal Rodrigo Borgia walked briskly from the Vatican to the three-story stucco house on the Piazza de Merlo where he'd come to claim three of his young children: his sons Cesare and Juan and his daughter Lucrezia, flesh of his flesh, blood of his blood. On this fortuitous day the vice-chancellor to the Pope, the second most powerful man in the Holy Roman Catholic Church, felt especially blessed.

At the house of their mother, Vanozza Cattanei, he found himself whistling happily. As a son of the church he was forbidden to marry, but as a man of God he felt certain that he knew the Good Lord's plan. For did not the Heavenly Father create Eve to complete Adam, even in Paradise? So did it not follow that on this treacherous earth filled with unhappiness, a man needed the comfort of a woman even more? He'd had three previous children when he was a young bishop, but these last children he had sired, those of Vanozza, held a special place in his heart. They seemed to ignite in him the same high passions that she had. And even now, while they were still so young, he envisioned them standing on his shoulders, forming a great giant, helping him to unite the Papal States and extend the Holy Roman Catholic Church far across the world.

Over the years, whenever he had come to visit, the children always called him "Papa," seeing no compromise in his devotion to them and his loyalty to the Holy See. They saw nothing strange about the fact he was a cardinal and their father too. For didn't Pope Innocent's son and daughter often parade through the streets of Rome for celebrations with great ceremony?

Cardinal Rodrigo Borgia had been with his mistress, Vanozza, for more than ten years, and he smiled when he thought how few women had brought him such excitement and kept his interest for so long. Not that Vanozza had been the only woman in his life, for he was a man of large appetites in all worldly pleasures. But she had been by far the most important. She was intelligent, to his eye beautiful—and someone he could talk to about earthly and heavenly matters. She had often given him wise counsel, and in return he had been a generous lover and a doting father to their children.

Vanozza stood in the doorway of her house and smiled bravely as she waved good-bye to her three children.

One of her great strengths now that she had reached her fortieth year was that she understood the man who wore the robes of the cardinal. She knew he had a burning ambition, a fire that flamed in his belly that would not be extinguished. He also had a military strategy for the Holy Catholic Church that would expand its reach, political alliances that would strengthen it, and promises of treaties that would cement his position as well as his power. He had talked to her about all these things. Ideas marched across his mind as relentlessly as his armies would march through new territories. He was destined to become one of the greatest leaders of men, and with his rise would come her children's. Vanozza tried to comfort herself with the knowledge that one day, as the cardinal's legitimate heirs, they would have wealth, power, and opportunity. And so she could let them go.

Now she held tight to her infant son, Jofre, her only remaining child—too young to take from her, for he was still at the breast. Yet he too must go before long. Her dark eyes were shiny with tears as she watched her other children walk away. Only once did Lucrezia look back, but the boys never turned around.

Vanozza saw the handsome, imposing figure of the cardinal reach for the small hand of his younger son, Juan, and the tiny hand of his three-year-old daughter, Lucrezia. Their eldest son, Cesare, left out, already looked upset. That meant trouble, she thought, but in time Rodrigo would know them as well as she did. Hesitantly, she closed the heavy wooden front door.

They had taken only a few steps when Cesare, angry now, pushed his brother so hard that Juan, losing his grip on his father's hand, stumbled and almost fell to the ground. The cardinal stopped the small boy's fall, then turned and said, "Cesare, my son, could you not ask for what you want, rather than pushing your brother?"

Juan, a year younger but much more slightly built than the seven-year-old Cesare, snickered proudly at his father's defense. But before he could bask in his satisfaction, Cesare moved closer and stomped hard upon his foot.

Juan cried out in pain.

The cardinal grabbed Cesare by the back of his shirt with one of his large hands—lifting him off the cobblestone street—and shook him so hard that his auburn curls tumbled across his face. Then he stood the child on his feet again. Kneeling in front of the small boy, his brown eyes softened. He asked, "What is it, Cesare? What has displeased you so?"

The boy's eyes, darker and more penetrating, glowed like coals as he stared at his father. "I hate him, Papa," he said in an impassioned voice. "You choose him always . . ."

"Now, now, Cesare," the cardinal said, amused. "The strength of a family, like the strength of an army, is in its loyalty to each other. Besides, it's a mortal sin to hate one's own brother, and there is no reason to endanger your immortal soul over such emotions." He stood now, towering over them. Then he smiled as he patted his portly belly. "There is certainly enough of me for all of you . . . is there not?"

Rodrigo Borgia was a mountainous man, tall enough to

carry his weight, handsome in a rugged rather than aristocratic way. His dark eyes often glimmered with amusement;
his nose, though large, was not offensive looking; and his
full sensual lips, usually smiling, gave him a generous appearance. But it was his personal magnetism, the intangible
energy he radiated, that made everyone agree he was one of
the most attractive men of his time.

"Chez, you can have my place," his daughter now said to
Cesare, in a voice so clear that the cardinal turned toward
her with fascination. Lucrezia, standing with arms folded in
front of her, her long blond ringlets hanging down over her
shoulders, wore an expression of hard determination on her
angelic face.

"You do not wish to hold your papa's hand?" the cardinal
asked, pretending a pout.

"It does not make me cry not to hold your hand," she said.
"And it does not make me angry."

"Crezia," Cesare said with real affection, "don't be a don-
key. Juan is just being a baby; he is most capable on his
own." He stared with distaste at his brother, who was
quickly drying his tears with the smooth silk of his shirt
sleeve.

The cardinal tousled Juan's dark hair and reassured him.
"Stop weeping. You may take my hand." He turned to Cesare and said, "And my small warrior, you may take the
other." Then he looked at Lucrezia and gave her a broad
smile. "And you, my sweet child? What shall your papa do
with you?"

When the child's expression remained unchanged and she
showed no emotion, the cardinal was enchanted. He smiled
with appreciation. "You are truly Papa's girl, and as a reward
for your generosity and bravery, you may sit in the single
place of honor."

Rodrigo Borgia reached down and quickly lifted the
small girl high into the air to place her on his shoulders.
And he laughed with pure joy. Now, as he walked with his
elegant garments flowing gracefully, his daughter looked

like another new and beautiful crown on the head of the cardinal.

That same day, Rodrigo Borgia moved his children into the Orsini Palace, across from his own at the Vatican. His widowed cousin, Adriana Orsini, cared for them and acted as governess, taking charge of their education. When Adriana's young son, Orso, became engaged at thirteen, his fiancée, Julia Farnese, fifteen, moved into the palace to help Adriana care for the children.

Though the cardinal had the day-to-day responsibility of his children, they still visited their mother, who was now married to her third husband, Carlo Canale. As Rodrigo Borgia had chosen Vanozza's two former husbands, he had chosen Canale, knowing a widow must have a husband to offer her protection and the reputation of a respectable house. The cardinal had been good to her, and what she hadn't received from him, she had inherited from her two previous husbands. Unlike the beautiful but empty-headed courtesans of some of the aristocracy, Vanozza was a practical woman, which Rodrigo admired. She owned several well-kept inns and a country estate, which provided her with a significant income—and being a pious woman, she had built a chapel dedicated to the Madonna, in which she said her daily prayers.

Still, after ten years, their passion for each other seemed to cool and they became good friends.

Within weeks, Vanozza was forced to relinquish the baby, Jofre, to join his brothers and sister, for he had become inconsolable without them. And so it was that all of Rodrigo Borgia's children were together under his cousin's care.

As befitted the children of a cardinal, over the next few years they were taught by the most talented tutors in Rome. They were schooled in the humanities, astronomy and astrology, ancient history, and several languages including Spanish, French, English, and of course the language of the

church, Latin. Cesare excelled because of his intelligence
and competitive nature, but it was Lucrezia who showed the
most promise, for above everything else, she had character
and true virtue.

Though many young girls were sent to convents to be educated and dedicated to the saints, Lucrezia—with the cardinal's permission, on the advice of Adriana—was dedicated
to the Muses and taught by the same talented tutors as her
brothers. Because she loved the arts, she learned to play the
lute, to dance, and to draw. She excelled in embroidery—on
fabrics of silver and gold.

As was her obligation, Lucrezia developed charms and
talents that would increase her value in the marital alliances
which would serve the Borgia family in the future. One of
her favorite pastimes was writing poetry, and she spent
long hours on verses of love and rapture for God as well as
those of romantic love. She was particularly inspired by the
saints, her heart often too full for words.

Julia Farnese indulged Lucrezia as a younger sister; Adriana and the cardinal both lavished Lucrezia with attention,
and so she grew into a happy child with a pleasant disposition. Curious and easy to get along with, she disliked dishar-
mony and made every effort to help keep the family peace.

One beautiful Sunday, after he had served High Mass at
Saint Peter's Basilica, Cardinal Borgia invited his children to join him at the Vatican. This was a rare and courageous act, for until the time of Pope Innocent all children of
the clergy were proclaimed to be their nephews and nieces.
To openly acknowledge paternity could endanger an important appointment to any high church office. Of course, the
people knew that cardinals and even Popes had children—
everyone knew they sinned—but as long as it was hidden
beneath the mantle of "family" and the truth of the relationship posted only in secret parchments, the honor of the office was not tarnished. Everyone could believe as they

wished, but the cardinal had little patience for hypocrisy. There were times, of course, that he himself was forced to alter or embellish the truth. But that was understandable, for he was after all a diplomat.

Adriana dressed the children in their finest garments for this special occasion: Cesare in black satin and Juan in white silk, and two-year-old Jofre in a blue velvet jumper edged with rich embroidery. Julia dressed Lucrezia in a long peach lace dress, and placed a small jeweled headpiece upon the little girl's white-blond curls.

The cardinal had just finished reading an official document brought to him from Florence by his senior advisor, Duarte Brandao. The document concerned a certain Dominican friar known as Savonarola. It was rumored that he was a prophet, inspired by the Holy Ghost, but far more dangerous to the purposes of the cardinal, every ordinary citizen of Florence rushed to hear Savonarola's sermons and responded with great fervor. He was an acclaimed visionary and an eloquent preacher whose fiery speeches often raged against the carnal and financial excesses of the papacy in Rome.

"We must keep an eye on this simple friar," Rodrigo Borgia said. "For great dynasties have often been brought down by simple men who believe they have a holy truth."

Brandao was tall and thin, with long black hair and elegant features. He appeared gentle and amiable, yet it was rumored about Rome that no one could match his wrath when faced with disloyalty or insolence. Everyone agreed that only a fool would dare to make an enemy of him. Now, Duarte brushed his mustache with his index finger as he considered the implications of what Rodrigo Borgia had just told him.

Duarte told the cardinal, "There is word that the friar also attacks the Medici from the pulpit, and the citizens of Florence cheer."

When the children entered Rodrigo Borgia's private chambers, the conversation halted. Duarte Brandao greeted them with a smile, then stood aside.

Lucrezia rushed into the cardinal's arms with excitement, but the boys stood back, their hands behind them. "Come, my sons," Rodrigo said, still holding his daughter in his arms. "Come and give Papa a kiss." He waved them toward him with a warm and welcoming smile.

Cesare reached his father first. Rodrigo Borgia lowered Lucrezia onto the small golden stool at his feet, and embraced his son. He was a strong boy, tall and muscular. The father liked the feel of this son; it reassured him about his own future. Rodrigo loosened his hold on the boy and then held him at arm's length so he could look at him. "Cesare," he said, fondly, "I say a prayer of thanks to Our Blessed Madonna each day, for you gladden my heart each time I behold you." Cesare smiled happily, pleased at his father's approval.

Then Cesare moved aside to make way for Juan. It may have been the speed of the younger boy's heart or its frantic beating against his own chest, it may have been the quickness of his breath, signaling his nervousness, but some part of Rodrigo responded to Juan's frailty. And when the cardinal embraced this son, he hugged him more gently but held onto him a little longer.

Usually, when the cardinal ate alone in his chambers, he ate sparsely, only bread, fruit, and cheese. But on this day he had instructed his servants to provide a table filled to excess with pasta and poultry, oxen with special sweetmeats, and round mounds of candied chestnuts.

As the children, Adriana and her son Orso, and the beautiful and charming Julia Farnese sat around the table laughing and chattering, Rodrigo Borgia felt like a fortunate man. Surrounded by family and friends, life on this earth was good. Silently he said a prayer of gratitude. When his manservant poured the blood-red wine into his silver goblet, he was filled with goodwill. And so, in a gesture of affection, he offered the first sip to his son Juan, who was seated next to him.

But Juan tasted the wine and made a face. "It's too bitter, Papa," he said. "I don't like it."

Rodrigo Borgia, always alert, suddenly froze with fear. This was a sweet wine; there should be no bitterness . . .

Almost immediately the child complained of feeling sick, and doubled over with stomach pains. Both his father and Adriana tried to reassure him, but only moments later Juan began to vomit violently. The cardinal lifted the boy from his seat, carried him into an anteroom, and placed him on the brocade couch.

The Vatican physician was called immediately, but before he could make his way to the chambers Juan had lost consciousness.

"Poison," the physician declared, after examining the child.

Juan was white as death and already feverish, a thin stream of black bile running from his lips. He looked quite small and helpless.

Now Rodrigo Borgia lost his holy composure. He became furious. "A poison meant for me . . ." he said.

Duarte Brandao, who had been standing by, now drew his sword, alert and watchful for any further attempts to harm the cardinal or his family.

The cardinal turned to him. "There is an enemy inside the palace. Gather everyone together in the Main Chamber. Pour them each a goblet of wine and insist that they drink it. Then bring me the one who refuses."

Adriana, concerned, whispered, "My dear cousin, Your Worthiness, I understand your grief, but in this way you will lose your most trusted servants, for many will become sick and some will die . . ."

Rodrigo turned to her. "I will not offer them the wine that was offered my poor innocent son. The wine they are offered will be pure. But only the sinner will refuse to drink, for his fear will choke him before he lifts the cup to his lips."

Duarte left at once to carry out the cardinal's orders.

Juan lay still as stone, pale as death. Adriana, Julia, and

Lucrezia sat at his side, wiping his forehead with wet cloths and healing ointments.

Cardinal Rodrigo Borgia lifted his son's small limp hand and kissed it; then he walked to his private chapel and knelt before the statue of the Madonna to pray. He reasoned with her, for he knew she understood the loss of a son and the pain it caused. And he vowed, "I will do everything in my power, everything humanly possible, to bring the immortal souls of thousands to the one true church. Your church, Holy Mother. I will see to it that they worship your son, if only you will spare the life of mine . . ."

Young Cesare was standing in the doorway to the chapel, and when the cardinal turned to see him there, he had tears in his eyes. "Come, Cesare. Come, my son. Pray for your brother," the cardinal said. And Cesare went to kneel beside his father.

Back in the cardinal's chambers, everyone sat in silence until Duarte came back to announce, "The culprit has been discovered. He is but a kitchen boy, formerly in the employ of the House of Rimini."

Rimini was a small feudal province on the eastern coast of Italy, and its ruler, a local duke, Gaspare Malatesta, was a formidable enemy of Rome and the papacy. He was a big man, his body huge enough to hold the souls of two, and his massive face was pitted and craggy, but it was for his hair, crinkled wild and red, that he was known as "The Lion."

Cardinal Borgia moved away from the side of his ailing son, and whispered to Duarte, "Ask the kitchen boy why he holds His Holiness in such contempt. Then be certain he drinks the bottle of wine from our table. Be certain he drinks it all."

Duarte nodded. "And what would you have us do with him once the wine has taken effect?" he asked.

The cardinal, his eyes glowing, his face flushed, said, "Place him on an ass, tether him tight, and send him with a message to the Lion of Rimini. Tell him to begin to pray for forgiveness and make his peace with God."

Juan lay as though in a deep sleep for several weeks, and the cardinal insisted he stay at his palace in the Vatican to be treated by his personal physician. While Adriana sat by his side, and several maidservants cared for him, Rodrigo Borgia spent hours in the chapel praying to the Madonna. "I will bring to the one true church the souls of thousands," he promised fervently. "If only you will plead with the Christ to spare the life of my son."

When his prayers were answered, and Juan recovered, the cardinal became even more committed to the Holy Catholic Church and to his family.

But Rodrigo Borgia knew that heaven alone could no longer secure his family's safety. And so he understood there was one more action to be taken: he must send to Spain for Miguel Corello, also known as Don Michelotto.

This bastard nephew of Cardinal Rodrigo Borgia had felt the tug of fate from his beginnings. As a child in Valencia he was neither mean nor sadistic, yet he often found himself defending those souls whose goodness made them vulnerable to the bullying nature of others. For often, kindness is mistaken for weakness.

Miguel, from the time he was a child, accepted his destiny: to protect those who carried the torch of God and the Holy Roman Church into the world.

But Miguel was a strong boy, and as ferocious in his loyalty as in his actions. As a burly teenager it was said that he had been attacked by the most savage bandit in his village when he stood to defend the house of his mother, the cardinal's sister.

Miguel was but sixteen at the time, when the bandit leader and several young vandals entered their house and tried to move the boy away from the wooden chest in which his mother's precious holy relics and family linens were hidden. When Miguel, who seldom spoke, cursed the bandits and refused to move away, the leader slashed his face with a stiletto, cutting across his mouth deep into his cheek. As blood ran in great streams down his face and onto his chest, his mother screamed, his sister began to cry in loud sobs— but Miguel stood fast.

Finally, as neighbors gathered in the streets and began shouting, the bandit and his gang, fearing capture, ran out of the village and into the hills.

Several days later, when this same pack of bandits tried to reenter the village, they were met with resistance; and while most fled, the leader of the pack was captured by Miguel. In the morning this unfortunate bandit was found with a heavy rope around his neck, hanging from a large tree in the village square.

From that day forward, Miguel Corello's reputation for fierceness spread throughout the principality of Valencia, and no one dared do injury to him or any of his friends or family for fear of retaliation. His face healed, though it scarred so that his mouth was set in a constant grimace; but no other damage had been done. Though on any other man this sneer would be a frightening sight, Miguel's reputation for fairness, and the look of mercy that radiated from his golden brown eyes, made everyone who saw him recognize his good soul. It was then that the villagers fondly began to call him Don Michelotto, and he became well known as a man to be respected.

Cardinal Rodrigo Borgia reasoned that in each family some must stand forward in the light and preach the word of God. Yet behind them must be others, to provide safety and ensure them success in their holy endeavors. Those who sat on the throne of the church could not defend themselves from the evil of others without the help of a human hand, for this was the nature of the world in which they lived.

That young Don Michelotto had been called upon to play

the role of the evildoer did not surprise either of them, for he was a superior man. His love of, and loyalty to, both the Heavenly Father and the Holy See was never in question, no matter the slurs to his character whispered by his enemies. For Rodrigo Borgia had no doubt that Don Michelotto would always surrender his will to that of the Heavenly Father and willingly act on the commands of the Holy Mother Church.

And as the cardinal believed that his actions were guided by divine inspiration, so Don Michelotto believed that his hands were guided by the same heavenly force, and so there was no question of sin. For each time he stopped the breath of an enemy of the cardinal or the church, was he not just returning those souls home to the judgment of the Heavenly Father?

And so it was, shortly after Juan's recovery, that Rodrigo Borgia, who had grown up in Valencia and knew the blood that coursed through the heart of this Spaniard, called his nephew to Rome. Aware of the dangers in this foreign land, he now entrusted twenty-one-year-old Don Michelotto with the well-being of his family. And as the cardinal's children grew older, they seldom turned without finding the shadow of Don Michelotto behind them.

Now, whenever the cardinal was in Rome and his duties as vice-chancellor didn't force him away, he visited his children daily to talk and play with them, Don Michelotto often at his side. And at the first opportunity, he fled the fetid choking summer heat of Rome, with its narrow crowded streets, to take them to his magnificent retreat in the rich green countryside.

2

Hidden in the foothills of the Apennines, a day's ride from Rome, was a vast tract of land with a magnificent forest of cedar and pine surrounding a small clear lake. Rodrigo Borgia had acquired it as a gift from his uncle, Pope Calixtus III, and over the past few years he had built it into an opulent country retreat for himself and his family.

This was Silverlake, a magical place. Filled with the sounds of nature and the colors of creation, it was to him an earthly paradise. At dawn and again at dusk, when the blue had gone from the sky, the surface of the lake turned a silvery gray. From the first moment he laid eyes upon it, the cardinal was enchanted. And his hope was that he and his children would spend their happiest moments there.

During the hot lemon-colored days of summer, the children swam in the lake to cool themselves and then ran wild in the lush green fields while the cardinal strolled through the fragrant citrus groves, golden prayer beads in hand. During those peaceful times, he marveled at the beauty of life, and especially at the beauty of *his* life. Certainly he had worked hard, was painstaking in his attention to detail from the time he was a young bishop, but how much did that determine one's good fortune? For how many poor souls labored yet were not rewarded on earth by the heavens? Gratitude filled his heart, and the cardinal looked up at the clear blue skies to say a prayer and beg a blessing. For beneath the surface of his faith, after all these years of grace, there remained the hidden terror that for such a life as his, a man must one day pay a steep price. There was no question that the abundance of God was freely given, but to be worthy to lead souls to the Holy Church, the sincerity of a man's soul must be tested. For how else would the Heavenly Father judge the man worthy? The cardinal hoped to prove equal to this challenge.

One evening, after he and his children ate a sumptuous meal seated by the lake, he provided for them an extravagant display of fireworks. Rodrigo held the baby, Jofre, in his arms, and Juan hung tight to his father's robes.

Silver stars lit the skies in huge luminescent arcs and sparkling cascades of gay color. Cesare held his sister's hand and felt her tremble and cry out at the sound of gunpowder, as great bursts of light lit the sky above them.

But when the cardinal saw his daughter's fear, he handed the baby to Cesare, and reached down to take Lucrezia in his arms. "Papa will hold you," he said. "Papa will keep you safe."

Cesare stood close to his father, holding baby Jofre now, and listened to the cardinal explain with grand gestures and great eloquence the constellation of stars. He found the sound of his father's voice so great a comfort that even then he knew this time at Silverlake was a time he would always treasure. For on that night he was the happiest child in the world; and, suddenly, he felt all things were possible.

Cardinal Rodrigo Borgia enjoyed everything he did. He was one of those rare men of such high spirits that he drew everyone around him into the vortex of his enthusiasm. As his children grew older and their knowledge became more sophisticated, he discussed religion, politics, and philosophy with them in great detail, spending long hours discoursing to both Cesare and Juan in the art of diplomacy and the value of religious and political strategy. Though Cesare enjoyed these intellectual pursuits, Juan was often bored. Due to the cardinal's previous fright, he indulged Juan to such a degree that it became a disadvantage, for the boy grew surly and spoiled. But it was his son Cesare in whom he placed his greatest hope, and his expectations of this son were high indeed.

Rodrigo enjoyed his visits to the Orsini Palace, for both his cousin Adriana and young Julia admired him and paid him much attention. Julia was growing into quite a beautiful woman, her hair more golden than Lucrezia's, reaching almost to the floor. With her wide blue eyes and full lips, it seemed fitting that she was referred to as *La Bella* throughout Rome. The cardinal began to feel a certain fondness for her.

Julia Farnese had come from minor nobility, and had brought a dowry of three hundred florins with her—quite a sum—for her betrothal to Orsini, who was a few years younger than she was. Though Rodrigo's children were always very happy to see him, Julia too began to look forward to his visits. His appearance brought a flush to her cheeks, as it did to most of the women he'd met in his life. And often after she'd helped Lucrezia wash her hair and dress in her finest outfits to greet her father, Julia herself made a special effort to appear her most attractive. Rodrigo Borgia, despite the difference in their ages, was charmed by this young woman.

When it was time for the official ceremony of the civil marriage of his godson, Orso, and Julia Farnese, respect for his cousin Adriana and affection for the young bride inspired him to offer to preside over the ceremony of their marriage in the Star Chamber of his own palace.

On that day, young Julia, dressed in a white satin bridal gown with a silver seed-pearl veil draped over her sweet face, seemed to him transformed from a mere child to the most beautiful woman he had ever seen. So fresh, so full of life, that the cardinal had to restrain his own passion.

It was not long before young Orso was sent to the cardinal's country retreat in Bassanello, with his advisors, and placed in training to become a leader of soldiers. As for Julia

Farnese, she willingly found herself first in the cardinal's arms, and then in his bed.

When Cesare and Juan reached their teens, both were sent away to begin to fulfill their destinies. Juan struggled with his lessons, and the cardinal reasoned that the life of a priest or a scholar was not this son's future. Instead, he would be a soldier. But Cesare's startling intelligence drove him on to school in Perugia. After two years of mastering his subjects there, for which he had a talent, Cesare was sent to the University of Pisa to further his study of theology and canon law. The cardinal hoped that Cesare would follow in his footsteps and rise to great honor in the church.

Though he had done his duty to his three earlier children by courtesans, Rodrigo Borgia focused his future aspirations on the children he'd had with Vanozza. Cesare, Juan, and Lucrezia. He had a much more difficult time establishing a strong connection to his youngest son, Jofre. Then to excuse himself for this lack of fatherly affection, he would attempt to reason. It was then that he would wonder if this youngest boy was his own. For who can truly know what secrets lie hidden in the heart of a woman?

Cardinal Borgia had been vice-chancellor, or papal lawyer, for several Popes. He had served the reigning Pope, Pope Innocent, for eight years, and during that time he had done everything possible to increase the power and legitimacy of the papacy.

But when poor Pope Innocent lay dying, not even fresh mother's milk or transfusions of blood from three young boys could save his life. The boys had been paid one ducat each, but when the medical experiment failed and led to disaster, they were rewarded by elaborate funerals and their families were given forty ducats each.

Unfortunately Pope Innocent had left the papal treasury

empty, and the Holy Church bare to the insults of the Catholic king of Spain and the most Christian king of France. Papal finances were in such disorder that the Holy Father himself had been forced to pawn his miter, or sacred hat, in order to buy palms to distribute on Palm Sunday. Contrary to the advice of Rodrigo Borgia, he had allowed the rulers of Milan, Naples, Venice, Florence, and the other city-states and fiefdoms to delay their tributes to the church treasuries, and he himself had squandered fortunes preparing for Crusades on which no one wished to venture.

Only a mastermind of strategy and finance would be able to restore the Holy Catholic Church to its former glory. But who would that be? Everyone wondered. Yet it was only the sacred college of cardinals, guided by the Holy Ghost and inspired by the divine, that would be left to decide. For a Pope could be no ordinary man, he must be one sent from the heavens.

On August 6, 1492, in the great hall of the Sistine Chapel, with a Swiss Guard, Roman noblemen, and foreign ambassadors to protect them from influence or intruders, the conclave of the college of cardinals began to do the work of electing the new Pope.

According to tradition, once Pope Innocent had died, all the princes of the church, the twenty-three members of the sacred college, gathered to elect the God-man who would serve as the Keeper of the Keys, the successor to Saint Peter, the Holy Vicar of Christ on Earth. He must be not only the spiritual leader of the Holy Roman Catholic Church, but also the earthly leader of the Papal States. As such he must possess enormous intelligence, the ability to lead men and armies, and the talent to negotiate to his advantage with the rulers of the local provinces as well as foreign kings and princes.

The Holy Tiara of the Pope carried with it the prospect of vast riches as well as the responsibility to unify or fragment even further that conglomeration of feudal city-states and provinces that made up the center of the Italian peninsula. And so, even before Pope Innocent had died, deals had been made, properties and titles had been promised, and certain loyalties had been negotiated in order to ensure the election of particular cardinals.

Within the select group of cardinals considered *papable*, there were only a few who were worthy: Cardinal Ascanio Sforza from Milan, Cardinal Cibo of Venice, Cardinal della Rovere of Naples, and Cardinal Borgia of Valencia. But Rodrigo Borgia was a foreigner—his heritage Spanish—and so his chances were slim. Being considered a Catalan was his biggest disadvantage. And though he had changed his name from the Spanish "Borja" to the Italian "Borgia," it gained him no more acceptance from the old established families of Rome.

Still, consideration was given, for he had served the church in a superb manner for more than thirty-five years. As papal lawyer he had negotiated several difficult diplomatic situations to the advantage of the previous Popes, though with each victory for the Vatican he had also increased the riches and benefices of his own family. He had placed many of his relatives in positions of power, and had granted them properties that the older families of Italy felt did not rightfully belong to them. A Spanish Pope? Nonsense. The seat of the Holy See was in Rome, and so it stood to reason that the Pope must be from one of the provinces of Italy.

Now, surrounded by mystery, the conclave began to do God's work. Isolated in individual cells within the huge cold chapel, the cardinals could have no contact with each other or with the outside world. Their decision was to be made individually through prayer and Divine Inspiration, preferably while on their knees in front of the small altars with the hanging crucifix and burning candles as the only adornments. Within those damp, darkened rooms, there was a cot for those who must sleep to renew themselves, a commode for expelling the contents of the stomach, a urinal, a vessel of sugared almonds, marzipan, sweet biscuits, cane sugar, a jug of water, and salt, for provisions. Because there was no central cooking area, food had to be prepared in their own palaces, brought to them in wooden vessels, and passed through a hatch in the door. During this time, each cardinal struggled with his own conscience to determine which man would best serve his family, his province, and the Holy Mother Church. For if one was not careful, one could save one's worldly goods but lose one's immortal soul.

Time could not be wasted, for after one week rations would be cut; then only bread, wine, and water would be brought to the cardinals. For once the Pope had died, chaos reigned. Without a leader, the streets of Rome were in complete disorder. Shops were being looted, castles plundered, hundreds of citizens murdered. And that wasn't all. For as long as there was no head beneath the Holy Tiara, Rome itself was in danger of being conquered.

As the voting began, thousands of citizens gathered in the piazza in front of the chapel. They stood praying aloud, singing hymns and hoping that a new Pope would plead to the heavens to stop the hell in their streets. They waved flags, held banners, and waited for an emissary to come to the balcony to announce their salvation.

The first round lasted three days but no one cardinal received the necessary two-thirds majority. The vote was split between Cardinal Ascanio Sforza of Milan and Cardinal della Rovere of Naples. Each had eight votes. Rodrigo Borgia, with seven votes, was the second choice of most of the college. When the count was complete, and no clear winner emerged, the ballots were ceremoniously burned.

That morning, the crowd in the square watched expectantly as the smoke rose from the chimney to form what appeared to be a dark gray question mark in the clear blue sky over the Sistine Chapel. Seeing it as a sign, they blessed themselves and held up hand-forged crosses of wood to the heavens. When there was no announcement made from the

Vatican, the citizens began to pray more fervently and to chant more loudly.

The cardinals went back to their cells to reconsider.

The second count, two days later, was much the same as the first; no real concessions had been made, and this time when the black smoke rose from the chimney, the praying weakened and singing grew fainter. The piazza was eerie in the darkness, lit by only a few lanterns and flickering street lamps.

Wild rumors swept throughout Rome. Citizens vowed that as the sun rose the following morning there appeared in the sky three identical suns, which the astonished crowd took as a sign that the next Pope would balance the three powers of the papacy: temporal, spiritual, and heavenly. It seemed to them a good omen.

But that night, high up in the tower of Cardinal Giuliano della Rovere's palace where no one was allowed entry, it was said that sixteen torches spontaneously burst into flame—and, as the crowd watched, first with expectation and then with trepidation, all but one of them went out. A bad omen! Which power of the papacy would remain? An eerie silence covered the piazza.

Inside, the conclave was hopelessly deadlocked. Within the chapel the rooms were becoming colder and damper. Many of the older cardinals were beginning to feel the strain. It would be unbearable; how could anyone think properly with running bowels and sore knees?

That night, one by one, some of the cardinals came out of their rooms and stole into the rooms of the others. Renegotiations began; they struck new bargains for sacred possessions and positions. Promises were made. Tempting pledges of riches, of station, of opportunity could be traded for a single vote. Bright new loyalties were forged. But the minds and hearts of men are fickle, and difficulties may indeed arise. For if a man can sell his soul to one devil, can he not to another?

In the square, the crowd had thinned. Many citizens, tired

and discouraged, concerned about their own safety and the security of their houses, left the piazza to return home to their families. So, at six in the morning, when the smoke from the chimney finally turned white and the stones began falling away from the blocked-up windows of the Vatican so the announcement could be made, there were only a few left to hear it.

A cross of benediction was held high above their heads, and a barely distinguishable figure, dressed in fine robes, proclaimed, "With great joy I am here to say, we have a new Pope."

Those who knew about the deadlock wondered which of the two leading cardinals had been elected. Was it Cardinal Ascanio Sforza or Cardinal della Rovere? But then from the window another figure appeared, larger, more imposing, and he let fall from his hands small pieces of paper, thrown like confetti, with scribbled writing which read, "We have as Pope, Cardinal Rodrigo Borgia of Valencia, Pope Alexander VI. We are saved!"

3

When Cardinal Rodrigo Borgia became Pope Alexander VI, he knew the first thing he must do was bring order to the streets of Rome. During the time between the death of Innocent and his coronation, there had been over two hundred murders in the city. As their Holy Father, he knew he must stop this lawlessness; he must make an example of the sinners, for how else could the good souls of the city resume their prayers in peace?

The first assassin was captured and summarily hanged. Not only that, his brother was also hanged. And—in the greatest humiliation for any Roman citizen—his house was razed, burned, and brought down entirely, so that his household was left without shelter.

Within weeks order was restored to the streets of Rome, and the citizens were pleased to have such a strong and wise head beneath the Holy Tiara. The choice of the cardinals was now the choice of the people as well.

But Alexander had other decisions to make. And two most important problems to solve, neither of which was spiritual. Foremost, he had to create an army to establish the Catholic Church as a temporal power and regain control of the Papal States in Italy. Second, he had to establish and fortify the fortunes of his children.

Still, as he sat on his throne in the Hall of Faith in the palace of the Vatican, he pondered on the ways of God, of the world, of nations and families. For was he not God's infallible vicar here on earth? And therefore, was it not his problem to deal with the whole world, the nations and their kings, all the independent cities of Italy, republics, oligarchies? Yes, including the newly discovered Indies? And wasn't it his obligation to give them the finest counsel? Did they or did they not pose a danger to the rule of God?

And his own family, the Borgia, with countless relatives to be taken care of, and his own sons and daughters, sworn to him by blood but uncontrollable because of their own unruly passions—what of them? Where did his primary duty lie? And could his two objectives be accomplished without sacrificing one for the other?

Alexander's duty to God was clear. He must make the church strong. The memory of the Great Schism, seventy-five years before, when there had been two Popes and two churches—both weak—made his resolve stronger.

The cities of Italy that belonged to the church were now ruled by tyrants who thought more of enriching their family coffers than of paying their rent to the Holy Church which sanctified their rule. The kings had used the church as a tool to seek power for themselves. The saving of the immortal souls of humanity was forgotten. Even the wealthy kings of Spain and France withheld their church revenues when they were displeased with the Pope. They dared! What if the Holy Church withdrew its blessing of their rule? For the people who obeyed kings did so because they believed them to be anointed by God, and only the Pope, as the representative of the church and the Vicar of Christ, could confirm that blessing. Alexander knew he must continue to balance out the power of the kings of France and the kings of Spain. The dreaded Great Council, called by kings, must never happen again. The church and the Pope must have worldly power to enforce the will of God. In short, a great army. And so it followed that Alexander carefully considered his power as Pope. And he formed a plan.

Immediately after his coronation, he nominated his son Cesare for cardinal. While still a child, Cesare had been

given benefices by the church and the title of bishop had
been bestowed upon him, with an income of thousands of
ducats. Now, though Cesare was only seventeen years of
age, with all the carnal passions and vices of youth, he was
in body and mind a full-grown man. He had degrees in both
law and theology from the Universities of Perugia and Pisa,
and his disputation was considered one of the most brilliant
student works ever presented. But his great love was the
study of military history and strategy. He had in fact fought
in some minor battles, managing to distinguish himself in
one. He was well trained in the art of war.

Alexander was fortunate. God had blessed this son of his
with a quick wit, a firm purpose, and a natural ferocity, without which one could not survive in this wicked world.

Cesare Borgia received the news that he had been appointed a cardinal of the Holy Roman Catholic Church
while he was still a student of canon law at the University of
Pisa. The appointment was not unexpected, as he was the
son of the new Pope. But Cesare Borgia was not happy
about it. True, it would make him richer, but he was at heart
a soldier; he wished to lead troops into battle, to storm castles and overcome the fortresses of cities. And he wanted to
marry and have children who were not bastards like himself.

His two closest friends and fellow students, Gio Medici
and Tila Baglioni, congratulated him and then began to prepare an evening festival, for Cesare would have to leave the
following week for his investiture in Rome.

Gio had already been appointed cardinal at the age of thirteen, through the power of his father, the ruler of Florence,
the great Lorenzo the Magnificent. Tila Baglioni was the
only one of the three who had no religious office, but he was
one of the heirs to the dukedom of Perugia. Here at the University of Pisa the three were merely high-spirited students;
though they had servants and bodyguards all were well
equipped to guard themselves. Cesare was an accomplished
fighter with sword, ax, and hunting pike, but he did not yet
own full battle armor. He had tremendous physical strength,

and was taller than most men. He was brilliant in his studies, the pride of his mentors. But all of this was to be expected from the son of the Pope.

Gio was a good student, but not imposing physically. He was also witty, but careful of his wit with his two friends. Even at seventeen, Cesare's resolve provoked awe in his friends. Tila Baglioni, on the other hand, was too much of a bully, given to cruel rages when he perceived an offense.

The three celebrated that night at a Medici family villa just outside of Pisa. In consideration of Cesare's newly announced red hat, it was a discreet affair, a small feast with only six courtesans. They had a moderate dinner with mutton, wine, a few sweetmeats, and light and charming conversation.

They went to bed early, for it had been decided that the next day, before returning to their homes—Gio Medici to Florence, and Cesare Borgia to Rome—they would all go to Perugia with Tila Baglioni for a great festive occasion. Tila's first cousin was to be married, and his aunt, the Duchess Atalanta Baglioni, had sent him a special request to attend. Sensing a certain tension in her request, Tila agreed to go.

The next morning, the three set off for Perugia. Cesare rode his finest horse, a gift from Alfonso, the duke of Ferrara. Gio rode a white mule, for he was not a good horseman. Tila, in his bullying way, rode a battle charger whose ears had been trimmed to give it a ferocious appearance. Together, horse and rider were overwhelming. None of them wore armor, though all three were armed with swords and daggers. They were attended by a company of thirty armed and lightly armored men employed by Cesare, wearing his personal colors of yellow and scarlet.

The town of Perugia was on the way from Pisa to Rome, only a leg inward from the sea. The Baglioni family and Perugia itself were fiercely independent, in spite of the fact that the papacy had claimed it as one of its states. Cesare had faith in his own craftiness and physical gifts, but still he would never have dared to visit it except under the protection of Tila. Now he looked forward to enjoying the gaiety of a wedding before he took up his duties in Rome.

Perugia was an awesome and beautiful site. Its fortress, which rested on an enormous hill, was almost impregnable.

As the three young men entered the city, they could see that the churches and palaces were decorated for the wedding, the statues draped with cloths of gold. Cesare chatted happily, even joking with his friends; he carefully made note of the fortifications, and amused himself with plans on how to storm the city.

The ruler of Perugia was the widow, Duchess Atalanta Baglioni. Still a beautiful woman, she was noted for the ferocity with which she ruled, using her son, Netto, as her military captain. It was her dearest wish to see her nephew, Torino, be married to Lavina, one of her favorite ladies of the court. Torino, she felt, could be counted on to support the reign of the Baglioni family.

All the different branches of the physically powerful Baglioni clan assembled on the castle grounds. Musicians played and couples danced at the great feast. There was wrestling and jousting. Cesare, who prided himself on his strength, took on all challengers and won his matches.

When night fell the Baglioni clan retired to the fortress, while Gio, Cesare, and Tila gathered in Tila's apartments for a final bout of drinking.

It was near midnight, and they were drowsy from the wine, when they heard screams and shouting ring throughout the castle. Startled, Tila immediately jumped up and tried to rush out of the apartment, sword in hand, but Cesare restrained him. "Let me see what is happening. You may be in danger. I'll return quickly."

As soon as Cesare heard the screams, he knew by instinct that some great treachery had occurred. As he left Tila's apartment, he held his sword down at his side. Though the Baglioni clan had a reputation for murder, he knew they would not dare kill the son of a Pope. Cesare walked calmly through the corridors of the castle toward the screams, which continued. He found himself outside the bridal chamber.

There was blood everywhere. The statues of the Virgin Mary, the portrait of the Infant Jesus, the white sheets and pillowcases of the marriage bed—even its canopy—were drenched in blood. And on the floor lay the bodies of the bridal couple, Lavina and Torino, their nightgowns stained red, sword punctures ripped through fabric and flesh, mortal wounds to their heads and hearts.

Over them stood Netto with four armed men, all with scarlet swords. Netto's mother, the Duchess Atalanta, was screaming curses at her beloved son. As Netto tried to calm her, Cesare stood listening.

The son was explaining to his mother. "Mama, Torino was too powerful, and his family was plotting to overthrow you. I have killed all the members of his clan." Then he tried to reassure his mother that, though she would have to be deposed and he would become the ruler, she would always hold a position of honor in his government.

She slapped him. "A son's betrayal!" she screamed.

"Open your eyes, Mama. Not only Torino, but also Cousin Tila, has conspired against you," Netto insisted.

Cesare had heard enough. He took his leave and quickly returned to Tila's apartment.

After hearing what happened, Tila was enraged. "Gossip, gossip, all of it!" he shouted. "That bastard cousin of mine, Netto, is trying to steal the crown from his own mother. And he plans to murder me as well."

Cesare, Tila, and Gio barricaded the door and then went out through the window and up onto the roof of the palace, scaling the rough stone walls. Cesare and Tila jumped down into the dark of the rear courtyard, then helped Gio, who was not physically strong. Once on the ground, Cesare had to restrain Tila from trying to get back to the castle to fight Netto. He finally led them to the fields where their escort was encamped, where he knew he'd be safe because of his own thirty armed men. His only problem was Tila.

Should he stay to save his friend, or take him to Rome and safety?

Cesare offered Tila the alternatives but Tila refused. He asked only that Cesare protect him in getting to the Communal Palace in the center of Perugia, where he could rally his own followers to defend his honor and restore the castle to his aunt.

Cesare agreed, but first he told ten of his armed men to escort Gio Medici back safely to Florence. Then, with the rest of his men, he took Tila Baglioni to the Communal Palace.

There they found four armed men, faithful supporters of Tila, waiting for them. He immediately sent them out as messengers, and by dawn there were more than a hundred soldiers under Tila's command.

As the sun rose, they saw a troop of armed men on horses led by Netto riding through the public square. Cesare warned his own men not to take part in any battle. Then they watched as Tila surrounded the square with his men and rode alone to confront Netto.

The battle was quickly over. Tila rode directly into Netto, grabbing his sword arm and then stabbing him in the thigh with his dagger. Netto fell off his horse. Tila dismounted, and before Netto could stand, Tila impaled him on his sword. Netto's troops tried to flee, but were captured. Tila then mounted his clipped-ear warhorse and ordered the captured enemy to be brought to stand before him.

Fifteen of them were left alive. Most of them were wounded and could barely stand.

Cesare watched as Tila ordered Netto's men beheaded, and their heads spiked to the ramparts of the cathedral. He was amazed at the sight of Tila, the bullying student lout, who had been transformed that one day into a merciless executioner. Only seventeen, Tila Baglioni had become the Tyrant of Perugia.

When Cesare arrived in Rome and met with his father, he told the story and then asked, "If the Virgin Mary is the most beloved saint in Perugia, why are they so merciless?"

Pope Alexander smiled. He seemed more amused with the story than horrified. "The Baglioni are true believers," he said. "They believe in paradise. Such a great gift. How otherwise can man bear this mortal life? Unfortunately, such a belief also gives evil men the courage to commit great crimes in the name of good and God."

Pope Alexander did not love luxury only for itself. His palace, the Vatican, had to evoke the all-encompassing pleasures of the heavens themselves. He understood that even those who were spiritually elevated were impressed by the rich, earthly trappings of God, as represented by the Holy Catholic Church. The common people accepted the figure of the Pope as the Vicar of Christ, infallible and venerated, but kings and princes tended to be weaker in their faith. Those of noble blood had to be convinced with gold and gems, silks and rich brocades; by the huge miter the Pope wore on his head and the rich tapestry of his papal robes, the gold and silver embroidery of his vestments and cape, centuries old, lovingly preserved and valuable beyond imagination.

One of the grandest chambers in the Vatican was the huge Hall of Popes—thousands of square yards of ornately decorated walls and magnificently painted ceilings which held the promise of the afterlife for those of virtue. It was in this hall that the Pope received those who came on pilgrimages from all over Europe, ducats in hand, begging for a plenary indulgence. Here there were portraits of famous Popes crowning great kings such as Charlemagne, as well as Popes leading the Crusades and supplicating the Madonna to intercede for mankind.

In all these portraits it was clear that these great kings owed their power to the Pope who was anointing them. He was their earthly savior. The kings, with heads bowed, kneeled in front of the Pope, whose eyes were raised toward the heavens.

It was into his private chambers in the anteroom off the Great Hall in the Vatican that Alexander now called his son Juan. It was time to make known to him that his destiny as a part of Spanish nobility was at hand.

Juan Borgia was almost as tall as Cesare, but slighter of build. Like his brother and father, he was an attractive man but with a difference. He had the slightly slanted eyes and high cheekbones of his Spanish ancestors. His skin was bronzed from his long hours of riding and hunting but there was often a look of suspicion in his widely set dark eyes. By far his greatest disadvantage was that he had none of the charm of Cesare or Alexander. His dark lips were often curled in a cynical smile, but they were not now, as he knelt before his father.

"How may I serve you, Papa?" he asked.

Alexander smiled with affection at this child of his. For it was this young man—like those souls in limbo, lost and confused—who most needed his guidance to gain salvation. "The time has now come for you to take over the responsibility left to you when your half brother, Pedro Luis, died. As you have been told, he bequeathed to you his duchy and his title of duke of Gandia. At the time of his death he was betrothed to Maria Enriquez, cousin of King Ferdinand of Spain, and I, as your father—and as the Holy Father—have decided to honor this commitment, in order to ensure our alliance with newly united Spain and to reassure the house of Aragon of our friendship. Therefore, within a short period of time, you will go to Spain to claim your royal bride. Do you understand?"

"Yes, Papa," he said, but he scowled.

"You are unhappy with my decision?" the Pope asked. "It is an advantage to us, and to you. The family has wealth and station and we will benefit politically from this alliance. Also, there is a great Spanish castle in Gandia, and many wealthy territories that will now belong to you."

"Will I have riches to take with me, so that they can see I also must be respected?" Juan asked.

Alexander frowned. "If you wish to be respected, you must be pious and God-fearing. You must serve the king faithfully, honor your wife, and avoid gambling and games of chance."

"Is that all, Father?" Juan asked sardonically.

"When there is more, I will call for you again," Pope Alexander said curtly. He was seldom annoyed with this son, but at this moment he found himself extremely irritated. He tried to remind himself that Juan was young and had no flair for diplomacy. When he spoke again, it was with constrained warmth. "In the meantime, enjoy your life, my son. It will be a grand adventure if you approach it properly."

On the day Cesare Borgia was to be ordained a cardinal of the Holy Roman Catholic Church, the huge chapel of Saint Peter's Basilica overflowed with fashionably dressed nobility. All the great aristocratic families of Italy were in attendance.

From Milan came the swarthy Ludovico Sforza, "Il Moro," and his brother, Ascanio. Ascanio Sforza, now Alexander's vice-chancellor, dressed in the rich ivory brocade ecclesiastical vestments and red hat of a cardinal. Everyone in the crowded basilica murmured at the sight.

From Ferrara came the d'Este, one of the most regal and conservative old families of Italy. Their robes, simple black and gray, showcased the dazzling jewelry that hung from their necks. They had made the difficult journey not only to show their respect, but to impress themselves upon the Pope and this new cardinal—for they would need his favors.

But none turned the heads of the crowd as sharply as the young man who walked behind them. From the illustrious city of Florence, Piero Medici, solemn and autocratic, wore an emerald green doublet embroidered with fantastic pinwheels of twenty-two-karat gold that cast a luminous glow around his face, making him appear almost saintly. He led seven of his proud relatives, including his brother, Cesare's good friend Gio Medici, down the long center aisle. Piero was the power in Florence now, but the talk was that the Medici's control of the city had truly ceased with the death of his father, Lorenzo the Magnificent. It was rumored that it would not be long before this young prince was overthrown and the Medici rule would end.

From the city of Rome, both the Orsini and the Colonna had come. Bitter rivals for many decades, the two families were momentarily at peace. They were, however, careful to seat themselves on opposite sides of the basilica. And for good reason: a bloody fight between the two had disrupted the coronation of an earlier cardinal.

In the front row, Guido Feltra, the powerful duke of Urbino, spoke quietly with the Pope's most cunning adversary, Cardinal Giuliano della Rovere, nephew of the late Pope Sixtus IV and now papal delegate to France.

Feltra leaned close to the cardinal. "I suspect our Cesare is more a soldier than a scholar," he whispered. "Would make a great general some day, that boy, if he weren't destined to be Pope."

Della Rovere bristled. "Like his father, he's hardly above matters of the flesh. And a bit of a rake in other ways as well. Fights bulls, wrestles peasants at local fairs. Very unseemly . . ."

Feltra nodded. "I've heard his horse just won the Palio in Siena."

Cardinal della Rovere looked annoyed. "With trickery rather than honor. He had his rider jump off near the finish, which made the horse lighter and faster. The result was protested, of course. Still, it stood."

Feltra smiled. "Amazing . . ."

But della Rovere frowned and said, "Heed my warning, Guido Feltra. He's full of the devil, this son of the church."

Giuliano della Rovere was now a dedicated enemy of the Borgia. What increased his fury, even more than his failed election, was the number of pro-Borgia cardinals Pope Alexander had just named. But failure to attend this ceremony would have been unthinkable, and della Rovere's eyes were firmly focused on his future.

Pope Alexander VI stood at the altar, a towering vision, tall, broad-shouldered, and mesmerizing. The stark drama of his white robes enhanced by the scarlet and gold *opus anglicanum* stole made him a commanding presence. At this moment his eyes shone with pride and certainty; here he reigned, alone and infallible, from this massive house of God built centuries before above the tomb of Saint Peter.

As the mighty organ roared a triumphant Te Deum—the hymn of praise to the Lord—Alexander stepped forward, raised the red cardinal's hat high in the air with both his hands, and with a sonorous blessing chanted in Latin solemnly placed it on the head of his son who knelt before him.

Cesare Borgia's eyes were cast downward as he received the Holy Benediction. Then he stood, a proud and imposing figure, as two elderly cardinals draped the purple robe of office around his broad shoulders. When they had finished, he walked forward and joined the Pope. The two holy men faced the congregation.

Cesare was darkly handsome and powerfully built. He was taller even than his massive father, with an angular face and prominent cheekbones. His long aquiline nose was as fine as in any marble sculpture, and his dark brown eyes radiated intelligence. A hush fell over the crowd.

But in the shadowed last row of the basilica, sitting alone in a pew, was a very fat man opulently dressed in silver and white: Gaspare Malatesta, the Lion of Rimini. Malatesta had an issue with this Spanish Pope—over a young boy who had arrived at his gate, murdered and tethered to an ass. What did he care for a Pope or his threats? Nothing. What did he care for this God? Nothing! The Lion believed none of it. Alexander was only a man—and men can die. The Lion indulged his imagination as he reminisced again on pouring ink into the holy water founts, as he had done during the

Lenten season, to stain the fine garments of the cardinal and his guests to bring them all down to earth. The thought appealed to him, but now he had more important business to attend to. He leaned back smiling.

Behind him, hidden in the shadows, Don Michelotto stood watching. And as the final glorious notes of the great Te Deum swelled to a deafening crescendo, the short, powerfully built man dressed in dark clothes slipped unseen into the narrow, unlit space behind Gaspare Malatesta. Soundlessly, he looped a garrote over Gaspare's head and in one fluid movement pulled the lethal noose tight around the fat man's neck.

The Lion of Rimini gasped, his breath stopped in his throat by the grip of the rope. He tried to struggle, but his muscles, starved for blood and oxygen, twitched lamely. The last words he heard, as darkness blotted all thoughts from his brain, were whispered in his ear: "A message from the Holy Father." Then the strangler slipped into the crowd, as quickly as he had appeared.

Cesare Borgia followed his father, the Pope, up the aisle; in their wake were Cesare's mother, Vanozza, his sister, Lucrezia, and his brothers, Juan and Jofre. Behind them were other family celebrants. All walked past the pew in the back row of the basilica without notice or comment. There, Gaspare Malatesta's chin rested on his huge belly as if he were asleep.

Finally, several women stopped and pointed at the comic sight, and Gaspare's sister-in-law, mortified by what she thought to be another of his practical jokes, leaned in to awaken him. As Gaspare's heavy body fell into the aisle, his bulging eyes staring blindly at the basilica's magnificent ceiling, she screamed.

4

Cardinal Giuliano della Rovere's desire for vengeance grew toward obsession. Often he woke in the night cold and shivering, for Alexander had invaded his dreams. And so, as he said his prayers each morning, even as he knelt in the chapel under the watchful eyes of gigantic marble statues of merciful saints and richly colored portraits of holy martyrs, he plotted the Pope's destruction.

It was not only della Rovere's defeat in his bid for the papacy that fostered these feelings, though it certainly played a part. It was his belief that Alexander was at his very core an immoral man.

The Pope's easygoing charm and charisma seemed to render those around him indifferent to the importance of saving souls, and helpless to resist as he placed his children in high-ranking church positions. Many of the cardinals and most kings, as well as the citizens of Rome, forgave him his excesses; they seemed to enjoy his gigantic processions, balls, banquets, spectacles, and elaborate festivities, which depleted monies that could better be used to defend the Papal States and move the armies of the church into new territories.

In contrast to the amiable Pope Alexander, della Rovere was an impatient man with a violent temper, who never seemed happy except when hunting or at war. He worked unceasingly and could not abide play in any form. It was because of this defect in character that he considered himself a virtuous man. He cared little for anything or anyone, though he had three daughters. And in his entire life, he had truly loved only once.

Cardinal della Rovere carried himself with a certain dignity, which would have been reassuring if not for the glimmer of the fanatic in his large dark eyes. The stiff bearing of his massive head, with its strong square cheekbones, made his face a canvas of stark lines and angles. He seldom smiled to show the beauty of his small, even teeth, and only his dimpled chin added softness. It was a face set in the Middle Ages, a living portrait of the Day of Judgment. Even the stony squareness of his body gave the impression of unbending opinion rather than strength. That he had courage and intelligence no one contested. But he was not particularly liked because of his rude and insulting language, which contrasted so sharply with the Pope's easy elegance. Still, he was a formidable enemy.

In della Rovere's many missives to the French King Charles, to King Ferrante of Naples, and to others, he constantly accused Alexander of practicing simony—buying the papal office; of being a swindler; of bribery, nepotism, greed, gluttony, and all manner of carnal sins. The fact that he, himself, had committed many of the same sins he accused Alexander of, seemed not to alter his judgment in any way.

And some of his accusations were true. Following the election, Alexander had turned over valuable castles to the cardinals who had supported him, and he had bestowed upon them the most important Vatican positions. Ascanio Sforza received the office of vice-chancellor because he helped cement the Pope's position on the last ballot. He was also given a castle, churches, and several fiefdoms. It was rumored that in the dark night before the election two donkeys were seen carrying heavy sacks of silver from the palace of Cardinal Rodrigo Borgia to the palace of Cardinal Ascanio Sforza. Cardinal Antonio Orsini's vote secured two cities with the value of thousands of ducats, and other cardinals received church offices or benefices and fiefdoms. Giuliano della Rovere himself was granted the role of the Pope's legate of Avignon, the large fortress of Ostia, and the Adriatic port of Senigallia, a castle and other offices, as well as the canonry of Florence.

This practice of distribution of benefices and territories was not new. It was customary for Popes to endow others with their possessions following their election, for their castles and other properties would otherwise be pillaged immediately by the citizens of Rome. And who would be more logical to reward than those who had shown their loyalty by casting their ballots for him? And so it was more a testament to Alexander's generosity that della Rovere received such benefices, for it was well known that he had cast his vote for himself.

But the charge of simony was outrageous. For Cardinal della Rovere came from a wealthier family and had far more prominent connections than Rodrigo Borgia. If the office of Pope could be purchased, and lavish gifts could win the election, della Rovere could easily have outspent Alexander and the outcome would have been altered.

Now, with gall overriding all reason and political sense, Giuliano della Rovere, accompanied by other dissident cardinals, planned to implore King Charles of France to call a General Council.

Many years before, a General Council could command or even depose a Pope: comprised of cardinals, bishops, and lay leaders, this assembly was once used to balance the power and limit the supremacy of the papacy. But it had become an extinct weapon since Pius II struck it down thirty years before.

Yet, the vision of the new Pope crowning his son Cesare as a cardinal so outraged della Rovere that he and his allies sought to breathe new life into the concept of the General Council as a means of destroying Alexander.

Wanting to distance himself, della Rovere left Rome soon after the coronation of Cesare, retreating to his official see in Ostia to begin his offense on Alexander. Once his alliances were set and his plans were in place, he would travel to France to put himself under the protection of King Charles.

Pope Alexander VI, having set the destinies of his sons in motion, knew he must now begin to establish his daughter's position in his grand plan. He carefully considered what he must do. Lucrezia was not yet a woman, just thirteen, but he could wait no longer. He must promise to betroth her to Giovanni Sforza, duke of Pesaro. He had already promised her to two young Spaniards when he was cardinal. But his political position had changed once he became Pope, and he had to plan carefully in order to secure the accommodation of Milan. His previous promises to the young men from Spain must be broken as amicably as possible.

Lucrezia was the most valuable asset he had in his marital alliances. And the twenty-six-year-old Giovanni, just widowed, his wife dead from childbirth, was a natural prospect. He must work quickly, for Giovanni's uncle, Il Moro, was the most powerful man in Milan. He must be made a friend before he aligned with the foreign kings of either Spain or France.

Alexander knew that if he was unable to unite the many feudal city-states into one Italy ruled by the laws of the Holy See, the Turkish barbarians—the Infidel—would surely conquer them. They would move toward the Roman territories if they were given an opportunity. So many souls would be lost, and so much revenue would leave the one true church. But most important, if he could not maintain the people's loyalty and protect Rome from the invasion of foreigners, if he could not use his papacy to increase the power of the Holy Mother Church, another cardinal—no doubt, Giuliano della Rovere—would take his place as Pope and his entire family would be in grave danger. Surely they would be accused of heresy and tortured in order to dispose of them. The fortune in possessions he had worked so hard for, over so many years, would be stolen, and they would be left with nothing. That was a far worse fate than the one his lovely daughter was about to endure.

After spending a sleepless night pacing up and down in his chambers, kneeling at his altar praying for divine guidance and considering his plan from all sides, he called for his children: Cesare, Juan, and Lucrezia. Jofre was still too young, and not the brightest of his boys. This strategy would only confuse him.

When they were in the company of strangers Lucrezia would curtsy to her father, kiss his ring, and kneel before him to show her respect, but whenever they were alone, she would run to him and throw her arms around his neck, kissing him sweetly. Oh, that dear child did pull at his heart.

Today, instead of embracing her in return, Pope Alexander pushed her back and held her arms until she stood straight in front of him.

"What's wrong, Papa?" she asked, her expression showing her surprise. She was desolate whenever she thought her father was unhappy with her. At thirteen, she was tall for a girl, and a true beauty, with skin as pale as porcelain and features so fine they looked as though they had been painted by Raphael. Her light eyes sparkled with intelligence, and she flowed gracefully each time she moved. Lucrezia was the light of her father's life; when she was present it was much more difficult for the Pope to think of scripture and strategy.

"Papa," Lucrezia repeated impatiently, "what's wrong? What have I done to displease you?"

"You must marry soon," he told her simply.

"Oh, Papa," Lucrezia said, falling to her knees, "I can't leave you yet. I will not live."

Alexander stood up and lifted his daughter from her knees, holding her close, comforting the crying child. "Shh, shh," he whispered. "Lucrezia, I must make this alliance, but that does not mean you must go away just yet. Now, dry your tears and allow Papa to explain."

She sat at his feet on a gold cushion and listened as he spoke. "The Sforza family of Milan is very powerful, and Il

Moro's nephew, young Giovanni, has just lost his wife in childbirth. He has agreed to a marital alliance. You know Papa wants the best for all of us. And you are old enough to understand that without these alliances with the great powerful established families, my reign as Pope will not endure. Then we will all be in danger, and that I cannot allow."

Lucrezia bowed her head and nodded in understanding. She looked very young.

When Alexander had finished, he stood up and began to walk around the large room, wondering how to present his new proposal most delicately.

Finally he turned toward his daughter and asked, "Do you know yet how to bed a man? Has anyone explained?"

"No, Papa," she said, and for the first time, she smiled wickedly at him, as she had seen many of the courtesans do . . .

Alexander shook his head in wonder at this child of his. She was so full of emotion, as was her mother, and yet could be so clever and playful even at this early age.

He motioned to his sons, Cesare and Juan. They both moved close and kneeled in front of him, bowing their heads in respect. "Rise, my sons," he said. "We must speak. We have important decisions to make, for the future of all of us will depend on what we speak about this day."

Cesare was thoughtful and introspective though not as easygoing and pleasant as his sister. Fiercely competitive since early childhood, he insisted on winning at all things by whatever means he could avail himself. Juan, on the other hand, was more sensitive to personal injury, though quite insensitive when it came to others. He had a cruel streak, and most of the time wore a sardonic expression. He had none of Lucrezia's easy grace, and none of the charisma of his older brother. Still, Alexander was very fond of him, sensing in him a vulnerability that Cesare and Lucrezia did not have.

"Papa, why have you called us here?" Cesare asked, looking out the window. He was feeling full of energy, and it was a beautiful day; he wanted to be outside in the city.

"There is a fine carnival this noon in the square that we should attend . . ."

Alexander moved over to his favorite chair in the corner of the large chamber. "Sit, my children, sit with me," he gently ordered them. All three sat at his feet on large silk pillows.

He smiled as he waved his arm over them. "This is the greatest family in all of Christendom," he said. "We will rise with the great deeds we do for the Holy Roman Catholic Church, we will save many souls, and we will live quite well while we are doing God's work. But as each of you knows, this entails sacrifice. As we have learned from the lives of many of our saints . . . great deeds require great sacrifice." He made the sign of the cross.

He looked at Lucrezia, who was sitting on the rug at his feet leaning against the shoulder of her brother Cesare. Next to him, but separate from them, sat Juan, polishing a new dagger he had been given. "Cesare, Juan? I expect that each of you has bedded a woman?"

Juan frowned. "Of course, Papa. Why would you ask such a question?"

"One should have as much information as possible before one makes an important decision," he said. Then he turned to his eldest son. "Cesare, and you? Have you bedded a woman?" he asked.

"Many," Cesare said simply.

"And were they pleased?" he asked both his sons.

Juan frowned impatiently. "How would I know?" he asked, laughing. "Was I obliged to ask?"

The Pope lowered his head and spoke. "Cesare, were the women you bedded pleased?"

Cesare, with a small smile and an open countenance, answered, "I imagine they were, Father," he said. "For each of them begged to see me again."

Pope Alexander looked at his daughter, who was watching him with a mixture of curiosity and expectation. Then he turned his gaze back to his sons. "Which of you will agree to bed your sister?"

Juan now looked bored. "Papa," he said, "I would rather join a monastery."

Alexander smiled, but said, "You're a foolish young man."

But Lucrezia was frowning now. "Why would you ask my brothers without asking me first?" she asked. "If one of them is to bed me, should it not be my choice?" she said.

Cesare patted her hand to reassure her, and said, "Papa, what is the reason for this? Why would you make such a request? And are you not worried that we shall find our souls doomed to hell for such an action?"

Pope Alexander got up and walked across his chamber to the arch of the ornate doorway leading from one great room to another. He pointed to the five panels of the great arcade and then asked, "In your studies have you learned nothing about the great Egyptian dynasties, where brother and sister wed in order to keep the bloodline pure? Do you not know about the young Isis, who wed her brother, the king Osiris, elder son of Heaven and Earth? Isis and Osiris had a child called Horus, and they became the great Trinity, the one that preceded the Christian Trinity of the Father, Son, and Holy Ghost. They helped men escape the wiles of the devil, and ensured that good souls were reborn for eternity. The only difference between them and our Holy Trinity is that one of them was a female." Here he smiled at Lucrezia. "Egypt was one of the most advanced civilizations in history, and we might well take their example."

"That cannot be the only reason, Father," Cesare said. "They were pagans and had pagan gods. There is something you have considered that you have not told us."

Alexander walked over to Lucrezia, stroked his daughter's long blond hair, and felt a twinge of conscience. He could not tell any of them his real consideration: that he understood the heart of a woman. He knew that the man to whom she first surrendered would be the man who would command her love and loyalty. For once she gave herself to a man, she would offer the keys to her heart and soul as well.

But he must find a way to ensure that she did not also offer the keys to the kingdom. And so it followed that, as Alexander would never allow a stranger to claim his best territory, the time had come for he himself to set claim.

"We are a family," he told his children. "And the loyalty of the family must come before everything and everyone else. We must learn from each other, protect each other, and be bound first and foremost to each other. For if we honor that commitment, we will never be vanquished—but if we falter in that loyalty, we will all be condemned." The Pope turned to Lucrezia now. "And you are correct, my child. For it is your choice in this instance. You cannot choose to whom you will be betrothed, but you may choose now who will bed you first."

Lucrezia looked at Juan and tilted her head coyly. "I would rather be sent to a convent than be bedded by Juan." Then she turned to Cesare. "You must promise you'll be gentle, for this is love, not war, we are engaging in, my dear brother."

Cesare smiled and bowed playfully. "You have my word. And you, my sister, may teach me more about love and loyalty than I have learned so far, and that will serve me as well."

"Papa?" she asked, turning to her father, her eyes wide. "Will you be there to be certain everything goes well? I will not be brave enough without you. For I have heard stories, from both Julia and my ladies in waiting."

Alexander looked at her. "I will be there," he said. "As I will be on the night you are officially wed. For a contract is not valid if it is not witnessed . . ."

"Thank you, Papa," she said. Jumping up to hug him, she asked, "May I have a fine new costume and a ruby ring as a gift for this celebration?"

"Of course," he said. "You may have two . . ."

The following week, Alexander sat on his throne wrapped in his dazzling robes of white satin, free of the weight of his heavy tiara. On his head he wore only a small satin cap. The platform built high above the ground, opposite the bed, rested against a backdrop of exquisite beauty in one of the more ornately decorated rooms of the newly renovated Borgia apartments. Cesare and Lucrezia were summoned, but the servants were instructed to remove themselves until Alexander beckoned them.

The Pope watched his son and his daughter as they undressed. Lucrezia giggled when her brother, Cesare, finally stepped out of his costume.

He looked up at her and smiled. Alexander thought how strange and somehow touching it was that the only time he saw real tenderness on his son's face was when he was with his sister. Though in every other instance he was the aggressor, with her—even here—he seemed under her power.

She was a treasure, Lucrezia—and not only for her beauty, though there was no silk finer than the golden ringlets that framed her face. Her eyes glistened so brightly that they always seemed to hold a secret. Now the Pope wondered what it was that made them shine so. She was built in perfect proportion, though still a slight bit thin, with budding breasts and smooth unblemished skin. A joy to behold, a perfect dream for any man who would possess her.

And his son Cesare? No Olympian god of antiquity had more perfect stature. Tall and sinewy, he was the picture of strength in young manhood. Ah, that he had the other virtues, to serve him more effectively than his driving ambition. But in this moment Cesare's face softened as he looked at his sister standing across from him.

"Am I quite beautiful?" Crezia asked her brother. And when he nodded, she turned her head toward her father. "Am I, Papa? Do you think I'm as fine as any young woman you have ever seen?"

The Pope nodded and smiled slightly. "You are beautiful, my child. Truly one of God's finest creations." He raised his right hand slowly, drawing the sign of the cross in the air, and ministered a blessing. Then he instructed them to begin.

Alexander's heart was filled with joy and gratitude for

these children whom he loved so deeply. He imagined that God the Father must have felt much the same way as he watched Adam and Eve in the garden. But after only a few moments' amusement he was intrigued by that thought. Was this the *hubris* that so many of the pagan heroes suffered, he wondered, and quickly crossed himself again, asking for forgiveness. But they looked so innocent, his children, so free of guilt, their young faces bright with curiosity and pleasure, that they would never visit a paradise like this again. And was that not the purpose of man and woman? To feel God's joy? Had not religion caused enough suffering? Was that the only way to honor the Creator? The world of men was so full of treachery; only here in their father's palace, in Christ's Holy See, would his children ever feel as safe and protected. It was his duty to see to that. These times of great pleasure would carry them through the trials and travails they must eventually encounter.

The large feather bed was covered with silk sheets and fine linens, and so when Lucrezia fell onto it she squealed with enjoyment. His manhood already aroused, Cesare leapt quickly onto his sister, startling her. "Papa?" she cried aloud. "Papa, Cesare is hurting me . . ."

Pope Alexander stood. "Cesare, is that the way you've learned to bed a woman? What a pity. Surely I have failed you, for if not me, who should have shown you how to bring Heaven to Earth?"

Cesare got up and stood by the bed, eyes blazing. He felt rejected by his sister and reproached by his father, but still he was a young man and so his ardor had not cooled.

Alexander approached the bed as Cesare moved aside. "Come here, my son," he said to the boy. "Come here. Crezia, come closer to the edge." He motioned to her, and she moved gingerly over toward them. Then, with his hand placed over his son's, he began to stroke his daughter's body, slowly, tenderly. First her face, then down her neck and across her small firm breasts, as he instructed Cesare. "Don't be in such a hurry, my son. Take the time to enjoy beauty. There is nothing as exquisite in the world as the body of a woman, the smell of a woman as she surrenders . . . willingly. But if you move too quickly you will miss the very essence of the lovemaking, and startle the poor things . . ."

Lucrezia was lying quietly now, her eyes half closed, her breathing quickening, as she felt the pleasure of the stroking of her brother's hands on her body. When he reached her belly and began to move downward, her eyes opened and she tried to call out, but her voice was stopped by the quivering of her body as wave after wave of pleasure shook her to her very soul. "Papa?" she whispered, "Papa? Is it not sinful to feel such pleasure? I shall not go to hell, shall I?"

"Would Papa endanger your immortal soul?" he asked.

Pope Alexander, still leading the hand of Cesare, was close enough to Lucrezia to smell her warm breath upon his face, and the force of his own response to her frightened him. He suddenly dropped Cesare's hand and said in a husky voice to his son, "Now take her, but take her slowly. Gently. Be a lover, be a man, honor her . . . but take her."

Shaken, he turned quickly and walked across the room to sit again on his throne. But when he heard his daughter moan, when she moaned again and then again in pleasure, he suddenly was afraid for himself. His heart was beating hard and too fast; he felt himself becoming dizzy. He had never before felt such intense emotion, such arousal at witnessing a carnal act, and in one brief moment he knew. He understood completely. Though Cesare might endure, might be saved in spite of this, he himself—the Vicar of Christ on Earth—had just seen the snake in the garden of Eden. And he had been tempted. His head throbbed with the knowledge that if ever he were to touch that child again, he would be damned for all time. For the pleasure he felt was of no earthly kind, and there was no doubt that it would mean his fall from grace.

He prayed on that day, to the Father, the Son, and the Holy Ghost, to lead him not into temptation ever again. "Deliver me from evil," he whispered earnestly, and when he looked up again his two children were lying on the bed, naked and spent.

"Children," he said, his voice devoid of all strength. "Put on your robes and come to me . . ."

And when they knelt before him, Lucrezia looked up to her father with tears in her eyes. "Thank you, Father. I can't imagine giving myself to another in the same way without knowing this first. I would have been so frightened, and yet I felt such pleasure." Then she turned to her brother. "Cesare," she said. "My brother. I thank you too. I can't imagine loving anyone as I love you in this moment."

Cesare smiled, but said nothing.

And as Pope Alexander looked down at his children, he saw an expression in Cesare's eyes that troubled him. He had not thought to warn his son of love's one pitfall: true love empowers a woman and imperils a man. And now he could see, that though this day might have been a blessing to his daughter and strengthened the Borgia dynasty, it might one day prove to be a curse to his son.

5

On the day that Lucrezia's husband-to-be, Giovanni Sforza, duke of Pesaro, was to arrive in the city of Rome, Pope Alexander arranged for a large procession in celebration. For he knew that Giovanni's uncle, Il Moro, would consider this gesture a sign of respect; proof of Alexander's sincerity in his alliance with Milan.

But Alexander also had other considerations in mind. As the Holy Father he understood the hearts and souls of his people, and he knew they enjoyed pageantry. It reassured them of his benevolence, as well as the benevolence of their Heavenly Father, and helped relieve the torpor of their drab, dull lives. Any cause for celebration brought new hope to the city, and often kept the more desperate among his citizens from murdering each other over minor disputes.

The lives of his less fortunate citizens were so devoid of pleasure that he felt responsible for providing them with some small happiness in order to feed their souls. For what else could ensure their support of the papacy? If the seeds of jealousy were repeatedly sown in the hearts of men who were forced to watch the pleasures of those less worthy but more fortunate, how could a ruler ask for their loyalty? Pleasure must be shared, for only in that way was it possible to keep the desperation of the poor at bay.

It was on this warm, balmy day, a day filled with the scent of roses, that Cesare, Juan, and Jofre Borgia rode to the high stone gates of Rome to greet the duke of Pesaro.

Accompanying them was the entire Roman senate and the regally adorned ambassadors of Florence, Naples, Venice, and Milan, as well as the representatives of France and Spain.

The procession would follow this envoy on its return, past the palace of his uncle, Ascanio Sforza, the vice-chancellor, where the young duke would stay until his wedding night. It would then continue through the streets until it reached the Vatican. Alexander had instructed his sons to ride past Lucrezia's palace in order to allow her to see her future husband. Though her father had tried to allay her fears by promising her that she could stay in her own palace at Santa Maria of Portico with Julia and Adriana after her marriage, and not be required to travel to Pesaro for a year, Lucrezia still seemed upset. And Alexander was never at peace when his daughter was unhappy.

The preparations for the procession had taken many weeks, but now everything was in place. There were jesters in green and bright yellow velvet suits, jugglers twirling gaily colored sticks and tossing gaudy papier-mâché balls into the air while the intoxicating tempo from the fife and trumpet brigades rang out musical notes to brighten the spirits of the crowds of Roman citizens who had gathered along the route to see this duke of Pesaro who was to wed the Pope's young daughter . . .

But early that morning Cesare had awakened in a foul humor, with an ache that made his head throb wickedly. He tried to excuse himself from greeting his future brother-in-law, for he thought it an unpleasant obligation, but his father would hear none of it. "As a representative of the Holy Father, you will not be released from your duty unless you are on your deathbed from plague or malaria," the Pope had said sternly. Then he stormed out.

Cesare would have argued had not his sister come into his room to plead with him. She had run through the tunnel from her own palace as soon as she heard he was ill. Now she sat on his bed, rubbing his head gently, and asked,

"Chez, who but you will tell me the truth about this man I am to marry? Who else can I trust?"

"Crezia, what difference can it make?" he asked. "You are already promised, and about that I can do nothing."

Lucrezia smiled at her brother and ran her fingers through his hair. She bent to kiss his lips tenderly and smiled. "Is this as difficult for you as it is for me?" she asked. "For I hate the idea of another man in my bed. I will weep and cover my eyes, and though I will not be able to keep him from the contract, I will refuse to kiss him. I swear I will, my brother."

Cesare took a deep breath and resolved to do as his sister wished. "I hope he is not a beast, for both our sakes," he said. "Or I shall have to kill him before he ever touches you."

Lucrezia giggled. "You and I will begin a holy war," she said, pleased by Cesare's reaction. "Papa will have even more to do than he does now. He will have to pacify Milan once you've killed Giovanni; then Naples will come to beg for alliance. Il Moro may capture you and take you to the dungeon of Milan to torture you. While Papa is using the papal army to try and save you, Venice will surely have something up their sleeve in order to conquer our territories. And Florence will have their finest artists paint unflattering portraits of us, and their prophets curse us with eternal damnation!" She laughed so hard she fell backward onto the bed.

Cesare loved to hear his sister laugh. It made him forget all others existed, and even soothed his anger toward his father. Now the throbbing in his head seemed to subside. And so he agreed to go . . .

As soon as Lucrezia heard the music of the approaching procession, she ran up the stairs to the second floor, to the main room of the castle from which the *loggia,* or balcony, extended like the hand of a great giant, fingers curled. Julia Farnese, who had been the Pope's mistress for more than two years now, helped Lucrezia choose a gown of deep green satin with cream-colored sleeves and a jeweled bodice. Then she dressed Lucrezia's hair and pulled her blond curls atop her head, allowing a few wisps to fall on her forehead and at her neckline to enhance her look of sophistication.

Julia had tried for months to instruct Lucrezia about what to expect on her wedding night, but Lucrezia paid little attention. As Julia explained in great detail how to please a man, Lucrezia's heart and mind went straight to Cesare. Though she never said a word to anyone, her love for him filled many of her thoughts each day.

Now, as Lucrezia Borgia walked out onto her balcony, she was surprised to see the crowds awaiting her. Her father had provided guards to protect her, but they could not save her from the petals of flowers that blanketed her and carpeted the grand balcony. She smiled and waved at the citizens.

As Lucrezia watched the procession approach, she laughed at the jester who passed before her, and joyfully clapped as the trumpeters and flutists played their merriest tunes. Then, from behind, she saw them.

First her brother Cesare, handsome and noble astride his white horse, his back straight and his expression serious. He raised his head to look at her and smiled. Juan followed, taking no notice of her, leaning down on his horse to gather the flowers from ladies of the street who called to him. Her younger brother, Jofre, waved to her with a dull but happy smile.

Behind them she saw him: Giovanni Sforza. He had long, dark locks and a well-trimmed beard, a fine nose and a shorter, stockier build than any of her brothers. She felt self-conscious and embarrassed when she first saw him, but when he looked toward the balcony, reined in his horse, and saluted her, she curtsied back as she'd been taught.

In three days she would be married, and as the procession passed her on its way to her father's house, she couldn't wait to hear what Adriana and Julia had to say about her betrothed. Though Adriana would console her and tell her all would be fine, she knew Julia would tell her the truth.

Once inside her palace again, Lucrezia asked them, "What did you think? Do you think him a beast?"

Julia laughed. "I think he's good-looking enough, though quite a large man . . . maybe too large for you," she teased, and Lucrezia knew just what she meant. Then Julia hugged her. "He'll be fine. It's only for the Holy Father, and the Heavenly Father, that you must marry. It has little to do with the rest of your life."

Once Alexander had established official residence in the papal palace, he had taken a suite of bare rooms built and abandoned long before, and made of them the fabulous Borgia apartments. The walls of his private reception room, the *Sala dei Misteri,* were covered with great murals painted by his favorite artist, Pinturicchio.

In one of these murals, Alexander himself was painted as part of the Ascension, one of the chosen few who watched Christ's ascent to heaven. Attired in his great jewel-studded cloak, he has placed his golden tiara on the ground beside him. He stands with eyes raised upward as he is blessed by the ascending Savior.

In other murals, likenesses of other Borgia were shown as the faces of long-dead saints, martyrs, and other religious figures: Lucrezia strikingly beautiful as a slender, blond Saint Catherine, Cesare as an emperor on a golden throne, Juan as an oriental potentate, and Jofre as an innocent cherub. And throughout the murals there roamed the charging red bull that was the symbol of the Borgia family.

On the door of the second Borgia room, Pinturicchio had painted a portrait of the Madonna, the Virgin Mary, in all her serene beauty. The Madonna was Alexander's favorite among the holy figures, so the artist had used Julia Farnese as his model, satisfying two passions of Alexander's with one painting.

There was also the Hall of Faith, a thousand yards square. This room was vaulted, with frescoes filling the lunettes and medallions on the ceiling. There was one fresco for each apostle, every one of them reading a scroll to the eager prophets who would spread the word of the divinity of Christ. The faces of the prophets were Alexander, Cesare, Juan, and Jofre.

All of these rooms were richly decorated with elaborate tapestries and gold trim. In the Hall of Faith was the papal throne, on which Alexander sat to receive important persons. Alongside the throne were ornate footstools on which the nobles knelt to kiss his ring and his feet, as well as divans on which those in power could sit for longer audiences while making plans for future crusades or discussing who should rule the cities of Italy and how.

Now the duke of Pesaro, Giovanni Sforza, was led into the Pope's chambers. He bent to kiss the holy foot, and then the Pope's sacred ring. He was enormously impressed by the beauty of the Vatican, and by the riches he would soon possess. For with his young bride had come a dowry of thirty thousand ducats, enough for him to beautify much of his home in Pesaro and provide him with other luxuries.

As Pope Alexander welcomed him into the family, Giovanni thought about his new wife's brothers. Of the two oldest, he was drawn much more strongly to Juan than to Cesare; Jofre was too young to consider. Cesare did not seem at all welcoming, but Juan had promised the duke a good time in the city before his wedding, and so he came to believe it might not be as bad as he had imagined. Whatever the circumstances, of course, he could never have argued with his uncle, Il Moro, or Milan would take back Pesaro and he would lose his duchy as quickly as he had gained it.

That afternoon, once everyone had arrived at the Vatican for the beginning of the celebrations, Cesare quickly disappeared. He left the palace on horseback and galloped out of Rome into the countryside. He had spent almost no time with Sforza, and yet he already hated the bastard. He was a lout, a braggart, an ass. Duller than Jofre, if that was possible, and more arrogant than Juan. What would his sweet sister do with such a husband? And what could he tell her when he saw her again?

As intensely as Cesare objected to his soon-to-be brother-in-law, Juan was drawn to him. Juan had few friends at the court; his only constant companion was the Turkish Prince Djem, who was being held hostage by the Pope at the request of Djem's brother, the reigning sultan.

Sultan Bayezid had made an arrangement with Pope Innocent when he feared the Christian Crusades were planning to overthrow him under the pretext of restoring his brother, Djem. In exchange for keeping Djem hostage in the Vatican, the Pope was paid forty thousand ducats a year. Once Innocent had died, Pope Alexander upheld the promise, treating him as an honored guest of the palace. For how better to fill the coffers of the Holy Roman Catholic Church than by taking the money of the Infidel Turks?

The thirty-year-old Djem, dark-skinned and surly-looking to the Roman citizens, with his turban and dark curled mustache, insisted on wearing his oriental costumes about the Vatican, and soon Juan, when not at official occasions, began to dress as he did. Though Djem was almost twice the age of Juan, they began to go everywhere together, and the prince exerted a great deal of influence on the spoiled and protected son of the Pope. Alexander tolerated their friendship not only because of the revenue Djem brought to the Vatican, but because the companionship of the prince seemed to bring a smile to Juan's otherwise sullen face. But Cesare found being in their company unbearable.

The night before the wedding, Juan invited Giovanni Sforza to accompany him and Djem into the city of Rome in order to visit the local inns and bed some bawdy whores. Giovanni agreed immediately. Djem and the duke of Pesaro seemed to get along well, exchanging stories and chatting amiably as they ate and drank in abundance. The citizens of

Rome stayed as far away as possible, and did not invite the trio into their shops or houses.

The prostitutes were a different matter. Juan was familiar to them, and many placed small bets on who could bed him most often. There were rumors he was Djem's lover, but the courtesans who earned their daily bread by bedding men of high rank didn't care, for when he visited them for his pleasure he paid them generously.

One of the girls Juan most frequented was about fifteen years old, with long dark hair and curly lashes. Her name was Avalona. The daughter of one of the innkeepers, she was truly fond of Juan. But on the night the three young men from the Vatican came to the city, Juan offered Avalona first to his brother-in-law, then to Djem. Both men took her upstairs to bed her while Juan looked on, but he was too drunk to consider how she felt. Instead, when he came to her expecting her familiar warmth and affection, she turned away and refused to kiss him. Juan, with his usual prickly sensitivity, was enraged at the thought that she enjoyed his brother-in-law better than himself. He slapped her for this insult, and she refused to speak to him. Juan sulked the entire return to the palace. But both Giovanni Sforza and Prince Djem had a fine evening, and hardly noticed that Juan was offended.

The day of the wedding arrived quickly. Lucrezia looked regal in a gown of red velvet trimmed with fur, her white-blond hair spun gold and ornamented with rubies and diamonds. Julia Farnese wore a simple rose-colored satin gown, which illuminated her pale beauty. And Adriana had chosen a deep blue velvet gown, unadorned, so as not to compete with the ruby-jeweled bodice of Lucrezia's gown. Only the bridegroom, Giovanni Sforza, wearing a thick borrowed gold collar, her brother Juan, and his friend Djem were dressed in clothes more richly fashioned than her own. The three wore turbans of cream satin and golden brocade stoles, ornate enough to outshine not only the garments of the bride, but the Pope's ecclesiastical vestments as well.

Alexander had chosen her brother Juan to accompany her down the aisle, and she knew Cesare was angry. But Lucrezia thought it better, for she knew that Cesare never could give her away gracefully. She wondered now if he would even attend, though orders from their father would leave him little choice. If there was a disagreement, she knew Cesare would gallop away again and ride into the country. But she prayed this time he wouldn't, for it was Cesare she wanted there most; it was him she loved above all.

The wedding took place in the Great Hall of the Vatican over the objections of the traditional church leaders and the other princes of the church, who believed the holy halls should be peopled only by men concerned with official church business. But the Pope wanted Lucrezia married at the Vatican, and so it was.

On a raised platform placed at the very front of the hall stood the throne of the Pope, with six burgundy velvet seats on each side for the Pope's twelve newly elected cardinals. In the Pope's private chapel, which was smaller and sparser than the Main Chapel of Saint Peter, he had instructed there be placed rows and rows of tall silver and gold torches, to burn before statues of enormous marble saints which graced the sides of the altar.

The presiding bishop, dressed in flowing ceremonial vestments, his silver miter crowning his head, chanted his prayers aloud in Latin, and offered the bride and bridegroom holy blessings.

The incense burning during the benediction seemed especially pungent. It had arrived from the East just a few days before, as a gift from Prince Djem's brother, the Turkish Sultan Bayezid II. The thick white smoke burned Lucrezia's throat, compelling her to hide a cough with her lace handkerchief. The vision of the crucified Jesus on the huge wooden cross seemed as ominous to Lucrezia as the great sword of fidelity the bishop held above her head as the young couple exchanged their vows.

Finally, she caught a glimpse of her brother Cesare at the entrance of the chapel. She had been troubled that his seat at the altar alongside the other cardinals had been conspicuously empty.

Lucrezia had spent the night before on her knees in prayer to the Madonna, asking for forgiveness, after sneaking through the tunnel into her brother Cesare's room to have him claim her once again. She wondered why she felt such joy with him, and such dread at the thought of another. She didn't even know this man who was to be her husband. She had seen him only once, from her balcony, and when they had been in the same room the day before, he had not spoken a word to her, or in any way acknowledged her existence.

Now, as they knelt on small golden stools in front of the altar and she heard the first words from her bridegroom—"I will take this woman as my wife"—she thought his voice a graceless and unpleasant sound.

As though in a trance, Lucrezia agreed to honor him as her husband. But her gaze and her heart were fixed on Cesare, dressed in solemn priestly black, now standing alongside her brother Juan. He never looked at her.

Afterward, in one of the great halls of the Vatican—the Sala Reale—Lucrezia Borgia sat in splendor at the special raised table. Alongside her were her bridegroom, Giovanni, her governess, Adriana, and Julia Farnese, whom she had chosen as her maid of honor. The granddaughter of the late Pope Innocent, Battestina, also shared her table, as did other bridesmaids, but her three brothers sat at a table across the room. Many of the guests were seated on the hundreds of pillows placed on the floor. Around the perimeter of the hall there were several huge tables filled with food and sweetmeats, and once the guests had eaten the center of the hall was cleared so that they could watch the theater players perform. Later, there would be dancers and singers to entertain them.

Several times Lucrezia looked at her bridegroom, but he ignored her and spent much of his time stuffing food and spilling wine into his mouth. Disgusted, she looked away.

On this day that was meant to be a great celebration, Lucrezia, for one of the few times in her life, missed her mother. For now that Julia was the mistress of the Pope, there was no place for Vanozza at the palace.

As she glanced again at her new husband, she wondered if she might ever get used to his grim expression. The thought of leaving her home in Rome to live with him in Pesaro filled her with despair, and she was grateful for her father's promise that she would not have to leave for a year.

Surrounded by the gaiety and laughter of the guests, Lucrezia felt incredibly lonely. She wasn't hungry, but she did take several sips of the fine red wine that had been poured into her silver goblet, and soon felt giddy. She began to chatter to her bridesmaids and finally she began to have a good time. For after all it was a party, and she was thirteen years old.

Later, Pope Alexander announced there would be a dinner that evening in his private apartments, where the gifts for the bride and groom could be presented. Before he left the Vatican hall for his own chambers, he instructed his servants to toss the remaining sweets from the balcony to the crowds of citizens in the piazza below so that they could share in the festivities.

It was well past midnight when Lucrezia had a chance to speak to her father. He was sitting alone at his desk, for most of the guests had gone and only her brothers and a few of the cardinals were left waiting in the antechamber.

Lucrezia approached the Pope hesitantly, for she did not want to offend him, but this was far too important to wait. She kneeled in front of him and bent her head waiting for permission to speak.

Pope Alexander smiled and encouraged her. "Come, my child. Tell Papa what is on your mind."

Lucrezia looked up, her eyes glistening but her face pale from the events of the day. "Papa," she said, in a barely audible voice. "Papa, must I go to the bedchamber with Giovanni this very night? Must you witness the contract so soon?"

The Pope raised his eyes to the heavens. He too had been thinking about the bedchamber, for more hours than he cared to acknowledge. "If not now, when?" he asked the child.

"Just a little while longer," she said.

"It is best to get unpleasantries over with as soon as possible," he said, smiling gently at his daughter. "Then you may continue your life without the sword hanging over your head."

Lucrezia took a deep breath and sighed. "Must my brother Cesare be present?" she asked.

Pope Alexander frowned. "What does it matter?" he asked. "As long as your papa is there. For the contract to be valid, any three witnesses will serve."

Lucrezia nodded then and said with determination, "I prefer he not be there."

"If that is your wish," the Pope said, "that is how it shall be."

Both Giovanni and Lucrezia were reluctant as they made their way into the bridal chamber: he because he still missed his first wife who had died, and she because she was embarrassed to be watched, and loath to allow anyone but Cesare to touch her. Now, she was so dizzy nothing seemed to matter. She had looked for her brother, but he had slipped away, and so she had quickly swallowed three more goblets of wine before she could avail herself of the courage to do what she knew she must.

Inside the chamber she and Giovanni undressed with the help of their servants, and both slipped under the white satin sheets, being careful not to allow their flesh to touch before the witnesses arrived.

When the Pope entered he sat on the velvet chair, facing a large tapestry of the Crusades on which he could focus and pray. In his hands he held jeweled rosary beads. The second seat was taken by Cardinal Ascanio Sforza and the third by Julia's brother, Cardinal Farnese, who had suffered the humiliation of being called the "petticoat cardinal" after his investiture by Alexander.

Giovanni Sforza didn't say a word to Lucrezia; instead he just leaned over, his face too close to hers, and grabbed her shoulder roughly to pull her toward him. He tried to kiss her, but she turned her face away and hid in his neck. He smelled like an ox. And when he began to run his hands over her, she felt her body shiver with revulsion. For an instant she was afraid she would be sick to her stomach, and hoped someone had thought to place a chamberpot alongside the bed. When suddenly she felt an overwhelming sadness, she thought she might weep. But by the time he mounted her, she felt nothing. She had closed her eyes and willed herself away, to a place in her mind where she ran through tall reeds and rolled in a meadow of soft green grass . . . to Silverlake, the one place she felt free.

The following morning, when Lucrezia rushed to greet Cesare as he walked from the Vatican Palace to the stables, she could see at once that he was upset. She tried to reassure him but he couldn't listen. And so she stood silent and still as she watched him harness his horse to leave.

It was two days before Cesare returned. He told her he had spent time in the country thinking about his future, and her. He had forgiven her, he said, but that made her angry. "What is there to forgive? I did what I must, as you do. You are always complaining about being a cardinal," she said. "But I would rather be a cardinal than a woman!"

Cesare shot back, "We must both be what the Holy Father wishes us to be, for I would rather be a soldier than a cardinal! So neither of us has what we want!"

Cesare understood that the most important battle he must fight would be the exercise of his own free will. For love can steal free will using no weapon but itself. And Cesare did love his father. Yet he had studied his father's strategies long enough to know what Alexander was capable of, and he knew that he himself would never stoop to such treachery. In Cesare's mind, to take from a man his possessions, his riches, even his life, was a far lesser crime than to rob him of his free will. For without that he is a mere puppet of his own need, a beast of burden yielding to the snap of another man's whip. And he swore he would not be that beast.

Though Cesare understood what his father had done by asking him to bed Lucrezia, he thought himself equal to the task of loving her. After that first claim, he tricked himself into believing that it had been his choice. And yet there was a hidden card. Lucrezia loved with a heart full enough to tame the wildest beast, and so, without knowing it, she became the whip used by her father.

Lucrezia began to cry, and Cesare hugged her then, and tried to comfort her. "It will be all right, Crezia," he said. He stood for a long time, smoothing her blond curls, holding her. Finally, he dried her tears and said, "Don't concern yourself with that three-legged quail Sforza. For despite all, we'll always have each other."

6

Ludovico Sforza, the man known as Il Moro, was the power in the great city-state of Milan. Though he was the regent, not the duke, he ruled. He had claimed his authority by default of his weak and spiritless nephew.

Though the name *Il Moro* conjured up a swarthy darkness, he was a tall elegant man with the light blond good looks of the Italians of the north, intelligent and sensitive to the world of the mind and reason. It could be said that he was more enamored of ancient myth than of religion. He was confident and self-assured when things were going well, less confident during times of adversity. He commanded the respect of his citizens, and though he was sometimes unscrupulous and often devious in his political dealings, he was a merciful ruler whose compassion imposed a tax upon his wealthier citizens to support homes and hospitals for the poor.

The citizens of Milan, a city considered the home of discovery, embraced the new culture of humanism, and Il Moro and his wife, Beatrice d'Este, did many things to improve conditions. They renovated and decorated the castles, painted the drab houses of the city in the bright colors of the new art, and cleaned the streets to remove the stench so that the air could be breathed without lemon-scented gloves or half-cut oranges held under the noses of the nobility. Moreover, he paid the finest tutors to teach at the universities, for he appreciated the importance of education.

It was Il Moro's wife—the beautiful and ambitious Beatrice d'Este of Ferrara—who, many years before, had encouraged him to claim the crown from his nephew, Gian. For once Beatrice had a son, she was troubled that her heirs would have no legal right to their kingdom.

For thirteen years, Ludovico ruled as regent without opposition from his nephew, the duke, and Milan grew to be a city filled with art and culture. But then Gian married a young woman of hot temper and resolve: Avia of Naples, the granddaughter of the dreaded King Ferrante.

Once Avia had two sons—who she swore were forced to live as commoners because of Il Moro—she complained to her husband, the duke. But he was quite content to have his uncle rule Milan and offered no resistance. Now Avia had no choice. She took the matter to her grandfather, King Ferrante. She wrote letter after letter and had them brought daily by messenger to Naples. Finally, Ferrante was outraged, both at the slight to his family, and by the annoying content and frequency of the letters. He was, after all, a king, and a king could not tolerate this insult to his granddaughter. And so he determined to exact vengeance on Milan and restore Avia to her rightful place on the throne.

Now, informed of the king's anger by his secret advisors, and fearing Ferrante's ruthless tactics, Il Moro re-examined his position. The military force of Naples was legendary—strong and skilled. Milan would have no chance to defend itself without help.

Then, as though sent from the heavens by benevolent forces, Il Moro received word that King Charles of France was preparing his army for an invasion to claim the crown of Naples. Taking drastic action, Il Moro broke with tradition and immediately sent an invitation to King Charles, offering him and his troops safe passage through Milan on his way south to conquer Naples.

At the Vatican, Pope Alexander was reassessing his political position in light of the news of the French invasion and Il Moro's shortsightedness. He had called for

Cesare early that morning to discuss new strategies when Duarte Brandao visited his chambers to inform him of the new threat to the papacy.

"It has come to my attention," he explained, "that King Ferrante of Naples has sent a message to his cousin, King Ferdinand of Spain, stating his concerns about your allegiance to Il Moro, and the Vatican's position in regard to Milan now that France is readying its troops."

Cesare nodded knowingly. "He's heard about my sister's betrothal to Giovanni Sforza, no doubt. And he's distressed about our alliance with Milan."

Alexander nodded. "As well he might be. And what was the good King Ferdinand's response?"

"He refused to interfere in our affairs, for the time," Duarte said.

Pope Alexander laughed. "He is an honorable man. He remembers that it was I who delivered the dispensation allowing him to marry his first cousin, Isabella of Castile. And it was because of that proclamation that the countries of Spain and Castile were united, expanding the Aragonese empire."

"It would be wise to consider sending an ambassador to Naples with an accommodation . . ." Duarte suggested. "And to reassure him of our loyalty to Spain and the house of Aragon."

Alexander agreed. "We will offer Ferrante a marital alliance as well. For should Milan have what Naples does not?"

"Father, it is to my regret that here I can do you no good," Cesare, now enjoying himself, said. "For I am, after all, a cardinal of the Holy Roman Catholic Church."

Later that night, Alexander, alone in his chambers, stared into the dark night sky and pondered the ways of men. As the Holy Father he came to a chilling conclusion: fear makes men act even against their own best interest. It changes them from men of reason to blubbering fools, or why else would Il Moro align himself with France where there was no chance of victory for him? Could he not divine that once an army entered the city, every citizen was in danger? The women, the children, the men were at risk. Now, the Pope sighed. It was at these times that he found the knowledge of his own infallibility a comfort.

Even in the most treacherous of times, some men prove to be more evil than other men. Cruelty pulses through their hearts and veins, bringing them to life and awakening their senses. And so they suffer the same exhilaration when torturing their fellow man that most men feel when making love. They hold to a punishing and powerful God, one of their own invention, and with warped religious fervor create themselves in the vision of this illusion. King Ferrante of Naples was one of those men. And in an unfortunate circumstance for his enemies, he found even more rapture in mental torture than in physical.

He was a man of short stature, bulky and olive-skinned with unruly coarse black eyebrows so thick they concealed his eyes and made him look thoroughly menacing. That same coarse hair covered his entire body, ofttimes emerging from the neckline of his royal garments and from his sleeves like the fur of some primitive beast. When he was a young man, he had removed his own two front teeth when he contracted an almost fatal infection. Later, because of his vanity, he had ordered the royal blacksmith to forge him new teeth of gold. He seldom smiled, but when he did, he looked particularly sinister. It was rumored throughout all of Italy that Ferrante never carried a weapon and had little need of bodyguards, for with those gold teeth, he could tear the flesh from the bodies of his enemies.

As ruler of Naples, the most powerful territory on the Italian mainland, Ferrante inspired unholy dread in everyone. When enemies fell into his hands he chained them in cages, and strolled through his dungeons each day gloating with pleasure over his "zoo." And once the torn and broken bodies of his prisoners finally gave up their will and released their souls to heaven, Ferrante would have them embalmed and placed back in their cages, to remind those who still clung to life that stopping their hearts would not stop his pleasure.

Even his most loyal servants did not escape Ferrante's rapacious appetite for cruelty. He took from them what he could, in both favors and money, and then cut them down while they slept in their beds, so they had not one moment's peace while they lived.

To add to the impossibility of the situation, he was a superb and accomplished statesman, who had managed to keep the papacy from claiming any portion of his territory. For many years he had refused to pay his tithes to the church, agreeing only to send the traditional gift of one white horse to Rome for the papal army.

It was in his role as the statesman rather than the cruel warrior that King Ferrante considered the alliance with the Pope. But to make certain there were no surprises, and to insure that he would have the help he needed in his conquest, he dispatched another letter to his cousin, King Ferdinand of Spain. "If the Pope offers nothing to my satisfaction," he announced, "and refuses to assist us, we will ready our troops, and on the way to Milan we will also take Rome."

King Ferdinand of Spain, aware of the tension between Rome, Milan, and Naples, knew he must intervene. He needed the help of this Pope to keep peace, which was for him always better than war. If everything went well, he would also inform Alexander of a significant deception that had come to his attention by way of his cousin Ferrante.

Ferdinand was a tall, imperious man who took his position as monarch of Spain quite seriously. He was a Christian king, with no uncertainty about his God, and bowed to the infallibility of the Pope without question. But his belief did not rise to the level of evangelistic fervor that his wife, Queen Isabella's, did; he had no need to prosecute those who didn't believe. In essence he was a reasonable man, and held to doctrine only inasmuch as it served the Aragonese empire. He and Alexander respected each other, thought each other worthy of trust—as much as any mortal man could be trusted.

King Ferdinand, dressed in a simple cloak of dark blue satin with fur trim, looked elegant as he sat across from the Pope in the huge sitting room. He sipped his wine. "In a gesture of goodwill," he said, "King Ferrante has asked me to inform you of a circumstance he has recently been made aware of which may be of help to you, Your Holiness. As he is certain the church is an ally—not only to Spain but to Naples as well."

Alexander smiled, but his eyes were filled with wariness as he said, "Heaven always rewards its faithful."

Ferdinand spoke softly. "Shortly after the conclave, Ferrante's commander general, Virginio Orsini, met with Cardinal Cibo to execute the purchase of three castles Cibo inherited from his father, Pope Innocent."

Pope Alexander now frowned but sat silent for several moments before speaking. "This transaction took place without my knowledge? Without the authority of the Holy See? This treachery committed by a prince of the Holy Catholic Church?"

In truth, Alexander was more puzzled at the betrayal by Orsini than by Cardinal Cibo; for Commander Orsini was not only Adriana's brother-in-law; the Pope had always considered him a friend. And even in the most wicked times, there are some men who inspire confidence. Virginio Orsini was one of those men.

That evening over dinner, King Ferdinand supplied the missing piece. "The agreement for the purchase of the castles took place in Ostia, at the Palace of Giuliano della Rovere."

Ah, now Alexander understood. It was della Rovere who stood behind this unholy deed! Whoever owned those castles—all impregnable fortresses north of Rome—held the safety of Rome in his hands.

"This is a difficulty that must be overcome," Alexander said.

King Ferdinand agreed. "I will travel to Naples to speak to Ferrante on your behalf, to see what can be done."

The king kissed the Pope's ring before he left, assuring Alexander that he would use all his influence to resolve the matter. Then, almost as an afterthought, Ferdinand said, "There is one more problem, Your Holiness. The New World is in dispute. Both Portugal and Spain claim the new territories. Your mediation would be greatly appreciated by the queen and myself, for the necessity of divine guidance is apparent in this situation."

King Ferdinand of Spain traveled to Naples and spoke to his cousin, Ferrante. Almost immediately upon his arrival dispatches began to be sent back and forth between Rome and Naples. Messengers rode day and night. Finally, King Ferrante graciously assured the Pope that no injury to Alexander's person had been intended by Virginio Orsini; rather, the castles in question could be held to keep Rome safe. They were just outside the city and therefore could act as protection in the event of a French invasion.

And so it was agreed that Virginio Orsini could keep his castles, but he would be required to pay a tax or tithe of forty thousand ducats each year to the Vatican as proof of his sincerity and loyalty to Pope Alexander.

Now the question was asked, what was the Pope willing to offer in return for the support of both King Ferdinand and King Ferrante?

King Ferrante wanted Cesare Borgia as a husband for his sixteen-year-old granddaughter, Sancia.

Alexander refused, reminding Ferrante that his oldest son had a calling to holy office. Instead he offered his youngest son, Jofre.

Ferrante refused. For who would want the younger rather than the older son?

Though most previous Popes had feared denying Ferrante anything he asked for, Pope Alexander was intractable. He had plans for Cesare, and would not trade his gold for common metal.

Ferrante had heard much about Alexander's skill and cunning in negotiations, and now he was completely vexed. He knew that if he let this opportunity for an alliance pass, Alexander would quickly forge another that would put Naples at risk. After much deliberation and little hope of victory any other way, Ferrante grudgingly accepted. He only hoped that twelve-year-old Jofre would be able to bed his sixteen-year-old Sancia, and legitimize the contract before Alexander found a better match.

But five months after the proxy marriage, King Ferrante, the most fearsome man in Naples, died. And his son Masino, not nearly as clever or as cruel as his father, was left at the mercy of Pope Alexander. Because Naples was a papal territory and the Pope their *suzerain* or feudal lord, the crown could only be bestowed by him, and displeasing him might force him to choose another.

At this time it happened that Alexander too was compromised. Young King Charles VIII of France, who proclaimed Naples as his own, also wanted the crown. He sent an embassy to warn Alexander, to threaten to divest him of his power and name another Pope if he favored Masino, Ferrante's heir. But the Pope knew that French control of Naples would be fatal to the independence of the Papal States.

To add to the Pope's distress, a spiraling unrest began to grow among the Spanish-haters and traditional enemies of the papacy, which he knew could lead to the breakup of the fragile peace that existed throughout Italy since he took office.

Then he received the news which helped him decide.

Duarte Brandao returned to the Pope's chambers to tell him, "There are rumors of a new French invasion. King Charles is fervent and enthusiastic, and quite determined to be the greatest Christian monarch of his time. He plans to lead another Crusade to conquer Jerusalem."

Alexander understood. "So this young king must first conquer Naples, for it borders on the lands of the Infidel.

And he must ride through the Papal States on his way to Naples."

Duarte nodded. "Charles has also made clear his wish to reform the papacy, and there is only one way that can be accomplished, Your Worthiness."

The Pope pondered what Duarte said. "He must depose me in order to do what he wishes . . ."

Now, Pope Alexander was determined not to alienate Ferrante's son, Masino, for he needed the military force of Naples to come north to Rome in order to stave off any attack by King Charles.

Soon Alexander began to form another plan: In order to protect his position in the Vatican, and Rome itself, from foreign invasion, the Pope grew certain he must unify the city-states of Italy. It was then he conceived the concept of a Holy League. His plan was to unify and lead several of the larger city-states—that would allow them more power together than each could have alone.

But the moment he presented his plan to the rulers of these city-states, there were difficulties. Venice, as always, remained neutral; Milan was already on the side of the French; and Florence had a weak military—as well as the prophet called Savonarola, who had enough influence to discourage the Medici from joining.

Alexander, having met with strong resistance, concluded he must quickly crown Masino—or another man would soon wear the Holy Tiara.

Four days after Masino was crowned king of Naples, Jofre Borgia married Masino's daughter, Sancia.

At the altar of the chapel of Castel Nuovo, twelve-year-old Jofre tried to appear older than he was as he stood near his sixteen-year-old bride. Though he was taller than she and handsome enough, with his thick dark blond hair and light eyes, he had no wit or charm. Sancia, a beautiful and spirited girl, was annoyed at her father's choice. She refused to be fitted for any new finery for her wedding, and during the ceremony she stared impatiently at the guests in the crowded chapel. When the bishop asked Jofre, "Will you take this woman—" he was unable to finish his sentence before the enthusiastic Jofre interrupted, breathlessly, "I will . . ."

The guests laughed aloud. Sancia was humiliated, and her response to her vows was barely audible. What was she doing with this silly child?

At the reception, however, once she saw the many golden coins and jewels he had brought and offered, Sancia's expression softened. And as he allowed her bridesmaids to choose more gold coins from his pockets, the dark-haired Sancia smiled at him.

That evening in the bridal chamber, with King Masino and two other witnesses, Jofre Borgia climbed atop his new bride and rode her as he would a new pony. She lay there stubbornly, stiff as a corpse. Again and again—four times— he mounted her, until the king himself called a halt, and agreed the marriage contract was valid.

Now Alexander called for Cesare and Juan to join him in the Hall of Faith, where according to the agreement he had made with King Ferdinand concerning Naples he had promised to meet the ambassadors of Spain and Portugal to mediate a dispute over new lands.

As Cesare and Juan entered the ornate room, their father looked regal, wearing the papal miter and his richly embroidered red and gold cape. He told his sons, "This may be an exercise in diplomacy from which you can learn, for each of you will take part in many negotiations in the positions that you hold for the church."

What he didn't say was that King Ferdinand's plea for papal arbitration was not an empty gesture but reflected the papal influence in both the religion and politics in the new Age of Discovery. Now, it would gain the Pope the support of Spain, which he would sorely need in the event King Charles of France chose to invade the Italian territories.

Alexander looked up when the ambassadors entered the room. He greeted them warmly and said, "We think you know our sons, Cardinal Borgia and the duke of Gandia?"

"Yes, Holy Father, we do," replied the Spaniard, a portly Castilian grandee in a black, heavily brocaded tunic. He nodded to Cesare, and then to Juan, as did the elderly Portuguese emissary.

Alexander had spread a map out on the large inlaid table. He and the two ambassadors were pointing to various locations. "My sons, we have solved a problem that has been causing great concern between the nations of these two worthies."

The two men nodded again and Alexander continued, "Both these great nations have sent brave explorers to the farthest reaches of the unknown seas. Both have laid claims to the riches of the New World. Our holy church, through Calixtus the Third, had decreed that the kingdom of Portugal was entitled to all non-Christian lands on the coast of the Atlantic. Therefore, Portugal claims this entitles their country to the entire New World. Spain, on the other hand, insists that Calixtus meant only those lands on the *eastern* coast of the great ocean, not the newly discovered lands in the west.

"In order to avoid conflict between these great peoples, King Ferdinand has asked that we arbitrate their differences. And both nations, hoping for divine guidance, have agreed to accept our decision. Is that so?"

The two emissaries nodded.

"Well then," Alexander continued, "we have considered the matter carefully and spent long hours on our knees in prayer. And we have come to a decision. We must divide the New World along this longitudinal line."

He pointed to a line on the map which was one hundred leagues west of the Azores and Cape Verde Islands. "All non-Christian lands east of this line, which include many valuable islands, will belong to the Portuguese kingdom. Henceforth the peoples there will speak Portuguese. All such lands to the west of the line will belong to Their Catholic Majesties Ferdinand and Isabella."

Alexander looked at the ambassadors. "We have already issued our bull, *Inter Caetera,* issuing out our ruling on the matter. Plandini, the Vatican clerk, will give you each a copy as you depart. I hope this is satisfactory and that many souls will be saved rather than sacrificed because of our agreement." He smiled his brilliant charismatic smile, and both men bent to kiss his ring as he gave them leave to withdraw.

When they had gone, Alexander turned to Cesare. "What did you think of my decision?"

"I think, Father, that the Portuguese are at a disadvantage, for they have received far less of the territory."

Alexander's face lit up with a wolfish grin. "Well, son, it was King Ferdinand of Spain who asked us to intervene, and at the heart of our family we *are* Spanish. We must also consider that Spain is probably the most powerful country in the world today. With the king of France considering an invasion and planning to move his troops across the Alps on the advice of our enemy Cardinal della Rovere, we may need Spanish help. The Portuguese, on the other hand, tend to produce hardy seafarers, but not much of an army."

Before Cesare and Juan left the Pope, he placed his hand on Juan's shoulder and said, "My son, due to our successful mediation, your promised betrothal to Maria Enriquez has been moved forward. Again, I say, prepare yourself. Do not offend our friend King Ferdinand, for it has taken much diplomacy to ensure our alliances. We thank God each day for the good fortune of our family, the opportunities to spread the word of Christ across the globe in order to strengthen the papacy for the bodies and souls of the faithful."

Within a week, accompanied by a caravan of vast riches,

Juan was en route to Spain, and a rendezvous with the Enriquez family in Barcelona.

In Rome, the Pope felt weary from the weight of the world; both heaven and earth seemed to rest on his shoulders. Yet, one small pleasure could revive him . . .

That night Alexander readied himself to appear in his finest silk sleeping costume, for his young mistress, Julia Farnese, had been invited to spend the night in his bed. As his manservant bathed him and washed his hair with perfumed soap, he found himself smiling at the thought of her sweet face gazing at him with admiration and, he believed, genuine fondness.

Though it puzzled him how a young woman of such beauty and charm could find herself enchanted by a man whose prime had passed, he accepted it as he had many of the other puzzlements in his life. Certainly, he was wise enough to know that his power and his favors could inspire a certain devotion. And her relationship with him as the Holy Father could improve the condition and the wealth of her entire family and therefore increase her own status. But there was more, and in his heart he knew it. For when Julia and he made love, it was a priceless gift. Her innocence was captivating; her need to learn and please and her curiosity for all manner of sensual exploration gave her special appeal.

Alexander had been with many beautiful courtesans who had far more experience, who knew how to please a man using pure craft. But Julia's uninhibited response to sensual pleasure was that of a joyful child, and somehow, though he could not describe it as the most passionate relationship he'd had, it brought him immense satisfaction.

Now Julia, wearing a gown of purple velvet, was led into his bedchamber. Her golden hair fell loosely down her back, and on her neck she wore a simple necklace of small pearls that he had given her the first time they made love.

As he sat on the side of his large bed, Julia began to unlace her gown. Without a word, she turned her back and asked, "My dear Holiness, please lift my hair?"

Alexander stood, his huge body close behind her, filling his senses with the lavender scent of her hair. He held her blond curls in his large hands, the ones that held the fate of the souls of so many, as she stepped out of her gown and it dropped to the floor.

When she turned to raise her face to accept his kiss, he had to bend to reach her lips. She was not even as tall as Lucrezia, and more delicate of form. She put her arms around his neck, and when he stood, he lifted her off the floor.

"My sweet Julia, I've been waiting for so many hours for your arrival. To hold you in my arms will bring me as much pleasure as serving Mass—though it would be a sacrilege for me to admit that truth aloud to anyone but you, my sweet."

Julia smiled at him and lay down next to him between the satin sheets. "I received a message from Orso today," she said, "and he wishes to come back to Rome to visit for a time."

Alexander tried not to show his displeasure, for it was much too beautiful a night. "It is unfortunate, but I believe your young husband's presence in Bassanello is important for a short time more. I may need to call upon him to lead one of my military troops."

Julia knew the Pope was jealous, for his every expression shone in his eyes. To reassure him, she leaned over and placed her lips upon his, kissing him hard. She had the sweet cool lips of someone young and inexperienced, but he was careful to treat her quite gently for above all things he didn't want to frighten her. They had made love several times before, but he had put his own pleasure aside to be sure he was aware when she reached hers. He didn't want to lose himself completely and have his passion drive him into her too hard, for she would stiffen then and all pleasure would elude them.

"Would it please you to have me lie on my stomach?" she asked him. "And then, you above me?"

"I fear to damage you," he told her. "I prefer that I lie on my back and you ride me as you will. In that way you may control the amount of your own passion, and receive as much pleasure as you can bear."

He'd considered it often, the childlike innocence of Julia as she let down her hair like those goddesses of ancient myth and story, those temptresses who cast a spell to keep a prince imprisoned against his will forever.

Each time he lay on his back and looked up at her face, her eyes closed with pleasure, her head thrown back in abandon, he believed the carnal pleasure he felt was a gift of surrender to the Heavenly Father. For who else except a Beneficent Father would provide man such heavenly grace on earth?

Before Julia left his chambers that morning, he gave her a gold filigree cross he had commissioned from one of the finest goldsmiths in Florence. She sat on the bed, unclothed, and let him place it around her neck. Sitting there, she looked the image of grace, and in the beauty of her face and body, Pope Alexander was again assured there was a Heavenly Father, for no one on earth could conceive of such perfection.

7

The Pope's physician rushed to the Vatican with an urgent report of an outbreak of plague in the city of Rome. Now, sitting at his throne, in the Hall of Faith, and hearing of the coming of the Black Death, Alexander was alarmed. He quickly called his daughter to his chambers.

"It is time for you to leave for Pesaro, to seek sanctuary with your husband," he said simply.

"But Papa," she cried, kneeling at his feet and holding to his legs, "how can I leave you? How can I leave my brothers, and my dearest Adriana, and our Julia? How can I live in that place so far from this city I love?"

Under normal circumstances Alexander would have bargained for more time with his precious daughter, but now, with this new and dangerous circumstance, he found he must insist that she go. "Papa will send Madonna Adriana and dear Julia with you to Pesaro," he told her. "And we will send messages each day, so neither of us will be lonely, my sweet child."

But Lucrezia was inconsolable. She stood now, her usual soft eyes blazing. "I would prefer to die a Black Death in Rome than live with Giovanni Sforza in Pesaro. He is impossible. He never looks at me, rarely speaks to me, and when he does it is all about himself, or to order me to do something I hate."

Pope Alexander drew her into an affectionate embrace

and tried to comfort her. "Have we not spoken of this before? Of the sacrifices we each must make in order to maintain the well-being of the family and the power of God in the world? Our dear Julia has told me of your admiration of Saint Catherine. Would she object, as you are doing, to the call of the Heavenly Father? And is not your papa the voice of the Heavenly Father on earth?"

Lucrezia stood back and looked at her father. With her lower lip still in a pout, she said, "But Catherine of Siena is a saint; I am but a girl. It is not necessary for girls to do as saints do. For being the daughter of a Pope should not make me a martyr."

Pope Alexander's eyes lit up. Only a rare man would have been able to resist his daughter's passionate argument, yet he found himself enchanted and amused by her reluctance to leave him.

He took her delicate hand in his. "Ah, your papa too has to sacrifice for the Heavenly Father, for there is no one in this world whom I love above you, my child."

Now Lucrezia looked at her father coyly. "Not even Julia?"

The Pope made the sign of the cross over his chest. "With the Lord as my witness, I say again, there is no one I love above you."

"Oh, Papa," Lucrezia said, throwing her arms around his neck and breathing in the scent of incense from his golden garments. "Will you promise to send message after message without ever stopping? And will you promise to send for me whenever you see I cannot bear it any longer? For if not I will fade away from despair, and you will never lay eyes on me again."

"I promise," he said. "Now gather your ladies-in-waiting, and I will inform your husband that you will be leaving immediately for Pesaro."

As Lucrezia left she bent to kiss the Pope's ring, and when she lifted her head she asked, "Shall I tell our Julia or will you?"

The Pope smiled. "You may tell her," he said, pretending seriousness. "Now go . . ."

O n the last day of their five-day journey to Pesaro, the rain was falling in heavy sheets, drenching Lucrezia, Julia, and Adriana, as well as all their servants and supplies.

Lucrezia was disappointed, for she had hoped to look her very best on her arrival; after all, she was their duchess. With the pride and excitement of a child pretending, Lucrezia wanted to enjoy the admiration and affection she hoped to see on the faces of those people who now would be her subjects.

A caravan of horses carried their precious cargo in peasant carts as they journeyed through the beautiful countryside along the rough dirt road. Though Michelotto and several of his armed men accompanied Lucrezia and her company to protect them from the dangers of attack by bandits, and the hazards of robbery, they were still forced to stop each night when darkness fell. But there were few accommodations along the road from Rome to Pesaro, and often they had to set up an encampment.

Several hours before they arrived, Lucrezia asked her envoy to put up shelter so she and Julia could prepare themselves. They had been on the road for many days now, and her fresh young face and clean hair had wilted with the weather—to say nothing of the mud caked on her shoes and gown. She asked her ladies-in-waiting to take down her hair, dry it with new cotton cloths, and apply balm to her tresses to give the gold a special sheen. But when she slipped out of her gown to put on another, she suddenly felt dizzy. "I have a chill," she told her lady, and then reached out to grab the shoulder of the girl in order to steady herself.

Adriana looked concerned, for Lucrezia's cheeks appeared rosy with fever. "Are you feeling sickly?" she asked.

Lucrezia smiled, her eyes shinier than usual. "I feel well," she lied, but Adriana noticed the gooseflesh on her arms.

"As soon as we arrive and I have some hot tea, I'm sure I'll feel better. But let us get started, for I'm certain there are festivities awaiting us, and we do not want to weary the loyal citizens."

They traveled on) to Pesaro, where miles before they reached the gates they saw the crowds of men, women, and children who had gathered, some holding boards or cloth above their heads to shelter themselves from the hard driving rain. But still they sang to her and clapped for her while they shouted happy greetings. They threw flowers and lifted children for her to touch.

But by the time they arrived at the gate, Lucrezia's head was spinning. And when Giovanni greeted her with a smile, and said, "Welcome, my duchess," she hardly heard him before she swooned from weakness and slipped from her horse.

One of the manservants caught her in his arms, and carried her into the palace. Amazed at how little she weighed and impressed by her blond beauty, he placed her gently on the feather bed in the grand bedroom and went back to tell the others all about the duke's new bride. Adriana and Julia fussed about her, asking for tea and soup to help warm her, but by then Giovanni had gone back to the crowds, telling them that the duchess would formally greet them the following day once she had rested and managed to renew herself.

That night, in the darkened room in a strange city, Lucrezia lay in bed, said her prayers, and tried to sleep. She missed her father terribly, but even more she missed her brother Cesare.

On the day she left Rome Cesare had promised to visit her in Pesaro, but if for any reason that became impossible, he promised he would send Don Michelotto to accompany her to meet him at Silverlake, which was halfway between Rome and Pesaro. There they could spend time alone. They could speak without anyone hearing; they could play in the fields as they did as children, far from the prying eyes of the Pope and those others who were sworn to safeguard them.

The thought of Cesare comforted her, and finally, when she closed her eyes and imagined her brother's lips upon hers, she fell asleep.

When she awoke the following morning she still felt feverish, but refused to stay in bed, for she didn't want to waste another day without seeing Pesaro and greeting the citizens she knew had been waiting to see her. The rain had cleared and now the sun was shining into her room, making it look warm and cozy. Some of the citizens had stayed through the night and were still standing in the square outside the castle; she could hear them singing through her open windows.

Giovanni had promised Lucrezia that there would be grand balls and parties to attend. She had to prepare. With Julia and Adriana and the ladies-in-waiting, she managed to choose a gown that was both simple and elegant, of pink satin with a bodice of fine Venetian lace. She wore a beaded headdress of gold and pearls, with her hair tied up at the sides, but left long and flowing in back. When she presented herself to Julia, she spun around joyfully. "Do I look like a duchess?"

Julia, her blue eyes shining, said, "Rather like a princess to me."

Adriana agreed. "A perfect angel."

Lucrezia walked out onto the balcony and waved to the crowd in the square. They clapped and cheered for her, and threw crowns woven of flowers. She bent and lifted one from the floor of the balcony and placed it on her head. And the crowd cheered even louder.

Then there was music in the city, with jugglers, jousters, and jesters running through the streets just as there had been in Rome, and again she was overcome with happiness at all the attention being paid to her. She had always wondered why her father and her brothers so enjoyed the marches through the city and the power of position, but now she felt she understood. Looking into the faces of all the men, women, and children gazing up at her, Lucrezia felt much less lonely. Maybe she too had been born to this.

Pesaro was beautiful; its countryside, dotted with olive trees, was lush and green. Surrounding it, protecting it, the huge and graceful Apennine Mountains cradled the city. Lucrezia knew she could be truly happy here—happier still if she could find a way to tolerate her husband, Giovanni.

It was well known throughout France that King Charles placed great faith not only in the Holy Roman Catholic Church, but also in the alignment of the stars in the heavens. And so it followed that his most trusted advisor was the physician and astrologer Simon of Pavia. Simon had read the celestial map on the occasion of Charles's birth, and it was he who proclaimed the young king's future destiny as leader of the new Crusade against the Infidel Turks. From the time Charles was a child, he embarked upon no important assignment without the counsel of his astrologer.

It was due not only to great skill but also to great fortune that Duarte Brandao came upon this important piece of information, and conceived of a brilliant strategy. He was in such high spirits, he rushed into the Pope's chambers to speak to him.

Pope Alexander was sitting at his desk, signing a large pile of papal bulls. When he looked up and saw Duarte, he smiled amiably and dismissed everyone else in the room.

Alexander stood and walked over to his favorite chair. But when Duarte bent to kiss his ring, the Pope pulled his hand away impatiently. "My friend, save all this ceremony for public occasions or when we are in the company of others, for in private I acknowledge that it is you that I trust above all—even my children. And that responsibility imposes a certain equality, even upon the Vicar of Christ. For I, Alexander the man, cherish your loyalty and value your friendship."

He waved his hand to indicate a chair opposite him, but Duarte was unable to sit still as he explained what he had learned.

Pope Alexander listened carefully. Then he asked, "Do you, yourself, believe the stars rule?"

Duarte shook his head. "Your Holiness, what I believe can hardly matter."

"And yet it does," the Pope said.

"I believe the stars affect one's life, yet no one but the man himself and our Heavenly Father *rules* his life."

The Pope reached to touch the amber amulet that always hung around his neck, and rubbed it affectionately. "Each of us believes there is a charm to our life, and so this Charles is not much different." He smiled at Duarte. "But you must have a plan you have brought me, for I can see it on your face, so speak of it now."

Duarte's voice was almost a whisper. "Let me go to this man, this Simon of Pavia, in advance of the invasion, with a 'professional fee.' An act of confidence."

"In what amount?" Alexander asked.

Duarte hesitated a moment, for he knew of the Pope's frugal nature when dealing with anything but state ceremony and family. "I would offer twenty thousand ducats . . ."

Alexander's eyes widened, and he tried to control the surprise in his voice. "Duarte? We could outfit an army with horses for such a sum. Twenty thousand ducats is not a professional fee, it is a colossal bribe . . ."

Brandao smiled. "Holiness, we must not quibble over a few pieces of gold. We must ensure a favorable reading by this physician, for he has earned the trust of the king of France."

The Pope sat in quiet consideration for several minutes, and then he agreed. "Duarte, as usual, you are correct. Pay the *dottore* his *fee,* as you suggest. Astrology itself denies the God-given gift of free will. It is forbidden by canon law. So it is not as though we are opposing a lawful Christian process. Our interference with it does not stain our immortal soul."

That very night Duarte rode in disguise through the French lines. He rode for several days to reach his destination—a small cottage in the woods. There he arrived in time to find Simon of Pavia frolicking in the arms of a very rotund whore. Brandao, always a gentleman, politely convinced Simon to excuse himself from the lady and join him in the living quarters, for he had a message of great importance to deliver.

It only took a few moments for Duarte to present the agreement and pay the physician his fee.

Still in disguise, assured of the success of his mission, Brandao mounted his horse and rode back to Rome.

A h, that a Pope could have only the heart and soul of a saint instead of the worldly desires of a mortal man. But as embroiled as Alexander was in political intrigue, he was now constantly distracted by his personal affairs. His young mistress, Julia Farnese, who had traveled with Lucrezia to Pesaro, had been forced to stay away weeks longer than expected after Lucrezia fell ill, in order to care for her. Once Lucrezia had recovered enough for Julia to leave with a clear conscience, she decided to visit her husband, Orso, at the Castel of Bassanello, for a reason Alexander could not comprehend. But first, she implored the Pope, she must stop to visit her mother and sick brother at Capodimonte.

When Alexander read Julia's request, he forbade it; her husband, Orso, was a soldier, he insisted, and had been sent away on papal business. But Julia, young and spirited, rebelled against the Pope's instructions to return to Rome immediately. She penned a second letter begging Alexander's forgiveness for her disobedience, but insisted she could not return just yet. And to add to her betrayal, she took her mother-in-law, Adriana, along with her to Capodimonte.

When Alexander received her next message, he was furious. If he could not bear to be without his Julia, how then could she bear to be without him? Faithless girl! Now the Pope flew into a rage at everyone in his service. He lay awake at night, sleepless, not over any political threat, but out of longing for the touch of Julia's hand, the scent of her hair, the comfort of her warm body. Finally, when he could bear it no longer, he kneeled at his altar and prayed that the demon of his insatiable appetites be shriven from his heart. When Cardinal Farnese tried to reason with him—explaining that his sister had no choice, for Orso had sent for her and he was after all her husband—the Pope dismissed him with a shout. *"Ingrazia!"*

For days Alexander fumed. He paced his chambers and repeated long lists of the vices of his mistress, her husband, and his favorite cousin. He would excommunicate them. They would surely be sent to hell for this betrayal.

But it was young Orso who finally helped relieve the Pope's anguish. Hearing of Alexander's distress, and fearing for his own position, he forbade his wife to come to Bassanello. Instead he instructed her to return home to Rome at once, for there was danger on the roads of Rome from the French invasion. And, because he was her husband, she was obliged to obey.

When King Charles moved his powerful army across the Alps into Italian territory, the bitter, angry Cardinal della Rovere was at his side, goading him, insisting that an attack on the Borgia Pope was more important than any against the Infidel Turks.

As the French troops moved southward toward Naples, no one took action to stop them—not Milan, not Bologna, not Florence.

Pope Alexander, hearing of their approach, prepared to defend Rome and the Vatican. He set his trust in King Ferrante's captain general, Virginio Orsini, head of the Orsini family. Virginio had convinced the Pope of his good faith by paying the necessary tax on his castles; Alexander knew that Virginio could call upon more than twenty thousand vassals, and with his great fortress, the impregnable Bracciano, they were almost invincible.

But the seeds of treachery and avarice can hide in the hearts of the most courageous of men, and even the Holy Father could not portend their development.

Duarte Brandao now rushed into the chambers of Pope Alexander. "I have received word, Your Worthiness, that our former friend Virginio Orsini has gone over to the French."

Pope Alexander, hearing the news, said, "He must have lost his wits . . ."

Duarte, whose composure was legendary, now looked upset.

"What is it, my friend?" the Pope asked. "It is just a change of strategy that is needed here. Now, rather than fight this King Charles, we must just outthink him."

Duarte lowered his head and his voice. "There is more distressing news, Your Omnipotence. The French have captured Julia Farnese and Madonna Adriana on their way back from Capodimonte. They are being held at the headquarters of the cavalry, even now."

Pope Alexander went pale with rage. For long moments he was speechless, his mind dark with worry and fear. Finally he spoke. "Duarte, the fall of Rome would be a tragedy, but if my dear Julia were harmed, it would be a complete calamity. You must arrange for her release, for they will surely wish to ransom her."

"What are your terms?" Duarte asked.

"Pay whatever you must," Alexander said. "For Charles now has in his hands my heart and my eyes."

The French, as well as being fine soldiers, were also known for their chivalry. Once they captured Julia Farnese and Adriana Orsini, they released all the servants who had accompanied them. Then they tried to charm the beautiful ladies with both food and amusing stories. But when Charles found out who the captives were, he immediately ordered that they be returned to the Pope.

"For what ransom?" the chief cavalryman asked.

Charles felt generous. "Three thousand ducats," he said.

The commander protested. "Pope Alexander will pay fifty times that."

"But we are here to gain the crown of Naples," Charles reminded the general, "which is worth far more."

Within three days, Julia Farnese and Adriana were returned to Rome unharmed, accompanied by four hundred French troops. And waiting at the gates joyful and relieved was Alexander.

Later, in his chambers, dressed as a cavalier with sword and dagger at his side, wearing shiny black boots from Valencia and a black cloak with gold brocade, he made love to Julia. And for the first time since she'd been gone, he felt at peace.

Pope Alexander, given the outrageous treachery of Virginio Orsini, knew that resisting the French was now hopeless. Without his fortresses to guard the entrance to Rome, there would be no stopping Charles. He needed time to develop a strategy to outsmart the young king, rather than to try to defeat the French in battle.

With his usual farsightedness, as soon as Alexander was made Pope, he had prepared for the possibility of a foreign invasion. He had commissioned a secure corridor between the rooms in the Vatican and the Castel Sant' Angelo which could offer him protection. He had supplied it with enough food and water to last for at least one winter, and now he resolved to resist that long if necessary.

Now, under the watchful eyes of Duarte Brandao and Don Michelotto, Alexander and Cesare instructed their servants to gather their valuables—the gold tiaras, papal jewels, relics, beds, chests and tapestries—for their retreat to Castel Sant' Angelo, an impregnable fortress. Their families came with them; even Vanozza abandoned her palace for the safety of Sant' Angelo. And with great wisdom and sensitivity Cardinal Farnese whisked his sister, Julia, out of Rome, preventing any opportunity for discomfort to the Pope. The confrontation between past and present mistresses could cause Alexander more distress than the arrival of King Charles, for though Vanozza accepted Julia—never quite able to take her seriously—Julia was quite jealous of the mother of the Pope's children.

On Christmas Day, the Pope ordered all troops from Naples to leave Rome at once. They were not strong enough to overcome the French troops, and Alexander feared that their presence in the city would make Rome seem a hostile place. Then Charles might resort to sacking the city, looting and pillaging all the valuables as they took capture—or, at the very least, failing to restrain his troops as they did so.

He told Duarte, "Please get a message to Charles. Tell him His Holiness, Pope Alexander, wishes to welcome him as he passes through our city on the way to Naples."

Duarte frowned, his eyes narrowed. "Passes through?"

"In a manner of speaking," Alexander said, but he looked concerned when he added, "though I'm not certain that is what the good king has in mind."

In December, as falling snow turned everything gray, the distressed Pope Alexander and his son Cesare watched from the window of their fortress as the French army, in orderly ranks, marched through the gates of Rome.

Swiss troopers with lethal ten-foot pikes and spears, Gascons with crossbows and the small-caliber long guns they called harquebuses, German mercenaries with axes and spikes, and light cavalry with fearsome lances flooded the city. They were accompanied by heavily armored men at arms with swords and iron maces, and taking up the rear came row after row of marching French artillerymen walking beside gigantic bronze cannons.

In preparation for the king's arrival, Alexander had set aside the lavish Palazzo Venezia for Charles. He would be attended to by the finest chef the Pope could commandeer, and hundreds of servants were enlisted to deliver all manner of luxury to the French monarch. In return for the Pope's hospitality, Charles gave his troops strict instructions that there was to be no looting or other violence in the city, under pain of death.

But while Charles was enjoying his "visit" to Rome, impressed by the respect the Pope had shown him, Cardinal della Rovere and his dissident cardinals were whispering in the king's ear, repeatedly warning Charles of the Pope's cunning and urging him to convene a General Council.

Alexander sent one of his many loyal cardinals, and one of his most persuasive, to speak to the king, to defend him against Cardinal della Rovere's charge of simony. And Charles seemed more persuaded by the arguments of Alexander's minister than by the harping of frantic della Rovere.

No General Council was called.

Instead, after several days, King Charles sent a sealed message to the Pope. As Alexander unrolled the parchment, he allowed himself a deep breath. He scanned the royal document carefully, and tried to apprehend the mood of the writer. It was a request. King Charles wanted an audience with him.

The Pope was relieved. He had accomplished what he hoped for. His strategy was working; now it appeared that this almost impossible situation could be negotiated to his advantage. Though his territory had been breached by Charles and his troops, the Pope knew he must maintain an air of superiority with this impetuous French king. He didn't want to appear arrogant; still, he understood he must avoid making his relief obvious.

The Pope arranged for a meeting in the Vatican gardens. But timing would be crucial. Alexander knew he could not arrive before the king and appear to be waiting, yet it was just as important that the king not arrive first and be kept waiting. This is where Alexander's genius was its most refined.

He was carried by litter from Castel Sant' Angelo to the meeting place in the garden. But he instructed his bearers to hide him behind a large bush alongside one of the stone buildings. There he waited soundlessly for twenty minutes. Then, just as he saw King Charles enter the garden and begin to walk the long path lined with scarlet roses, Alexander's bearers brought forward his litter.

Pope Alexander was outfitted in one of his most imposing garments: the three golden crowns a sparkling beacon on his mitered headdress, a great jeweled crucifix dangling against his chest.

Charles, the mighty king of France, the most powerful military nation in Christendom, was a tiny, almost dwarflike man, who walked on elevated boots and seemed to conceal his person in voluminous garments in all the colors of the rainbow. He was so obviously awed by the stature of Pope Alexander that a trickle of saliva ran from his mouth.

And so it was, within this garden filled with holy roses, that Pope Alexander negotiated to save Rome.

The following day, Pope and king met again to finalize their agreement, this time in the Hall of Popes. Alexander knew this would allow him the advantage. Charles would consider it a holy place, as sacred a venue as there could be.

Alexander dictated that the preamble read in such a way that Charles could never move to depose him. "Our Holy Father," it stated, "shall remain the good father of the king of France, and the king of France shall remain a devoted son to our Holy Father." Then it was time to get to the other business at hand.

Alexander would provide the French army with free passage through all the Papal States, with provisions to boot. In short, if Charles could win Naples with arms, Alexander would give him the approval of the church. To ensure this, the Pope would hand over his dearly beloved son Cesare to

King Charles as a hostage. Cesare Borgia would also be given authority to crown Charles as king of Naples once the city was conquered.

Prince Djem, still held captive by the Pope, would also be handed over to Charles, but the Pope would be permitted to keep the forty thousand ducats that the sultan of Turkey paid each year to keep his brother captive. Charles would use Djem as one of the leaders of the Crusade, to blunt the vigor of the defending Infidel.

King Charles's foremost desire was to be named by the Pope as the official commander of the Crusades. Alexander agreed, but insisted first Charles must swear obedience to him, and acknowledge him as the true Vicar of Christ.

It was agreed, with the exception that Charles would be named commander of the Crusades only *after* he had conquered Naples.

Charles bowed several times as was necessary, and kissed Alexander's ring. Then he said, "I swear obedience and reverence to Your Holiness, as have all the kings of France. I acknowledge you, Holy Father, as the pontiff of all Christians, and the successor of the apostles Peter and Paul. Now I offer everything I own to the Holy See."

Alexander rose, clasped Charles in his arms, and said, "I will grant you three favors," as was the custom. Before a vassal swore obedience and reverence to a new lord, he had the right to ask favors. To avoid indignity to the holy office, it was understood that the favors would be negotiated beforehand and thus would not seem to be bargaining.

Charles continued. "I ask that you confirm my family in all its royal privileges, that you decree we rule by God's will. Second, that you bless my expedition to Naples. And third, that you name three of my designees as cardinals, allowing Cardinal della Rovere to reside in France."

Pope Alexander agreed to the terms, and so, with great joy, King Charles called from his company a tall, reed-thin man with a long face and mournful eyes. "Your Holiness, I wish to introduce my physician and astrologer, Simon of

Pavia. His reading of the stars influenced my decision more than any other factor, and led me to reject the urgings of Cardinal della Rovere and to place my trust in you."

Thus, from a position of helplessness, Alexander had negotiated a reasonable peace.

Later that evening, Alexander called Cesare into his chambers to explain the afternoon's agreement with King Charles.

Cesare felt a quick rush of anger as he listened, but he bowed his head. He knew that, as a cardinal and the Pope's son, he was logically an appropriate hostage. His brother Juan, who would soon become captain general of the papal army, could not be the primary hostage. Cesare's anger had less to do with the danger of the situation than with the way the transaction reminded him that he was a pawn to be traded on the whim of others.

Alexander sat down on the beautifully carved chest at the foot of his bed, the lid intricately carved by Pinturicchio. Inside that chest were drinking goblets, many nightclothes, extra perfumes and essences—all necessary when Pope Alexander brought his mistresses to his sleeping chambers at the Borgia apartments. He preferred sitting on this chest more than on any of the chairs in his chambers.

"My son, you know I am not able to send your brother Juan to be hostage, for he is to become the captain general of the papal army. Therefore, it must be you," Alexander told his son, acknowledging Cesare's irritation. "Charles has also demanded Djem as a hostage, so you will have a companion. Cheer up! Naples is an enjoyable city for a young fellow like yourself." Alexander paused for a moment, his dark eyes merry. Then he said to Cesare, "You are not fond of your brother Juan."

But Cesare was used to this trick of his father—the joviality that masked a serious intent. "He is my brother," Cesare said respectfully. "So I am fond of him as my brother."

Cesare had far more terrible secrets to hide than his hatred of his brother—secrets that could ruin his life, and his relationship with his father, the church, and his fellow men. So he did not try too hard to conceal his dislike for Juan. Instead he laughed. "Of course, if he were not my brother, he would be my enemy."

Alexander frowned with annoyance. He knew he was missing something of importance. "Never say that, even in jest. The Borgia family has many enemies, and we can only survive holding faith with each other." He rose from the chest and came to Cesare and embraced him. "I know you would rather be a soldier than a priest. But believe me, you are more important in the family plans than Juan, and you know how much I love your brother. But when I die, everything falls unless you are there to succeed me. You are the only one of my children who can accomplish this. You have the wits, the daring, and the fighting skill. There have been warrior Popes before, and surely you can be one."

"I am too young," Cesare said impatiently. "You would have to live another twenty years . . ."

Alexander gave him a push with his hand. "And why not?" He grinned at Cesare, that roguish grin which so endeared him to his children and his mistresses. His deep baritone voice rolled off at full measure. "Who enjoys a banquet more than I? Who can hunt more hours a day than myself? Who loves women better? If it were not so strictly against canon law for a Pope to father children, how many more bastards would I now have? I will live another twenty years, and you shall be Pope. I have already planned it."

"I would rather fight than pray," Cesare said. "It is my nature."

"As you have proven," Alexander sighed. "But I tell you all this to prove my love for you. You are my dear son and my greatest hope. Someday *you*, not Charles, will regain Jerusalem." He paused for a moment, overcome by emotion.

Alexander's most formidable weapon was his ability to inspire a feeling of well-being in his company—it was this ability to make each person believe that their welfare was of the greatest importance to him that gained their trust, and made them believe more in him than they did in themselves. This was his true treachery.

And so it was in his dealings with royalty, his children, and his subjects: for as long as he was Pope, the entirety of earth was under his dominion.

For a moment the charm of Alexander entranced Cesare. But the reference to another Crusade broke the spell. Popes and kings had often used the hope of another Crusade to extract money from the believing people; it was another source of revenue. But the time for a Crusade had passed, for Islam was now too strong. It threatened Europe itself. Venice lived in fear that its worldwide trade would be cut off by such a war and that the Turks might even attack their city. France and Spain were constantly at each other's throats for the crown of Naples, and the Pope himself had all he could do to maintain its temporal power in the Papal States of Italy. And his father was too clever not to know all this. But Cesare also knew that Juan was first in his father's heart—and rightly so, he thought. Juan had the wiles of a devious woman and the fickle heart of a courtier. At times he could even charm Cesare himself, though Cesare despised him because he thought him a coward. Commander of the papal army? A joke!

"When I lead the Crusade, I will have my head tonsured," Cesare said. It was a joke between his father and himself. Cesare had never worn his hair in the priestly tonsure.

Alexander laughed. "After you lead the Crusade, perhaps you can persuade the church to do away with both celibacy and tonsure for priests. Perhaps they are both healthy practices, but still they are unnatural." Alexander was silent for a moment, lost in thought. Then he said, "Let me remind you of one thing. When you accompany the army of France to Naples, you must guard the life of your fellow hostage, Djem. Remember, the sultan of Turkey pays me forty thousand ducats each year for his keep. If he dies, no more money; if he escapes, no more money. And he brings in more money than a cardinal's hat."

"I will guard him and myself," Cesare said. "I trust that you will restrain my brother Juan in Spain. He must do nothing to alienate King Ferdinand and thus endanger our safety with the French king."

"Your brother acts under my orders only," Alexander said. "And my orders will always be to protect you. After all, you, my son, hold in your hand the future of the Borgia."

"I will do my best for you always," Cesare said. "And for the church."

K nowing that by afternoon he would be taken hostage and forced to leave Rome, Cesare left the Vatican before dawn and rode far into the countryside. He had only one purpose in mind.

After riding for quite some time, over hills and through a forest alive with the rustling of animals and the hooting of owls, he reached the outskirts of the small village just as the sun was rising to push away the shadows of night. His horse was sweaty from the speed and strain of the journey.

When he came upon the small stone cottage, he called out. "Noni, Noni," he shouted, but no one answered. As far as he could see, the fields were empty. He rode around the back.

There an old woman, nearly doubled forward by age, rested heavily on a hawthorn stick. She shuffled as she walked through the garden, a wicker basket on one arm filled with freshly picked herbs and flowers. For a moment she stopped and stood with her head bent so low she almost toppled over; then slyly she raised her head and looked around in all directions. But through her clouded eyes she didn't see him. She placed her basket on the wet ground, picked one more small bundle of herbs, and placed them carefully on the very top of the flowers. She cast her gaze upward and crossed herself. Then, as though confused, she shuffled off, her sandals dragging through the mud.

"Noni," Cesare called to the old woman again as he rode up closer to her. "Noni!"

The woman stopped when she saw him and quickly raised her hawthorn stick to strike. But then through squinting eyes she recognized him. Only then did she smile. "Come down, my boy," she said, her voice strained with age and emotion. "Come here and let me touch you."

Cesare dismounted and put his arms around the old woman, holding her gently for fear her brittle bones would break.

"What can I do for you, my son?" she asked.

"I need your help," he told her. "An herb that will put a large man to sleep for many hours, but do him no harm. It must be tasteless, and colorless as well."

The old woman cackled and reached up to touch Cesare's cheek affectionately. "A good boy. You're a good boy," she repeated. "No poison? Not like your father . . ." she muttered. Then she cackled again, and her face wrinkled like a thin sheet of brown parchment.

Cesare had known Noni all his life. It was rumored throughout Rome that she had been his father's wet nurse in Spain, and that Alexander felt such affection for her that he had brought her to Rome and provided her with this small cottage in the countryside and a garden in which to grow her herbs.

For as long as anyone could remember she had lived alone, yet no one had disturbed her—not even the night bandits or gangs of unruly street vandals who sometimes wandered out into the countryside to sack and pillage the weak and helpless villagers. It was a wonder that she had survived so long. And yet, if other rumors were to be believed, Noni had far greater protection than even the Holy Father. For it was also said that in the dark of night, a strange howling could often be heard coming from her house—and not only when the moon was full. And this much Cesare knew to be true: never did she have to hunt or shop to eat. For dead birds and small animals seemed to appear at her doorstep or in her garden fresh and ready for her pot.

Cesare seldom heard his father speak of her, and then it

was with warmth and kindness. But each year, ceremoniously, Alexander came to this cottage in the far countryside to be bathed by Noni in the small clear pond at the back. Those who had accompanied him stood far away, but all swore they heard the sound of wild winds and flapping wings and saw a great spiraling of stars.

There were other stories, too. Around his neck Alexander wore an amber amulet that Noni had given him when he was a young cardinal, and once when it was lost he had become frantic. That very afternoon during a hunt he fell off his horse, hit his head, and lay unconscious for hours. Everyone thought he would die.

On that day, all the servants in his castle and many cardinals searched for the missing amulet, and after many promises and fervent prayer it was found. Alexander recovered, and as soon as he was able he had a strong lock placed on a thick gold chain by the Vatican goldsmith, on which to hang the amber amulet. Later he had the lock soldered so he could never remove it. He swore it protected him from evil, and there was no one who could convince him otherwise.

Now Noni walked slowly inside as Cesare followed her. On several small spikes lining the walls of the darkened cottage there were ribbon-tied bunches of herbs of all kinds. From one of these bunches the old woman carefully pulled off some leaves, and with her knarled and crooked fingers wrapped around the stone pestle she placed the leaves in a mortar and mashed them into a fine powder. This she put in a small sack and handed to Cesare. "That is the horielzitel plant's great secret," she told him. "It can induce a dreamless sleep. You need only one pinch for a man, but here I have given you enough for an army."

Cesare thanked the old woman, and embraced her again. But as he mounted his horse, she put her hand on his arm and cautioned, "There is death in your house. Someone young. Protect yourself, for you too are at risk."

Cesare nodded and tried to reassure her. "Death is always at hand, for we live in dangerous times."

8

Cesare, riding with the French cavalry, watched the well-disciplined troops chew up vast chunks of territory, stopping only to conquer hostile castles as they carved a path toward Naples with the military precision of a gigantic scythe.

Although Cesare was meant to be a hostage, he was treated with great respect by the soldiers and loosely guarded even at night. During the long days his love of the field was apparent, and he watched the French commanders plan their military tactics and studied their strategies. Here on the battlefields he was not a cardinal but a warrior, and for the first time in his life Cesare felt at home.

If Cesare's only interest was his own, he could have been content to ride with the French until they had conquered Naples. But both as a son and as a prince of the Holy Church, he had other matters to consider. He knew that despite Pope Alexander's pact with King Charles, his father did not want the French or any foreign power to control even the smallest fiefdom of Italy. He was certain that as he rode through these fields on his way to Naples, Alexander was meeting with the ambassadors of Spain, Venice, Milan, and Florence, attempting to put in place a Holy League of city-states to resist foreign aggression in Italy.

He also knew that even as he rode with the French to Naples, Spain was preparing ships and readying troops to stop them. And if by some chance French troops did reach Naples, and Charles's army managed to withstand the attacks by the ferocious and bloodthirsty Neapolitan troops long enough to conquer Naples and overthrow King Masino, Pope Alexander, backed by King Ferdinand of Spain with the help of Venice, could recover the crown and force the French to withdraw.

But there was one very difficult consideration. All of this could be accomplished if—and it was a troubling *if*—if Cesare's life was not at stake. Now that he was a hostage, he felt that his father might hesitate, might even refuse to consider taking action against the French because of him. Of course, the solution was obvious. He must escape. But the question of Djem still remained. Could he take him? Would he agree to go?

Over the last several days, Djem himself had appeared to be enjoying his situation as a French hostage. In fact just the night before Cesare had heard him talking to the troops, drinking with them and excitedly planning to help overthrow his own brother, the sultan. It would not be an easy task to convince Djem to return with him to Rome, and it would be a danger to confide in him.

Now, Cesare examined his options: a double escape would double the danger, and he could not afford to fail. Djem was in no danger from the French, for alive he had value as a means to compromise the Pope, and if Alexander and Spain failed in their plan, he would certainly be a help to Charles in his Crusade. Dead, of course, he would have no value at all. And so Cesare made his decision.

That night, near midnight, he stepped outside his tent. Two guards—young men he was familiar with, for they had spent many nights together—were sitting on the ground around a small campfire.

Cesare greeted them. "It is a beautiful night. Clear and crisp, is it not?" When they agreed, he pretended to study the skies. "A full moon," he said, "and yet I hear no howling . . ." Then he laughed so they would understand he was being playful.

One of the young men held out a flask and offered it to

him. But Cesare shook his head. "I have something better," he said. And he stepped back into his tent, returning with a bottle of fine red wine and three silver goblets.

The eyes of the soldiers glimmered in the moonlight as he handed them each a goblet and poured one for himself.

The men toasted each other in the dark, outside the tent, gazing together at the stars. But within a short time the two young men began to yawn. Cesare bade them good night and walked inside his tent, where he returned the small brown sack Noni had given him to its hiding place and sat to wait.

Within twenty minutes Cesare peered outside the tent to find both guards in a deep sleep.

Then, fully dressed, he slipped silently through the long row of tents to the place the horses were tied. There another guard sat with his back toward Cesare, watching the sleeping troops. Cesare silently slipped behind him, putting his hand over the guard's mouth to make certain no sound escaped. Then he quickly applied a headlock, and with his forearm placed heavy pressure on the soldier's throat and neck. Within moments the young man lost consciousness.

Cesare found his horse, a swift, strong black stallion, and carefully walked him to the edge of the encampment, trying not to make a sound. There he mounted the stallion, riding bareback as he had done so many times before at Silverlake. Once he reached the roadway, Cesare flew through the night toward Rome.

The following day, after a bath and change of clothes, Cesare was led into his father's study. Alexander rose to greet him with tears in his eyes. And when the Pope embraced him, it was with such strength that Cesare found himself surprised.

Alexander had true affection in his voice. "Cesare, my son, you can't imagine my torture these last days. You saved me from the most terrible choice of my life. Once I had gathered the members of the Holy League, I knew that Charles would consider it a breach of our agreement, and so I feared for your safety. For one of the few times in my life, I was tormented by indecision. Was I to stop my plans for the league and sacrifice our territories and the papacy? Or was I to move forward, at the risk of my dear son's life?"

Cesare had seldom seen his father so distressed, and he found himself amused. "And what did you decide?" he asked playfully.

"It hardly matters now, my son," Alexander said, smiling gently. "For you are safe and so have solved my dilemma."

King Charles's reaction to Cesare's escape was milder than the Pope had expected. And once Alexander learned the outcome of the king's Neapolitan campaign, he understood why.

The French troops had succeeded in occupying Naples; King Masino, without a struggle, had abdicated and fled. King Charles had won. He had overcome the first obstacle to his conquest of Jerusalem and the overthrow of the Infidel. And he had little interest in dampening his mood by worrying over Cesare's escape. All he wanted now was to enjoy the beauty of Naples, the food, the women, the wine.

But with Cesare free, Alexander moved quickly to put in motion his plans for the Holy League. Now that King Ferrante was dead, and there was no longer any threat of Naples invading Milan, Il Moro was willing to align with Rome again. Troops from Milan and Venice began to gather in the north: they had plans to join the Spanish, whose ships would land below Naples, and move up the Italian peninsula.

Alexander, seated on his throne, called Cesare and Duarte Brandao to his chambers to review his military strategy and plans for the Holy League.

"Are you not concerned, Father," Cesare asked, "that King Charles will consider it a terrible offense that you have broken your word about Naples?"

Alexander looked puzzled for a moment, then frowned. "Broken my word?" he said. "What are you speaking of, Cesare? I vowed not to interfere with his conquest of Naples. Not once did I say I would allow him to *keep* it."

Duarte smiled. "I doubt the young king is able to grasp that subtlety."

Cesare continued, "So it is your plan that the forces of the Holy League should cut off the escape route, so that the French army will be crushed between the Spanish in the south and the troops from Venice and Milan in the north? Father, that is to be caught between a hammer and an anvil."

Duarte asked, "And if the French army makes it past the Spanish and Neapolitan troops to Rome?"

Alexander was thoughtful. "If they escape our troops in the south and find their way to our city—if only for a few days—they could still do considerable damage. They would certainly sack the city . . ."

Duarte said, "And, Holy Father, this time I have grave doubt that King Charles would stop them . . ."

Cesare thought a moment, then made a suggestion. "Charles must realize that if he wishes to reclaim Naples, he must convince you to break your alliance with the Holy League. He also must be crowned by you and receive your blessings, for you are the suzerain."

Alexander was impressed by his son's analysis, yet he felt there was something Cesare was not saying. "And, my son, your strategy would be?"

Cesare smiled slyly. "If the French king finds Your Holiness here in Rome as he retreats, he might seize the opportunity to force you to make concessions. But if you are elsewhere . . ."

When the French advance guard entered the city, they reported back to Charles that the Pope had gone north to Orvieto. King Charles, determined to convince the Pope to do his bidding, ordered his army through Rome and

on to Orvieto. But when Alexander's scouts spotted the
French advance guard approaching Orvieto, Alexander was
ready. Before long he and his envoy were on the road, racing
to Perugia, where he would meet with Lucrezia.

From Orvieto, Alexander had already sent Don Michelotto to accompany his daughter back across the mountains,
for he had not seen her in several months and needed to reassure himself of her well-being and talk to her about her
husband. The Pope felt it would be pleasant to have Lucrezia's company; it would help pass the time while he
waited for the outcome of the French invasion.

King Charles entered Orvieto anxious to convince
Alexander to sign another treaty. But frustrated by the news
that the Pope had moved on to Perugia, Charles angrily ordered his army out of Orvieto and on to Perugia.

Suddenly on the road ahead he recognized one of his advance guards. The soldier, breathless, stammered with the
news that troops of the Holy League, in serious numbers,
were concentrated in the north. Charles had to change his
plans. Then he received another piece of bad news. His new
ally, Virginio Orsini, had been captured by Spanish troops.
They were now moving south, right behind Charles.

Charles could waste no more time in pursuit of this elu-
sive Pope. The trap he had feared was about to be sprung,
and his army was its prey. With not a moment to spare he
pushed his troops mercilessly toward the Alps in a series of
forced marches. They arrived just in time. As it was, his
troops had to fight Holy League infantrymen with pikes in
order to cross the border to safety.

King Charles, badly shaken and defeated, was going
home to France.

9

Now that Rome was temporarily quiet, the Pope traveled to Silverlake for a necessary respite. And he immediately sent for his children to join him there for a family celebration.

Lucrezia came from Pesaro; Juan came from Spain without his Maria, Jofre and Sancia left Naples to be part of the festivities. Again, the Borgia family was together. Julia Farnese and Adriana would arrive within the week, for Alexander planned to spend the first few days with his children and wanted no distractions.

At Silverlake Rodrigo Borgia had built a majestic stone villa, a hunting lodge with stables for his prize horses, and several small cottages to house the women and children who often accompanied him when he fled the choking summer heat of the city. Pope Alexander loved to surround himself with beautiful women dressed in finery, and to listen to the sound of those delicate creatures laughing happily. And so, with their husbands gone to far-off places, many of these young court pretties accompanied him, some with their children. The bright faces of the children, so new and untarnished, filled him with a sense of hope.

His entourage of noblemen and their wives, men and ladies in waiting, servants and palace cooks to prepare the lavish meals to be served, together with the members of his court, numbered more than one hundred. There were musicians and actors, jugglers and jesters, all to assist in those comedies and performances that the Pope so enjoyed.

Pope Alexander spent many days sitting alongside the

lake with his children. During those peaceful times, he often regaled them with tales of the great miracles that occurred as sinners from Rome came to bathe themselves in the waters of the lake to wash away their sinful desires.

Years before, the first time he told these stories, Cesare had asked, "Did you too bathe in the waters, Father?"

The cardinal smiled. "Never," he'd said. "For what sins have I committed?"

Cesare laughed. "Then I, as my father, have no desire to bathe."

Lucrezia looked at them both and said slyly, "I suppose neither of you have need of a miracle?"

Rodrigo Borgia had thrown his head back and laughed with pure joy. "Quite the contrary, my child," he said. And then with his hand to his mouth, he whispered, "But I've a greater need for my earthly desires at the moment, and live in horror of them being washed away too soon. There will come a time. But not while the hunger in my belly for the fullness of life is greater than the hunger in my soul for salvation . . ." He blessed himself then, as though fearing sacrilege.

Now, each day began with an early morning hunt. Though the Pope was forbidden by canon law to hunt, he quoted his doctors as saying that he must have exercise. To himself, he reasoned silently, he did other things that were forbidden, most of which he enjoyed less than hunting. When chastised by his valet because he wore boots that made it impossible for his subjects to show their respect by kissing his feet, he joked that at least it prevented the hunting dogs from taking off his toes.

Surrounding the hunting villa, a hundred acres had been sealed off by fences composed of wooden poles and thick sailcloth, forming an enclave in which the game naturally congregated. Before each hunt, pound after pound of raw meat was stacked near the wide gate of the pen for use in leading the animals to their fate.

Just as dawn was breaking, the hunters gathered. Once

they drank a cup of strong Frascati wine to thicken their blood and fortify themselves, Alexander dropped the papal banner. With trumpets blaring and the sounding of drums, the gates of the game pen were opened. A dozen gamesmen raced inside to scatter a trail of raw meat, and the animals rushed through the gates to what they thought was freedom. Stags, wolves, boars, hares, porcupines—all were met by the hunters. Wielding spears and swords—even battle-axes for the more bloodthirsty—the hunters chased down their prey.

Lucrezia and Sancia, with their ladies-in-waiting, were secure on a raised platform so that they could watch the slaughter in safety. Women at the hunt were meant to inspire and encourage the hunters, but Lucrezia, disgusted, hid her eyes and turned away. Something within her recoiled at the similarity between the destiny of those poor trapped animals and her own. Sancia, on the other hand, saw no deeper meaning in the display; she gloried in the spectacle as was expected of her, and even gave her silk handkerchief to her brother-in-law, Juan, to be dipped in the blood of a slain boar. For though not as skilled as Cesare with weapons, Juan had a taste for cruelty and a need to impress that made him the most dedicated hunter in the family. He made a show of courage by standing his ground when a huge boar charged, and then slew it with a spear and hammered it with his battle-ax.

Cesare rode through the hunting grounds with two of his favorite greyhounds, Heather and Hemp. Though pretending to hunt, in truth what he truly enjoyed was running with the hounds, and this day he was busy with his thoughts. He envied Juan. His brother could live a full life, a normal life, and look forward to a military career, while Cesare himself was committed to the church, a career he had not chosen and did not want. As the black bile rose in his throat, he felt a mounting hatred for his brother. But as quickly as it had come, he reproached himself for what he felt. A good man, especially a man of the cloth, could never hate his brother. Not only was it unnatural, not only would it make his father unhappy, but it was dangerous as well. Juan, as captain general of the papal army, had more power than any cardinal of the Catholic Church. And another truth remained: even after all these years and all his own efforts to please and excel, it was still Juan, not he, who was his father's favorite.

Cesare, deep in thought, was quickly brought to full attention by the screaming yelp of one of his greyhounds. As he rode toward the pitiful sound, he saw the magnificent animal pinned to the ground by a spear. When he dismounted to help the wounded hound, he saw the handsome face of his brother Juan disfigured by a fierce scowl. And suddenly he knew what had happened. Juan had missed the scuttling stag and hit his greyhound. For a moment Cesare thought it might have been intentional, but then his brother rode up to him and said in apology, "Brother, I'll buy you a pair to replace him." Still holding the dislodged spear in his hand, Cesare looked down on the slain greyhound, and for an instant felt a murderous rage.

Then he saw his father ride up to where a boar was entangled in a net of ropes awaiting the fatal thrust of his spear. The Pope rode past, shouting, "The work of the hunter has already been done with this animal, I must find another . . ." He kicked hard at his horse's side then took off to follow another large boar. Other hunters, concerned by the Pope's recklessness and speed, rode up to protect him; but by then the Pope, still a powerful man, had thrust his spear deep into the side of the boar, inflicting a mortal wound. Twice more the Pope thrust his spear, piercing the dying animal's heart. The boar stopped his last frantic thrashing, and the rest of the hunters fell upon the carcass and hacked it to pieces.

As Cesare watched his father's courageous display, and marveled at the strength of the man, he felt pride in his father. If Cesare himself wasn't doing what he wanted with his life, at least he was doing what his father wanted, and he knew that was a source of joy to Alexander. And as he looked at the fallen animal, he thought it was fortunate for him that he was the man his father wanted him to be.

A t twilight, Cesare and Lucrezia walked hand in hand beside the gleaming water of the lake. They were a very handsome couple, this brother and sister; his tall and darkly handsome good looks bore such a contrast to her blond hair and hazel eyes, which often shone with intelligence and amusement. On this night, though, she was upset.

Lucrezia said, "It was a mistake, Cesare, Papa forcing me to marry Giovanni. He's not a good man. He hardly ever speaks to me, and when he does, he's gruff and rude. I don't know what I hoped for. I knew ours was a marriage for political advantage, but I had no idea I'd be so unhappy."

Cesare tried to be gentle. "Crezia, you know that Ludovico Sforza is still the most powerful man in Milan. Giovanni helped cement our relationship with the family at a crucial time."

Lucrezia nodded. "I understand. Still, I thought somehow I would feel different. But even as we kneeled on those ridiculous gold footstools at that obscenely lavish wedding, and I looked over at the man who was to be my husband, I knew something was terribly wrong. I couldn't decide whether to laugh or cry when I saw all those purple-robed cardinals, and the grooms in Turkish costumes of silver brocade. It was meant to be a celebration, and yet I felt completely miserable."

"Was there nothing that pleased you?" he asked, smiling.

"Yes," she said. "You, clothed in black. And the Venetian gondolas fashioned from the twenty thousand roses."

Cesare stopped and faced his sister. "I could not bear it, Crezia," he said. "I could not bear the thought of you in the arms of another man, no matter the reason. Had I been able to stay away and not be part of that fiasco, I would have. But Papa insisted I be there. That day my heart was as black as my costume . . ."

Lucrezia kissed her brother gently on the lips.

"Giovanni is an arrogant braggart," she said. "And he is a terrible lover. I barely escaped his clutches except by weeping like a willow. I cannot even tolerate the smell of him."

Cesare tried to hide his smile. "To bed him is not the joy it is with me?" he asked.

Lucrezia giggled despite herself. "My dear love, it is the difference between heaven and hell for me."

As they began to walk again, they crossed a small bridge and entered the forest. "Your husband reminds me of our brother Juan," Cesare said.

Lucrezia shook her head. "Juan's young. Maybe he'll grow out of it. It is not the blessing for him it is for me, to have you as a brother."

Cesare was silent for a time, but when he spoke it was in a very serious tone. "In truth, I believe our brother Jofre is more of a curse to the family than Juan. I have accepted his stupidity, but the household he and Sancia have established is a scandal. Over a hundred servants for just the two of them? Gold dinner plates and jeweled goblets for two hundred guests whenever they choose? It's mad, and it reflects badly on our family. More important, it is dangerous for the son of a Pope to live so extravagantly."

Lucrezia agreed. "I know, Chez. Papa is upset by it too, though he seldom acknowledges it. But he loves Jofre less than he does the rest of us, and knowing his weakness and lack of comprehension, he is more forgiving."

Cesare stopped once more to gaze at Lucrezia in the moonlit sky. Her pale porcelain skin seemed more luminous than usual. Cesare gently lifted her face so he could look into her eyes. But he saw such sadness that he was forced to look away. "Crezia," he said then, "do you wish me to talk to Papa about a divorce from Giovanni? Father adores you. He might be willing. Would Giovanni consent?"

Lucrezia smiled at her brother. "I've no doubt that my husband could easily live without me; it is my dowry he would miss. It was always the gold in his hand, not the gold of my hair, that captured his affection."

Cesare smiled at her guilelessness. "I will wait for the proper time, and then I will present the problem to Papa."

As evening slowly descended on Silverlake, Juan set out to show Jofre's wife, Sancia, his father's old hunting lodge. It was rarely used now that the new, more elegant lodge had been completed.

Sancia was the same age as Juan, though she seemed far less mature. She was beautiful in a classic Aragonese way, with dark green eyes, long dark lashes, and lustrous jet-black hair. Her entire demeanor was light and impish, which gave everyone the impression of a playful wit. In truth it was a shallow pretension, an overused device to charm the innocent.

Juan took Sancia's hand as he led her down the overgrown path to a clearing in the forest. There she saw the cottage, of rough-hewn pine with a stone chimney.

"Not the proper place for a princess," Juan said, smiling at her. For she was after all the daughter of King Masino of Naples and therefore a true princess.

"I think it's charming," Sancia responded, still clinging to Juan's hand.

Once inside, Juan made a fire as Sancia walked around the room examining the many mounted trophies of animal heads on the wall. She stopped and stroked the fruitwood dresser, the headboard of the full feathered bed, and the other pieces of fine country furniture, its golden patina reflecting years of careful use and polish.

"Why does your father leave this place furnished if it's no longer used?" she asked.

Juan, who was kneeling in front of the fireplace, looked up and smiled. "Father still uses it on occasion, when he has a visitor with whom he wishes to be alone . . . just as I do now." Juan stood and crossed the room to her. He quickly pulled her close, his arm encircling her. Then he kissed her. For a moment she was silent, but then she leaned away, murmuring, "No, no, I can't. Jofre will . . ."

Juan's longing forced him to pull Sancia even closer as he said in a husky whisper, "Jofre will do nothing. He is capable of nothing!"

Juan may have disliked his brother Cesare, but he respected his intelligence and physical skills. For the frivolous Jofre, on the other hand, he had nothing but disdain.

Now, Juan pulled his brother's wife to him again. Moving his hand beneath her loose white skirt, he caressed her inner thigh, moving his fingers upward slowly until he felt her respond. Then he pulled her toward the nearby bed.

Within seconds they lay together. Lit only by the fire's flickering glow, Sancia's long black hair spread across the pillow made her look exquisite, and her skirt lifted high flamed Juan's desire. Juan quickly moved atop her. As he thrust into her, and then slowly withdrew, he heard her moan. But she didn't resist; instead she kissed him hard on his open lips again and again, drinking from his mouth as if with an unquenchable thirst. Juan began to push harder, thrust after long powerful thrust, sliding deeper and deeper into her, driving from Sancia's head all thoughts of "no" and of Jofre—spiraling her into a mindless oblivion.

That evening the Pope and his family ate a late dinner in the open air on the shores of Silverlake. Colored lanterns hung from the trees, and flaming torches flickered on tall wooden poles all along the shores. The game they had slain made a great feast, enough to feed the more than one hundred members of the Pope's entourage with plenty left over for the poor in the nearby towns. And after the jugglers and musicians had entertained them at the banquet, Juan and Sancia stood up and sang a duet.

Cesare, sitting alongside Lucrezia, wondered when the two had found time to practice together, for they sang very prettily. But Sancia's husband seemed pleased and applauded. Cesare wondered if Jofre could be as dense as he appeared.

Pope Alexander enjoyed good conversation as much as hunting, food, and beautiful women. After the evening banquet, when the comedy of actors and the dancing began, Alexander discoursed to his children. One of the actors, in a fit of daring common to those eccentric folk, had given a dialogue in which a poor suffering nobleman questioned how a merciful God could inflict natural misfortunes on faithful men. How could He permit floods, fires, plagues? How could He let innocent children suffer terrible cruelties? How could He permit man, created in His image, to wreak such havoc on his fellow man?

Alexander took up the challenge. Since he was with friends, he chose not to draw upon the words of Scripture to make his point. Rather he answered as a Greek philosopher or a Florentine merchant would.

"What if God promised a Heaven achieved so easily, and without pain, here on earth?" he said. "Heaven would not seem such a prize. What reason would test man's sincerity and faith? With no purgatory, there is no Heaven. Then, what inexhaustible evil would men engineer? Man would dream up so many ways to extinguish each other, there would not even be an earth. What is achieved without suffering is worthless. What is achieved easily is of no account. Man would be a trickster, playing the game of life with crooked dice and marked cards. He would be no better than the beasts we raise. Without all these obstacles we call misfortune, what pleasure would Heaven be? No, these misfortunes are proof of God, of his love for mankind. As for what men do to each other, we cannot blame that on our God. We must blame ourselves and do our time in purgatory."

"Father," Lucrezia asked him, for she was his child most concerned by the matters of faith and goodness, "but then what is evil?"

"Power is evil, my child," he said. "And it is our duty to erase the desire for it from the hearts and minds of men. That, the Holy Church can do. But we can never erase the power of society, in society. Therefore we can never erase evil from civilized society. It will always be unjust, it will always be cruel to the common man. It is possible that in five hundred years, men will not cheat and murder each other, oh, happy day!"

Then he looked directly at his sons Juan and Cesare and continued. "But it is in the very nature of society that, in order to hold a people together for their God and their country, a king must hang and burn his subjects in order to bend their will. For mankind is as intractable as nature, and some demons don't fear holy water."

Alexander raised his glass in toast then, "To the Holy Mother Church and to our family. May we flourish as we spread the word of God throughout the world."

They all raised their glasses now and shouted, "To Pope Alexander! May God bless him with health, happiness, and the wisdom of Solomon and the great philosophers."

Soon, most of the company retired to their quarters, settling into the lakeside cottages, each flying the charging red bull of the Borgia banner. Fires burned to give light, and many flaming torches fastened to wooden arcs sparkled on the shores of Silverlake.

In his quarters Jofre paced, sulking. Sancia had not returned with him that night. When he had approached her earlier at the festivities with his request that she accompany him back to their cottage, she had refused with a snigger and waved him away. As he searched the faces of the crowd around them, he felt the hot flush of embarrassment color his cheeks and sting his eyes.

That day at Silverlake had been a humiliation for him, though everyone else appeared to be drinking and laughing and having so good a time that he doubted they had noticed. He had clapped, of course, and smiled—as was required of him by royal protocol—but the vision of his wife and his arrogant brother, Juan, singing a duet, set his teeth to snapping and destroyed any enjoyment he could find in the sweet sound of her song.

Jofre had returned to their cottage by himself. After trying to sleep and finding himself unable to, he walked outside to quell his restlessness. The humming of the sleeping night creatures in the groves made him feel less alone. He sat on the ground, feeling its coolness, which calmed him. And he thought about his father, the Pope, and his brothers and sisters . . .

He had always known that he was not as smart as his brother Cesare, and no match in physical strength for Juan. But in the deep recesses of his soul, he understood something they did not. That the sins he committed—of gluttony and excess—were not as black as Juan's cruelty or Cesare's ambition.

As for a sharp mind, how important could that be in determining the direction of his life? His sister, Lucrezia, was far superior to him in mental ability, yet she had no greater choice in her life than he had. Reflecting on the condition of his family, Jofre concluded that intelligence was far less important than the counsel of a pure heart and a good soul.

Juan had always been the most unkind of his siblings, calling him names from the time he was a small child, and consenting only to play games he knew he could easily win. Cesare was sometimes driven by his obligation as a prince of the Holy Roman Catholic Church to reprimand Jofre for his excesses; yet he did so with a firm kindness, rather than with the cruelty and appetite for humiliation Juan so often showed. His sister, Lucrezia, was his favorite, for she treated him with a sweet and gentle affection, and always made him feel as though she was pleased to see him. His father, the Pope, hardly seemed to notice him.

Now, feeling restless again, Jofre resolved to go in search of Sancia. He would persuade her to return with him to their cottage. He stood and began to walk the narrow path between the trees, which served for a moment to calm him. But just outside the campgrounds, beneath the dark night sky, he saw two dark shadows. He was tempted to call out, to greet them, but something caused him to stop.

He heard her laugh before he saw her clearly. Then the bright night moon highlighted his brother Juan and his wife, Sancia, walking arm in arm. Soundlessly, he turned and followed them back toward the cottage. There he watched as Juan and Sancia stopped to embrace. Jofre felt his lip curl in disdain. He kept himself stiff and still as he watched his brother bend to kiss Sancia passionately in parting.

At that moment, Jofre found Juan contemptible. But more than that, he saw in Juan some unholy thing. And so, with complete resolve, he condemned him in his heart and vowed to denounce him as a brother. Suddenly he could see with a brilliant clarity; there was no longer any doubt. As the seed of the Christ had been sown in the womb of the Virgin Mother by the Holy Ghost, so the pit of evil can also be planted—unknown and unrecognized—until the time of discovery, when the fruit of the womb is exposed.

Now his brother began to walk away, and in a rare moment of high spirits Juan pulled his dagger from its sheath and waved it in a swift swirling motion. Then Juan laughed as he bragged loudly to Sancia, "Soon I will be captain general of the papal army, and then you shall see what I do!"

Jofre shook his head and tried to restrain his fury. After some time he managed to quiet himself. Then, with an unnatural dispassion, he tried to reason: Senseless battles for political gain didn't interest him; they were not enjoyable and in fact, they bored him. To use a weapon to take another's life, chancing eternal damnation for some military goal, made no sense. To risk that, he thought, the prize must be far more precious and personal.

Cesare, too, was restless. His conversation with Lucrezia weighed heavily on his heart, and he found that he could not fall asleep. When he inquired, he found that the Pope had already retired to his quarters. Still, he felt he must speak to his father.

In his suite the Pope was sitting at his desk, reading and signing official papers presented to him by a pair of secretaries, who were dismissed summarily at Cesare's entry into his father's chambers. Marveling at his father's energy, Cesare advanced toward him to receive an embrace. A five-log fire blazed in the enormous fireplace.

The Pope was already in his sleeping costume: a long woolen nightgown covered over by a richly embroidered silk robe lined with fur, which he claimed retained his body heat and protected him against the malarial winds of Rome. On his head was a small ruby-colored biretta, unadorned. Alexander often said that though a Pope, for reasons of state, must always show the riches of the church in public, he could at least sleep as simply as a peasant.

"And what did my daughter confide in her *favorite* brother?" the Pope said. "Does she complain of her husband?"

Cesare caught the knowing irony in his father's voice; still, he was surprised by his father's awareness of Lucrezia's feelings. Cesare answered, "She is unhappy with him."

Alexander looked thoughtful for a moment. "I must admit, I, myself, am no longer happy with my daughter's marriage. It doesn't serve politically as I had hoped." He seemed glad for the chance to talk about it. "What good is that Sforza boy to us anyway? I never truly liked him, and he was worthless as a soldier. And now Il Moro is not so valuable to us, for his loyalties are weak and he cannot always be trusted. He is a man to reckon with, certainly, for we need him in the Holy League. But he can be unpredictable. Still, we must consider your sister's feelings as well. Don't you agree?"

Cesare thought how happy Lucrezia would be, and that pleased him. She would think him a hero. "How shall we proceed?"

Alexander continued. "King Ferdinand has asked me to make a friend of the royal house of Naples. Surely, though Jofre's marriage to Sancia has already put him in the Neapolitan camp, that doesn't necessarily serve us. In fact, it may have done us damage. Unless . . ." The Pope smiled before he continued. "We may be able to repair that breach with some new alliance."

Cesare frowned. "Father? I don't quite understand."

Alexander's eyes glistened, and he looked amused at his most recent inspiration. "Sancia's brother. Alfonso. Now *that* could be a much more rewarding match for Lucrezia. It's always awkward to insult the Sforzas, but it may be worth considering. Tell your sister I'll consider altering her circumstance."

Alexander pushed his chair away from his desk and rose to walk across the room to stoke the fire with one of the cast-iron hooks that rested on the stone floor in front of him.

When he turned back to his son, he said, "Cesare, you understand we must control the Papal States. The papal vicars are like greedy warlords, always fighting each other, fighting the Pope's infallibility, draining and oppressing the people. We must do something to bring them back in line."

Cesare asked, "And you have a plan?"

"The kings of France and Spain are uniting their territories under a central authority. We must do the same. It is imperative for the people and for the papacy. But we must also do it for our family. For if we do not create a Borgia-controlled, unified government, which will force the locals to recognize the authority of Rome and the Pope, you and the rest of the family will be in grave peril." He became silent.

"We must have well-manned fortresses," Cesare said with determination. "To put down the local uprisings as well as to stop the foreign invaders who hope to make the central territories their own."

Alexander said nothing; he seemed deep in thought.

Cesare bowed his head. "I am at your service, Father. I am a cardinal of the church."

Pope Alexander spoke with grave intensity as he sat back down in his favorite leather chair. "I don't have to tell you how dangerous it will be for all of you if I die and a hostile Pope like della Rovere is elected. I can't begin to think of what will happen to your sister. Dante's hell has no match for the inferno she will face . . ."

Cesare said, "Father, why are you telling me this? We need not tremble yet, for you have not yet begun to do the good works you must for the Holy Church, and therefore I am certain you will live many more years."

Alexander lowered his voice. "No matter the peril, there are only two men in this court that you can trust completely. One is Don Michelotto . . ."

"That is no surprise, Father, for your affection for him has not escaped anyone's notice. And it is not difficult for me to trust him, for I have since I was a child." Now he paused. "Still, his life is rather a mystery to me. I have never asked you this, Father: How is it that a Valencian became so entrenched in the workings of Rome?"

And so Alexander told his son the story of Miguel Corello, now known as Don Michelotto.

"But he is also the one known as the strangler," Cesare said.

"Yes, my son, he is called the strangler, but he is much more than that. He is an accomplished leader of troops, a ferocious warrior—and, most important, he would die protecting our family. His loyalty is as fierce as his fury. So make no mistake, he is not only a killer. He can be trusted completely."

"And the other?" Cesare asked.

"The second man is Duarte Brandao. About his past I can tell you little, for he was captured and brought to me as a prisoner many years ago when I requested an English translator and my own was unavailable. But he had been beaten badly by our own troops, and swore he remembered nothing of his past."

"And still you kept him?" Cesare asked.

Alexander sat, remembering. "The first I saw of him he was filthy and disheveled, as any prisoner who had been locked in the dungeons would be, but once he was bathed and given proper clothing he was brought to me again. On that day, something in his demeanor sparked a memory of one Edward Brampton, a converted Jew, who rendered great service to Edward the Fourth of England. I had seen him only once, long before, but I took note of him, for he was the first Jew ever knighted. It is said he served the king's brother, Richard the Third, who as you know was slain by Henry Tudor's men. Brampton fought in great land and sea battles for Edward the Fourth, and literally saved the entire English fleet for Richard the Third. That's when Brampton disappeared from England, and about the time that Duarte Brandao was captured in Rome. The Tudors would have killed him had they caught him, and even now he is always in danger from Tudor agents."

"And that accounts for his change of name, Father?" Cesare asked. "But is Brandao a Jew?"

Alexander said, "If so he's a convert to the Holy Catholic Church, for I've seen him take Communion. And for these past seven years he has served me and the Holy Mother Church more religiously than any other man I know. He's the most courageous and intelligent man I've ever met, a fine soldier and oddly enough a highly skilled seaman too."

"I'm not objecting to him being a Jew, Father," Cesare said, with an amused expression. "I'm just wondering what anyone else will think when they find that you, the head of the Holy Roman Catholic Church, is being advised by a man who is not even a Christian."

Alexander smiled. "I'm glad you don't object, my son," he said sarcastically. Then his voice took on a more serious tone. "You know my views on the Jewish situation, Cesare. When Ferdinand and Isabella of Spain asked that I imprison, torture, and kill Jews who dared to practice their religion in secret, I refused. I told them I believed the Spanish Inquisition was an abomination, as was the treatment of Jews in their own country. After all, these people gave us the law; they gave us Jesus. Should I slaughter them because they don't believe he's the Son of God? I will not! I can't always prevent our citizens or even our officials from attacking or abusing them, but it certainly is not my policy."

Cesare knew that when Popes were elected, part of the ceremony was that the new Pope was offered the book of Hebrew laws by the head of Rome's Jewish community. Every other Pope had taken the book and thrown it to the ground in revulsion. Only his father had not. Alexander VI, too, had rejected it—but he had handed it back, with respect.

Now Cesare asked, "What is your policy, Father?"

"I will not harm them," the Pope said. "I will, however, tax them heavily."

10

Pope Alexander had been betrayed at the moment of his greatest need by Virginio Orsini, one of his papal barons, a man he trusted, and he did not suffer this betrayal lightly. The devil had claimed another soul, he reasoned, and the devil must be destroyed. The fact that Virginio himself had been captured, tortured, and killed in one of the most notorious dungeons of Naples did not rid Alexander of his need for revenge.

To the Pope, this became a very real battle between the Vicar of Christ on Earth and Satan himself. As the leader of the Papal States, he knew he must take action against the local barons, those greedy warlords who were always fighting each other—and, even more disastrous, fighting the dictates of the Holy Catholic Church. For if the word of the Holy Father was not honored and obeyed, if evil was allowed to flourish and men of virtue did nothing, the authority of the church itself would be weakened. Then who would save the souls of the good for God?

Alexander understood that spiritual power must be supported by temporal might. Though the French army had withdrawn, and what few troops were left had been conquered by the armies of the Holy League, Alexander knew he must devise a suitable punishment to ensure that such a betrayal would not happen again.

After much consideration, he reasoned that he must make an example of the Orsini, to forever discourage the rebellion of the other barons under his charge. In order to do that, he must use the most lethal weapon in his spiritual arsenal: excommunication. Alas, he had no choice. He must publicly banish the entire Orsini family from the Holy Roman Catholic Church.

Excommunication was the most extreme of proclamations, and the strongest implement of the Pope's power. For it was a punishment not only of this life but one which extended into the next. Once a man was exiled from the church, he could no longer gain the grace of the holy sacraments. His soul could not be cleansed of its sins by confession; the blackened stains must remain without forgiveness, the opportunity for absolution denied. A marriage could no longer be sanctified, a child could not be baptized, blessed, and protected from the devil by the sprinkling of holy water. Oh, sad day! No last rites could be performed to bring peace at the end of life, for burial in sacred ground was now forbidden. It was the most terrifying of all actions; at its core, it was a judgment that drove the soul into purgatory or even hell.

Having exiled the Orsini from the heavens, Alexander now concentrated on destroying their worldly power. He called his son, Juan, back from Spain to act as captain general of the papal army—despite the opposition of Juan's wife, Maria Enriquez, who was again with child. His son and heir, Juan II, was only a year old, she argued, and had need of his father.

But Pope Alexander insisted that Juan was to leave Spain immediately to lead the papal troops—for after Virginio's betrayal he no longer trusted any of the mercenaries, the *condottieri*. His son must return at once to seize all the towns and castles of the Orsini. Meanwhile, the Pope also sent a message to his son-in-law, Giovanni Sforza, in Pesaro, with orders to bring as many soldiers as he had, and offered to pay him an entire year's salary if he did so with haste.

From the time his brother Juan was sent to Spain, Cardinal Cesare Borgia had hoped that his father would consider a change in roles for him. After all, Cesare had been the one at the Pope's side, working on matters of state.

He understood Italy. Juan belonged in Spain. And no matter how often his father insisted on his position in the Holy Mother Church, Cesare constantly hoped he would reconsider.

Now, sitting in the Pope's chambers, Alexander told Cesare of his plans for Juan—that he was to conquer and keep the Orsini castles.

Cesare was furious. "Juan? Juan?" he said, unbelieving. "But Father, he knows nothing about leading troops. He knows nothing of strategy. His only concern is for himself. His strengths lie in the seduction of women, in the squandering of our family's fortune, and in his own vanity. As his brother I owe him allegiance, but Father, I could lead troops blindfolded and you would be assured of greater success."

Pope Alexander narrowed his eyes, and looked at his son. "I agree, Cesare. You do have a greater intelligence and ability for strategy. But you are a cardinal, a prince of the church, not a warrior of the battlefield. And who am I left with? Your brother Jofre? Unfortunately, he would lead his horse backward. I cannot even imagine a weapon in his hand. Therefore, what is my choice? A Borgia must appear to command this force, or we will lose the impact of this punishment for the Orsini betrayal on the other papal barons."

Cesare sat silent and thoughtful for a moment before responding. "You truly expect Juan to secure a victory for us? After his ridiculous behavior in Spain, despite our warnings not to gamble, not to bed prostitutes, and to pay proper respect to his wife and the Enriquez family, first cousins of King Ferdinand? Still you choose him?"

Alexander's deep baritone voice was soft and reassuring. "The real commander will be Guido Feltra. He is an experienced *condottiere* well known for his military skill and mastery."

Cesare had heard stories about Feltra. That he was a good man, a loyal man, there was no doubt; he was a famous patron of literature and the arts, and the beloved duke of

Urbino. But, in truth, his reputation was that of the son of a true *condottiere,* a professional soldier, who had gained the duchy as a reward for his military services. Young Guido himself had fought in too few battles, and had won them too easily, to challenge the experience of the ruthless Orsini soldiers. Especially at their main fortress of Bracciano. Certainly, if papal troops were to try to take Ostia, the home of Cardinal della Rovere, there was real danger for his father and for Rome. But Cesare said none of this to the Pope, for he knew that where Juan was concerned his father refused all reason.

Later that night, still angry, he sent a message to his sister. Then he secured a promise from Don Michelotto to accompany her from Pesaro, for he had asked Lucrezia to meet him the following week at Silverlake.

When Lucrezia arrived at the cottage, Cesare was waiting for her. She was dressed in a blue satin gown which highlighted her golden tresses and accentuated the blue in her eyes. It had been a long ride, taking over a day and a half, and her cheeks were flushed with heat and excitement. She ran into the cottage and put her arms around her brother's neck. "I have so missed you," she said. But when she pulled back to look at him, she saw the anguish in his eyes. "What is wrong, Chez? What is troubling you?"

Cesare sat on one of the large leather seats and patted the footstool in front of him. Lucrezia sat holding his hand, trying to comfort him. "Crezia, it is pure madness. Father has ordered Juan home to lead the troops as captain general, and I am so full of envy I could kill him . . ."

Lucrezia stood up, walked behind him, and began to rub his forehead to soothe him. "Chez," she said, "you must accept your destiny. It is not Juan alone who causes you such sadness. You also are to blame. It is as though you two are still children fighting over Mother Vanozza's Christmas cakes. I do understand how you feel, but it can only cause you harm, for Father will do as he has always done. Only what he wishes."

"But I am a better soldier than Juan, much more suited to leading troops, and I would guarantee a victory for the Holy Church and Rome. Why is it that Father would rather have a commander who is an arrogant braggart—a fool who just *appears* to be leading his army?"

Lucrezia kneeled in front of Cesare now, and looked up into his eyes. "Chez, why is it that Papa must also have a daughter who *appears* to be happily married to the ignorant duke of Pesaro?"

Cesare smiled. "Come," he said, drawing her close. "I need you now. For you are what is real in my life. I *appear* to be a man of God, but for the hat of a cardinal and the love of my father, I swear, Crezia, I fear I have sold my soul to the devil. I am not who I appear to be, and I find that unbearable."

When he kissed her, he tried to be gentle, but he had waited so long that he could not manage it. As he kissed her again and again, she began to tremble and then to cry.

Cesare stopped and lifted his head to look at her. There were tears in her eyes. "Forgive me," he said. "It was brutal of me."

"It is not the pain of your kisses you see," she said. "They are the tears of my longing for you. This time in Pesaro makes me dream of the glory of Rome, and you are a part of those dreams."

After they made love, they lay in bed a long time. Cesare seemed relaxed and Lucrezia could smile again. She rested her head on his shoulder and asked, "Do you believe, as Papa does, that it's God's will that his children should live without loving truly?"

"Is that what Papa thinks?" Cesare said, playing with his sister's hair. "One could not imagine that by his behavior."

"Well, I am married to a man I certainly don't love," she said. "And our brother Juan did not marry for love. Jofre loves easily, so he may be the lucky one, strange as that may seem. For only the hat of a cardinal has saved you from a fate like mine."

"It is a heavy hat," Cesare said.

"But not without benefit," Lucrezia reminded him.

Once they had dressed, they sat at the small wooden table to eat. Cesare poured his sister a fine wine he had brought and raised his goblet to toast. "To your happiness, my dear sister," he said, smiling. He always felt so safe with Lucrezia, so loved and accepted. He could not imagine a life without her.

He had brought a long loaf of freshly baked bread with a crisp golden crust from Rome—the very kind he knew his sister favored—and it lay alongside several wheels of fresh cheese. As he broke the bread and sliced the cheese to serve her, Cesare said, "I do hope that I will manage to control the way I feel when Juan appears again in Rome. For it takes all my restraint to treat him as a brother."

With a coy smile, Lucrezia said, "He may have what you *want*, Chez, but he doesn't have what you *have* . . ."

"I know that, my sweet," he said, kissing her nose. "I do know that, and it is my salvation."

Juan Borgia arrived in Rome to great celebration. He rode through the streets poised on a chestnut bay mare draped in a cloth of gold; in his hands he held the reins of her bridle, encrusted with fine jewels. He wore a rich brown velvet suit and a cape studded with precious emeralds. His dark eyes glittered with power, and his lips were set in the insolent smile of an already conquering hero.

When he reached the Vatican, the Pope embraced him, greeting him warmly. "My son, my son," Alexander repeated, making his way into the Hall of Popes, where he had called a meeting to map the strategy for the papal army.

Long hours were spent in discussion of military tactics with Guido Feltra, Alexander, Juan, Cesare, and Duarte Brandao in attendance.

The gatherings continued for three days. Cesare noticed at these meetings that Duarte seldom addressed Juan directly;

if he had a suggestion he addressed it to the Pope, and used Juan's title, "Captain General," rather than his name. It was the first time that Cesare suspected Duarte Brandao's displeasure, and it was so subtle that he was certain only he had noticed.

But that evening, after the final session, as Alexander sat alone with Duarte Brandao, he asked, "You believe it is a mistake to have my son Juan lead our troops against the Orsini?"

Duarte answered with both cleverness and respect. "I believe it is a pity that, by accident of the order of birth, a prince by nature must become a warrior and a true warrior must become a cardinal."

"But, my friend," Alexander asked, "do you not believe in destiny? In the plans of our Heavenly Father? In the infallibility of the Pope?"

Duarte Brandao said with good humor, "Who can know of the Heavenly Father's plan, and are we as mortal men not subject to an occasional error of interpretation? Even the most honorable and virtuous of us?"

"Duarte," Alexander said, "Pedro Luis, bless his soul, was my firstborn. Cesare is my second son. It is the custom that the second son is called to service in the Holy Church. That plan holds no error in interpretation, for it keeps the power of the royal families in check and yet allows them the advantage of special benefices from our Holy Father. And is a man's destiny not always both a gift and a burden? For who of us must not struggle with his own free will when praying, 'Thy will be done, Dear Lord, not mine'?"

Duarte's good-natured laughter rang out through the great hall. "Your Worthiness, forgive me. And it is with both awe and admiration that I present my point. How can one be certain that your young warrior, Cesare, is but your second son? Your attractiveness to women is legendary, and your vigor of heroic proportions. It is difficult for me to believe that there are not some others, hidden by their mothers, and hidden from you . . ."

At that, Alexander began to laugh. "You are a brilliant advisor, and a diplomat as well," he said. "And if the young cardinal's destiny is to be a holy warrior, the time will come that your argument will serve us. But for now it is Juan who is the captain general, and he must lead our troops. And so, for the present time, we must bend our knees and pray for victory."

Twenty-one-year-old Cesare, standing outside the Hall of Popes, clothed in the garments of a cardinal, overheard this conversation, and for the first time in memory he felt a certain hope. Was it possible that above all the treachery in the world, there truly was a heaven and a Father who had heard? He walked back to his apartments, his head filled with imaginings, for the first time daring to anticipate the day when he might be called upon to lead the troops of Rome.

Captain General Juan Borgia, and the *condottiere* Guido Feltra, led the papal army north from Rome toward the first of the Orsini castles. Though the Orsini were fierce soldiers, at this first bastion they were stunned by the sheer number of papal troops, and so the first two castles fell without a battle.

When the news was brought to Duarte, he met with Alexander. "I suspect this is a plan of the Orsini, to trick our new commanders into believing that this will be an easy victory. Only then will the Orsini show their true abilities."

Alexander nodded. "Then you have little confidence in Feltra?"

"I have seen the Orsini in battle . . ." Duarte said.

Cesare had been called by Alexander, for his father knew his skill in strategy. And now the Pope asked him, "You may speak the truth. To what do you ascribe the greatest danger in this situation?"

Careful to keep his emotions in check, Cesare responded with caution. "I fear that Feltra is not more skilled at military matters than the captain general. And I anticipate that this easy victory will place both off guard—leading to disaster at Bracciano, for there the Orsini will assemble their finest warriors. And there della Rovere will inspire them to think it a holy war, which will make them even stronger."

The Pope marveled at this son's assessment of the situation, but he did not yet know how accurate Cesare was. For it was not more than a few days before the Orsini resistance stiffened, and della Rovere, the most dangerous enemy of the Pope, called upon the distinguished artillery commander Vito Vitelli to raise an army to rescue the Orsini.

Vitelli's army moved quickly and descended upon the papal army at Soriano. There both Juan and Guido Feltra proved hopelessly incapable, and the papal forces suffered a stunning defeat. Guido Feltra was captured, taken prisoner, and thrown in a dungeon in one of the Orsini castles. Juan fled, escaping serious injury with only a cut to his face.

Hearing of this, and reassuring himself that his son was not badly hurt, Alexander again called Cesare and Duarte into the Hall of Popes.

"The war is not lost," Duarte reassured him, "for we have other resources available to us."

Cesare added, "And if the Holy Father determines we are in serious danger, he can always call in Gonsalvo de Córdoba's experienced Spanish troops from Naples . . ."

But after meeting with the ambassadors of Spain, France, and Venice—all of them urging peace—Pope Alexander, always a diplomat, agreed reluctantly to return the surrendered castles to the Orsini. Of course, they must be made to pay a price for this arrangement. After much negotiation, the Pope accepted fifty thousand ducats. For, after all, such compensation was necessary to fill the coffers of the Holy Catholic Church.

The outcome seemed a victory for the Pope. But when Juan returned, he complained bitterly that he had been stopped from his future conquests and deprived of the properties he would retain by Alexander's agreements. Therefore, he argued, it was he who deserved the fifty thousand ducats for his embarrassment. To Cesare's dismay, Alexander yielded.

But there was even more serious a problem, in Cesare's mind. In order to repair his reputation, Juan insisted on being assigned the task of retaking Ostia from the French army left there by King Charles.

Cesare rushed to his father's chambers to plead with him. "Father, there are only a few French troops left, I know that. But if there is a way to lose, Juan will, and with his defeat will come the damnation of the papacy and the Borgia family. For della Rovere is there, setting a trap, waiting for just such folly."

Alexander sighed. "Cesare, we have been over this time and again. Do you think your father such a fool that he cannot see what you can? This time I will assure a victory. I will call on Gonsalvo de Córdoba—for there is no better captain in the world."

Cesare's voice was filled with frustration. "That will not stop my brother. He will interfere. He will struggle with de Córdoba—you know he will. I beg of you, Holy Father, rethink your position."

But Alexander was adamant. "Juan will do no such thing. I have sent explicit instructions. He will simply ride out of Rome as the head of papal forces, and when the battle is over and we have won, he will ride back in victory, accompanied by the waving Borgia flag. Between those two shows of splendor he will give neither orders nor suggestions."

Juan obeyed his father. He rode out of the city on a spirited black charger, waving his cap to the crowds of Roman citizens who lined the streets along his way, and as he had been ordered, he played no role in the well-directed battle for Ostia.

Gonsalvo de Córdoba's men quickly overthrew the French garrison and conquered the city of Ostia, without any interference. And Juan rode back into the city of Rome, just as he had left it, this time to the cheers and shouts of victory from the throngs of Roman citizens lining the streets.

Three nights later at the Palazzo Borgia, Cardinal Ascanio Sforza held a huge ball to which he invited many important guests, including Alexander's children. Also in Rome at the time were the Medici brothers, Piero and Gio, Cesare's friend from the University; the Medici had been driven from their homes in Florence by the French, and the preachings of Savonarola.

Cardinal Sforza's massive palace had been the home of the Borgia while Rodrigo was still cardinal, but it was given as a gift to Ascanio when he became Pope. Everyone agreed it was the most beautiful palace in all of Rome.

That night Cesare returned to his father's former home with his friends, with whom he had spent the night before eating, gambling, and drinking in the city.

The walls of the vast entrance hall were hung with elaborate tapestries, thick with rich threads that brought the many great moments of history to life. Off this hall were many rooms also hung with intricate tapestries, their floors covered with priceless oriental carpets in colors that matched the velvet and satin seat coverings and complemented the ornately carved wooden cabinets, dressers, and tables.

But on this evening the great hall had been made into a ballroom, with a small orchestra playing from the mezzanine to accompany the many fine young couples as they danced.

Cesare, who was in the company of a beautiful and popular courtesan, had just finished dancing when Gonsalvo de Córdoba approached him. De Córdoba, a strong and always serious man, looked particularly disturbed on this night. He bowed in greeting and then asked Cesare if they might speak in private.

Cesare excused himself and led the Spanish captain to one of the open balconies on which he had played as a child. The balcony overlooked a private courtyard; beneath it several guests were milling around, talking and laughing while they ate hors d'oeuvres and drank the thick red wines being offered on bright silver trays by the servants.

But the merriment of the night was offset by the disposition of de Córdoba, whose usually pleasant face was contorted with anger. "Cesare, I am more furious with your brother than you can know. More than anyone can know."

Cesare put his hand on the captain's shoulder in a gesture of friendship and reassurance. "What has my brother done now?" he asked.

The captain's voice was hoarse with tension. "Do you understand that your brother had no hand in the fighting at Ostia?"

Cesare smiled broadly. "Yes, I assumed that, dear captain. For we won."

"And are you aware that Juan has been taking credit, claiming victory for this conquest?" Cesare listened with a sympathetic expression as the captain fumed on. "Juan describes it everywhere he goes, saying it was *he*—not even *we*—who put the French to flight."

"He is an empty-headed braggart," Cesare said, "and his claims are ridiculous. There is no one in Rome who would believe him. But let us reason what can be done to correct this terrible injustice."

Gonsalvo, still furious, would not be mollified. "In Spain, I would certainly challenge him to a duel. But here . . ." and he stopped to catch his breath. "Did you know that arrogant fool has actually commissioned the casting of a bronze medal to be distributed in his honor?"

Cesare frowned. "A medal?" he repeated, surprised. He had heard nothing of it.

"It will bear his profile. Beneath it, in elaborately carved letters, the inscription will read, 'Juan Borgia—Victor of Ostia.' "

Cesare was tempted to laugh at his brother's absurdity, but restrained himself in order not to inflame Gonsalvo further. Then he said, "There is not a soldier in the papal army, and certainly not one of the French troops, who does not know the truth. That you, Gonsalvo de Córdoba, and only you, are the victor of Ostia."

But the Spanish captain would not be consoled. Instead, he turned to Cesare with a look of rage. "Juan Borgia? Victor of Ostia? We will see! I should kill him. I may still . . ." Then he turned and walked away from the balcony back into the palazzo.

Cesare remained for several moments after de Córdoba's departure, staring into the dark night sky, and wondered how it was that he and this one they called his brother could have emerged from the same womb. It was a trick of fate, he was certain. But just before he turned back to enter the ballroom, something in the courtyard caught his attention.

Below him, standing around the central fountain and speaking in voices too low for him to hear, Cesare saw his brother Jofre talking to the Spanish captain and a younger man, tall and lean. De Córdoba was listening intently, fully engaged, while the younger man seemed to be looking around the courtyard as though searching for someone. But it was Jofre, usually so amiable and apathetic, who most startled Cesare. For on his face he wore an expression of ferociousness that Cesare had never before seen.

Cesare thought of calling out to them, until he felt a hand on his arm. Standing behind him, his finger to his lips, Don Michelotto pulled Cesare back from the ledge of the balcony to a place where they would not be seen. Hidden in the shadows, they watched for several moments until they saw the captain smile and shake young Jofre's hand. When Jofre reached for the hand of the younger man, Michelotto noticed a large, irregularly shaped blue topaz ring, which glistened in sharp shards caught by the light of the moon. He pointed it out. "Take notice, Cesare. For that man is Vanni, an Orsini nephew." And then, just as quickly as he had appeared, Michelotto was gone.

Inside the palazzo again, Cesare walked through the rooms trying to find Jofre, but he seemed to have disappeared. He nodded at his sister Lucrezia, who was dancing with that fool husband of hers, Giovanni; nearby, completely unaware of the chaos he was causing, Juan was dancing with his sister-in-law, Sancia. Both were laughing and having a wonderful time. But what concerned Cesare most was de Córdoba as he left the ball—for suddenly he seemed at peace.

11

Lucrezia had come to join her father and brothers for the Easter festivities at the Vatican, and so she was in her apartments at her Palace of Santa Maria in Portico when Giovanni Sforza's chamberlain came to her with an urgent message. Her husband had requested that she accompany him back to Pesaro, the man explained, for he found his stay in Rome oppressive and desired to escape the Pope's vigilance.

Lucrezia listened, upset, as Julia began choosing some of Lucrezia's things for her maidservant to pack. She had been incredibly lonely in Pesaro; here in Rome, she finally felt herself again.

"What am I to do?" she asked aloud as she paced. "In Pesaro, as in Rome, the duke seems not to care a goose's egg for me; when he looks at me, it is with anything but affection. Yet now he wants to leave, with me at his side."

Julia walked over to console her.

The chamberlain cleared his throat to summon his courage and asked for permission to speak. When it was granted he continued. "The duke of Pesaro indicates he is quite fond of the duchess. He longs for her company—if not in conversation, then just to be with him in his own duchy, where he is free to rule as he likes."

"Well, my good man," Lucrezia said, "that is his desire, and he wishes to have it his way. But what will become of me if I return? I will wither and die of loneliness. There is nothing to interest me in Pesaro."

Impatient with Lucrezia, for she knew the torment it

would cause Alexander, Julia excused herself and left the room.

Suddenly there was a knock at the door, and Lucrezia heard her brother's voice calling. "Crezia, it's Chez. May I enter?"

Quickly she ordered the chamberlain to conceal himself behind her dressing screen. She warned him not to move or make a sound, for his carelessness could cost him his life. Her brother's dislike for the duke had enraged him of late, and she didn't want another scene.

The little man moved silently behind the screen and covered himself with one of Lucrezia's robes, placing other garments over his head to hide himself completely should Cesare walk too close or choose to search his sister's chambers.

When Cesare entered, the first thing he did was kiss Lucrezia. He seemed pleased. "Father has decided to grant your wish for a divorce. He is quite certain that that swine Giovanni Sforza has not given us an advantage, and now that Milan is again aligned with the French, he is of no use to us. Also, and even more important, Father is displeased that he has not made you happy."

Lucrezia sat on the divan and offered Cesare a seat next to her. But he refused, and walked around the room instead.

"But what will you tell Giovanni?" she asked him. "How shall a divorce be accomplished? He is not a heretic, and has committed no treason except to cause me unhappiness . . ."

Cesare smiled. "And is that not crime enough?" he asked.

Lucrezia's eyes lit up with amusement. "Though I think it the most heinous, I fear it will not be seen through the same eyes by others."

Cesare became more serious. "Father will not chance a legal divorce. It would cause too great a scandal. He has ordered that Giovanni must be made to vanish."

Lucrezia stood and frowned at her brother. "Chez, you cannot allow that. Giovanni is a brute and a bore, certainly. But much of my unhappiness with him is that he is not you!

And though that too is a crime, it is not one that deserves the punishment you suggest."

"And would you choose to tell the Holy Father that you refuse to obey his orders? Would you bring the fires of hell down upon you for Giovanni, who acts like such a pig?" Cesare asked.

Lucrezia studied her brother. "Did anyone ask the duke of Pesaro if he would consider willingly dissolving this marriage before you consider the extreme measures of a dagger or poison?"

Cesare answered, "Father asked, Giovanni refused. There is nothing left to speak about."

Lucrezia's voice was filled with determination. "Then speak again to the Holy Father, and your own father as well, to say that I will not agree to endanger my soul with such an action. For hell is eternal, and despite many of my own sins, I hold the hope of a merciful God and an eternity in heaven."

Cesare lowered his head and rubbed his eyes with resignation. "Crezia, something must be done to end this masquerade, and it must be done quickly."

"There is nothing I wish more than to be rid of the duke," Lucrezia explained. "And this is no secret to you, my brother. But it is your soul, and Father's, that I am concerned about, as well as my own. I can play no part in taking the life of another for worldly advantage alone."

Cesare had been certain his sister would be pleased when he brought her the news of the Pope's decision on her marriage, and her reaction disappointed him. He had intended to free her from the beast who had kept them apart and make himself her savior. Now he was angry, and just before he stormed out of his sister's chambers, he shouted: "To be caught between you and Father, my dear sister, is to be caught in the grip of the metal tongs of a vise. There is no escape. So now I ask you—what would you have me do?"

"Do not betray yourself, my dear brother, not to betray another," Lucrezia warned.

Once she was certain Cesare had gone, Lucrezia went behind the screen to rescue Giovanni's chamberlain, who was shaking so forcefully that his trembling could be seen from beneath the garments he had heaped upon himself. As she began to uncover the poor man, she whispered, "Have you heard what was said?"

His eyes wide with fright, he answered quickly. "Not a word, Duchess. Not a single word."

"My God, are you a pod without seeds? Go quickly. Tell the duke all you have heard. Tell him to make haste. I, for one, do not want the stain of his blood on my hands. Now go . . ."

And with that she led the chamberlain out through a side door of the palace.

When the breathless chamberlain reached the Borgia apartments where Giovanni was staying and confided in him what he had overheard, Giovanni Sforza went quickly to the Pope. He asked the Pope to be excused from evening vespers, for he felt the need to ride to the church of Saint Onofrio, outside Rome, to make a holy confession.

This Alexander accepted, for it was Holy Week, and it was well known that during this time, at this particular church, a sinner could receive a special indulgence which would rid his soul of all sins. Both Cesare and the Pope, knowing what was being planned for Giovanni, felt it their obligation to permit him to confess at the church of his choice, and so he was allowed to go.

But the moment Giovanni reached the church, he mounted a prize Turkish horse that had been placed there by the commander of his own troops in Pesaro. Driven by his fear, he whipped the horse harshly, and rode without stopping for twenty-four hours until he reached Pesaro. There at the gates, the horse—exhausted from the journey, foam bubbling from his mouth—fell to his knees and quickly died.

Giovanni Sforza, who was fonder of animals than of men, was heartbroken. He instructed his stable master to have the horse buried with great ceremony, and for days thereafter he stayed in his rooms without eating or speaking to anyone. Not one of the citizens of Pesaro could determine whether he was more desolate over the loss of his wife or his horse.

Lucrezia was angry with her father for not speaking directly to her about his plans, and thereby denying her the opportunity to make known her concerns. Once she discovered that the Pope had sent a papal lawyer to Pesaro to demand an annulment from Giovanni on the only grounds a committee would accept—that of impotence—Lucrezia decided what she must do. Though she had no love for the duke, reason alone would dictate that if he were forced to admit to a weakness that was both embarrassing and untrue, he would resist with the truth he must suspect about herself and her brother. And especially at this time, she was loath to let that happen.

For it was she, because of Cesare, who had—after that first night—refused to sleep in his bed, and had seldom done her wifely duty. Though the admission of impotence was less lethal than poison or a dagger, it was still a mortal blow to one of such arrogance. He would be forced to retaliate, and that would endanger the Pope as well as the entire Borgia family.

The following morning she woke at dawn, and gathered several of her ladies-in-waiting to accompany her to the Convent of San Sisto—for she was aware that a convent was the only refuge for women who would escape the authority of both their husbands and their fathers. Her choice was both simple and virtuous.

But Julia and Adriana tried to convince her otherwise.

"The Holy Father will not rest while you are gone," Adriana told her. "And he will not accept your plan to leave without resistance."

Lucrezia was determined. "He will not prevent me, for he will not know until well after I am on my way."

Julia pleaded with her, for she knew how unhappy the Pope would be. "Dear sister, give the Holy Father a chance to dissuade you. Give our father an opportunity to explain his reasoning. You know how miserable he becomes whenever you are absent from the Vatican . . ."

But Lucrezia turned to her with annoyance. "I will not change the direction of my plans. And if, Julia, you wish the Holy Father, and my father as well, not to be unhappy, I suggest you entertain him in the ways he expects of you. I have no further need to please him, for he has considered neither my position nor the Heavenly Father's in his decisions."

Adriana tried once more. "Lucrezia, you have said so often that you are unhappy—and yet now when the father who loves you tries to extract the writ of divorce or annulment from the husband that you yourself have so slandered, you turn your back and reject your father as well. Where does reason lie in this?"

Lucrezia's eyes filled, but she could not afford to doubt herself, for then all she loved would be lost. Without a word, she embraced both Adriana and Julia, and gave them instructions. "Do not say a word to the Holy Father for half a day. If he asks, tell him I am in the chapel on my knees in prayer and do not wish to be disturbed."

Then she turned to one of her most loyal ladies-in-waiting and handed her a letter she had penned the night before. "Please take this to my brother, the cardinal. Be sure to place it in his own hand and no other."

Pope Alexander, in all matters of church and state, was a reasonable man. In matters of the heart and in his dealings with his children, he was far less reasonable. And so when he was informed of his daughter's departure from her palace and her intention to stay within the walls of the Convent of San Sisto, he was both grief-stricken and enraged.

What did it matter if a man became Pope if he couldn't command even his own daughter? How was it that his once-sweet child could kneel before the Holy Father and with true respect kiss his ring and his holy foot, and yet disobey her own father without consideration?

He called Cesare to him, and Duarte Brandao. Then he sent for Michelotto.

Once they were gathered in his chambers, he asked, "What is it that I have done to my own child, of whom I am so fond, to cause her to desert me in this way?"

Cesare, his head lowered, said nothing.

Duarte, his dark eyes compassionate, said, "It may be a call to the service of the Heavenly Father, Your Worthiness."

"Duarte, please," the Pope said. "Don't humor me, as though I'm a feeble old dunce. There is something I do not know, something that has escaped my understanding."

Duarte nodded. "My intention was not to humor you, Holy Father, for I meant no disrespect, but to dissuade you from blaming yourself for the actions of this child of yours. For, in truth, she is no longer a child. And she is either running toward a greater promise, or running from a greater threat."

"And what could that be?" Alexander asked as he turned to Cesare.

Cesare's gaze met his father's. And in that moment the fire in his father's eyes seared his own. They had never in all these years spoken of the love that mattered most to Cesare, for he feared it would matter even more to his father. And in any battle of love and power with Alexander, Cesare was certain he would lose. For the Pope expected their loyalty to him to count above all else on earth. To reveal the truth of the relationship between himself and his sister would ignite a spiritual inferno.

Cesare had spoken of it to no one; even when drunk and bedded down with courtesans, he had managed to hold his tongue. The servants of the court would certainly never speak of it, for fear they would be beheaded. But could his father, as the Holy Father, divinely inspired, see into the soul of his son? Cesare wondered.

Suddenly the fiery mask on the face of the Pope softened and he smiled. "My friend, Don Michelotto. Choose for me a messenger to travel daily to the convent. I have no doubt my daughter will relent. Make certain the young man is of good character, and intelligent. He must be well groomed and appealing, so my dear Lucrezia will accept my messages and eventually be convinced to return home."

Don Michelotto did as he was commanded. He chose for messenger a young man called Perotto, whom he knew Alexander favored. A musician and a poet, the boy served the Pope as a messenger in return for his keep and his salvation. More highly educated than many of the others in court, he had come from Spain to spend time in Rome after hearing of its beauty. He was honest and deeply devoted to the church, and Alexander trusted him completely.

When Alexander placed the first message to Lucrezia into Perotto's hand, he did so knowing that if Perotto could not bring it to her it was because he had been slaughtered in the hills on his way. That much trust he had in this young man.

When Lucrezia first met Perotto in the garden of the convent, she tried to refuse the message he brought from the Pope. "I do not wish to engage in any disagreements with the Holy Father," she told Perotto. "And the way to do that is never to begin."

Perotto, his long blond hair tied back, his light eyes sparkling, just nodded cheerfully. "I understand, Duchess. I only impose on your goodwill for I believe this message concerns an issue of importance."

Lucrezia looked at him, shook her head, and turned to walk away. She sat on one of the stone benches on the far side of the garden and considered what to do.

But instead of turning to go, or leaving the message where she could reach it, Perotto disappeared for a few moments and then returned with a guitar. He asked Lucrezia's permission to sit on the grass and play his music.

She frowned; but he had a sweet and pleasant face, and life in the convent bored her, so finally she consented. "Play if you will," she told him.

Lucrezia was surprised to find that when Perotto sang, his voice was as pleasing as his song. It had been so long since she had been in male company that she found herself smiling.

When he had finished, her spirits lifted, and she asked for the message. Perotto, smiling, gave it to her.

The message was quite formal. Her father told her that negotiations for her annulment were still under way, and that some progress had been made. That Giovanni was considering the benefices and compensation that had been offered. Alexander told her that if she had any concerns, she should pen them, for the messenger would return the following day with further news.

She went inside her apartments in the convent, sat at her desk, and wrote a short formal response to the Pope. In it she told him she hoped he was well, and she thanked him for his efforts on her behalf. But she signed it only "Lucrezia Borgia," and so when he received it and read it, he knew she was still angry with him.

The following day, Alexander awoke determined to put the matter of Lucrezia's divorce behind him. The business of the papacy was going reasonably well, and once he completed his morning prayers he was free to devote the rest of the day to settling family business.

Cesare also awoke in a pleasant mood, and so when he came to join his father, he said, "It may be time to consider another festival, for those in the city are restless, and they need something to celebrate before they cause themselves trouble."

"Yes," Alexander agreed. "I myself could use a carnival, for the business of the church has caused me to become far too serious."

Just then, Plandini, the chief clerk, announced the arrival of Ludovico Sforza and his nephew, Giovanni.

They all sat around a small marble table and were served platters of cheese, fruit, and wine. After exchanging some pleasantries, Alexander turned to Sforza with a sober expression. "Ludovico, I can no longer spin in circles. I have invited you here today to finalize plans for divorce."

Ludovico, his wine goblet frozen in midair, appeared surprised. But it took him only moments to recover. "Your Holiness, there is no need of divorce, if you are speaking of Giovanni and your sweet daughter, Lucrezia."

Giovanni nodded, but said nothing.

Alexander then removed himself from the table and began to pace around the room. "There *is* such a need for divorce, Ludovico. Giovanni left the city for months to stay in Pesaro. Lucrezia was left alone in Rome."

Ludovico stood up and moved into the sitting area, and Giovanni followed. "My nephew left Rome because of threats from your son, Excellency," Ludovico explained apologetically.

Cesare had not left the table; he sat finishing his wine.

Alexander turned to him. "Is this true, my son? Threats?"

Cesare responded with complete composure. "I never make threats. If a man angers me, I challenge him to a duel." He shook his head now. "I don't remember challenging you, Giovanni. Did I?" He looked at his brother-in-law, with eyes dark and cold.

The two men disliked each other enormously. "You must admit, you were not a gracious brother-in-law," Giovanni said arrogantly.

Ludovico, becoming nervous, addressed the Pope in a honeyed tone. "Your Holiness. Giovanni returned to Rome. The two young people could live happily together in Pesaro, as a married couple. But Lucrezia—no, Lucrezia refused. She wanted Rome."

Now all were seated in the Pope's study.

Alexander became impatient. "Ludovico, my friend. We

could argue all day, yet both of us have more to do. There can be only one conclusion here. Giovanni and Lucrezia must be divorced. We sympathize with both your concerns and your nephew's feelings. But for the good of the church, it must be done."

"The church?" Ludovico said, perplexed.

Now both he and Alexander stood and began to pace the floor, together. "Holy Father," Ludovico whispered. "I'm certain Giovanni would agree to a divorce, if it could be on the grounds that the marriage was never valid." He cleared his throat before he added, "For Lucrezia was already betrothed to the Spaniard."

Alexander turned and placed his hand on Ludovico's shoulder. "Ludovico, Ludovico," he said. "Oh, that this distraction could be cleared up so easily. But the ruling body, the holy commission, disagrees."

Ludovico's voice dropped lower still. "You could always issue a bull."

Alexander nodded. "You are correct, my friend," he said. "I could. If she were another man's daughter." Then the Pope turned to face Ludovico, and spoke in a voice of authority. "The only possible ground is impotence. The admission that the marriage was never consummated. This, both the citizens and the commission will understand. And we have Lucrezia's written statement."

Giovanni jumped to his feet, his face flushed and red. "She lies. I am not impotent, and I will never confess that I am."

Ludovico turned to him, and in a stern voice commanded him to relent. "Sit, Giovanni. We must find a way to accommodate the Holy Father." Il Moro knew that he needed the Pope, for he feared that Milan could be swallowed up by the French at any time, and he might one day need the papal armies and their Spanish support.

Now Cesare spoke in words of stone. "I believe I have a solution. Crezia says one thing, Giovanni says another. And I propose a test. We can gather the members of both families in a large reception room. And into that room we can move a comfortable bed. In that bed we will place an attractive courtesan, a healthy, enthusiastic one. Then Giovanni will slip into the bed next to her, and prove his manhood one way or another."

Giovanni was appalled. "In front of both families? I will not. I will not agree to any such thing!"

The Pope now approached Ludovico. "Well, then, the matter is settled. Giovanni has refused the opportunity to prove himself, and so we must conclude, as any court would, that Lucrezia's statement is true. Of course, we will treat Giovanni generously, for he did what he could as a husband, and we are not here to lay blame."

Giovanni tried to speak, but his uncle stopped him, pulling him aside. "Our entire family will disown you if you do not agree. You will lose your title and your land. At this moment, though you are no longer a husband, you are still a duke. And that is no small thing."

Later that day, Cesare sat at his desk in his own chambers and reread the message his sister had sent the day before. His handsome face reflected the sadness he felt, for to be separated from Lucrezia left him with a deep ache and longing. But there was something more he was concerned about. His hand trembled slightly as he read the message again and again.

One line seemed to stand out on the page: "I am not at liberty, at this time, to discuss the matter which is of utmost importance to us."

It was the formality of her letter, her insistence on not giving him any information, that drew his attention. It was all she didn't say. And he knew his sister well enough to understand she had a secret that, once told, could place them all in grave danger.

12

Vanozza Cattanei's guests sat at the gaily colored banquet tables and watched the blazing sun descend over the red stone ruins of the Roman Forum. She had invited several friends, as well as her children, to her country estate for a gathering in celebration of Cesare's departure for Naples the following week as the papal delegate.

Vanozza's Vineyard, as her children affectionately called it, sat on the nearly deserted Esquiline Hill opposite the stately fifth-century Church of San Pietro.

Juan, Jofre, and Cesare sat together for once, laughing and enjoying themselves. Then Cesare noticed his mother, across the courtyard, talking quite intimately with a young Swiss guard. He smiled to himself, for she was still quite beautiful. Though she was tall she was delicately built, with clear olive skin and rich auburn hair that as yet showed no silver. She looked splendid in a long black silk dress adorned with a single strand of South Sea pearls, a special gift from Alexander.

Cesare adored his mother, was proud of her beauty, intelligence, and obvious skill in business. For she was as successful with her inns as any man in the city of Rome. He looked again at the young guard, and in his heart he wished his mother well, for if she could still enjoy an active love, that is what he wished for her.

On this night, Vanozza brought in two senior chefs from her inns in the city to prepare a large variety of delectable dishes. They sautéed savory goose liver with sliced apples and raisins, simmered freshly caught lobster in a delicate tomato, basil, and cream sauce, and pan-fried tender veal scallops with rich truffles taken from the earth and fresh green olives plucked ripe from the local trees.

Some of the younger cardinals, including Gio Medici, shouted with enthusiasm as each new platter was served. Cardinal Ascanio Sforza remained sedate, but managed to help himself to more than one serving of each new dish, as did Alexander's cousin, the cardinal of Monreal.

Large porcelain carafes of wine, made from the plump burgundy grapes of Vanozza's own vineyards, were served during the meal, and Juan drank each goblet that was poured for him, hardly waiting for the first to be emptied before he lifted the next to his lips. During the meal, a very thin young man wearing a black mask sat down alongside him and whispered something in his ear.

Cesare had seen the masked man at the Vatican several times during the last month in the company of his brother, but when he had inquired about the stranger, no one seemed to know him. And when he asked Juan, Juan just laughed sardonically and walked away. Cesare assumed the young man was an eccentric artist from one of the city ghettos, where Juan often went to bed whores and squander his money.

Now, with his tunic unbuttoned and his hair matted with sweat, Juan stood up shakily—for he was quite drunk—and prepared to make a toast. He raised his goblet and held it before him, tipping it so the wine began to spill. Jofre reached to help steady it, but Juan roughly pushed him away. Then, with slurring speech, he turned to Cesare and said, "Here's to my brother's escape from the French. To his skill at avoiding danger wherever it arises. Whether it be by wearing a cardinal's hat or fleeing the French. Some call it daring . . . I call it cowardice . . ." and he began to laugh loudly.

Cesare leapt to his feet, his hand on his sword. He started for Juan, but his old friend Gio Medici grabbed him, and,

with the help of Jofre and the pleas of Vanozza, succeeded
in holding him back.

Vanozza pleaded with her son. "He doesn't know what
he's saying, Cesare. He doesn't mean it."

Cesare responded with blazing eyes and a set chin. "He
knows, Mother, and if it were not your home, I'd kill the insolent bastard at this very moment—though he is my brother
and your son."

Still shaken by his fury, Cesare allowed Gio to guide him
back to his seat. The guests, their enthusiasm tempered by
the discord of the brothers, sat now in quiet conversation.

Then the masked man stood, and once again whispered
something to Juan. And Juan, sobered by his brother's anger,
rose more steadily and announced, "You must excuse me,
for I have another appointment I must honor."

Helped into his dark blue velvet cloak by his page, he
quickly left the party accompanied by one of his squires and
the tall masked man.

Soon afterward the rest of the party disbanded, and Cesare left with his brother Jofre, Gio, and Ascanio Sforza. As
they rode away on horseback, Cesare waved good-bye to his
mother, Vanozza, who was left with the young Swiss guard
for company.

The men rode swiftly toward the city. Once they passed
through the gates of Rome—at the crossroads in front of
the Borgia Palace—they talked for quite a while about the
incident with Juan. Cesare made it known he could not
tolerate his brother's drunken arrogance and lack of family loyalty. He was determined to speak to Juan again, to
impress upon him the seriousness of the incident at
Vanozza's. He wanted to reason with Juan first, but if he
had to, he would challenge him to a duel to settle things
once and for all. Juan knew that in a duel, Cesare was the
more skilled, and Juan would be forced to repent his
ridiculous conduct—not only with Cesare, but with all
those others he had injured, bringing scandal upon the entire Borgia family.

Cesare also knew that it was Juan, not he, who was a coward, no matter his reckless accusations. In any battle, of wills or swords, Cesare would prevail.

Cardinal Ascanio Sforza complained as well—for only a few nights before, when Juan was again drunk, he had slain Ascanio's majordomo, unprovoked. Ascanio was still displeased about it, and swore that if he had not been wearing the red hat of a cardinal, and did not fear retaliation from the Pope, he himself would have settled the debt with Juan.

Sixteen-year-old Jofre never said a word against Juan, yet Cesare knew he was angry at his brother, for he was not ignorant of Sancia's relationship with Juan. He was a puzzle, this younger brother. At first, because his expression was so bland, he seemed less than bright. But Cesare had witnessed his transformation in the presence of de Córdoba that night in the garden, and would never see him in the same way again.

After they bid Ascanio good night, and Gio Medici left for his palace, Jofre told Cesare, "I think I will pay a visit to the ghetto and spend a few hours with a woman who will respond to my affections."

Cesare smiled at him, and slapped his shoulder with encouragement. "You'll get no argument from me, little brother," he said, laughing. "Have a pleasant night."

Cesare watched as his brother rode away. It was then that he witnessed something that aroused his concern. As young Jofre turned the corner toward the ghetto, three men on horseback slipped out from between the stone buildings behind him and appeared to follow him. One man, taller than the rest, rode a white stallion.

After waiting a few moments so they would take no notice of the gallop of his own horse behind them, Cesare rode to the square above the ghetto. Before him, several streets away, stretched the shadows of four men on horseback, his brother Jofre among them. He could hear them talking, their voices friendly and high-spirited. Convinced that his brother was in no danger, Cesare turned his horse around and returned to the Vatican alone.

Cesare had been asleep for hours when a frightful nightmare woke him. *Was it the sound of horsemen?* He tried to shake himself awake, but the lantern in his chambers had burned out and his room was dark as pitch.

Sweating, with his heart beating fast, he tried to calm himself, but nothing seemed to ease the panic he felt. Blindly, he stood and searched to find a match to strike, but his hands were unsteady and his mind was filled with irrational fears. In a terror, he called aloud for his manservant. But no one came.

Finally, without explanation, his lantern flickered and there was light again. Still half asleep, he sat back on his bed. But now dark shadows surrounded him, reaching toward him from the walls. Cesare wrapped a blanket around himself, for he felt cold as ice, and could not control the shivering of his body. Then, from nowhere, he heard the voice of Noni in his ears: *"There is death in your house . . ."*

He tried to shake the feeling, to dismiss the voice, but his mind was filled with dread. Could Crezia be in danger? No, he reassured himself. A convent was a safe place for her to be—her father had seen to that, by sending Don Michelotto to set a guard around the convent, carefully hidden so as not to alarm or enrage Lucrezia any further. Next he thought of Jofre. But remembering the sound of his voice with his companions, Cesare was reassured.

Juan? God knows, if there was any justice in the heavens, danger to Juan would cause him no nightmares. But then Cesare was seized with worry concerning his father. What would become of him if anything happened to Juan?

Cesare dressed quickly and approached the Pope's chambers. Standing before his father's room, two soldiers of the Holy Guard stood at attention, one on each side of the heavy metal doors.

"Is the Holy Father resting well?" Cesare asked, struggling to maintain his composure.

It was Jacamino, his father's favorite manservant, who answered from the anteroom. "He was sleeping only moments ago," he said. "All is well."

Cesare returned to his own chambers. Yet his restlessness persisted, and there was nothing left for him to do but ride out into the country, as he always did when the beat of his heart threatened to burst through his skin. He raced to the stables, and he was about to mount his favorite stallion when he saw Jofre's horse being rubbed down by one of the grooms. He noticed thick red river clay on the horse's shoes.

"So my brother Jofre has returned safely home?" Cesare asked.

"Yes, Cardinal," the young boy said.

"And my brother Juan? Has he returned?"

"No, Cardinal," the young boy said. "Not at this time."

Cesare left the city with a sense of foreboding. He did not know what he was looking for, but still he rode as though possessed by a demon. Everything around him appeared as though in a dream. It was in this altered state of mind that he rode through the country along the riverside, looking for his brother Juan.

The night was cool and damp, and the smell of salt from the Tiber cleared his head and calmed him. He searched the shores for evidence of disorder, but found none, and after a few hours of riding he reached the red clay of the riverside. Across from one of the large fishing docks there stood the palace of Count Mirandella, and a hospital with lanterns flickering in the windows. Still, all seemed quiet.

Cesare dismounted, looking around for someone who could have seen his brother. But both the dock and the shore seemed deserted, and the only sounds he heard were the splashing of the fish as they leapt through the shimmering glasslike surface of the river.

Cesare walked to the end of the dock and stood looking across the water. There were a few fishing boats anchored there, and the crews were either out at one of the local pubs in the village or deep asleep in the bowels of the boats. He thought how it might be to live as a fisherman, when the only thing to do each day was to throw a net and wait for the invited fish to come. He smiled then, feeling more at peace.

He was about to turn and leave when he noticed a small boat moored against the stack of timber logs, a man asleep inside. "Signor? Signor?" Cesare called.

As he walked toward the boat, the man sat up and looked at him warily. "I am Cardinal Borgia," Cesare said. "And I'm inquiring about my brother, the captain general. Did you observe anything that would cause you suspicion earlier this night?"

As Cesare stood talking to the fisherman, he spun a gold ducat between his fingers.

Seeing the coin, the man, whose name was Giorgio, was persuaded to talk freely to Cesare.

After half an hour, before he took leave of the fisherman, Cesare thanked him and handed him the gold piece. "No one must know we have spoken," he said. "I count on you for that."

"I have already forgotten, Cardinal," Giorgio vowed.

Cesare rode back to the Vatican. But he told no one what he had learned.

Pope Alexander awakened earlier than usual, with a feeling of uneasiness. He had called a meeting to review the military strategy that would be used in the upcoming battles, and was convinced that his discomfort might have arisen from his anxiety over their outcome.

After kneeling for morning vespers, praying for divine guidance, he arrived at the meeting to find only Duarte Brandao in attendance.

"Where are my sons, Duarte?" the Pope asked. "It is time to begin."

Duarte dreaded what he must tell Alexander. He had been awakened before dawn by a manservant of the captain general, who told Duarte that his master had not returned from his dinner at the vineyard. Even more ominous, the squire who had accompanied him was also missing.

Duarte had reassured the servant, instructing him to go back to the captain general's apartments, and inform him when the Pope's son arrived. But Duarte felt something strange in the air, and was unable to return to sleep. After lying awake for long moments, he finally got out of bed, dressed quickly, and before the golden light of day cut through the black night sky he rode through the streets of Rome, asking in the ghetto if anyone had seen Juan Borgia. But no one had.

When Duarte returned to the Vatican, he immediately woke Cesare to ask when Juan was last seen.

"He rode away from the party with his squire and the masked man," Cesare said. "He was meant to be returning to the Vatican. His squire was instructed to make certain he arrived, for he was still quite intoxicated."

"I have been unable to find the squire who accompanied him," Duarte told Cesare. "And I, myself, have searched all of the city looking for Juan."

"I will dress immediately," Cesare said. "In the event my father has need of me."

But Duarte noticed, as he left Cesare's apartments, that Cesare's boots were still wet and covered with fresh red mud.

After several hours more, Alexander became increasingly upset about Juan's absence. He paced back and forth within his chambers, golden rosary in hand. "That boy is impossible," he told Duarte. "We must find him. He has much to answer for."

Duarte tried to reassure the Pope. "He is young, Your Holiness, and the city is filled with pretty women. He may be passed out in some bedroom in Trastevere that we have not yet discovered."

Alexander nodded, but then Cesare entered with sinister news. "Father, Juan's squire has been found, mortally wounded, and it seems the wounds inflicted are so dreadful that he is unable to speak."

"I will go to this man, and ask about my son," the Pope said, "for if this man can speak to anyone, he will speak to me."

Cesare's head was bowed, and his voice was low. "Not without a tongue, Father."

The Pope felt his knees weaken.

"And he is too wounded to pen this information?" the Pope asked.

"He cannot, Father," Cesare said. "For he is without fingers."

"Where was this squire found?" the Pope asked his son.

"In the Piazza della Giudecca," Cesare said, "and he must have lain there for hours, in front of hundreds of passersby, who in their fear did not report the incident."

"And there is still no news of your brother?" Alexander asked, now, sitting down.

"No, Father," Cesare said. "There has been no word."

After they rode throughout Rome gathering information from the captains of the Holy Guard, the commander of the Spanish force, and the Swiss Guard, as well as the foot police in the city, both Cesare and Duarte returned to the Vatican.

Alexander was still sitting silently, his golden rosary beads now clutched tight between his fingers. When they entered the Pope's chambers, Cesare looked toward Duarte Brandao. He felt it would be kinder to his father to hear the most recent news from a trusted friend.

Duarte stood next to the Pope and placed a strong hand on his shoulder to help brace him. "It has in these last moments been brought to my attention, Your Holiness, that the captain general's horse has been found, wandering with one stirrup cut by what appears to be a sword."

The Pope felt his breath taken away, as though he had received a sharp blow to the stomach. "And the rider?" he asked softly.

"No rider was found, Father," Cesare said.

Pope Alexander lifted his head, his eyes clouded, and turned to Cesare. "Call together the Holy Guard and have them search the streets and the countryside outside Rome. Tell them they are forbidden to return until they have found my son."

Cesare left, as he was asked, to instruct the troops. In the hallway to the palace he passed his brother Jofre. "Juan is gone," Cesare said, "and Father is desolate. I would speak very carefully if I were you, and under no circumstances allow him to know your whereabouts last evening."

Jofre nodded to his brother, and said, "I understand."

But he offered nothing more.

Rumors spread throughout the city about the Pope's son Juan: that he was missing, and that the Pope was in severe distress, threatening dire punishment if it were found that he had been harmed.

Storefronts were boarded up and shops shut down as Spanish soldiers ran through the streets with swords drawn. The enemies of Alexander, including the Orsini and the Colonna, fearing they would be blamed, also took up arms. Runners were sent into all the alleys in the city of Rome to search, and all soldiers were threatened with death should Juan not be found.

Early the following morning, the police awoke a fisherman they discovered sleeping on his boat. His name was Giorgio Schiavi, and he claimed that on the night of the party he had seen four riders, one of them masked. He had watched from his boat as a fifth horse was brought forward—a body draped across its back—and led to the place in the Tiber where the filth of the city was dumped. There the body was lifted from the horse, and heaved into the river.

The police asked, "What did these men look like? What can you tell us?"

Giorgio said, "It was very dark . . ."

On further questioning, he admitted that he had heard the voice of one, the master, order the others to throw several stones upon the corpse when his blue velvet cape floated to the surface. And he told them, of course, that one of the horses was white.

But he kept his vow to the cardinal, and never described the man who had spoken, the man who had been there. When the police became more aggressive, asking why he had not reported such a happening, Giorgio replied, annoyed, "I've seen hundreds of bodies thrown into the Tiber over these past years. To report each time to the police would leave me no time to fish, nor to eat!"

B y noon, divers searched the riverbed from bank to bank with dragging nets and huge grappling hooks. But it was three o'clock before one of the hooks thrown by a local fisherman caught on something solid, and a bloated body floated to the surface, faceup, with a blue velvet cloak swirling around in the current.

He still wore his boots and spurs. His gloves were tucked in his belt, and his purse contained thirty ducats, so the motive had not been to rob him. But once he was taken from the water and examined, it was found that he had nine deep stab wounds in his body, and that his throat had been slashed.

Duarte Brandao came to identify the body. There was no question. It was the Pope's son, Juan Borgia.

J uan's body was taken by boat at once to the Castel Sant' Angelo. And on seeing the corpse of his favorite son Alexander fell to his knees, distraught and distracted by grief. He sobbed and sobbed, so that his cries to his God could be heard throughout the Vatican.

When Alexander was able to collect himself, he ordered the funeral to be held that very evening. Juan's body was prepared and laid out in state, dressed in the rich brocade uniform of the captain general of the Holy Roman Catholic Church.

At six o'clock that evening, Juan, looking handsome and as though asleep, was placed on a magnificent bier and carried by the noblemen of his household across the bridge while the Pope stood alone, watching from the tower of Castel Sant' Angelo.

The procession was led by 120 torch and shield bearers, followed by hundreds of church chamberlains and ecclesiastics, weeping and in great disorder.

That night, accompanied by a thousand mourners, all carrying torches, borne between lines of Spanish troopers, their unsheathed swords held before them, the procession reached the Church of Santa Maria del Popolo, where Juan was laid to rest in the chapel his mother, Vanozza, had prepared as her own tomb.

Alexander was still in the throes of great grief when, immediately after the funeral, he called for his son Cesare to come to his chambers.

Anxious to be of help to his father, Cesare went at once.

Entering the Pope's private study, he found Alexander sitting at his desk, his face pale, his eyes rimmed red from weeping. Cesare had only seen him like this once before— when he was a child and Juan's life was in danger. He wondered in that moment whether prayer could ever change destiny, but rather just postpone the inescapable.

When Alexander saw this son, in the darkness of his dimly lit room, he approached Cesare, positioning his mountainous body just inches away. He was beside himself with grief and rage. He had always known that Cesare had no love for his brother; he understood that Juan had taken the life that Cesare wanted for himself. He'd heard that they had quarreled bitterly two nights before at Vanozza's, the night Juan disappeared. Now he wanted the truth from Cesare. And he spoke in a harsh, commanding tone. "Swear to me that you did not kill your brother. Swear on your immortal soul. And know if you keep the truth from me, you will burn in hell forever."

The shock of his father's accusation almost took his breath away. In truth, he was not sorry his brother was dead. But it was also the truth that he himself did not kill Juan. And yet he could not blame his father for suspecting him.

Cesare moved even closer, locking his eyes with his father's gaze. He put his hand to his chest, and addressed Alexander with sincerity. "Father, I did not kill my brother. I swear to it. And if I am not speaking the truth, I shall willingly burn in hell forever." He saw the confusion in the face of the Pope, and so he repeated the words. "I did not kill Juan."

It was the Pope who looked away first. He sat again then, seemed to collapse into his large leather chair, his hand over his eyes. When he spoke his voice was soft and sad. "Thank you. Thank you, my son," he said. "As you can see I am desolate over the loss of my boy. And I am enormously relieved by what you have said. For I must tell you—and these are not the words of a grieving father that may be dismissed—that if you had killed your brother, I would have had the limbs torn from your body. Now leave me, for I must pray and try to find some solace in my grief."

There is a time in every human life when a decision one makes helps carve the path to his destiny. It is at that crossroads, without knowing what lies ahead, that a choice is made which influences all events to follow. And so it was that Cesare chose not to tell his father about the fisherman who found the blue topaz ring—and that he knew his brother Jofre had killed his brother Juan. For what possible purpose could telling him serve?

Juan had brought his fate upon himself. That Jofre was used as an instrument of justice seemed a fit outcome of Juan's pathetic life. He had contributed nothing to the Borgia family; on the contrary, he had endangered them. And so Jofre's murder of his brother seemed a fitting penance for the many Borgia sins.

It was not that he was surprised to find his father suspected him, though the impact of Alexander's doubting his allegiance and love wounded Cesare more than he had imagined it could.

But if Alexander chose to blame him, then that was how it must be, for to strike back at his father with the truth would only wound him more. As the Holy Father, the Pope must be infallible, for it was that infallibility that held his power. In this case, Cesare reasoned, the truth would deny the very quality that was the mainstay of the papacy.

Cesare knew his father doubted him, but would it serve to have his father doubt himself? No, that would weaken him. And in so doing, it would weaken the entire Borgia family. This Cesare could never allow.

And so it was, with Juan's death, and his decision, that Cesare assumed the mantle of guardianship for Rome, as well as for the family.

Lucrezia was praying before the large marble statue in the chapel of the Convent of San Sisto when she was summoned by one of the young nuns, a nervous young girl from one of the royal families of Naples. There were as many wealthy young women from the aristocratic families of Europe sent to the convents for sanctuary as there were poor peasant girls who had a true religious calling. Both served the church. The families of the wealthy girls paid large sums to the church, and the peasant girls prayed for the salvation of the wealthy.

Now the young girl stuttered as she told Lucrezia that someone was waiting for her with an important message.

Lucrezia, her heart already racing with apprehension, walked as fast as she could, her shoes echoing on the stone pathways of the empty corridors.

She was wearing a simple gray wool dress with a high waist, and over it a plain cotton jumper. Thank God, she thought each morning as she dressed, that the clothes were large and unflattering enough that they hid her belly, which was becoming fuller each day.

A thousand thoughts ran through her mind in the minutes it took her to reach the entrance hall. Was her father well? Her brother Cesare? Had he been unable to live without her these many months, and gone away for good? Or was it just another message from the Holy Father, her father, pleading with her to return to Rome and take up her place again in the court?

She had opened only one of those messages the young page, Perotto, had brought to her. After that she feared it was all the same: her father demanding her obedience, and Lucrezia herself being unable to obey even if she wanted to. It certainly would not serve anyone to show herself in such condition, especially since she knew from young Perotto that her father had insisted on the annulment of her marriage to Giovanni on the grounds of impotence. She patted her belly gently as she walked. "And how then will he explain you to everyone?"

The entrance hall was stark and cold, with bare marble floors, windows covered with dark curtains, and several crucifixes hanging on the unadorned walls. When Lucrezia reached it, she stopped, stunned by what she saw. Her brother Cesare, dressed in his ecclesiastical vestments, awaited her alone in the front hall.

She was so happy to see him that she rushed to him, throwing herself upon him, not caring if anyone saw them. But Cesare pushed her away, stood her in front of him and looked at her sternly, his handsome face in a scowl.

"Chez?" she said, almost in tears. "What is it?" She could not believe he had noticed so soon, or heard about her condition from anyone else. But as she stood before her brother, a thousand thoughts running through her mind, he bent his head and said, "Juan is dead. He was murdered in the night."

Her knees failing her, Lucrezia fell forward, almost hitting the hard marble floor before Cesare caught her. Kneeling next to her, he noticed the paleness of her skin, the small vessels in her closed eyelids more prominent than ever before. He called to her gently—"Crezia, Crezia . . ."—but she wouldn't wake. Then, removing his velvet cape, he placed it on the floor and rested her head upon it.

Lucrezia's eyes fluttered and began to open just as Cesare ran his hand over her belly to soothe her, to wake her. And as her eyes began to focus, all she could see were his eyes.

"Are you feeling better?" he asked.

"It is a terrible nightmare," she said. "Juan is dead? And Father? Is Father able to bear it?"

"Not well," Cesare said to her. But then he placed his hand on her stomach and frowned. "There is a change in your condition that I was unaware of."

"Yes."

"With Father pursuing an annulment, this has not come at the most fortuitous time. Now no one will believe that swine Giovanni is impotent, and your annulment will not be granted."

Lucrezia sat up quickly. There was an edge to her brother's voice; he was displeased with her. She was still shattered by the news of the death of her brother Juan, and now to have Cesare angry with her confused her. "My condition has nothing to do with Giovanni," she said coolly. "I bedded him once, and that was on a marriage bed."

Cesare looked angry. "Now what scoundrel shall I slay?"

Lucrezia reached up to touch her brother's cheek. "This child is yours, my sweet," she said. "And can it be more bitter?"

He stared silent and thoughtful for long minutes.

Then he said, "I must rid myself of the hat of a cardinal. For no child of mine shall be a bastard."

Lucrezia covered his lips with her finger. "But no child of yours can ever be mine."

"We must think, and we must plan," he said. "Does anyone else know?"

"Not a soul," Lucrezia said. "For on the day I was certain, I left Rome."

The Pope locked himself away after Juan's death. Despite the pleas of Duarte, Don Michelotto, Cesare, and all those who loved him, he refused to eat, or to speak to anyone for days—not even Julia. From outside his chambers his prayers could be heard, and his shrieks of remorse as he begged for forgiveness.

But first he shook his fist and ranted at God. "Heavenly Father, of what benefit is saving the souls of thousands when the loss of this one is the cause of so much pain?" Alexander raged on and on. "To punish me for the loss of virtue, with the life of my son, is unjust. A man is subject to human frailty, but *a God is meant to be merciful!*" He sounded as though lunacy had taken hold of him.

Those cardinals whom he favored took turns knocking on the doors to his chambers to beg for entry, to help him in his suffering. But again and again he refused. Finally, a shout was heard throughout the Vatican. "Yes, yes, Heavenly Father, I know—Your Son was martyred too . . ." And there was silence for two days more.

When Alexander finally opened the doors to his chambers he was thin and pale, but still he seemed at peace. He announced to all who waited: "I have made a vow to the Madonna to reform the church, and I will begin immediately. Call the consistory together so I may address them."

The Pope proclaimed his love for his son publicly, and told the cardinals in attendance that he would give up seven tiaras to have him back. But because that was not possible, he said, he would instead initiate reform of the church, as

Juan's murder had awakened him and made him all too aware of his own sins.

His anguish was apparent as he talked about his grief, and as he confessed his own wickedness and the wickedness of his family he swore to make amends. He told the entire gathering of cardinals and ambassadors that he understood he had offended Providence, and he asked that a committee be set up to make suggestions for change.

The following day, the Pope wrote to the Christian rulers recording both his tragedy and his new understanding of the need for reform. Everyone was so convinced of Alexander's intention that there were speeches of sympathy given throughout Rome, and both Cardinal della Rovere and the prophet Savonarola, two of the Pope's greatest enemies, sent letters of condolence.

And so it seemed a new era was about to begin.

II

13

Alexander was still in mourning for Juan, and so it was that Duarte came to Cesare Borgia to suggest that once he had crowned the king of Naples he must visit the city of Florence, which had been turned upside down during the French invasion. For now, in order to cement the relationship between the city's largest lawmaking body—the Signoria—and the Pope, to attempt to reinstate the Medici, and to assess the danger from the prophet Savonarola, someone trusted must be sent to evaluate the truth of the rumors that were reaching Rome.

"It is being said," Duarte told Cesare, "that the Dominican friar, Savonarola, has become even more inflammatory and influential in these last months, and that he is turning the people of Florence against the Pope—unless there are stringent reforms." Alexander had already sent an interdict to Florence forbidding the friar from preaching if he planned to continue undermining the people's faith in the papacy. He had ordered that Savonarola not preach again until he could make his way to Rome to speak with the Pope himself; he had even imposed sanctions on the merchants of Florence to prevent them from listening to the friar's speeches. Yet nothing stopped the zealous prophet.

Piero Medici's arrogance had alienated the citizens of Florence as well as the members of his court. And now from the pulpits and in the squares, Girolamo Savonarola's inflammatory speeches against the Medici had the throngs of people in a fervor for reform. The growing power of the wealthy commoners, who resented the Medici and felt their money entitled them to a voice in the affairs of Florence, added to the clamor and threatened to undermine the power of the Pope.

Cesare smiled. "Can you guarantee, my friend, that I myself will not be slaughtered if I visit Florence? They may wish to make an example of me. I have heard it said that according to the prophet and the citizens of Florence, I am almost as evil as the Holy Father."

"You have friends there, as well as enemies," Duarte said. "And even some allies. The brilliant orator Machiavelli is one. During this time of weakness in the papacy, a sharp eye is needed to separate the true from the false dangers to the Borgia family."

"I appreciate your concern, Duarte," Cesare said. "And if I am able, you have my word, I will visit Florence when I have finished in Naples."

"The hat of a cardinal will protect you," Duarte said. "Even from one as zealous as the prophet. And it might serve us to hear directly of what he is accusing the Pope, so that we may properly refute it."

Now, fearing that with the loss of the ruling Medici family, and the election of a new Signoria, the Pope would be in greater danger, Cesare consented to go to Florence to see how he could alter the situation to Rome's advantage.

"As soon as possible," Cesare said, "I will do as you ask."

In Florence, Niccolò Machiavelli had just returned from Rome, where he had gone as an emissary for the Signoria to investigate the murder of Juan Borgia.

Machiavelli stood in the enormous room of the Palazzo della Signoria, surrounded by extraordinary tapestries and priceless paintings. Giottos, Botticellis and many other treasures donated by the late Lorenzo the Magnificent decorated the room.

Sitting in a large red velvet chair among the eight members of the Signoria, and fidgeting nervously, the aging president listened intently as Machiavelli prepared to report what he had discovered.

All of the members dreaded the prospect of what they would discover, about both Florence and themselves. For though they were often impressed by this young man's ability to present an argument, they were also concerned by the degree of concentration they must maintain in order to fully understand his presentation. They could not rest their eyes for a moment.

Machiavelli was slightly built; he looked even younger than his twenty-five years. Now, with his body dramatically wrapped in a long black cloak, he paced up and down in front of them as he spoke. "All of Rome believes that it was Cesare Borgia who murdered his own brother. But I do not. The Pope himself may believe it, but still I disagree. Certainly Cesare Borgia had a motive, and we all know the relationship between the brothers was at the very least strained. It is said they nearly fought a duel on the night of the murder. But still I say no."

The president waved his withered hand impatiently. "I don't care a Tuscan fig what Rome thinks, young man. In Florence we make up our own minds. You were sent to assess the situation, not to bring back gossip that could be heard on any Roman street."

Machiavelli remained unflustered by the president's attack. With a sly smile, he continued. "I do not believe Cesare Borgia killed his brother, Excellency. There are many others who had strong motives. The Orsini, for one, who are still bitter over the death of Virginio and the attack on their fortresses. Giovanni Sforza, due to the divorce proceedings over the Pope's daughter, Lucrezia."

"Hurry, young man," the president said. "Or I shall die of advanced age before you finish your presentation."

Machiavelli didn't flinch. He spoke passionately, though he had been interrupted. "There is the duke of Urbino, Guido Feltra, who was imprisoned in the dungeons of the

Orsini due to the captain general's incompetence—and left there for months, for due to his greed, Juan Borgia would not pay the ransom. And let us not overlook the Spanish commander de Córdoba, who was robbed of both the money and the glory of the conquest of the Orsini. But perhaps more than any other, there is the Count Mirandella. His fourteen-year-old daughter was seduced and used by Juan, who immediately afterward boasted of it to the crowds in the public square. You can understand a father's shame. And it is his palace that is just opposite the site on the Tiber where Juan Borgia was thrown into the river."

The president began to doze, and Machiavelli raised his voice to seize his attention. "But there are still more enemies . . . Cardinal Ascanio Sforza could have done it, for his majordomo was slain just the week before. And let us not overlook—the man whose wife he had seduced . . ." He stopped in a well-choreographed pause, then continued in a voice one had to strain to hear: "His younger brother, Jofre . . ."

"Enough, enough," the president said, annoyed. Then, with a clarity remarkable for his age, he argued, "We are concerned only about the threat to Florence from Rome. Juan Borgia, the captain general of the papal army, has been murdered. There is the question of who has murdered him. Some say his brother, Cesare, may be guilty. It is reasonable to assume that if Cesare Borgia *is* guilty, Florence is in danger. For if this is the truth, he is a patriot filled with ambition, and it follows that he will one day attempt to claim Florence as his own. To put it simply, young man, what we find necessary to know is the answer to the question, 'Did Cesare Borgia murder his brother?' "

Machiavelli shook his head. Then, in a voice both impassioned and sincere, he argued, "I do not believe he is guilty, Your Excellency. And I will state my reasons. The evidence shows that Juan Borgia was stabbed nine times. . . . in the back. That is not the style of Cesare Borgia. He is a warrior, and a strong one, who requires only one thrust to an enemy. And for a man such as Cesare Borgia to claim victory, the battle must be face-to-face. Midnight murders in dark alleys and bodies tossed in the Tiber are actions not consistent with his nature. It is this above all else that persuades me of his innocence."

For months after Juan's death, Alexander repeatedly fell into deep bouts of depression. When grief took hold of him, he would retreat to his chambers and refuse to see anyone, or even conduct papal business. Then, once again inspired, he would emerge from his quarters filled with energy, determined to proceed with his mission of reforming the church.

Finally, Alexander called for his chief clerk, Plandini, and dictated his request that the commission of cardinals be convened to bring him their advisements.

Alexander called Duarte and confessed that reform could not stop at the church alone. That he was ready to reform his own life, and that of Rome as well. He needed no authorization, for in this matter he would need only divine guidance.

Certainly Rome needed reform. In all areas of commerce, fraud and theft were common. Robbery, lechery, homosexuality, and pedophilia were rampant on the streets, in every shop and alley. Even cardinals and bishops paraded through the streets with their favorite young catamites dressed in lavish oriental costumes.

Sixty-eight hundred prostitutes roamed through the streets of the city, causing a new medical as well as a moral threat to the people. Syphilis was becoming prevalent; having begun in Naples, it was spread by the French troops, moved northward to Bologna, and was then carried by the army across the Alps. The wealthier Romans, infected with the "French pox," paid olive oil dealers vast sums of money to allow them to soak for hours in the barrels of oil in order to relieve the pain of their sores. Later, that same oil was sold in fashionable shops as "pure extra-virgin" olive oil. Such travesty!

But Alexander knew he must change the practices of the church itself, and for that he needed the work of the committee. The Holy Roman Catholic Church was a large and wealthy enterprise with an enormous number of accounts. The chancellery alone sent out more than ten thousand letters a year. The cardinal in charge of the financial branch, the Apostolic Camera, was responsible for paying thousands of bills, as well as collecting payments in ducats, florins, and other currencies. The large staff of the curia, which was growing more each year, was salaried, and there were valuable offices to be sold and traded, both legitimate and otherwise.

Yet much had to be considered. Over the years, both the Pope and the cardinals vied for control. Reform would mean the power of the Pope would be weakened while the power of the college of cardinals would be strengthened. This had been the cause of tension between them for over a century.

And so it stood to reason that one of the areas of disagreement would be the number of cardinals ordained. By flooding the college with family members, a Pope could increase his own power. He could, in fact, through them, control the future papal elections, guarantee and protect a family's interest, and increase its wealth.

Of course, limiting the number of cardinals any one Pope could appoint would give each existing cardinal more individual power, as well as greater revenue—for the benefices of the college of cardinals itself were shared equally.

And so it was that five weeks after its work had begun, the committee that Alexander had commissioned to investigate reform gathered in the Great Hall of the Vatican to report their findings and offer their recommendations to the Pope.

Cardinal Grimani, a short, blond Venetian, rose to speak for the group. He spoke carefully with a well-modulated voice. "We have explored the suggestions of reform from previous papal committees, and considered those we feel are necessary at this time. We will begin with the reforms for the cardinals. It has been decided that we must reduce our earthly pleasures. We must limit the number of dinners at which meat is served. The Bible must be read at each meal . . ."

Alexander waited, for there was nothing startling here.

Cardinal Grimani continued by proposing to curb all simony and gifts of church property, as well as limiting the income of cardinals—though not the personal income from private or family sources, only from certain church benefices. Since most of the cardinals were wealthy, this would cause no hardship.

Ah, but then Grimani's recommendations became more aggressive, as Alexander knew they would. "There must be limits to the powers given the Pope," Grimani began softly. "The cardinals will have approval over the appointment of bishops. The Pope is forbidden to sell or barter any administrative offices without the consent of the college of cardinals. Upon the death of any cardinal now in service, no new cardinal will be appointed."

Alexander frowned as he listened.

Grimani, his voice lowered now so that the Pope was forced to lean forward and strain to hear, said, "No prince of the church should have more than eighty servants, no more than thirty horses, no jugglers, jesters, or musicians. None should employ young boys as valets. And whatever their rank, all clergy must give up entertaining concubines, or all benefices would be lost."

The Pope now fingered his rosary beads as he sat listening impassively. These were worthless suggestions, most adding nothing to the good of the soul or the good of the church. Still, he remained silent.

When he finished at last, Grimani asked courteously, "Does the Holy Father have any questions?"

Alexander's fervor for reform had diminished over the last month; now, having heard the commission's proposal, it had disappeared completely.

The Pope rose from his throne and faced the committee. "I have nothing to say at the moment, Grimani. But of course I wish to thank you all for your diligence. I will now study the reports carefully, and my chief clerk, Plandini, will notify the commission when I am prepared to discuss the matters presented."

Alexander made the sign of the cross, blessed the committee, and quickly turned and left the hall.

One of the other Venetian cardinals, Sangiorgio, approached Grimani, who was still standing at the lectern. "Well, Grimani," he whispered, "I doubt that we should rush to make arrangements for a return trip to Rome. I suspect the reform suggested by the Pope is ready to be given last rites."

B ack in his quarters, Alexander called for Duarte Brandao. He was sipping a goblet of strong wine when Duarte entered, and he insisted Duarte sit so that they could discuss the afternoon's events.

Duarte accepted the wine offered to him, and sat attentively.

"It is unbelievable," Alexander said, "that human nature consistently goes against itself for lofty principles."

Duarte asked, "And so you found nothing worth considering in the committee's report?"

Alexander stood and began to pace, an amused expression on his face. "Outrageous, Duarte. Their suggestions go against all earthly pleasures. To be moderate is one thing, but to be an ascetic? What joy will God feel if we feel none?"

"Of their recommendations, Your Holiness, which did you find the most objectionable?"

Alexander stood and faced Duarte. "My friend, they suggested no 'concubines.' As Pope I cannot marry, and therefore my dear Julia would have no place in my bed or at my side. I could never allow that. And even more treacherous, no properties for my children? No entertainment for the citizens? It is nonsense, Duarte, pure nonsense, and I find it worrisome that our cardinals have become so indifferent to the needs of our people."

Duarte smiled. "Am I to assume, then, that you will not accept the suggestions of the committee?"

Alexander sat again, more relaxed. "I must have been mad with grief, my friend. For a reform of the church in this way would distance a Pope from his children, his love, and his people. And therefore, fewer souls will be saved. We will wait one more month, but then all talk of reform must cease."

Duarte rubbed his chin thoughtfully. "So you were surprised by the report?"

Alexander shook his head. "Horrified, my dear friend, horrified."

In the Roman countryside, rumors grew like weeds. And it was said that Providence had exacted the price of Juan's life because the wicked Borgia brothers, as well as the Pope, had each bedded Lucrezia.

Giovanni Sforza had agreed to the divorce, but not graciously, and so he began to fight the rumors of the reasons for his annulment with his accusations of incest within the Borgia family. Not only had she slept with her brother, Cesare, he insisted, but also with her father, the Pope. The rumors were so scandalous that they enlivened the streets of Rome, and finally Florence as well. Savonarola began to preach with new fervor about the "evil that will befall the followers of the false Pope."

Seemingly unfazed by all that was being said, Pope Alexander was considering a number of suitors for his daughter. Of all, Alfonso of Aragon, son of the king of Naples, seemed the most desirable.

Alfonso was a handsome young man, tall and blond, with a pleasant, easygoing manner. Like his sister, Sancia, he was illegitimate, but his father had agreed to make him duke of

Bisceglie, to give him added income and status. Even more important, Alfonso's family's relationship to Ferdinand would unite the Pope and the Spanish king, giving Alexander a tactical advantage in his disputes with the barons and warlords south of Rome.

As Alexander made his plans for Lucrezia, young Perotto carried daily messages to her concerning the divorce proceeding and the ongoing marital negotiations between the Convent of San Sisto and the Vatican.

During this time, Lucrezia and the gentle Perotto became good friends. Each day they shared stories and music, and walked together through the convent gardens. He encouraged her to explore her freedom, for it was the first time in her life that she had not been under the domination of her father, and therefore could be herself.

Lucrezia, still so young, and the charming Perotto held hands and told secrets, and often after they had lunched together on the grass Perotto spent the afternoons weaving gaily colored flowers into Lucrezia's long blond hair. She began to laugh, to come alive again, to feel young.

On the day Perotto delivered the announcement that Lucrezia was to return to the Vatican to take part in the ceremonial annulment of her marriage in front of the Roman Rota—the highest ecclesiastical court—she was beside herself with dread. As she held the parchment in her trembling hands, she began to weep. Perotto, who had by this time fallen deeply in love with Lucrezia—though he had not yet spoken of it to her—held her close to comfort her.

"What is it, my sweet?" he asked, breaking with his usual formality. "What could cause you such pain?"

She hung tight to him, her head buried in his shoulder. She had told no one except Cesare of her condition, but to be called upon to declare herself a virgin now seemed an impossible feat. If her father or anyone else discovered her true state, the new alliance with Prince Alfonso of the House of Aragon in Naples would be endangered; even worse, she and her brother could be put to death by their enemies, for they had put the papacy itself in danger.

And so it was that Lucrezia, having no one else to confide in, confessed to the young Perotto her predicament. And he, an honorable knight, suggested that rather than admit her relationship with her brother, she should claim that he, Perotto, was the father of her unborn child. There would still be some consequences for her action, but certainly not of the seriousness that a charge of incest would incur.

Lucrezia was both touched and frightened by his suggestion. "But Father will have you tortured, for to endanger the alliance he has planned will weaken his position in the Romagna. Of course the rumors are bad enough without proof, but now . . ." and she patted her belly, and sighed.

"I am willing to give my life for you and for the church," Perotto said simply. "I have no doubt that with the goodness of my intentions the Heavenly Father will reward me, no matter what the Holy Father decrees."

"I must tell my brother the cardinal," Lucrezia mused aloud.

Perotto with his even temper and good nature said, "Tell him what you feel you must, and I will suffer the consequence all true love must bear. For a gift of such wonder as I have known these past months is worth whatever it may cost."

He bowed, and took leave of her. But not before she handed him a letter to deliver to her brother. "Make certain it is he who receives this message and only he, for you know the danger should it fall into anyone else's hand."

Perotto arrived in Rome, and immediately met with the Pope to inform him that Lucrezia was six months pregnant, and that he was the father of her baby. He begged the Pope's forgiveness for the betrayal of his trust, and vowed to make amends in whatever way the Pope decreed.

Alexander listened intently to what Perotto had to say. He

seemed puzzled for a moment, then became quiet; but to Perotto's surprise he didn't appear angry. He simply gave the young Spaniard orders. He instructed Perotto to speak to no one about the situation; there could be no exceptions. He explained that Lucrezia would remain in the convent, where she would bear the child assisted by those brides of Christ who had sworn allegiance to the church and therefore could be counted on to protect its secrets.

But what to do about the infant? Certainly Alfonso and his family must never know the truth. Nor should anyone else but Alexander, Lucrezia, and of course, Cesare. Even Jofre and Sancia could be in danger if this was discovered. And it was understood that even under torture Perotto would not betray this truth.

As Perotto was readying himself to take leave of the Pope, Alexander asked, "You have told no one about this, I assume?"

"Not a soul," Perotto admitted. "For my love of your daughter has imposed its own silence upon my lips."

Alexander embraced the young man then, and sent him on his way. "Take care," he called after Perotto. "I appreciate your candor and your courage."

After his visit to the Pope, Perotto stopped to see the cardinal to deliver the message from Lucrezia. Cesare paled as he read the parchment, then looked at Perotto with surprise. "What is the purpose of this admission?" he asked the young Spaniard.

Perotto, his guitar slung over his shoulder, smiled and said, "Love is its own reward."

Cesare's heart was racing. "Have you told anyone?"

Perotto nodded. "Only His Holiness . . ."

Cesare maintained his composure with difficulty. "And his reaction?"

"He was quite gracious," Perotto said.

Now Cesare was alarmed. He knew his father was most quiet when he was most angry. "Then go quickly to a place in the ghetto of Trastevere and remain hidden," he told Perotto. "And if you have any regard for your life, make no further mention of this to anyone. I will consider what to do, and the moment I return from Naples I will call for you."

Perotto bowed as he left the room, but Cesare called after him, "You are a noble soul, Perotto. Go with my blessings!"

In Rome Lucrezia rose before the twelve judges, seven months pregnant. And even disguised by her loose clothing, the change in her appearance was apparent. But she had made certain to tie her golden hair neatly back in a ribbon, and to scrub her rosy complexion clean. From her months spent in the convent, eating modestly, praying often, and sleeping many hours each night, she looked quite young and innocent.

On seeing her, three of the judges whispered and leaned in to confer. But the vice-chancellor, plump and puffy Cardinal Ascanio Sforza, now waved his hand to silence them. When he asked Lucrezia to speak, her speech, written by her brother Cesare, delivered in Latin, haltingly and with extreme modesty, was so effective that each of the cardinals found himself enchanted by the sweet young daughter of the Pope.

Still seated before them, as they conferred with each other, Lucrezia raised her linen handkerchief to her eyes and began to shed brokenhearted tears. "You will pardon me, Your Excellencies, if I may beg one more indulgence of you." She lowered her head, and when she raised it again, to look at the cardinals, her eyes were still shiny with tears. "Please consider what my life will be, without babies to hold and care for. And will you sentence me to live without knowing the passion of a husband's lovemaking? Would you impose upon me a curse that is not my own? I beg of you, in all your goodness and mercy, please spare my life by annulling this unfortunate marriage—that by its very nature must remain loveless."

Not one objection was raised when Ascanio, turning to

Lucrezia, pronounced her, loudly and firmly, *"Femina in-tacta!"* A virgin. By that evening, she was on her way back to the convent to await the birth of her baby.

When Perotto arrived at San Sisto to bring Lucrezia the news that her divorce was final, and that the negotiations for her marriage to Alfonso, duke of Bisceglie, had been concluded, she felt tears well up in her eyes.

"After the birth, my baby will be taken from me," Lucrezia told Perotto sadly as they sat in the convent garden. "And I will not be permitted to see you again, for in a very short time I will again be married. So this is both a happy day and a sad day for me. On the one hand I am no longer married to a man I dislike, but on the other I will lose both my child and my dearest friend."

Perotto put his arm around her to comfort and reassure her. "Until the day I reach the heavens, I will hold you in my heart."

"And you in mine, my good friend," she said.

As Cesare prepared to leave for Naples, he and Alexander met in the Pope's quarters to discuss the situation of Lucrezia and her baby.

Cesare spoke first. "I believe, Father, I have solved the problem. Immediately after the birth, the infant can be brought to live in my apartments, since yours or Lucrezia's are out of the question. I will issue a statement that the child is mine, and that the mother is a married courtesan whom I prefer not to name. They'll believe that, for it suits the rumors of my character."

Alexander looked at his son with admiration and smiled broadly.

Cesare asked, "Why are you smiling, Father? Is that so funny not to be believable?"

The Pope's eyes shone with amusement. "It is quite

funny," he said, "*and* believable. I am smiling because I, too, have a reputation that fits the situation. And today I signed a bull—not yet made public—referring to the child as the "*Infans Romanus*" and declaring that *I* am the father. Also by an unnamed woman."

Alexander and Cesare embraced, both still laughing.

And Alexander agreed that to declare Cesare the father of the child was a better solution. He then promised that on the day of the baby's birth, he would issue another bull, declaring Cesare the father of "*Infans Romanus.*" And the original bull declaring Alexander as the father would be hidden away in a Vatican drawer.

On the very day that Lucrezia gave birth to her baby, a healthy baby boy, Alexander had the infant taken immediately from San Sisto to Cesare's home while Lucrezia was left at the convent to recover. It was agreed that later Lucrezia would claim him as her nephew, and raise him as her own. But there remained a dangerous loose end for Alexander—one more detail that required careful handling.

Though he felt some regret, he knew what he must do. He sent for Don Michelotto. An hour before midnight, the short, powerfully built man with a chest like a barrel stood at the door of his study.

The Pope embraced Michelotto as a brother and told him of the crisis that had befallen them.

"It is the young man who states he is the father of this child," the Pope said. "A fine young Spaniard, a noble young man . . . and yet . . ."

Don Michelotto looked at Alexander and placed his fingers to his own lips. "Not another word need be spoken," he said. "I am at the service of the Holy Father. And if this good soul is as fine as he appears, then there is no question that the Heavenly Father will greet him with great joy."

"I have considered exiling him," Alexander said. "For he has been a loyal servant. But there is no way to know what temptation in life will force his tongue loose, and cause the fall of our family."

Don Michelotto's expression was one of sympathy. "It is your duty to keep him from temptation, and it is mine to help in any way I am able."

"Thank you, my friend," Alexander said. And then, hesitating, he added, "Be as kind as possible, for he truly is a good lad, and to have been seduced by the wiles of a woman is understandable."

Don Michelotto bowed to kiss the ring of the Pope and then took his leave, assuring him that the task was as good as done.

Michelotto slipped into the night and rode with haste across the fields and out into the countryside, over rough paths and hills, until he reached the dunes at Ostia. From there he could see the small farm, with its tiny patches of odd vegetation, its rows and rows of rootlike vegetables, and a number of beds filled with strange herbs and tall bushes laden with purple and black berries and exotic-looking flowers.

Michelotto rode around to the back behind the small cottage. There he found the old woman doubled over, resting heavily on a hawthorn stick. Seeing Michelotto, she raised it, and squinted her eyes. "Noni," he called, soothingly, "I've come for some medicine."

"Go away," the old woman said. "I don't know you."

"Noni," he said, coming closer. "The clouds are thick, tonight. I am sent by the Holy Father . . ."

She smiled then, a wrinkled mask. "Ah, so it is you, Miguel. You've grown older . . ."

"It's true, Noni," he said, chuckling. "It's true. And I've come to ask for your help to save another soul."

Standing next to her now, towering over her, he reached for her wicker basket to carry it, but she pulled it back. "Is this an evil man you wish to send to hell, or a good man who stands in the way of the church?"

Don Michelotto's eyes were soft when he said, "He is a man who in any case will see the face of God."

The old woman nodded, and beckoned to him to follow her into the cottage. There she studied several of the herbs hanging on her wall, and finally carefully chose one wrapped with the sheerest silk. "This will place him in a gentle dreamless sleep," she said. "He will not struggle." Before she handed it to Michelotto, she sprinkled it with holy water. "It is a blessing," she said.

As the old woman watched him ride away, she bowed her head and made the sign of the cross upon her chest.

In the ghetto of Trastevere, the owner of a dingy tavern had difficulty waking a drunken patron at closing time. The young man's blond head was resting facedown on his arms and he had been in that position since his companion left an hour before. The proprietor tried to shake the man awake, more vigorously this time, and his head fell from his arms. The tavern owner, seeing this, pulled back in horror. The young man's face was bloated and blue, with purple lips and bulging eyes, blood red, but most shocking was his tongue, so swollen it protruded from his mouth, making his handsome face that of a gargoyle.

Within minutes the police arrived. The tavern owner remembered little of the young man's companion, just that he was short and barrel-chested. He could be any of a thousand Roman citizens.

But not the young man. Several citizens of the city identified him. His name was Pedro Calderon, and he was called "Perotto."

14

On the day Cesare Borgia crowned the king of Naples, he received an urgent message from his sister. It was brought by her secret messenger and handed to him when he was walking alone on the castle grounds. He was to meet her at Silverlake within a few days, it said, for she must speak to him before either of them could return to Rome.

Cesare spent that evening at the lavish coronation celebration. All the aristocracy of Naples was there to meet him, including many beautiful women, fascinated by his good looks and easy charm, who surrounded him in spite of his cardinal's robes.

He visited with his brother Jofre and sister-in-law Sancia, and noticed that Jofre seemed to be walking with a different, surer step since Juan's death. He wondered if anyone else noticed. Sancia, too, had changed. She was still flirtatious, but seemed more willing to please, a little less spirited than she was before.

It was Jofre who, during the evening, introduced him to a tall, handsome young man who would impress Cesare with his intelligence and courtliness. "My brother, Cardinal Borgia, this is the duke of Bisceglie, Alfonso of Aragon. Have you met?"

When Alfonso reached for Cesare's hand, Cesare found himself intrigued by the look of the young man. He had an athletic build, but his features were so fine and his smile so radiant that one could no more keep from staring at him than from studying a beautiful painting.

"It is my honor to meet you," Alfonso said, bowing, and his voice was as pleasing as his appearance.

Cesare nodded his head in acknowledgment. And for the next several hours the two men excused themselves from the crowd to walk through the gardens and become familiar with each other. Alfonso's intelligence matched Cesare's own, and his sense of humor was refreshing. They discussed theology, philosophy, and of course, politics. By the time Cesare said his farewell he felt a certain fondness for the young man, and so as they parted, he said, "I've no doubt you are worthy of my sister. And I am certain she will be happy with you."

Alfonso's blue eyes glittered. "I will do all in my power to see that it is so."

Cesare found himself looking forward to meeting his sister at Silverlake. It had been months since he and Lucrezia were alone together, and now that she had recovered from childbirth he found himself thinking about making love to her again. He wondered, as he rode as quickly as he could, what it was she had to tell him. He had not heard a word from his father or Duarte in recent weeks, and so he suspected it was something more personal than political.

Arriving at the lake before she did, he took a moment to stand back and gaze upon the clear blue of the sky, enjoying the peace of the countryside before going inside the cottage. There, after bathing and changing his clothes, he sat, sipping a goblet of wine, and reflecting on his life.

So much had happened of late, and yet he knew even more was meant to happen in the near future. He was determined, once he had returned to Rome from Florence, to ask the Holy Father to relieve him of his duties as cardinal. He could no longer bear the hypocrisy that the cardinal's hat imposed on him. He knew that convincing the Holy Father would be a formidable task, that it would add tension to their already strained relationship. Since Juan's death, instead of growing closer, his father had seemed to be drifting away from Cesare.

Cesare was filled with ambition and passion; he wanted to live his life to the fullest. And yet he felt thwarted. Now that his sister was to be married again, he found himself struggling. Alfonso was an honorable man, one he liked, and though he wanted the best for Lucrezia, he found himself feeling jealous. Now his sister would have children she could love and claim as her own. As a cardinal, his children would be denied—or worse yet be bastards, as he was. He tried to calm down, to talk himself out of his feelings, chastising himself for his shortsightedness. Cesare reminded himself that Lucrezia's betrothal to the son of the king of Naples was a great alliance for the church and Rome. Yet he grew impatient, full of frustration that the course of his life had been decided by mere accident of birth.

The Pope, too, had always enjoyed his life; he felt genuinely fulfilled by his mission in the church, and the saving of the souls of humanity. But Cesare struggled with believing, and felt no such passion. Spending his nights with courtesans rarely brought him pleasure; all at once he found he wanted more. Jofre and Sancia seemed happy, with their material luxury and commitments to court life. And even his brother Juan had certainly had a good life—one of freedom, riches, and distinction—until at last he was defeated by the death he deserved.

By the time Lucrezia arrived, Cesare was sullen. But once she rushed into his arms and he smelled her hair again and felt her warm body against his, all his discontent began to disappear. It was only when he pushed her back to look at her, to see her face, that he noticed she'd been crying.

"What is it?" he asked her. "What is it, my love?"

"Papa killed Perotto," she said. She hadn't called him Papa for years, since she'd been a child.

"Perotto is dead?" Cesare said, stunned by the news. "I instructed him to hide until I returned." He took a deep breath, and asked softly, "Where was he found?"

Lucrezia held tight to her brother. "In the ghetto. In a tavern in the ghetto. A place where he would never go."

And Cesare realized that even as he tried to help Perotto, he was already too late. They talked together then about the sweetness of the man, his willingness to sacrifice himself for love. "He truly was a poet," Lucrezia said.

"His goodness makes me feel ashamed," Cesare said. "For were it different, I could not count upon myself to make the choice he did, though I do love you."

Lucrezia spoke with clear-eyed certainty. "There is justice in the heavens, I've no doubt. And his courage will be honored."

Hours passed as they walked by the lake, and more hours as they talked by the roaring fire in the cottage.

Later they made love. And it was better than ever before. They lay together for a very long time, before either of them was willing to break the bond of silence, and then it was Lucrezia who spoke first. "Our baby is the most beautiful cherub I have ever seen," she said, smiling. "And he looks just like . . ."

Cesare leaned on his arm and looked into his sister's clear blue eyes. "Just like who?" he asked.

Lucrezia laughed. "Just like . . . us!" she said, and laughed again. "I think we will be happy together, even if he is your son, and can never be mine."

"But we are most important," Cesare reassured her. "And we know the truth."

Lucrezia sat up then, wrapping a silk robe around herself, and slid out of bed. In a voice both hard and cold, she asked, "Cesare, do you think the Holy Father evil?"

Cesare felt a shiver run throughout his body. "There are times I'm not sure I know what evil is," he said. "Are you always certain?"

Lucrezia turned and looked at him. "Yes, I am certain, my brother. I know evil. It can't disguise itself from me . . ."

The following morning Lucrezia left to return to Rome, but Cesare could not. It was too soon for him to face his father, for he was filled with both anger and guilt. And now that young Perotto was dead, there was no reason to hurry.

Disguised in the plain clothes of a peasant, Cesare rode up to the gates of Florence. It had been so long, it seemed, since he'd been to this city. As he rode alone, his entourage left outside the gates, he remembered his first visit to Florence. He had gone there from school, when he was just a boy, with Gio Medici. And then it was so different . . .

There was a time when Florence had been a proud republic, so proud that it had forbidden anyone of noble blood to take part in the government. But the Medici family, with its great banking house and its monies, actually ruled Florence through its influence with the elected officials. It did so by making rich those who formed the ruling committees elected by its citizens. And so Gio's father, Lorenzo the Magnificent, had cemented the Medici family power.

For young Cesare Borgia, it was a new experience to live in a great city where its ruler was almost universally beloved. Lorenzo was one of the richest men in the world, and one of the most generous. He gave poor girls dowries so they could be wed. He gave painters and sculptors money and facilities in which to work. There the great Michelangelo lived in the Medici palace in his youth, and was treated as a son.

Lorenzo Medici bought books from all over the world, and had them translated and copied at great cost so that they could be made available to scholars in Italy. He endowed chairs of philosophy and Greek at Italian universities. He wrote poetry that was acclaimed by the severest critics, and compositions for music to be played at the great carnivals. The finest scholars and poets, artists, and musicians were often guests at the Medici table in the palace.

When Cesare was a guest there, though he was only a boy of fifteen, he was treated with exquisite courtesy by Lorenzo and the other men in his company. But Cesare's fondest memories of Florence were the tales he was told of the Medici family's rise to power—especially the story Gio told him of his father Lorenzo's narrow escape from the coils of a great conspiracy when he was a young man.

At the age of twenty, on the death of his own father, Lorenzo had become head of the Medici family. By this time the Medici family was banker to the Pope and various kings, the most powerful financial institution in the world. But Lorenzo saw that unless he wanted to jeopardize that position he would have to consolidate his own personal power.

He did so by financing great festivities as entertainment for the people. He staged mock sea battles on the river Arno, and financed musical dramas in the great Piazza of Santa Croce; he sponsored parades of the cathedral's holy relics, with a thorn of the crown Jesus had worn, a nail from his cross, and a fragment of the spear that had been thrust into his side by a Roman soldier. All the shops in Florence were decorated with the Medici banner, its three red balls recognizable throughout the city.

Lorenzo was both bawdy and religious. On carnival days, gaily decorated floats carried the prettiest prostitutes of the city through the streets; on Good Friday the Stations of the Cross—portraying the life and death of Christ—were reenacted. Life-size figures of Christ, the Virgin Mary, and various saints were carried to the cathedral, and captive white doves were released and floated through the air like angels. There were beauty pageants for young women of respectable families, and processions of monks to warn people of hell.

Lorenzo was perhaps the ugliest man in Florence, but because of his wit and charm had many love affairs. His younger brother and best companion, Giuliano, on the other hand, was acclaimed the city's most handsome man in a festival held in his honor, on his twenty-second birthday in 1475. Little surprise that he won: his costume for the event was designed by Botticelli and his helmet by Verrocio, at the cost of twenty thousand florins. It delighted the people of Florence to see the ugly but generous Lorenzo embrace his brother without a trace of envy.

But at the height of Lorenzo's power in Florence, at the height of his happiness, the Medici family became the target of a powerful conspiracy.

The trouble began when Lorenzo refused to grant a huge loan demanded by a previous Pope, the monies to be used to purchase the strategic town of Imola in the Romagna. Pope Sixtus was enraged by this refusal. This Pope, too, was devoted to his family; he had already given seven of his nephews each a cardinal's hat, and he had wanted the town of Imola for his natural son, Girolamo. When Lorenzo refused the loan, the Pope in retaliation turned instead to the Pazzi family, the great rivals of the Medici.

The Pazzi family and its bank gave the fifty thousand ducats to the Pope with utmost speed, and then applied for other accounts with the papacy, especially the account of the alum mines of Silverlake just outside of Rome. But this the Pope was not willing to do, perhaps because Lorenzo had sent him rich gifts to placate him. And yet the friction between Lorenzo and the Pope still festered.

When the Pope nominated Francisco Salviata as archbishop of Pisa, a Florentine possession—violating an agreement that all such posts would be subject to approval by officials of Florence—Lorenzo barred the archbishop from taking up his post.

The Pazzi family had much older roots in Florence, a longer lineage of fame, than the Medici. And its leader, Jacopo, a much older and more sober man, hated the young Lorenzo.

The Archbishop Salviata and Francisco Pazzi also burned with ambition and hatred. These two men engineered a meeting with Pope Sixtus and convinced him they could overthrow the Medici. He gave his approval. This convinced the old man, Jacopo Pazzi, a ruthless and mean-spirited man, to join the conspiracy.

The plan was to kill Lorenzo and his brother, Giuliano, as they attended Sunday Mass; then, Pazzi supporters and troops hidden outside the wall would swarm in and take over the city.

To get everyone into the church at the same time, it was arranged that the unsuspecting Cardinal Raphael Riario, the seventeen-year-old grandnephew of the Pope, would pay a visit to Lorenzo. As expected, Lorenzo planned a great banquet in the cardinal's honor, and accompanied him to Mass in the morning. Behind them were two priests named Maffei and Stefano, who under their vestments had each concealed daggers.

Upon hearing the sound of the sacristy bell ringing for the elevation of the Host—when all the faithful in the church would lower their eyes—the priests were to pull their daggers and commence their unholy act. But Lorenzo's brother, Giuliano, was not there, and the conspirators had been instructed to kill both. Francisco Pazzi rushed to Giuliano's home to hurry him to church; on the return trip he poked at Giuliano's torso as if in fun, in order to confirm that he wore no armor beneath his clothing.

In the church, Lorenzo stood at the far side of the altar. He saw his brother Giuliano enter the church with Francisco Pazzi behind him, and then he heard the sacristy bell ring. To his horror he saw Francisco draw a dagger and plunge it into Giuliano's body. At that very moment, he felt a hand grab his shoulder. He recoiled as he felt cold steel touch his throat, drawing blood. But instinctively his body flinched away, and now he threw off his cloak and used it to repel the thrust of the other priest's dagger.

Lorenzo drew his own sword then and fought both of them off, jumping over the altar rail and running to the side door. Three of his friends had gathered around him. He led them into the sacristy and pulled the heavy doors closed behind them. For that moment, he was safe.

Meanwhile, outside, the Archbishop Salviata and the assassin, Francisco Pazzi, ran out of the cathedral to shout that the Medici were dead and Florence was free. But the populace of the city ran to take up arms. The archbishop's troops in the square were overwhelmed and slaughtered.

Lorenzo emerged from the sacristy to the cheers of his friends and supporters. He first made sure that no harm had come to the young Cardinal Riario, but he did nothing to stop the execution of the archbishop and Francisco, who were hanged from the windows of the cathedral.

The two priests, Maffei and Stefano, were castrated and beheaded. Jacopo Pazzi was hunted down, stripped naked, and hanged beside the archbishop. The Pazzi family palace was looted, and all members of the Pazzi clan were banished from Florence forever.

Now, as Cesare returned to the city so many years later, in place of that city of justice and luxury he found a completely different Florence.

The streets themselves were in complete disorder, with filth and sewage flowing freely. Dead and rotting animals lay in the alleys; the smell itself was worse than Rome's. It was true that the plague had been found in Florence—but only a few cases; still, the very spirit of the people seemed to have been overcome by disease. As Cesare rode the streets, he heard fierce arguments and watched vicious stick fights while angry shouts rather than church bells filled his ears.

When he stopped at the most respectable inn to find a room in which to rest until nightfall, he was reassured that the innkeeper didn't recognize him—even tried to turn him away, until Cesare forced a gold ducat into his grasping hand.

Once he had done so, the innkeeper was polite and indulgent. He led Cesare to a room where, though the furniture was sparse, it was clean and of good quality. From the window Cesare could see the square in front of the Church of San Marcos, and the monastery of the prophet Savonarola. He determined to wait until evening before he walked out into the streets to see what he could discover.

Moments later, the innkeeper returned with a large carafe of wine and a huge platter of fresh fruit and cheese. And so Cesare rested on the bed, and dreamed . . .

It was a disturbing dream, a nightmare in which crosses and chalices, holy vestments and religious objects swirled around him, just outside his reach. A thunderous voice overhead instructed him to take hold of a golden chalice, but when he grasped for it he found a pistol in his hand. Though he tried to control it, it seemed to fire on its own. Then, as in all dreams, the scenery changed, and he was at a celebration, seated across from his father, his sister, and her newly betrothed, Prince Alfonso. The smile on his face turned to a grimace, and the golden pistol went off and shattered the face of either his sister or Alfonso—he could no longer see well enough to tell.

Cesare awoke, drenched in sweat, to hear the voices and shouts of the citizens in the square beneath his window. He got out of bed, still shaken, and looked outside. There, on a makeshift wooden pulpit, stood the preacher, Savonarola. He began with a fervent prayer to the Lord, his voice trembling with passion, and followed with a hymn of holy praise. In the square, the voices of the citizens were raised in adoration. But within a short time, the preacher began his fiery invective against Rome.

"Pope Alexander is a false Pope," the friar shouted, and his voice was rich and filled with passion. "The minds of the humanists can twist the truth and make sense out of nonsense. But as there is black and white, there is good and evil, and it stands to reason: that which is not good is evil!"

Cesare studied the man. Thin, ascetic, and clothed in the brown hooded robes of the Dominican Order; his features coarse, yet not unpleasant. His tonsured head moved with conviction, and his hands spoke parables as he waved them to punctuate his words. "This Pope has courtesans," he shouted. "He kills and poisons. The clergy in Rome keeps boys, and steals from the poor to feather the beds of the rich. They eat from golden plates, and ride on the backs of those who live in poverty."

The citizens continued to gather, and Cesare found himself strangely fascinated by this man, entranced, as though he didn't know the people the friar was railing about.

As a large crowd began to form, there were angry shouts, but the moment the friar began to speak again there was such silence that a star could be heard as it fell from the sky. "The God of heaven will cast your souls to hell for eternity, and those who follow these pagan priests will be damned. Give up your worldly goods and follow the path of Saint Dominic."

Someone shouted from the crowd. "But in the monastery you have food donated by the wealthy! Your plates are not of wood, and your chairs have plush cushions. You dance to the tune of the fiddler who pays!"

Savonarola shuddered, and made a vow. "All money from the rich will be refused from this day forward. The friars in San Marco will only eat what the good citizens of Florence provide. One meal a day is enough. Any more shall be given to the poor who gather in the square each evening. No one will go hungry. But that will care only for your body! To preserve your souls you must renounce the Pope in Rome. He is a fornicator; his daughter is a prostitute who sleeps with both her father and brother—and poets as well."

Cesare had witnessed enough. Once the Pope heard of this, he would not only excommunicate Savonarola—he would accuse him of heresy.

Cesare found his own reaction to the man confounding. He believed the man had vision, but also that he was crazy. For who would martyr himself in this way, knowing the outcome? Still, he allowed, who can know what images and icons spill within the brains of others? Despite all his logic, he knew the man was dangerous, and something must be done about him. For the new Signoria in Florence could be influenced, and if they forbade Florence from joining the Holy League, his father's plans to unite the Romagna would be thwarted.

This could not be allowed.

Cesare dressed quickly. Outside, as he was moving among the crowd in the street toward the square, a thin, pale young man in a black cape, a head shorter than he was, came up beside him. "Cardinal?" the young man whispered.

Cesare turned, his hand already poised on the sword hidden beneath his robe.

But the young man bowed his head in acknowledgment. "My name is Niccolò Machiavelli. And we should speak. There is danger in the streets of Florence for you at this time. Come with me?" Cesare's eyes softened, and so Machiavelli took him by the arm, and led him to his apartment away from the square.

Inside, the well-furnished rooms were cluttered with books; the desks overflowed, and papers were scattered on the chairs and floor. There was a small fire burning in the stone fireplace.

Machiavelli cleared off one of the chairs and offered it to Cesare. When Cesare looked around the room, he found himself strangely comfortable. Machiavelli poured a glass of wine for each of them, and took a chair opposite Cesare.

"You are in danger, Cardinal," Machiavelli warned. "For Savonarola believes he is entrusted with a mission, a holy one. In order to fulfill his part in it the Borgia Pope must be dethroned, the Borgia family destroyed."

"I am aware of his religious objections to our pagan ways," Cesare said, sardonically.

"Savonarola has visions," Machiavelli warned. "First there was a sun falling from the sky, and Lorenzo the Magnificent was dead. Then there was the swift sword of the Lord, from the north, striking the tyrant, and the French invasion followed. He holds power over our citizens; they fear for themselves and their families, and believe this prophet has the gift of sight. He tells that the only mercy will come with angels in white robes, after the destruction of the wicked iniquities, when the souls of the good hold to the rule of God and repent."

Cesare recognized in Savonarola this spark of truth. But

no man could endure the visions this friar claimed and still
live in the world. Once he chose to speak, if he had vision,
he must be able to predict his fate. To Cesare these visions
could never be his truth, for they would deny free will. If
destiny always held the winning hand, then what part did
man play? It was a fixed game, one in which he would take
no part.

Cesare turned his attention back to Machiavelli. "The
Pope has already excommunicated the friar. If he continues
to inflame the populace he will be put to death, for there will
be nothing else the Holy Father can do to silence him."

Late that night, back in his room at the inn, Cesare could
still hear the voice of Savonarola sounding through his window. The friar's voice remained strong. "Alexander Borgia
is a pagan Pope who looks to the pagan gods of Egypt for
inspiration! He fills himself with pagan pleasures, while we
of true faith bear the suffering. Each year, to enrich their
own chest of riches, the cardinals in Rome impose heavier
burdens on our citizens. We are not asses, to be used as
beasts of burden!"

As Cesare began to drift into sleep, he heard the friar's
passionate voice, and its words of doom: "In the early
church the chalices were made of wood, but the virtue of the
clergy was of gold. At this dark time, with the Pope and the
cardinals in Rome, the chalices are of gold, and virtue of our
clergy is of wood!"

15

The moment Alexander entered the comfortable country home of Vanozza Cattanei, he was reminded of all the years they'd spent together, all the times they'd shared. The many evenings they'd spent supping in the candlelit dining room, the warm summer nights he had spent with her in the luxurious bedroom upstairs, his senses alive with the scent of jasmine wafting through the open window filling the darkened room. The sense of peace and love he felt, the comfort and warmth of her flesh against his own. It was on those nights of complete ecstasy, he reflected, that his belief in God was at its height, and that he had made his greatest and most sincere vows of service to the Holy Mother Church.

Vanozza greeted him with her usual warmth. And the Pope, smiling, remembering, stepped back to look at her with fondness and admiration. "You are one of God's miracles," he said. "You become more and more beautiful each year."

Vanozza embraced him and laughed. "Not quite young enough for you, Rodrigo, eh?"

Alexander's voice was soft and reassuring. "I am Pope now, Vee. It is different from when we were younger."

"And is it 'different' with La Bella?" she teased. Alexander's face reddened, but Vanozza gave him a broad smile. "Don't be so serious, Rigo, I'm joking. You know I have no resentment toward Julia, or any of the others. We were good together as lovers, yet we are even better as friends, for true friends are rarer than lovers any time."

Vanozza led him into the library and poured them each a goblet of wine.

It was Alexander who spoke first. "So Vee, why is it that you sent for me? Are the vineyards or the inns not doing well?"

Vanozza sat across from the Pope, and spoke pleasantly. "On the contrary, both are doing extremely well. And both are making money. There is hardly a day that passes when I don't feel grateful for your generosity. Still, I would have loved you had you bought me nothing. And would have showered you with gifts had I been able to."

Alexander said with affection, "I know that, Vee. But if it is not that, then what concerns you and how can I help?"

Vanozza's eyes were dark and serious now. "It's our son, Rigo. It's Cesare. You must see him for who he is."

Alexander frowned as he explained. "I see him quite clearly. He is the most intelligent of all our children. And one day he will be Pope. At my death he'll be elected— for if he isn't, his life, and perhaps even yours, will be in danger."

Vanozza listened as Alexander spoke, but once he had finished, she insisted, "Cesare doesn't want to be Pope, Rigo. He doesn't even want to be a cardinal. You must know that. He is a soldier, a lover, a man who wishes a full life. All the wealth and mistresses you give him don't fill his heart; all the benefices and properties still leave him empty. He wants to *fight* bulls, Rigo, not issue them."

Alexander was silent, thoughtful. Then he said, "He told you this?"

Vanozza smiled and moved to sit closer to him. "I am his mother," she said. "He doesn't have to say it to me. I know it, as you should."

Suddenly Alexander's expression hardened. "If I were as much his father as you are his mother, it is possible it would be as clear to me . . ."

Vanozza Cattanei lowered her head for a moment, as though in prayer. When she lifted it again, her eyes were clear and her voice strong. "Rigo, I will say this only once, for I feel no need to defend myself. Yet, I feel you have a right to know. Yes, it is true that Giuliano della Rovere and I were lovers before you and I met. In fact, until my heart jumped at the first sight of you. And I will not patronize you by pretending I was a virgin then, for you know this not to be true. But, on my honor, and under the clear gaze of the Madonna, I swear to you that Cesare is your son, and no other man's."

Alexander shook his head, and his eyes softened. "I could never before be sure, Vee—you knew that. I could never feel certain. And so I could not trust what I felt for the boy, or what he felt for me."

Vanozza reached for Alexander's hand. "We could never speak of this before. For in order to protect both you and our son, I had to allow Giuliano to believe that Cesare was his son. But I swear to the Christ that was a lie. I did it to keep Giuliano at bay, for his heart is neither as good nor as forgiving as your own. The only protection from his treachery was for him to believe that your son was his."

Alexander struggled with himself for a moment. "And how can either of us believe what is true? How can either of us know for certain?"

Vanozza took the Pope's hand in her own and held it up before his eyes. She turned it slowly before him. "I want you to study this hand, Rigo. I want you to examine it carefully, in its every angle and form. And then I want you to study the hand of your son. For from the moment he was born, I lived with the fear that someone else would see what was so apparent to me, and then all would be lost."

Suddenly Alexander understood Giuliano della Rovere's hostility toward him, understood his jealousy and hatred. For he had everything that della Rovere had believed was his—the papacy, the lover, the son.

It was no secret among the cardinals that della Rovere had only loved once, that Vanozza was the great love of his life. He felt considerable humiliation when she left him for Rodrigo Borgia. Until then he'd had a spark of joy in his eyes, and a ready laugh. It was only after Vanozza was gone that he became so bitter, angry, and zealous a man. It did not help that he had never had a son; all his children were daughters. How God had tested him.

Alexander felt a wave of relief wash over him, for he understood so much more now that he admitted to himself what he had always suspected—that he had never been certain about Cesare. Had he not loved Vanozza with such passion, and admired her as well, he might have asked the question earlier and spared himself and Cesare great suffering. But to live without her, to risk losing her, was too great a cost, and so he never had.

"I'll consider what you have suggested about our son," Alexander told Vanozza. "And I will speak to Cesare about his choice of vocation. If he will ever speak to me."

Vanozza's voice was filled with compassion. "Our son Juan is dead, Rigo. Without him life will never be the same. But our Cesare is alive, and you need him to lead your armies. If not him, who will? Jofre? No, Rigo. It must be Cesare, for he is a warrior. But in order to claim his life you must use your love to free him. Let someone else be Pope. We have had happy lives."

As Alexander stood and bent to kiss Vanozza's cheek, he caught the scent of her perfume. And when he turned to leave, it was not without regret.

Vanozza stood at the doorway, and smiled as she waved. "Look at his hands, Rigo. Be at peace."

On the day Cesare returned to Rome from Florence, he immediately came to confer with his father and Duarte Brandao. They retired to an inner chamber hung with tapestries and decorated with the intricately carved chests that held the raiments of his office. There were no formalities here. Alexander embraced his son, but there was a warmth in that embrace which made Cesare wary.

Duarte spoke first. "Have you found the prophet as dangerous to us as has been rumored?" he asked.

Cesare sat on a cushioned chair opposite Duarte and his father. "He is an impassioned speaker, and the citizens gather in great crowds, as though at a carnival, to hear him preach."

Alexander looked interested. "And he speaks about?"

"Reform," Cesare said. "And the indulgences of the Borgia family. He accuses us of all manner of evil deeds, and frightens the people into believing that to follow the Holy Church in Rome and to honor the papacy will doom them to eternal damnation."

Alexander stood and began to pace. "It is unfortunate that a mind so bright as his has been invaded by such demons. I've often enjoyed his writings. And I've heard it said he admires the world of nature—that often on clear nights he will awaken everyone in the monastery to call them into the courtyard to gaze at the stars."

Cesare interrupted Alexander. "Father, he is a danger to us now. He insists on stringent reform. He is aligned with the French. And he insists that the papacy be returned to someone of true virtue. No doubt that someone would be Giuliano della Rovere."

Alexander bristled. He turned to Duarte and said, "I hesitate to force a man to confess to his sins when he has served the church well, but I fear this must be done. Duarte, see if there is a way to solve this quickly, for it is necessary that some order be brought to Florence before more damage is done."

Duarte bowed and took his leave.

Alexander finally reclined on a divan and motioned Cesare to an upholstered velvet stool. His face was impassive, but his eyes had that look of shrewdness which he never showed in public. He said, almost formally, "Now is the time when you must tell me what is in your heart. Do you love the Holy Church as I do? Will you continue to devote your life to it as I have?"

This was going in the direction that Cesare had hoped. He had shown clearly and deliberately to his father that he was a soldier, not a priest. He considered his answer carefully. The Pope must trust him absolutely. Cesare knew that his father did not love him as much as he had loved Juan, but he was certain of his father's love in some measure. He knew also that he must be wary of his father's cunning, a weapon used on even the most loved or worshipped. And so Cesare felt compelled to guard his most terrible secrets.

"Father," he said finally, "I must confess that I have too many unholy appetites to serve the church as you wish. And I do not wish to damn my soul to hell."

Alexander raised himself up on the divan so that he could look directly into Cesare's eyes. "I was much like you when I was young," he said. "Nobody dreamed I would become a Pope. But I labored for forty years and I became a better man, and a better priest. The same could happen to you."

"I do not desire it," Cesare said quietly.

"Why not?" Alexander asked. "You love power; you love money. In this world, men must work to survive. And with your gifts you can raise the church to its proper eminence." He paused for a moment. "Is there some great crime on your conscience that makes you believe that you cannot serve the church?"

In that moment, Cesare divined everything. His father wanted him to confess to the truth about his carnal relationship with Lucrezia. But if he confessed, he knew his father would never forgive him. Though he found it difficult to conceal the truth, Cesare realized that his father wanted to be lied to, but in a convincing fashion.

"Yes," Cesare said. "There is a great crime. But if I confess it you will condemn me in your heart."

Alexander leaned forward. His eyes were hard, piercing, with nothing in them of forgiveness. At that moment, though Cesare was sure his father guessed that he had remained Lucrezia's lover for all these years, he could not help but feel a surge of triumph at outwitting him.

"There is nothing that God will not forgive,"Alexander said.

Cesare spoke softly, for he knew the impact his words would have. "I do not believe in a God. I do not believe in Christ, the Virgin Mary, or any of the saints."

Alexander seemed amazed for a moment, then recovered. "Many sinners say that because they fear punishment after death," he said. "So they try to renounce truth. Is there anything else?"

Cesare couldn't restrain his smile. "Yes. Fornication. Love of power. Murder, but only of dangerous enemies. Telling lies. But you already know them all. There is nothing else for me to confess."

Alexander took Cesare's hands in his. And studied them carefully. "Listen, my son," he said. "Men lose their faith; when the cruelties of this world become too much for them, they question an everlasting and loving God. They question his infinite mercy. They question the Holy Church. But faith must be revived with action. Even the saints themselves were persons of action. I think nothing of those holy men who scourge themselves and ponder the mysterious ways of mankind for scores of years while they live in their monasteries. They do nothing for the living church; they will not help it to endure in this temporal world. It is men like you, and myself, who must do our own particular duty. Even though," and here Alexander raised a commanding papal finger, "our souls may rest for a time in purgatory. Think how many souls of Christians yet unborn we will save in the next hundreds of years. Those who will find salvation in a strong Holy Catholic Church. When I say my prayers, when I confess my sins, that is my consolation for some of the things I have done. It does not matter that our humanists— those believers in the Greek philosophers—believe that mankind is all that exists. There is an Almighty God, and he is merciful and he is understanding. That is our faith. And you must believe. Live with your sins, confess them or not, but never lose faith—for there is nothing else."

This speech moved Cesare not at all. Faith would not solve his problems. He had to wrest power on this earth, or his head would decorate the walls of Rome. He wanted a wife and children, so it followed that he must live a life of power and richness and not become one of the powerless herd. And to do that, he must commit acts for which his father's God would make him suffer. Why should he believe in such a God? And he was so alive himself, a man of twenty-three: the taste of wine, food, and women so strongly in his blood that he could not believe in the possibility of his own death, though it had been proven over and over in the death of others.

But Cesare bowed his head. "I believe in Rome, Father," he said. "I will give my life for it, if you give me the means to fight for it."

Alexander sighed again. Finally he could fight against this son no longer, for he recognized that Cesare could be his most powerful instrument.

"Then we must make our plans," he said. "I will appoint you captain general of the papal army, and you will regain the Papal States and become the duke of Romagna. Someday we will unite all the great cities of Italy, impossible as it may seem: Venice, its people living in the water like serpents; those sly sodomites of Florence; haughty Bologna so ungrateful to Mother Church. But we must begin at the beginning. You must be master of the Romagna, and for that you must first marry. We will meet with the consistory of cardinals in a few days, and you will give them back the red hat. Then I will make you captain general. What you lose in your churchly benefices, you will make up for in war."

Cesare bowed his head. In thanks he attempted to kiss the foot of the Pope, his father, but slowly enough that Alexander moved his body impatiently and said, "Love the church more, Cesare, and your father less. Show your obedience to me with deeds, and not these formal gestures. You are my son and I forgive you all your sins—as any natural father would."

For the first time in longer than he could remember, Cesare was filled with certainty that he was master of his own fate.

On the night the final contract for the marriage of the Pope's daughter and Prince Alfonso was signed, Alexander spoke with Duarte. "I wish to hear Lucrezia laugh again," he said. "She has been solemn for far too long."

It had not escaped his notice how difficult this past year had been for his daughter, and he hoped to make amends in order to secure her continued loyalty. Knowing it was claimed that Alfonso of Aragon was the "handsomest man in the Imperial City," the Pope wished to surprise his daughter, and so he insisted Alfonso's arrival in Rome must remain secret.

Young Alfonso entered the city of Rome early one morning, accompanied by just seven of his envoy. The rest of the fifty who had traveled with him from Naples had been left outside the gates in Marino. He was met by the emissaries of the Pope, who immediately brought him to the Vatican, and once Alexander was reassured by his good looks and forthright manner he was then led on horseback to the Palace of Santa Maria in Portico.

Lucrezia was standing on her balcony humming softly to herself as she watched some children playing tag in the streets below. It was a beautiful summer's day and she was thinking of the man she was to marry, for her father had informed her he was due to arrive before the week's end. She found herself looking forward to meeting him, for there had been no one before of whom her brother Cesare spoke with such extravagance.

Suddenly Alfonso rode up and was before her. Lucrezia's eyes fell on the young prince, and her heart began to race as it had only once before. Her knees weakened and she had to be kept from swooning by Julia and one of her ladies-in-

waiting, who had come to warn her of Alfonso's arrival. But
they had come too late.

"Glory to God," Julia said, smiling. "Is he the most handsome creature you have ever seen?"

Lucrezia was silent. Just then Alfonso looked up and saw
her there, and he too seemed struck dumb and placed in a
trance as though by a wizard.

For the next six days until the marriage ceremony could
take place, Lucrezia and Alfonso attended parties and spent
long hours walking in the countryside. They explored the
finest shops and streets in Rome, stayed up late and rose
early.

Like a child, Lucrezia once again ran to her father's quarters and embraced him joyfully. "Papa, how can I thank
you? How can you know how happy you've made me?"

Alexander's heart felt full again. He told his daughter, "I
want for you everything you want for yourself . . . and even
greater treasures than you can imagine."

The marriage ceremony was much like Lucrezia's first,
complete with pomp and ceremony. But this time she took
her vows willingly, and hardly noticed the unsheathed sword
held above her head by the Spanish captain, Cervillon.

That night, after the celebration, Lucrezia and Alfonso
happily fulfilled their marriage contract in front of the Pope,
another cardinal, and Ascanio Sforza, and as soon as was allowed by protocol, the young couple quickly retired to Santa
Maria in Portico to spend the next three days and nights together. They needed nothing but each other. And for the first
time in her life, Lucrezia felt the freedom of a love that was
allowed.

After the wedding celebration, a solitary Cesare walked
the floors of his quarters at the Vatican. His head was
spinning with thoughts and plans for himself as captain general, but his heart had turned to stone.

He had conducted himself with great restraint during his

sister's wedding, even contributing to the good-humored
ceremony by appearing in the costume of a magic unicorn—
representing the mythic symbols of chastity and purity—in
the stage play Alexander requested after watching Lucrezia
and Sancia dance before him. The Pope loved to watch
young women in their colorful outfits, as they swirled in the
fast-paced Spanish dances he remembered from his childhood, while he listened to the sound of their quick-tapping
feet on the marble floor.

Cesare had drunk too much, but the wine made the night
bearable. Now, as it wore off, he found himself lonely and
agitated.

Lucrezia was more beautiful than usual that day. Her dark
red wedding gown, studded with jewels, embroidered with
black velvet, and girdled with pearls, made her look like an
empress. She looked regal now, no longer a child. Since her
last wedding, she had become mistress of her own house,
had a child, and was now at ease in society. Until that day,
Cesare had hardly noticed the change in his sister. Dressed
as a cardinal, he had blessed her and wished her well, but in
his heart he was aware of a growing anger.

Several times after the ceremony she had caught Cesare's
eye and smiled to reassure him. But later, as the night wore
on, she became less and less accessible. Each time he approached to speak to her, she was engaged in conversation
with Alfonso. Animated and smiling, twice she had failed
even to notice him. And as she left the hall that night to fulfill her marriage contract, she had not even thought to say
good night to him.

Cesare told himself that in time he would forget how he
felt on this night. That once he had put down the purple and
had a life of his own, once he had married and had children,
once he became captain general and fought great battles as
he had always dreamed, then he would stop dreaming of her.

His mind tried to trick him then. He convinced himself
that Lucrezia's marriage to Alfonso was just a ploy set up by
his father to align Rome with Naples, so that Cesare could

marry a Neapolitan princess. He knew Rosetta, daughter of
the king, would serve. He had heard she was quite pretty and
smiled easily. And once he was entrenched and given property and titles in Naples, he could begin to wage war on the
vicars and barons and conquer the rest of the Romagna for
the Pope and the Borgia family.

He tried to fall asleep that night with visions of glory in
his head, but he woke again and again longing for his sister.

16

Francis Saluti, interrogator for the Florentine Council of Ten, knew that this would be the most important task of his official life, the questioning by torture of Girolamo Savonarola.

That Savonarola was a priest, and an important one, did not lessen his sense of purpose. True, he had often listened to the man's sermons and had been moved by them. But Savonarola had attacked the Pope himself and challenged the ruling class of Florence. He had conspired with the enemies of the republic. And so he must stand trial. The truth of his treason must be ripped from his body.

In the special chamber, guarded by soldiers, Saluti directed his staff. The rack was ready; the artisan had checked its mechanisms, the various wheels, straps, pulleys, and weights. They were in order. A small stove, its belly red and its opening speared by various pincers, heated the room so thoroughly it made Saluti sweat. Or perhaps it was because he knew that this was a day on which he would earn a generous pay.

Saluti had the pride of a professional, but he did not enjoy his work. He did not enjoy the fact that his occupation was an official secret, kept for his own protection. Florence was a city filled with vengeful people. He always went armed to his house, which was surrounded by the houses of the members of his extended family, who would rally to his defense if he was attacked.

His job was much sought after. It paid sixty florins a year, twice that of a cashier at the Florentine banks, plus a bonus of twenty florins for every job to which he was assigned by the council.

Saluti was dressed in tight-fitting silk hose and a blouse the color of burnet, a blue, almost black, fabric color made only in Florence. That color dignified his office, but it was not so severe that it offended his own personal taste. For Saluti, despite frequent stomach upsets and insomnia, was a cheerful, thoughtful man. He attended lectures on Plato at the university. He never missed a sermon of Savonarola's, and he regularly visited the studios of the great artists to take in the newest paintings and sculptures. He had even been invited once to tour the magical gardens of Lorenzo Medici, when Il Magnifico was still alive. It had been the greatest day of his life.

He never enjoyed the suffering of his victims. He resented such accusations. Still, he never was tormented by pangs of conscience. After all, the infallible Pope Innocent had published a bull ruling torture justified in the search for heresy. True, the screams of his subjects were heartrending. True, the nights of Francis Saluti were long, but he always drank a full bottle of wine before retiring, and that helped him sleep.

What really bothered him was the unaccountable stubbornness of his victims. Why did they refuse to admit their guilt at once? Why did they wait and make everyone suffer with them? Why did men refuse to listen to reason? Especially in Florence, where beauty and reason flourished more than in any other place, except possibly ancient Athens.

It was a pity, really a pity, that Francis Saluti himself was to be an instrument of their suffering. But wasn't it true, as Plato had said, that in the life of every single person, no matter how good his intent, there were persons in this mortal world they made suffer?

More to the point: the legal documents were impeccable. Under the great republic of Florence, no citizen could be subjected to torture unless there was proof of his guilt. The documents had been signed by the responsible officials of the Signoria, the ruling council. He had read them carefully, more than once. Pope Alexander had approved, and sent church dignitaries as official observers. There were even rumors that the great Cardinal Cesare Borgia was in Florence secretly to observe. In that case there was no hope for the sainted friar. Silently, the man who must torture prayed for the holy man's quick release from this earth.

His mind and soul prepared, Francis Saluti waited at the open door of the torture chamber for the defeated Hammer of God, Fra Girolamo Savonarola. At last, the famous orator was dragged into the room. It appeared that he already had been beaten, a fact that disappointed Saluti. This was an insult to his skill.

Like the professionals they were, Saluti and his assistant fastened Savonarola securely to the rack. Unwilling to leave the critical task to a subordinate, Saluti himself turned the iron wheels that moved the gears that, in turn, pulled the subject's limbs ever so slowly from his body. All through this process, neither Saluti nor Savonarola said a word. This pleased Saluti. He considered this room to be like a church, a place for silence, prayer, and, finally, confession, not idle conversation.

Soon Saluti heard the familiar crunching pop, as the priest's forearms broke loose at his elbows. The senior cardinal of Florence, who sat nearby, turned pale, shocked by the ghastly sound.

"Do you, Girolamo Savonarola, confess that your spoken message was false and heretical—a defiance of our Lord?" Saluti asked.

Savonarola's face was pale as death, his eyes rolled toward heaven like the sainted martyrs in religious frescoes. Still, he made no reply.

The cardinal nodded to Saluti, who turned the wheel once again. After a moment there was a fierce ripping sound, accompanied by a high-pitched animal-like scream, as the bones and muscles of Savonarola's arms were torn from his shoulders.

Again Saluti intoned his question. "Do you, Girolamo Savonarola, confess that your spoken message was false and heretical—a defiance of our Lord?"

The whispered words were barely audible when Savonarola whispered, "I confess."

It was over.

Savonarola had acknowledged his heresy, and so the end was preordained. There was no protest from the Florentines. They had once adored him, but now were glad to be rid of him. Within the week the Hammer of God was hanged, his broken body twisting on the ropes until he was almost dead. Then he was cut down and burned at the stake in the piazza in front of the Church of San Marco where he had spewed forth his fire and brimstone—where he had almost driven the Pope himself to death and destruction.

Pope Alexander, on this workday morning, considered the ways of the world, the trickeries of nations, the treacheries of families, and the odd, satanic ways hidden in the hearts of every individual on earth. Still, he did not despair. The ways of God he never had to ponder, since he was Christ's Vicar on Earth and his faith was immeasurable. He knew that above all God was merciful, and would forgive all sinners. That was the bedrock of his faith. He never doubted that the purpose of God was to create happiness and joy in this temporal world.

But a Pope's duties were different. Above all, he had to make the Holy Church stronger so that it could carry the word of Christ everywhere in the world—and, even more important, over the vastness of time into the future. The greatest calamity for man would be to have the voice of Christ silenced.

In this way his son Cesare could serve. Though he would no longer be a cardinal, he was certain to help unify the Papal States, for he was an excellent military strategist and a patriot as well. The only question was, did he have the character to withstand the temptations of power? Did he know mercy? For if not, he could save the souls of many and yet lose his own. This troubled Alexander.

But now, there were other decisions to be made. Details of his office, boring administrative rulings. Today there were three, only one of which caused him true conflict. He had to decide on the life or death of his chief secretary, Plandini, who had been convicted of selling papal bulls. Then he would have to decide whether one of the members of a great and noble family should be canonized as a saint of the church. And third, together with his son and Duarte, he had to go over the plans and amassed funds that he had allocated to start a new campaign to unite the Papal States.

Alexander was dressed in formal style, but simply—as a Pope who would dispense favors, not demand them. His white robe was plain, lined only in red silk, and on his head he wore the light linen miter. On his hand was only the ring of Saint Peter, the papal ring, to be kissed. Nothing more.

Today, in order to justify the actions that he was about to take, he was to represent the church as merciful. And for this he used the reception room whose walls were adorned with the paintings of the Virgin Mary, the Madonna who intercedes with God for all sinners.

He called for Cesare to sit by his side, for he understood some men must be taught the virtuous application of mercy.

His first client was his most loyal of twenty years, Stiri Plandini, who had been discovered forging papal bulls. Cesare knew him well, for he had been at the court from the time Cesare was a child.

The man was wheeled into the chamber in a prisoner's chair—a stuffed chair in which he was immobilized by chains, covered with robes out of respect for the Pope's tender eyes.

Alexander ordered the chains on the man's arms removed at once, and then ordered that he be given a glass of wine. For Plandini had tried to speak, but could only croak hoarsely.

Then the Pope spoke, with compassion. "Plandini, you are convicted and sentenced. You have served me faithfully these many years, yet I cannot help you now. But you begged for an audience and I could not refuse you. So, speak."

Stiri Plandini was a typical scrivener. His eyes were squinted from reading, and his face had that looseness which bespeaks a man who has never hunted or worn armor. His body was so slim it held only a small space in the chair. And when he spoke, his voice was very weak.

"Holy Father," he said. "Have mercy on my wife and children. Do not let them suffer for my sins."

Alexander said, "I will see that they come to no harm. Now, have you given up all your conspirators?" He hoped that Plandini could name one of the cardinals he held in special disfavor.

"Yes, Holy Father," Plandini said. "I repent for my sin and I beg you, in the name of the Holy Virgin, for my life. Let me live and care for my family."

Alexander considered this. A pardon for this man would encourage others to violate his trust. But he felt pity. How many mornings had he dictated letters to Plandini and exchanged a jest, or inquired as to the health of his children? The man had been a perfect secretary and a devout Christian.

"You are well paid. Why did you commit such a grievous crime?" the Pope asked.

Plandini was holding his head in his hands, his whole body shaking as he was wracked with sobs. "My sons. My sons," he said. "They are young and wild and I had to pay their debts. I had to keep them close to me. I had to bring them back to the faith."

Alexander looked toward Cesare, but his expression remained impassive. True or not, it was a clever response by Plandini. The Pope's fondness for his own children was well known in Rome. The man had touched him.

Standing there in the bright sunlight that streamed through the stained-glass windows, surrounded by portraits of the forgiving Madonna, Alexander felt overwhelmed by

his responsibility. This very day, this very man before him
would be hanging from a gibbet in the public square, deaf
and dumb forever to the pleasures of earth—his five sons
and three daughters torn to pieces with grief. And certainly
the three conspirators must die, even if he pardoned this
man. Would it be just to kill him as well?

Alexander lifted the linen miter from his head; light as it
was, he could not bear its weight any longer. He ordered his
papal guards to free the prisoner and help him stand up.
Then he saw Plandini's warped torso, his shoulders twisted
from the rack during interrogation.

Overcome not so much with sadness for this single sinner,
but for all the evil in the world itself, he stood and embraced
Plandini. "The Holy Mother of Compassion has spoken to
me. You will not die. I pardon you. But you must leave
Rome and leave your family. You will live the rest of your
life in a monastery far from here, and devote your life to
God to earn his mercy."

Gently, he pushed Plandini back into his chair and motioned for him to be taken away. All would be well; the pardon would be cloaked in secrecy, the other conspirators
would hang, and both the church and God would be served.

Suddenly he felt a joy that he had rarely felt—not even
with his children, the women he loved, the treasures he
counted for the Crusades. He felt a belief in his Christ that
was so pure that all the pomp, all the power vanished, and it
seemed he was all of light. As that feeling faded, he wondered if his son Cesare could ever feel this ecstasy of mercy.

The next petitioner was an altogether different kettle of
fish, Alexander thought. He would have to keep his wits
about him and not go soft. A hard bargain had to be made,
and he must not weaken. This client would inspire not a drop
of mercy. He replaced the miter on his head.

"Shall I wait in the anteroom?" Cesare asked, but the
Pope beckoned Cesare to follow him.

"You may find this interesting," he said.

For this meeting, Alexander selected another reception room that was not so forgiving. Its walls were painted with the portraits of warrior Popes, striking down the enemies of the church with sword and holy water. Depictions of saints being beheaded by the Infidel, Christs on crosses with thorned crowns and halls painted bright red. It was the Salon of Martyrs, more than appropriate to this interview.

The man presented to the Pope was the head of the noble and rich Venetian family of Rosamundi. He owned a hundred ships that traded all over the world. Like a true Venetian, his wealth was a closely guarded secret.

This Baldo Rosamundi, a man over seventy, was dressed respectfully in black and white, but wore precious stones as buttons. And on his face was the look of a man prepared to do serious business, as the two men had done together when Alexander was a cardinal.

"So you think your granddaughter should be canonized," Alexander said cheerfully.

Baldo Rosamundi spoke respectfully. "Holy Father, that would be presumptuous of me. It is the people of Venice who began the petition to make her a saint. It is the holy officers of your church who investigated the claim and pushed it forward. I understand that it is only you, the Holy Father, who can give the final approval."

Alexander had been briefed by the bishop designated as Protector of the Faith, whose role it was to investigate claims for canonization. It was quite an ordinary case. Doria Rosamundi would be a white saint, not a red saint. That is, she would be elevated to sainthood on the grounds of an impeccably virtuous life: a life of poverty, chastity, and good works, with an improbable miracle or two thrown in. There were hundreds of such claims each year. Alexander had no affection for white saints; he preferred those who died as martyrs for the Holy Church—the red saints.

The documentation showed that Doria Rosamundi had scorned the good life of her rich family. She had ministered

to the poor, and since there were not enough of them in
Venice—a city that did not allow even the freedom of
poverty—she had traveled throughout the small towns of
Sicily gathering orphan children to care for. She had been
chaste, she had lived in poverty, and most important she had
fearlessly tended victims of the plagues that constantly
struck the general population. And then she herself had died
at the age of twenty-five of one of these plagues. She had
been dead only ten years when her family initiated the
process of canonization.

Of course, as proof, there had been miracles. During the
last plague, some of the victims had been pronounced dead
and put on the stacks of corpses for burning. But when Doria
had prayed over them, they had miraculously come back to
life.

After her death, prayers at her tomb had produced some
cures for deadly illnesses. And on the blue Mediterranean
waters, sailors saw her face hovering over their ships in great
storms. Document after document attested to these miracles.
Everything had been investigated, and none had been dis-
proven. And it helped that the great wealth of the
Rosamundi could help to push this petition up through all
the levels of the church.

Alexander said, "What you ask is great, my responsibility
even greater. Once your granddaughter is made a saint, by
definition she resides in heaven seated at the side of God and
therefore can intercede for all her loved ones. Her shrines
will be in your church; pilgrims will come from all over the
world to worship. It is a weighty decision. What can you add
to all this evidence?"

Baldo Rosamundi bowed his head in reverence. "My personal experience," he said. "When she was just a little girl, I
was at the height of my good fortune and yet it meant nothing to me. It was all ashes. And yet when Doria was only
seven years old, she saw my sadness and implored me to
pray to God for happiness. I did, and I became happy. She
was never selfish as a child; she was never selfish as a young

woman. I delighted in buying her expensive jewels, but she never wore them. She sold them and gave the money to the poor. After her death, I was very ill. The doctors bled me until I was white as a ghost, but still I was failing. Then one night I saw her face, and she spoke to me. She said, 'You must live to serve God.' "

Alexander raised his hands in respectful benediction and then lifted the miter from his head. He placed it on the table between them. "And have you lived to serve God?" he said.

"You must know I have," Baldo Rosamundi said. "I have built three churches in Venice. I have supported a home for foundlings in memory of my granddaughter. I have renounced worldly pleasures unsuitable to men of my age, and I have found renewed love for Christ and the Blessed Madonna." He paused for a moment and then faced the Pope with a benign smile that Alexander remembered well. "Holy Father, you have but to command me as to how to serve the church."

Alexander pretended to ponder this, then spoke. "You must know that since I have been elected to this holy office, my greatest hope has been to lead another Crusade. To lead a Christian army into Jerusalem to recapture the birthplace of Christ."

"Yes, yes," Rosamundi said eagerly. "I will use all my influence in Venice so that you will have the finest fleet of ships. You can count on me."

Alexander shrugged. "Venice is hand in glove with the Turks, as you know. They cannot jeopardize their trade routes and colonies by giving lavish support to a Crusade for the Holy Church. I understand that, as you surely do. What I really need is gold, to pay the soldiers and supply them with provisions. The sacred fund is not plentiful. Even with revenues from the jubilee, the extra tax I have extracted from all the members of the clergy, high and low, and the tax of ten percent for the Crusade from every Christian. From the Jews of Rome I've asked twenty percent. But the sacred fund is still a little meager." He smiled and then added, "And so you can serve."

Baldo Rosamundi nodded thoughtfully as though this were a surprise to him. He even dared to raise his eyebrows slightly. Then he said, "Holy Father, give some idea what you require and I will obey, even if I have to mortgage my fleet."

Alexander had already given some thought to what sum he could extract from Rosamundi. To have a saint in the family would make the Rosamundi welcome in every court in the Christian world. It would protect them from powerful enemies to a great degree. It did not matter that there were almost ten thousand saints in the history of the Catholic Church; only a few hundred of them had the certification of the papacy in Rome.

Alexander spoke slowly. "Your granddaughter was certainly blessed by the Holy Spirit. She was beyond reproach as a Christian, she added glory to God's kingdom on earth. But it is perhaps too soon after her death to canonize her. There are many other candidates waiting, some as long as fifty or one hundred years. I do not want to be hasty. It is an irrevocable act."

Baldo Rosamundi, who had radiated hope and confidence only moments before, seemed to shrink in his chair. He said, in an almost inaudible whisper, "I want to pray at her shrine before I die, and I have not so long to live. I want her to intercede for me in heaven. I am a true believer in Christ and I truly believe that my Doria is a saint. I wish to worship her while I am here on earth. I beg you, Holy Father, ask me what you wish."

At that moment Alexander saw that the man was sincere, that he truly did believe. So, with the gaiety of a gambler, Alexander asked for double the amount he had planned. "Our fund for the Crusade needs five hundred thousand ducats," he said. "Then the Christian world can sail for Jerusalem."

Baldo Rosamundi's body seemed to jump into the air, as if struck by lightning. For a moment he pressed his hands over his ears as if not to hear, but he was concentrating his mind and trying to answer. Then he became calm, and a beautiful serenity transformed his face. "Thank you, Holy Father," he said. "But you must come to Venice personally to dedicate her shrine and perform the necessary ceremonies."

Alexander said quietly, "That was my intent. A saint is greater than any Pope. And now we will pray together to ask her to intercede for us in heaven."

17

Cesare awoke that morning with mounting excitement. He could already feel the change in himself. Today was the day he was to appear before the consistory of cardinals who had been selected by the Pope to "consider" releasing him from his vows, and allowing him to resign his status as cardinal.

A commission of fifteen was appointed, and all but two were present. A Spanish cardinal had fallen ill with malaria, and one of the Italian cardinals had fallen from his horse.

None of the remaining cardinals had ever before faced such a request, for to be a cardinal was the dream of most men throughout Italy. To be selected was to rise high in the ranks of the church, and to be held in the greatest esteem, for each was in a position to be considered as a future Pope. Most of the cardinals present had committed themselves to long years of exhaustive work, prayer—and occasional sin—to reach their position, and so Cesare's request was considered both puzzling and an impertinence. To lay down the purple voluntarily was an affront to their honor.

Each member of the commission sat stiffly on a high-backed, ornately carved wooden chair in the Hall of Faith. Dressed in their formal vestments, the long line of red hats appeared as a huge ribbon hung before the portrait of the Last Judgment, the faces of the cardinals masks contorted with disbelief: stark, white, and ghostly.

Cesare rose to address them. "I stand here before you in order that you understand why I am about to ask your indulgence in this matter. I must confess that I have never wished a life in the church. My own father, his Holiness Alexander VI, made this choice for me with every good intention. Still, it has never been my choice and will never be my vocation."

The cardinals looked at each other nervously, surprised by his candor. Now Cesare explained. "My choice is to lead the papal army, to defend the church and Rome. And to that I must add that I wish to marry and have legitimate children. This being my true vocation and my greatest conviction, my colleagues, I ask humbly that you free me from my vows and permit me to resign."

One of the Spanish cardinals protested. "If this is allowed, there may be a danger. For what if the cardinal becomes a prince and then feels able to form new alliances, serve a new king, and become an enemy of the present church and Spain?"

Alexander stood impassively before them, unmoved. The cardinals had been made aware of his wishes, but now each looked to him for confirmation in this important decision. He spoke. "It is only for the good of his soul that my son makes this request. For, as he confessed, his true calling is to marry and to be a soldier, not to be a man of the cloth. His temporal appetites and worldliness have caused the papacy universal scandal, for he seems unable to subdue his passions. And we must agree that does not serve the Holy Mother Church or Rome. We must consider also that on the cardinal's resignation over thirty-five thousand ducats in territories and benefices will fall vacant and be returned to us. In view of the benefits of this action, and because we are committed to saving souls, we must honor this request."

The vote was unanimous, the amount of the benefices casting away any doubt.

In a short ceremony, Pope Alexander released his son from his vows and authorized him to marry, bestowing upon him a special papal blessing.

And so it was that Cesare Borgia carefully laid down his

great purple cloak and red hat in front of the consistory, bowing in acknowledgment to the cardinals of the committee and to the Holy Father. Then, with his head held high, Cesare strode from the room into the golden sunlight of Rome. He was now a man of the world, not of the church, and his new life could begin.

Afterward, Alexander felt a sense of grief, for he had built his life upon the hope that his son Cesare would eventually become Pope. But now that Juan was dead and he needed a commander he could trust to lead the papal army, he resolved to bend to the will of the Heavenly Father and accept the decision of his son.

He felt himself falling into a depression, quite uncommon for a man of his buoyant nature, and so he reasoned that he needed some pleasure to lift his spirits and offset his heavy heart. He determined to have a massage, for the pleasures of the body always helped to cheer him.

Alexander called for Duarte and informed him that he would conduct any emergency afternoon meetings in his private salon. As he did in other situations which brought him pleasure but would be frowned upon by others, he told Duarte to make known to his staff that a long afternoon massage had been prescribed as a health measure by his personal physician.

He had been in the salon for less than an hour when Duarte entered and announced, "There is someone who wishes to see you. He claims it is a matter of great importance."

The Pope, lying prone, covered only by a light cotton towel, spoke without raising his head. "Ah, Duarte, you must have these young women relax you when they are finished with me. It drives the devil from your body, and brings new light to your soul."

"There are other ways I find more effective," Duarte said, laughing.

Alexander asked, "Who wishes this audience?"

"The French ambassador, Georges d'Amboise," Duarte announced. "Do you wish me to ask him to wait until you are clothed?"

"Tell him if it is important enough, he will have to speak to me as I am, for I have no inclination to end this session more quickly than I had planned," Alexander said. "After all, Duarte, even a Pope must have a moment to honor the temple of his body. For is it not a creation of the Lord?"

Duarte said, "Theology is not my strength, Worthiness. But I will send him in. For the French are seldom horrified by pleasures of the flesh."

And so it was, lying unclothed on a high table, with two attractive young girls massaging Alexander's back and rubbing his muscular legs, that the French ambassador, Georges d'Amboise, found the Pope. He was ushered into the salon by an amused Duarte, who quickly took leave of them.

Though cynical and highly sophisticated, Georges d'Amboise was taken aback at this sight. But his face, set in practiced diplomacy, revealed nothing.

The Pope said, "It's safe to speak, Ambassador. These girls pay no attention."

But d'Amboise refused. He told Alexander, "The king's instructions are that no one but Your Holiness must hear this."

Pope Alexander impatiently waved the girls away, slid off the table, and stood up. The ambassador attempted to avert his eyes.

"D'Amboise, you French make such a thing of secrecy, yet all rumors fly on the wind, and nothing escapes us. Your court can keep nothing to itself, nor can ours. But now we are alone. You may speak."

Georges d'Amboise found it difficult to approach a matter of such great importance while the Pope stood naked before him, and in his attempt to compose himself he began to cough and sputter.

Alexander looked down at himself and smiled. "And the French are said to be so free . . ." he said, with some sarcasm. "I will dress so you may stop stammering and get to the point."

A short while later, dressed in formal attire, the Pope joined d'Amboise in his study. D'Amboise began. "King Charles is dead. In an unfortunate accident, in which he hit his head on a large ceiling beam, he swiftly fell into unconsciousness, and within hours, despite his physicians and the attentions of the court, he died. Nothing could be done. His relative, Louis the Twelfth, has now ascended to the throne as king. Under his rule, I am sent with information: that the situation with both Naples and Milan is now changed, for this king claims them. They are rightfully his."

Alexander thought a moment, and frowned. "Am I to understand that your new king claims *both* kingdoms?"

"Yes, Your Worthiness. One claim is set on the grounds of his forebears, the other on that of King Charles. But be assured, he means no harm to you or the Holy Mother Church."

The Pope feigned surprise. "Really? And how can we be certain?"

The ambassador placed his hand over his heart in a gesture of sincerity. "I had hoped that you would accept my word and the word of the king."

Alexander sat silently, thoughtfully, for a moment. "What is it that your king wishes from me? For to come to me with this information, and offer assurances as well, he must desire something dear . . ."

"Well," d'Amboise said, "he has a wish that only Your Holiness can grant. And it has to do with his marriage to Jeanne of France. He has asked me to tell you that he is not content, Holiness."

"My dear d'Amboise," Alexander said with a look of amusement. "Not content with his marriage to the deformed, misshapen daughter of Louis the Eleventh? What a surprise! Though he disappoints me, for I expected more of him. He is not as charitable as I presumed."

The ambassador's voice became cold and more formal.

He was affronted by Alexander's remarks. "It is not a matter of her beauty, Holy Father, I assure you. Their marriage has never been consummated, and the young king strongly desires an heir."

"Has he another wife in mind?" Alexander asked, already suspecting the answer.

The ambassador nodded. "He wishes to marry Anne of Brittany, the widow of his late cousin, Charles the Eighth."

The Pope laughed good-naturedly. "Ah," he said. "Now it becomes clearer to me. He wishes to marry his sister-in-law, and so he asks for a dispensation from the Holy Father. In exchange, he will offer a treaty protecting our lands."

D'Amboise's body seemed to fold in on itself with relief. "In substance, Holy Father, though I would put it more delicately . . ."

Pope Alexander's sonorous voice resounded throughout the hall. "This is a serious matter you come to me with. For it is written in the holy Commandments: 'Thou shalt not covet thy brother's wife.'"

The ambassador stammered, "But with your dispensation, Your Holiness, even a commandment can be altered in some measure."

The Pope sat back in his chair and rested, and his voice became much more conversational. "This is true, Ambassador. Still, before I can agree, there is something more I desire than the safety of our lands, for your king is requesting a great indulgence." D'Amboise said nothing, and Alexander continued. "You must be aware that my son, Cesare Borgia, has given up the hat of a cardinal. And so it is imperative that he must soon marry. The daughter of King Federigo of Naples, Princess Rosetta, seems a suitable match, and one who would be greatly influenced by your king, do you not agree? I assume we can count on his support?"

"I will do my utmost, Your Holiness, to see that the king understands your wishes, and grants an accommodation.

Until we speak again, I beg Your Holiness to consider the king's request, for he has waited patiently for this."

The Pope looked at the ambassador slyly. "Go, d'Amboise, bring Louis my message. For perhaps both France and the papacy can celebrate, if indeed there are to be two weddings."

Cesare had sent several messages to Lucrezia at Santa Maria in Portico, asking that she meet him in private, but in each case she had replied that she had other pressing engagements, though she would come as quickly as possible. At first Cesare felt slighted, but before long he became angry.

His sister was not only his lover, but his dearest friend. Now that there were so many things about his life and his plans that were changing, he wanted to share them with her. Yet for months she did nothing but spend every minute of the day and night with her new husband, Prince Alfonso, throwing parties, entertaining poets and artists, taking outings in the countryside. Her palace had become an artists' gathering place, attracting visitors far and wide.

Cesare stopped himself from imagining the young couple making love, for he had heard rumors of her wedding night, and in this case—unlike her experience with Giovanni Sforza—he had heard that she was filled with joy and enthusiasm.

Now that Cesare was no longer a cardinal, he had little to do. To pass the time he spent hours studying military strategy, and trying to determine the best marital alliance he could form in order to help his father expand the papal territories. And he wished to speak about the matter with his sister, to gain counsel not only from his father and his advisors but from her as well—for who knew him better?

Unfettered by the robes of a cardinal, he began to spend days and nights drinking in the city with courtesans, managing in several incautious encounters to contract the French pox. And he paid dearly for his indiscretions, for his own physician used him as a guinea pig to construct a cure, forcing him to spend weeks soaking the pustules that covered his body with all manner of herbs and boiling pumice packs. He was cut and scrubbed and soaked until finally the sores disappeared, leaving him with a host of small round scars that were hidden beneath his clothes. And for that his physician was credited with a cure.

Once Cesare was well, he again sent for Lucrezia. And for two days he received no answer. Then, as he was raging in his bedchambers, determined to take himself to her palace and insist on a meeting, he heard a knock at the door to the secret passage. He sat up alert, on the side of the bed.

Suddenly Lucrezia was standing before him, radiant and more beautiful than ever before. She ran to him and he stood to kiss her, to embrace her with all his pent-up passion, but their lips met for only a moment before she pulled away. It was a sweet kiss, an affectionate embrace, but one completely without lust.

"This is what you come to bring me?" Cesare asked her. "Now that you have someone else to enchant?"

He turned before she answered, and stood with his back to her. She begged him to turn and look at her, but he refused, and she found herself pleading with him. "Cesare, my dearest brother, my love, please don't be angry with me. All things change. And now that you are no longer a cardinal, you will find a love as complete as I have."

Cesare turned toward her again, his chest heavy, as though he had swallowed a stone. His dark eyes glowed with anger. "This is what you feel after all our years together? In just a few months you have given your heart to another? And what has he given you?"

She tried to approach him again, this time with tears in her eyes. "Chez, he lavishes me with kindness, conversation, and affection. It is a love that fills my heart and my life, but more than that, it is a love I don't have to hide. It is not forbidden, it is blessed, and that is something you and I could never have."

Cesare sneered. "All your promises about never loving anyone as you loved me—all that has changed in this short time? Just because you have a blessing, you can give yourself wholly to another? Your lips can be kissed as I kissed them? Your flesh responds with the same fire?"

Lucrezia's voice trembled. "There will never be anyone like you for me, for you were my first love. It was with you I first shared the secrets of my body, as well as the secrets of my heart and the most intimate thoughts of my mind." She walked to him then, and he allowed it. She held his face in her hands, and he did not pull away as she looked into his eyes. Her voice was soft but strong when she continued. "But my dear Chez, you are my brother. And our love has always been tainted by sin, for though the Holy Father sanctioned it, the Heavenly Father would not. One does not have to be a cardinal or a Pope to know the truth of sin."

She covered her face as he shouted, "A sin? Our love, a sin? I will never accept that. It was the only true thing in my life, and I forbid you to make less of it. I lived and breathed for you. I could live with Papa loving Juan more than he loved me; I could live with Papa loving you more than he loved me, for I knew you loved me above all things. But now that your love for another is greater than for me, how do I make that right with myself?" Cesare began to pace.

Lucrezia sat on his bed and shook her head. "I don't love another more than I love you. I love Alfonso differently. He is my husband. Chez, your life has just begun. Papa will ordain you captain general of the papal army, and you will have great battles to fight, as you have always dreamed. You will marry and have children you can claim as your own. You will be master of your own house. Cesare, my brother, your whole life is before you, for finally you are free. Don't allow me to be the cause of your unhappiness, for you are more special to me than the Holy Father himself."

He bent to kiss her then, a gentle kiss, the kiss of a

brother for his sister . . . and some part of him turned hard
and cold. What would he do without her? For until that
night, whenever he'd thought of love he always thought of
her; whenever he'd thought of God he always thought of
her. Now he feared that whenever he thought of war, he'd
always think of her.

18

Cesare spent the following weeks dressed in solemn black, pacing the halls of the Vatican, sullen and angry, as he waited impatiently for his new life to begin. Each day he anxiously marked time as he looked forward to an invitation from Louis XII, king of France. He was restless and wanted to escape the familiar landscape of Rome, to leave behind all memories of his sister, and his life as cardinal.

During these weeks his night terrors returned, and he was reluctant to fall asleep for fear he would wake in a cold sweat with a half-scream upon his lips. No matter how hard he tried to banish his sister from his heart and mind, he was possessed by her. And each time he closed his eyes to try to rest, he imagined making love to her.

When the Pope, with great pleasure, informed him that Lucrezia was pregnant again, he spent the entire day riding through the countryside almost mad with jealousy and rage.

That night, as he tossed and turned in his sleep, a bright yellow flame burst forth in his dreams. Suddenly the sweet face of his sister appeared, and he saw it as a sign, a symbol of their love. It had warmed him, then burned him, but still it burned bright. He made his commitment during that dark night, that he would wear that flame as his personal insignia and place it alongside the Borgia bull. From that day forward, in peace or in war, the flame of his love would now flame his ambition.

Cardinal Giuliano della Rovere had been the most bitter enemy of Pope Alexander for many years. But following his exile to France—after the failed and humiliating attempt to unseat the Pope and align himself with the unfortunate Charles VIII—della Rovere discovered that his contentious attitude had brought him nothing but misery. A man like himself was much more comfortable in the cramped and crowded passages of the Vatican, where he could make subtle plans for his own future and assess his position while speaking directly to both his friends and enemies. There, in an expression of a face or an inflection of a voice, he could learn more than from all the written agreements.

Once della Rovere determined that his stance against the Pope no longer served to his advantage, he was quick to attempt a reconciliation. The opportunity had come with the death of the Pope's son Juan, when he penned a letter of condolence to Alexander. The Pope's grief, and his resolution to reform himself as well as the Church, had moved him to accept the cardinal's message with grace. When the Pope wrote back it was with appreciation, and an invitation for Cardinal della Rovere to act as papal delegate in France. For even in his desolation the Pope was aware of della Rovere's importance in the court, and envisioned that he might one day have to call upon him for assistance.

When at last Cesare received the invitation to visit King Louis at Chinon, he had two important missions to accomplish: First he must bring the requested papal dispensation to the king—and then he must convince Princess Rosetta to be his wife.

Alexander called him into his chambers before he was to leave for France. After embracing his son, he handed Cesare the parchment with the red wax papal seal. "This is the dispensation for the king, annulling his marriage and permitting him to marry Queen Anne of Brittany. It is most important, for this is not only the case of a man who wishes a more beautiful wife, but rather, a delicate political matter. For if the king cannot marry Anne, she will withdraw Brittany from the control of the French, which will be a serious blow to Louis's plan for 'la grandeur de la France.' "

"Can he not just divorce Jeanne or prove grounds for annulment?" Cesare asked.

Alexander smiled. "It would seem a simple matter, but it is not. For though Jeanne of France is short and misshapen, she has true stature, and a clever mind. She has brought in witnesses who swear they heard Louis state publicly that he mounted her more than three times on their marriage night. To add to that, he claims to have been less than fourteen, beneath the age of consent, but no one can be found who will swear to the date of his birth."

"And how will you solve this problem?" Cesare asked slyly.

"Ah," Alexander said, sighing. "To be a Pope, and infallible, is a true blessing. I will just place his age where I feel it must be, and state any evidence to the contrary to be false."

"Is there anything more I must carry to France to ensure my welcome?" Cesare asked.

Alexander's voice grew serious. "The red hat of a cardinal for our friend Georges d'Amboise."

"D'Amboise wants to be a cardinal, but he is a fine ambassador," Cesare said.

"He wants it desperately," the Pope said, "but only his mistress is certain of his reasons."

The Pope embraced Cesare warmly. "I will be quite lost without you, my son. But I have seen to it that you will be treated well. For our papal legate to France, Cardinal della Rovere, will be there to meet you and protect you from any unseen danger. I have given him clear instructions to guard you with great care, and to treat you as a son."

And so it was that in October, when Cesare arrived by sea in Marseilles accompanied by an enormous entourage, Cardinal della Rovere and his embassy were there to greet him. Cesare was dressed in black velvet and gold brocade, each garment lavishly decorated with delicate jewels and diamonds. His hat was embroidered with gold and plumed with white feathers. Even his horses had shoes of silver, for the papal treasury had been plundered to equip him.

Cardinal della Rovere embraced him and said, "My son, I am here to dedicate myself to your comfort and honor. If there is anything you desire, you may be certain I will provide it." Della Rovere had managed to convince the Council of Avignon to raise a loan to arrange a fitting reception for the arriving dignitary.

The following day, at a fabled French castle, Cesare's display was even more outrageous. He wore a white doublet over his velvet black, encrusted with pearls and rubies. His own horse was a dappled gray stallion, its saddle, bridle, and stirrups studded with gold. He was preceded by twenty trumpeters each in scarlet, mounted on a white horse, and behind Cesare rode a troop of Swiss cavalry in crimson and gold papal uniforms. They were followed in turn by Cesare's thirty gentlemen servants, who came before his numerous aides, pages, and other servants, all brilliantly costumed. Last came musicians, jugglers, tumblers, bears, monkeys, and seventy mules bearing the riches of his wardrobe and gifts for the king and members of his court. Such a grand and gaudy parade!

Before he left Rome, Brandao had cautioned him against such excess, telling him that the French would not be impressed by such a display. But Cesare believed he knew better.

Now della Rovere and his envoy took Cesare through the city, rich with hangings and triumphant arches decorated at great expense for his arrival. On the instructions of the cardinal, everyone treated the Pope's son as a royal prince. He was showered with gifts of silver platters and silver plate, then taken to the Maison de la Ville to enjoy a great celebration.

Della Rovere had invited many of the most beautiful girls and elegant ladies of the city to attend, for it was well known that Cesare enjoyed their company. Several days followed filled with sumptuous banquets and elaborate theater plays, and the nights passed as they drank fine wines amid entertainment and displays of dancing before Cesare and his company.

And for two months afterward it was the same, in every city, in every town. There was not a fair that Cesare did not attend, not a horse race he didn't bet, not a card game he was absent from.

France was cold that autumn, with bitter winds and lashing hail, yet in every municipality crowds appeared, and Cesare's arrival attracted great attention. Humility was never one of his virtues, and now, rather than seeing the curiosity of the people for a son of the Pope, he took their attention as a sign of their adoration for him, and his head filled with his new power. He became arrogant and overconfident, alienating those Frenchmen who could truly help him.

Finally Cesare reached the court of France in Chinon, and by then the king was furious. He was anxiously awaiting news of his annulment, and had not been sent any word whether or not the Pope had granted his request.

On the day he arrived Cesare was accompanied by a grand cavalcade, and a long line of heavily laden mules carrying many luxurious adornments. Each animal was covered in rich cloths of yellow and red, bearing the Borgia bull and Cesare's new insignia, the yellow flame. His envoy was lavishly bejeweled, and on several mules there were immense chests, which filled the citizens' imaginings. Some said they contained precious jewels for Cesare's future wife; some said holy shrines and relics for great blessings. Yet none of the aristocracy were impressed. In Italy this gaudy show would have told the tale of great wealth and station, but in France it inspired contempt.

The king himself had a penchant for parsimony, and the court followed his example. Before long Cesare faced laughter in the streets. Filled with a new sense of self-importance, and without either his father's wisdom or his sister's good sense to balance him, he remained unaware of their reactions.

At the first sight of Cesare, King Louis whispered to an advisor, "This is all too much." But still he greeted the Pope's son with great enthusiasm, and had to keep himself from inquiring immediately about his long-awaited dispensation from Alexander.

As Cesare, accompanied by Georges d'Amboise, passed down the formal reception line to be introduced to important members of the court, he seemed not to concern himself with their expressions of amusement. They could laugh if they wished, but their king must treat him well, for he held within his possession a decision that was critical to their king.

The young aristocrats foolish enough to mock Cesare were given a warning from the king so severe it surprised them. Obviously, they thought, this Borgia was someone the king cared about.

After the introductions had been made, Cesare, Louis, and the ambassador, Georges d'Amboise, retired to a delightful and intimate room in the king's quarters. Its walls were covered in panels of yellow silk and oak. Tall French windows looked out into a beautiful garden, its delicate splashing fountain abundant with gaily colored birds whose sweet song filled the room.

King Louis began by reassuring Cesare. "You do understand, my dear friend, that French soldiers moving into Italy will in no way challenge papal rights or threaten papal territories. Moreover, if there is any difficulty in unseating the local warlords or vicars in the Romagna, I can assure you that a sizable number of experienced French troops will be readied to assist you."

"Thank you, Your Highness," Cesare said. Pleased by the

king's generosity, Cesare immediately handed Louis the formal papal dispensation.

The king could not hide his delight, and when Cesare passed the wax-sealed parchment to Georges d'Amboise and he read it, his face radiated astonished pleasure at being named a cardinal, and being accepted as a prince of the Holy Mother Church.

Louis himself was now in an expansive mood. In light of the Pope's generosity, he would make it official: Cesare would be Duke of Valentinois. That title carried with it some of the finest castles and most profitable estates in France. Cesare was greatly relieved, for he had spent far too much on his entourage and he knew he would need to hire troops for his campaign in Romagna. The king's gift guaranteed he would never again have to concern himself about money.

The three men toasted each other. And then Cesare asked, "How goes the marital alliance?"

Suddenly, Louis seemed uneasy. "There is some problem with the Princess Rosetta. For though she is in France, a lady-in-waiting to my beloved Queen Anne, she is not one of my subjects but the daughter of the king of Naples—of Spanish heritage—therefore a subject of the house of Aragon. And a girl with a mind of her own. I cannot simply order her to marry you."

Cesare frowned, but then asked, "May I speak with the lady, Your Majesty?"

"Of course," the king said. "D'Amboise will arrange it."

Later that afternoon, Cesare and Princess Rosetta sat together on a stone bench in the garden surrounded by the fragrant smell of orange trees.

Rosetta was a tall girl, and not the prettiest that Cesare had seen, but regal in her bearing. Her dark hair, pulled back at the nape of her neck, made her look severe. But she had a pleasant and forthright approach, and was not at all reluctant to discuss their proposed match.

Rosetta smiled gently, but spoke firmly. "I do not wish to offend the duke in any manner, for until this moment, I have never even seen him. But the unfortunate truth is that I am desperately in love with a Breton nobleman, and therefore have no love left to give another."

Cesare tried to persuade her otherwise. "Often a desperate love is not the most trustworthy match for a life together," he said.

But Rosetta looked at him unflinchingly. "I must speak candidly, for I believe you are worthy of my trust. You are the son of the Pope, and papal views as well as papal armies are very important to my father. I believe that they are of such supreme importance that, if you insisted, my father would force me to marry you. But I beg you not to do that. I would never be able to love you, for my heart has already been given." Her eyes filled with tears.

Cesare admired the girl, for she stood for her truth. He handed her his handkerchief. "Not for a moment would I desire to force you into marriage. If my charm cannot win you, then I will not have you as a bride." He smiled then. "But you have true value as a friend . . . and, if I am ever to fall victim to the courts, I would ask you to present yourself as a lawyer to plead my case."

Rosetta laughed, amused and relieved. And the princess and Cesare spent the afternoon together enjoying each other's company.

That night Cesare reported to the king, explaining what had happened. Louis did not seem surprised by Rosetta's response, but he was pleased by Cesare's reaction.

"I thank you for your kindness and understanding," the king said.

"Do we have another princess who has not yet fallen in love?" Cesare asked pleasantly.

Still embarrassed by his inability to carry forth his promise to the Pope, the king said, "I have planned to offer an additional title as duke of Dinois, and present two estates of great significance to those I have already conferred upon you."

Cesare bowed his head in acknowledgment; then, with a glint in his eye, he asked, "I am grateful, of course—but will this gain me a wife?"

Louis was obviously distressed. "With the refusal of Princess Rosetta, and with your permission, we will begin a more extensive search immediately. We will scour the French royal houses for just the right princess."

Cesare stood to leave. "I will extend my stay," he said, "and visit your countryside until she is found."

In Rome, the Pope could think of nothing but his son's marriage. He called Cardinal Ascanio Sforza to him and asked that he return to Naples to plead again with the king.

But weeks later the cardinal returned without success, for Rosetta continued to refuse, and he had found no willing match among the other young women. And during his stay in Naples, Cardinal Sforza found more that was troubling. There was news in the south that Louis XII was planning another French invasion to claim his ancestral rights to both Milan and Naples.

"Is this true?" Ascanio Sforza asked Alexander. "And what do you mean to do about it?"

The Pope was enraged to be so questioned by Ascanio. But he was unable either to lie or tell the truth. Instead he said, "I would take action if my son, Cesare, was not hostage at the very court of France."

"A very well-dressed, well-kept, willing hostage," the cardinal remarked, "who carries with him the coffers of the Holy Mother Church filled with riches for his pleasure. Or to seduce a wife in order to form an alliance which will threaten Rome itself."

Pope Alexander was outraged now, and so he thundered, "My dear cardinal, it was your brother Il Moro, if you recall, who invited the first French invasion. And it is Rome that is betrayed—for not one of the members of the house of Aragon will offer a marital alliance. They give me little choice."

"So it is true that you have aligned with France against Aragon?" Ascanio asked, with some satisfaction.

Alexander struggled to compose himself. Then he stood up and pointed toward the door of his chambers and said, "Leave at once, for what you have spoken nears heresy. And I suggest that you pray for forgiveness for such slander, or I shall give you last rites and have you tossed into the dark waters of the Tiber on this very night."

Cardinal Ascanio Sforza fled, but the sound of the Pope's fiery invective and thunderous voice sent him racing down the steps so quickly that his heart in his chest was pounding. He tripped once but picked himself up, determined to leave Rome for Naples as soon as he was able.

During the months that followed, the Pope put aside all papal business. He could focus on nothing but a new alliance. He refused visiting ambassadors from Venice, Florence, Milan, and Naples—anyone who did not come to offer his son Cesare a wife.

In France, after several months, King Louis called Cesare into his chambers and happily announced, "I have brought some very good news. If you and the Holy Father agree, I have found a splendid match for you: Charlotte d'Albret, a beautiful and intelligent woman, and the sister of the king of Navarre."

Cesare, pleased and relieved, immediately sent a message to his father asking for permission to marry and to extend his stay in France.

After celebrating High Mass at Saint Peter's, Alexander was deeply troubled. He had received a message from his son, and as he knelt at the altar in the basilica under the watchful eye of the Holy Madonna he tried to reason . . .

During his thirty-five years as a vice-chancellor to Popes,

during his six years as Pope, and in all his years of life, Alexander had never been faced with such a terrible dilemma. His alliance with Spain had always been his strength, as a man of God and as a man of the world. He had managed to balance the foreign powers of Spain and France, and maintain support for the papacy in both countries.

But after Juan's death his widow, Maria Enriquez, had convinced Queen Isabella, and therefore King Ferdinand, that Cesare Borgia was the true killer of his brother. As a result, there was not one family in the house of Aragon—nor in Spain, Naples, or Milan—who would allow their daughter to wed the Pope's son.

Alexander had searched all the cities, had spoken to countless ambassadors and offered great benefices, but still he had been unable to find a suitable wife and a strong alliance for Cesare. Yet he must, or the Borgia themselves would fall.

He needed support for the papacy, and he needed the help of the armies of Naples and Spain in order to unify the lands and quell the uprisings by the greedy warlords. Even his daughter Lucrezia's marriage to Alfonso of Naples, under the house of Aragon, secretly rested on this intention to ensure the alliance of Cesare with Alfonso's sister, Princess Rosetta.

But now she had refused, and the son he had sent to marry a Spanish princess was instead offered a French princess for a wife. Was he losing his grip on the papacy?

He folded his hands, bowed his head before the great marble statue of the Madonna, and begged for her counsel.

"As you must already know, Holy Mother, my son, Cesare, asks if he can take for a wife a daughter of France. And His Catholic Majesty, Louis the Twelfth, offers to assist him in claiming the lands owed to your church. He will send French soldiers to accompany him in battle."

Alexander wrestled with his thoughts and pondered his choices. If he consented to the marriage of Cesare and Charlotte, must he now cut free not only from Spain and Naples, but his beloved daughter as well? For her husband, Alfonso, was a prince of Naples, and a French alliance would no doubt destroy Lucrezia's marriage. Yet what would happen to his family if he refused France? For surely this king would invade with or without his permission—and install Cardinal della Rovere as Pope.

If the French came through Milan, Alexander was certain, Ludovico would run without a fight. More important, though, once Naples had to take up arms, what would become of his son Jofre and his wife, Sancia?

The Pope searched desperately for just one reason to choose Spain over France, to deny Cesare his French wife. But after kneeling, praying, and pacing for hours, Alexander could find none. On the other hand, if the well-trained French soldiers rode with Cesare to overtake the territories now run by local barons and warlords, he could be crowned duke of the Romagna. The Borgia family would then be safe and the papacy secure.

He stayed all night, watching the flickering candles and pleading for divine inspiration. And when he left the chapel in the early hours of the morning, he had arrived at his decision, though reluctantly.

Duarte Brandao was waiting in the Pope's chambers on his return, for he understood Alexander's struggle.

"Duarte, my friend," the Pope said. "I have considered this as carefully as I am able. And I have come to a conclusion. I need one piece of parchment so that I may pen my reply in order that I may lay my head on a pillow and finally rest."

Duarte watched the Pope sit at his desk, and for the first time he looked aged and tired. He handed the Pope his pen.

Alexander's hand was firm, but his message to Cesare was short. It said only, "My dearest son. Match excellent. Proceed."

The holy city of Rome held great festivities on the day of Cesare Borgia's marriage to Charlotte d'Albret in France. The Pope ordered a huge display of fireworks, a gigantic streaming light show to brighten the sky, and bonfires to be set to lighten the streets. Ah, such jubilation!

Lucrezia, at home in Santa Maria in Portico with Prince Alfonso, watched in horror as one of the largest fires was lit before her palace. Not that she wasn't happy for her brother, for she loved him dearly—but what of her dear husband, for whom this new political alliance could only mean disaster?

When word reached them that Cardinal Ascanio Sforza had fled the city, accompanied by several other cardinals aligned with Naples, Alfonso was filled with fear and confusion about his future.

He pulled Lucrezia into his arms to hold her as he watched the fires rage. "My family is in danger if there is a French invasion," he said softly. "I must go to Naples to command the troops. My father and uncle will need me."

Lucrezia clung tight to him. "But the Holy Father assures me that we will not be in danger, for he will never let political discord interfere with our love."

Alfonso, though only eighteen, looked at Lucrezia with deep sadness. He brushed her hair from her eyes. "And you believe this, my sweet Lucrezia?"

That night, after they made love, they lay awake a long time before Lucrezia was able to fall asleep. And once Alfonso heard the soft sound of her easy breathing, he sneaked out of bed and walked carefully to the stables. There he mounted his horse and made his way south into the countryside, to the castle of the Colonna; from there, in the morning, he would leave for Naples.

But the Pope sent papal police to hound him, and he was forced to stay at the castle or return to Rome, for otherwise he would be carried back by papal troops. Day after day Alfonso wrote Lucrezia, begging her to join him, but his letters never reached her for they fell into the hands of the Vatican messengers and were brought instead to the Pope.

Lucrezia was more unhappy than she had ever been. She could not understand why Alfonso did not write, for she missed him desperately. If she had not been six months pregnant, she would have followed him to Naples. But now she dared not make such a strenuous trip, for she had already lost one baby early in that year, when she had fallen off a horse. And even to attempt such a journey would mean having to sneak out in the night past her father's guards—for they surrounded her palace.

Cesare stayed in France—not only long enough to marry Charlotte, but to spend months with her in a small château in the beautiful Loire Valley.

Charlotte was as beautiful and intelligent as the king had promised, and Cesare finally felt some peace. She radiated a remarkable serenity, and their lovemaking calmed Cesare. But each day he struggled with himself, for in his heart he still longed for Lucrezia.

For a time, Charlotte's presence in his life balanced Cesare's fierce urge to succeed, to achieve, to conquer. The young couple spent days together taking long walks, boating on the placid river, reading together. And they laughed in great measure as Cesare tried to teach Charlotte to swim and to fish.

One evening during this time, Charlotte confessed, "I truly love you as I have loved no other man."

Despite his usual cynicism, Cesare found he believed her—and yet her words did not matter as much as they should. It was puzzling: though he tried to fall in love again, something seemed to be standing in his way. As they spent their nights together making love by the fire and holding each other in comfort, Cesare began to wonder if he had been cursed, as his sister had suggested. Had his father truly sacrificed him to the serpent that first time in the Garden?

On the very night that Charlotte told him she was pregnant with his child, he received an urgent message from the Pope.

"Return to Rome immediately to fulfill your duties," it

read. "The vicars are conspiring, and the Sforza have invited Spain to Italy."

Cesare told Charlotte that he must return to Rome to lead the papal armies, to claim the territories in the Romagna and establish a strong central government for the papacy. Until he secured the Borgia power so completely that it would endure beyond his life and the life of the Pope, she and their children would be in danger. In the meantime, he told her that she and the child she was carrying must remain in France.

On the day Cesare left Charlotte tried to be gracious, but in the end she clung fiercely and tearfully to him as he mounted his horse. He stepped down, held her in his arms, and felt her body tremble. "My dear Lottie," he said, "I'll send for you and the infant as soon as I am able. And have no fear, for there is not an Italian alive who can kill me." He bent and kissed her gently.

Then Cesare mounted his sleek white charger, and with one last wave to Charlotte he rode through the castle gate.

19

Alexander could not bear Lucrezia's tears. And while she wore a brave face in public, each time they were alone she spoke little and then only in the most polite terms. Even his invitation to Julia and Adriana, who brought Lucrezia's firstborn to stay with her, didn't seem to lift her despair. Now, most evenings, they all sat in silence. He missed their lively conversations, and Lucrezia's enthusiasm—its absence weighed on him.

Lucrezia once again felt helpless to change her destiny, and though she did not blame her father for his alliance with France, she understood her husband's need to aid his family. Still, she mourned the truth—that because of political differences, she and her unborn babe were forced to do without Alfonso. It seemed an impossible plight. She tried to reason with her heart, but it refused all reason. And she asked herself one hundred times each day why her dear husband did not send a message.

After several weeks of witnessing his daughter's despair, Alexander was beside himself. And so he devised a plan that he believed might help. Lucrezia was an intelligent woman, gracious and blessed with many of his own leadership qualities. She certainly had inherited his charm, even if it had not been apparent of late.

Nonetheless, in his larger plan, he had always considered granting her some territories in the Romagna—once Cesare had conquered them—and so he reasoned that some practice in governing would provide an advantage in the future and take her mind off her immediate distress. That foolish husband of hers was still ensconced in the Colonna castle, stubbornly refusing to return to Rome. There was no question that he missed his wife, but having heard nothing from her in months, he believed she had forsaken him. The Pope was obliged to send Cervillon, the Spanish captain who held the sword over them at their wedding ceremony, to enlist the help of the king of Naples to recover Alfonso.

Of all this emotion Alexander was impatient. Though he was anything but stoic in his own love life, his suffering seemed more worthy than the suffering of these two young people. For God knows how many more lovers each would have in a lifetime! If one suffered over each to the same degree, there would be no time left to do one's work, or God's.

And so, after much deliberation and discussion with Duarte, Alexander determined that he would send Lucrezia to rule over the land called Nepi, a beautiful territory he had reclaimed from Cardinal Ascanio Sforza once he had fled to Naples.

Because Lucrezia was in the late stages of her pregnancy, Alexander knew they must take special care and allow more time for her journey. He would offer a large envoy to accompany her, a golden-covered litter in the event that riding her horse became too uncomfortable. He would send Michelotto to guard her in the early weeks and to make certain the territory was safe. Of course, she must also have an advisor when she arrived in Nepi, to teach her to govern.

Pope Alexander knew there were some in the church who would object, for she was, after all, a woman. But Lucrezia had been born and raised to statesmanship, and there was no reason to let her waste her gifts just because she had not been born a man. The Borgia blood coursed through her veins, and so her gifts must be utilized.

He felt no such fondness for his youngest son, Jofre, and was in fact quite angry with his wife, Sancia. Of course he realized that some of his ill will was due to his extreme displeasure at her uncle, the king of Naples, whose daughter

Rosetta refused to marry the Pope's son. It was an unbeliev-able arrogance. What gall! Moreover, Alexander was not fooled. He understood that a king could order his daughter to marry Cesare, and yet he had not. So it was the king, he concluded, who had rejected his son.

Sancia, the princess from Naples that his youngest son had married, was always a stubborn, willful girl; even more to the point, she had not yet given Jofre an heir. She was a seductress as well. They all would have fared far better had Jofre become the cardinal and Cesare become Sancia's hus-band—for he, no doubt, could have tamed her.

Alexander now called seventeen-year-old Jofre into his chambers. His son entered with a broad smile on his pleas-ant face, and though he did not complain, he was limping badly.

"What has happened?" Alexander asked him, without his usual concern or even a perfunctory embrace.

"It is nothing, Father," Jofre answered, head bowed. "I was injured in the thigh while fencing."

Alexander tried to keep himself from sounding impatient, but incompetence made him irritable.

Jofre had blond hair and an open countenance. His eyes did not hold the sparkling intelligence of his sister's, the dark glow of cunning his brother Juan's had had, or the fiery ambition one could see in the eyes of Cesare. In fact when the Pope looked into this son's eyes he saw nothing, and that he found disconcerting.

"I wish you to accompany your sister to Nepi," Alexander said. "She will need the company of someone she cares about, and some protection. She is a woman alone, about to bear a child, and she must have a man present she can count on."

Jofre smiled and nodded his head. "I will enjoy that, Your Holiness," he said. "And my wife will enjoy it, for she is quite fond of Lucrezia, and she is due a change of scenery."

Alexander watched to see if the expression on his son's face would change when he dealt him the next blow, though he was willing to bet that it wouldn't. "I said nothing about your wife, as you call her, accompanying you. She will not be going, for I have other plans where she is concerned."

"I will tell her," Jofre said dully, "but I am certain she will not be pleased."

Alexander smiled, for he had expected nothing from this son and his son had not disappointed.

One could not say the same, however, for Sancia. That afternoon, the moment she heard the news, she raged at Jofre. "Will you never become more my husband and less your father's son?" she shouted.

Jofre studied her, puzzled by her words. "He is not only my father," Jofre defended. "He is the Holy Father as well. There is more at stake if I refuse to obey him."

"There is more at stake if he forces me to stay and you to go, Jofre," Sancia warned, and then she began to cry with frustration. "I hated marrying you when I was made to, but now I've actually grown fond of you—and still you let your father keep you from me?"

Jofre smiled, but for the first time it was a cunning smile. "There were times where you were more than willing to be kept away . . . times you spent with my brother Juan."

Sancia stood perfectly still and stopped her tears. "You were a child, and I was lonely. Juan comforted me; it was nothing more."

Jofre remained calm. "I believe you loved him, for you cried more at his funeral than any other."

Sancia said, "Don't be a fool, Jofre. I cried because I was frightened for myself. I have never believed your brother died at the hands of a stranger."

Jofre looked alert. His eyes took on a look of cold intelligence and he looked taller, his shoulders broader, his stance stronger. "And are you suggesting then that you know who killed my dear brother?" he asked.

In that moment, Sancia recognized that something had changed about her husband. He now stood as someone completely different from the boy she knew. She moved toward him, and reached up to put her arms around his neck. "Don't let him send you away from me," she pleaded. "Tell him I must be with you."

Jofre stroked her hair and kissed her on the nose. "You may tell him," Jofre said, realizing then that after all this time he was still angry about her and Juan. "Say whatever you must, and let us see if you fare any better than the others who tried to argue with the Holy Father."

And so Sancia took herself over to the Pope's chambers and demanded an audience with him.

Alexander was sitting on his throne when she entered, having just finished a discussion with the ambassador from Venice, who left him in quite a foul humor.

Sancia stood before him, after the smallest of bows and without the kiss of respect to his ring or his holy foot. But for what he was about to do, he could forgive her those small slights.

Sancia spoke without waiting for permission, for after all she was the daughter and the granddaughter of kings. On this particular day she more closely resembled her grandfather, King Ferrante, than any other; her black hair was free and loose, unkempt and unrestrained. Her green eyes were penetrating, her voice accusing, when she spoke. "What is this I hear? I am not being sent with my husband and his sister to Nepi? Am I meant to stay in the Vatican without the company of those I enjoy?"

Alexander yawned deliberately. "You are meant, my dear, to do as you are requested, which is something that apparently does not come easily to you."

Sancia stamped her foot in a rage she could not control. This time he had gone too far. "Jofre is my husband, and I am his wife. My place is with him, for it is to him that I owe my loyalty."

The Pope laughed, but his eyes were steely. "My dear Sancia. You belong in Naples. With that foolhardy uncle of yours, in the land of that animal who was your grandfather, Ferrante. And I will send you there at once if you do not hold your tongue."

"You do not frighten me, Your Holiness," she said. "For I believe in a power higher than yours. And it is to my God that I pray."

"Beware of your words, child," Alexander warned. "For I can have you hanged or burned for heresy, and then your reunion with your dear husband will take even longer."

Sancia's jaw was set tight, and she was angry to the point of recklessness. "I will cause a scandal and you can burn me, if you wish, but that will not keep me from telling the truth. For nothing in Rome is what it seems, and the truth shall be known."

When Alexander stood, he was such an imposing figure that Sancia instinctively backed away. In a moment she regained her composure, marshaled her will, and held her ground. But when she refused to look down, to be intimidated by the Pope's holy gaze, he became infuriated with her. If his son couldn't tame her, then he would. "You will leave for Naples tomorrow," the Pope said. "And you will carry a message from me to the king. Tell him if he wants nothing of mine, I want nothing of his."

Before she left, with the smallest of escorts and almost no money to take on her trip, she told Jofre, "Your father has more enemies than you know. This will come to a bad end one day. I only pray that I am here to see it."

King Louis, clothed in rich brocade embroidered with golden bees, rode into Milan with Cesare at his side. They were accompanied by Cardinal della Rovere, Cardinal d'Amboise, the duke of Ferrara, Ercole d'Este, and a force of forty thousand occupation troops.

Ludovico Sforza, Il Moro, had reduced himself to poverty hiring mercenary soldiers, but they were no match for the skilled soldiers of the French army. Knowing his defeat was near, Ludovico had sent his two sons and his brother, Ascanio, to Germany to be placed under the protection of his sister's husband, the Emperor Maximilian.

And so it was that after an easy victory King Louis of France was declared the true duke of Milan. And for his help in the invasion, the king was thankful for the Pope's blessings—as well as for the help of his son Cesare.

In his inspection of the city, the first place the king visited was the great Sforza castle. There he searched for the oaken chests with the special locking devices designed by Leonardo da Vinci, which were rumored to be filled with precious jewels and gold. On opening them, the king found them empty. It appeared that Ludovico took the best of the jewels, and over 240,000 ducats, with him as he fled. But still there was enough of value left in the fortress to impress King Louis with the grandeur of Ludovico's court—from the Sforza stables, with their dazzling and detailed portraits of prize horses, to Leonardo's wall painting of the Last Supper in the Monastery of Santa Maria.

Yet the king took no notice when his archers used Leonardo's marvelous clay statue of a horse, stationed in the square, for target practice, destroying it completely. The cultured citizens of Milan thought the French soldiers barbarians, for they spit on the floors of the castles and laid waste to the streets.

Had the territories of the Romagna been unified, Louis's invasion of Italy might have been stopped there. But they were not. And so Alexander knew this was his moment to set claim to them, for they were, after all, Papal States, and it was only due to his generosity and indulgence that their greedy warlords had been able to rule them for this long.

Now Cesare had only to overthrow the petty princes to conquer the rest of the territories in the Papal States, in order to unify Italy and bring glory and riches to his family and Rome.

In Nepi, Lucrezia threw herself wholeheartedly into her administrative duties. She set up a lawmaking body, and a force of police to implement those laws and keep peace in the streets. As her father had done, each Thursday he was in

Rome, she invited the citizens into the castle to voice their discontents, and then did all she could to remedy those situations. She seemed to have a talent for ruling and her citizens became quite fond of her.

During this time Jofre was a comfort to Lucrezia when she longed for Alfonso, and she was a comfort to him. For Jofre was despondent over Sancia, difficult as she sometimes was. As Lucrezia learned to govern, Jofre hunted and rode through the beautiful countryside and the days grew easier for both of them.

As a reward for her excellence and service, one month after Lucrezia arrived in Nepi, the Pope managed to convince Alfonso to join her. For this, he generously bestowed upon the young couple the city, the castle, and the lands surrounding Nepi. The two young lovers were so filled with ecstasy at being together again that neither of them asked what the Pope wished in return.

Alexander gave Lucrezia and Alfonso several weeks before he paid them a visit. He could give them no more time, for there was none to give. On his second day in Nepi, during a sumptuous family lunch, the Pope asked Lucrezia if she would be willing to return to Rome to have her baby. He was most convincing when he explained that he was getting on in age, and having a new grandson would bring him great pleasure. Filled with happiness at being with her husband again, and relieved at the prospect of being with Julia and Adriana, she agreed to go. Having vowed that they would never again part, Alfonso agreed to go with her.

Lucrezia returned to Rome with her husband, Alfonso, and her brother Jofre, and found that the Pope had sent a musical band, mimes, and jugglers to meet them at the gates.

While she had been gone, Lucrezia's Palace of Santa Maria in Portico had been decorated with rich hangings of silk and intricate tapestries. The Pope himself wasted no time in coming to greet her and welcome her back. "What a happy day," he exclaimed, embracing her, until even in her delicate condition she was lifted off her feet. "My dear daughter returns, and before too long my son Cesare will arrive, a conquering hero." He even gave Jofre a reluctant embrace, for he could hardly restrain himself. On this day, he felt all of his prayers had been answered.

Shortly afterward his joy was unbounded when he received news of Cesare's invasion of Milan. Within a short time Lucrezia gave birth to a healthy baby boy, called Rodrigo in honor of her father, and Alexander was so exhilarated that an episode of syncope forced him to bed for the day. But the moment he recovered he began to prepare for the child's baptism.

20

Cesare Borgia, dressed in black armor and mounted on a magnificent white charger, met his commanders at the gates outside Bologna. There the army of Swiss and German mercenaries, Italian artillerymen, and Spanish officers were joined by a large contingent of veteran French troops.

The king had kept his promise.

With his standard bearer just behind him flying the white banner emblazoned with the charging Borgia bull, Cesare's army of fifteen thousand soldiers snaked its way down the Bologna-Rimini road toward the cities of Imola and Forli.

The golden bull carved on Cesare's black chestplate shone bright in the noonday sun. His new armor was made light to allow greater freedom and still offer vital protection. Now he could fight effectively even on foot if he were dismounted.

Cesare's men, heavily armored and atop powerful horses, were efficient fighting machines, difficult to stop and fearsome to oppose. His light cavalry was protected by chain mail and tough seasoned leather, armed with swords and lethal lances.

The infantry was made up of hardy Swiss soldiers with frightening ten-foot pikes, Italian troopers with various weapons, and swarthy Germans bearing crossbows and small-caliber long guns.

But the most devastating weapon of Cesare's entire arsenal was Captain Vito Vitelli's powerful Italian artillery.

Imola and Forli had always been a source of trouble in the

Romagna. These two lands had once been ruled by Girolamo Riario, the rude and brutish heir of a powerful north-
ern Italian family and the son of old Pope Sixtus. Girolamo
had married Caterina Sforza, a niece of Milan's Ludovico
Sforza, when she was only a girl. When Girolamo was murdered twelve years later, Caterina had grown up and grown
angry; instead of retiring to a convent, she mounted her
horse and led her soldiers in swift pursuit of her husband's
killers.

When they were captured and brought before her, Caterina exacted a fierce and terrible revenge on the aristocratic
assassins. She sliced off their genitals, lifted them with her
own hand to place them in a linen handkerchief, and, with
ribbons she had taken from her hair, tied their penises
around their necks, for she thought them a breed not to be
encouraged.

"These lands are mine," she said, standing over them. "I
had no wish to be a widow." Then she stayed to watch as
the blood from their bodies spilled onto the ground in
small spidery veins of red until the murderers turned stiff
and cold. Ah, what she would have done had she truly
loved him.

Immediately upon her return, Caterina had claimed both
Imola and Forli in the name of her son, Otto Riario, a godson of Pope Alexander. Once word spread throughout the
towns and territories of her ruthless punishment, Caterina
became as famous for her ferocity as she was for her
beauty. For truly she was as vicious as any warrior—and as
feminine as any duchess. Her long blond hair framed a
fine-featured face; her skin, as soft as sable, was her pride;
and though she was taller than many men, she was a beautiful woman. She spent much of her time with her children,
and for enjoyment she often created special salves for her
flawless pale skin, bleaches for her ash-blond hair, and lo-
tions for her large, firm breasts which she often displayed
almost uncovered. She used charcoal to shine her even
white teeth, and it was said that she kept a book in which

she journaled all her magic spells. It was well-known in the villages that she had an appetite for sensual pleasure that could equal any man's. She was, in Renaissance terms, a true virago—a woman to admire for her courage and culture, a testimony to her powerful steely mind and unscrupulous will.

When she married again—and her second husband was also murdered—she again took a furious revenge. This time she had the limbs torn from the bodies of the assassins, and then hacked their remains to pieces.

Three years later she had married Giovanni Medici, and together they had a son. Bando Neir was the name of the babe, and he was her favorite child. She enjoyed having Gio as a husband; even his ugliness appealed to her, for in the night, and in the bedchamber, he was more of a man than any she'd known. But in the year just passed she had again become a widow. Caterina was now thirty-six years old, and so fierce that she had become known as the She-Wolf.

Caterina Sforza despised the Borgia family for their betrayal of her after her husband Riario died, and had no intention of allowing them to take control of the territories that she and her son Otto Riario ruled. Months before, she had received the papal bull demanding the monies that were owed in taxes for her territories, and accusing her of withholding tithes to the Pope and the church. Having foreseen this papal ploy, Caterina sent her tithe in advance, and in full, to Rome by special messenger. But still Alexander was determined to claim her lands for the Romagna. And so she prepared for battle.

Her informers, well paid but not loyal, brought her word that Cesare was leading the army to conquer her cities. She in turn sent a gift to the Pope—a black shroud from a corpse who had died of the plague, which she twisted tight and placed in a hollowed-out cane. When Alexander opened her gift, she hoped, the sickness would befall him, and he would give up his plans for this conquest. But under torture her informers informed on her, and so while they were put to death, the Pope was saved.

Cesare's plan was first to take Imola, then Forli.
      As the papal army neared Imola, Cesare marshaled his troops, moved the artillery forward, and used the light cavalry and infantry as a barrier. Then he rode ahead with a special battalion of armed soldiers.

But his preparation was unnecessary, for as he approached, the gates of the city swung open and a worried group of citizens rushed forward. In an attempt to spare themselves and their city from being sacked, robbed, and pillaged by the papal army, they quickly surrendered.

Caterina Sforza, because of her well-known cruelty and ferociousness, was not a popular or beloved ruler. Her subjects had nothing to gain by fighting for her. On the first day two French lancers discovered a local carpenter who had been wronged by Caterina, and wanted his revenge. He asked to meet with Cesare. Hoping to spare himself, he eagerly pointed out the weakest points in the structure of the castle walls.

But there was a small fortress inside the city, and its commander, Dion Naldi, was a true soldier. Now he called out from the rooftop, "We will fight!"

And so Cesare's army prepared for a siege.

Vito Vitelli, the Italian commander, moved his cannons to the front line, readied his troops, and began to bombard the castle walls with continuous shots. Realizing his peril, Dion Naldi called a truce, and announced that if help hadn't arrived within three days he would surrender the city.

Knowing that negotiation would save both money and lives, Cesare set up camp, and for three days they waited.

No help came. Naldi, a skilled officer from a famous fighting family, also bore a grudge, and so he threw down his guns and dismissed his men. He would have fought till his death if he felt some loyalty to his ruler; but even now, as he stood in defense of her castle, Caterina Sforza held his wife and children hostage in the citadel at Forli. Naldi surrendered Imola, on one condition: that he himself could join Cesare and the papal forces when they rode into Forli.

Therefore Cesare Borgia accomplished the first goal of his campaign without losing a man . . . or facing Caterina Sforza.

Forli held Caterina's principal fortress, and it was there that Cesare would have to face the She-Wolf herself. The son of the Pope was younger and had much less experience than the ferocious Caterina and so he approached the gates with some caution. But once again the gates swung open, and a crowd of citizens rushed out to announce their surrender.

Atop the ramparts of the castle, Caterina Sforza stood dressed in full armor, wielding a sword with one hand and holding a falcon on the other. All along the rooftops her archers stood, their arrows set, their bows poised.

The moment Caterina saw her citizens with Cesare she became enraged, and shouted to her soldiers, "Shoot the citizens! Shoot the lily-livered cowards who abandon our good city!"

Arrows flew like flocks of birds, and her subjects fell at Cesare's feet.

"My God," Cesare said, turning to Vitelli. "The woman is mad. She is slaying her own people."

One of her commanders shouted from a tower window that the countess wished to meet with Cesare Borgia, to negotiate a peaceful surrender.

"Cross the drawbridge," the commander shouted. "The countess will meet you in the sheltered pathway."

Cesare watched the drawbridge slowly descend and the castle gates swing open. He and the Spanish captain, Porto Díaz, began to walk through the gates, but when Cesare looked up through the wide opening in the wooden roof above the entrance, he thought he heard something scurrying above them. Suddenly, he turned around in time to see several of Caterina's men raising the drawbridge. He turned back to see the iron grate dropping in front of him.

Cesare grabbed for Porto Díaz and shouted, "Be quick. A trap!"

He leapt atop the giant steel-toothed pulley that raised the bridge. It was only inches from crushing him as the bridge swung shut, and in a fit of daring Cesare dove sideways into the moat below. Dozens of crossbows shot heavy iron spearheads into the water, barely missing him as he desperately swam toward the far bank.

Three swarthy Swiss soldiers cursed Caterina loudly as they pulled Cesare from the water.

But Porto Díaz was not so lucky. He was trapped between the iron grating and the closed drawbridge. As soon as Cesare was on land again, Caterina ordered boiling oil to be poured upon Díaz from the opening in the roof above. Standing on the bank, Cesare listened to his bloodcurdling screams and vowed Caterina would not escape without punishment for the torture of this good captain.

Cesare knew she would not surrender without a deadly battle. And so he retreated to his camp to make a plan. Finally, after several hours, he believed he had a surprise that might change her mind. Two of her children had been captured in Imola, and he brought them to the bank of the moat in sight of the castle.

He called to her, "Caterina, I have something here that is yours."

She looked down to see him, and he pointed to her children.

"If this castle is not surrendered, and the torture of my commander stopped immediately, I will slaughter these children right before your eyes."

In the dim twilight, with the falling orange sun behind her, Caterina emerged, a dark shadow. She laughed raucously, and her laughter echoed menacingly. Then she lifted her skirt up to her chestplate to expose herself.

"Look, you son of a whore," she shouted at Cesare, and then pointed at her loins. "Do you see this? Go ahead and destroy them: I have the mold. I can make more children— many more—so do what you must."

Just then Caterina waved her arm, and Cesare heard a splash. The headless, scalded body of Porto Díaz had been thrown into the moat.

And so it was that Cesare Borgia, duke of Valentinois and son of the Pope, ordered the bombardment to begin. Vito Vitelli's cannons fired round after round at the castle walls.

In the dark of night, Dino Naldi approached him. "Are you going to order the children killed?" he asked Cesare.

Cesare looked surprised; he had forgotten. Quickly, he reassured Naldi. "It was only a threat. And it would have worked with any normal mother. Then we could have saved many lives. Now, because of this crazy woman, those lives will be lost. But killing two children won't serve. Take them away."

"What shall I do with them?" Naldi asked.

"Keep them," he said. "Raise them as your own."

Naldi smiled in gratitude, and crossed himself in prayer. Why they called this man a monster he could not imagine, for the woman who now held his sons was far worse indeed.

As soon as the sun appeared the following morning, Cesare bombarded the fortress. Still, Caterina stood on the ramparts brandishing her sword. Cesare turned away and ordered his men to cut nearby trees, to build square rafts to transport them.

"Each must hold thirty soldiers," he shouted. "For when the walls are breached, these will carry our soldiers across the moat."

The end did not come quickly. But finally the stone balls shot by Vitelli's cannons broke through the fortress wall, and Cesare heard the shout: "A breach! A breach!" The north wall had crumbled.

The French captain led his soldiers onto the rafts that

were already floating in the moat. Paddling rapidly, with their weapons at the ready, they disembarked and sent the rafts back to be reloaded. In all, more than three hundred of Cesare's men stormed the castle.

Once his soldiers lowered the drawbridge, Cesare and his men galloped across the bridge and into the castle, shouting, *"Attack!"*

It was then that Caterina, from her perch on the rooftop, took note of the stock of munitions and gunpowder heaped in great mounds in the center of the fortress. With all her might she dislodged one of the fiery torches from the ramparts, and tossed it into the hill of gunpowder. She would blow herself and her city up rather than fall captive to this enemy! The explosion rocked the castle, destroyed homes and shops, and killed over four hundred citizens of Forli. But Cesare and many of his soldiers remained unharmed. Caterina's soldiers emerged from the rooftops, towers, balconies, and other embankments. Wounded and bedraggled, they surrendered, relieved by Cesare's victory.

Unfortunately for her, Caterina Sforza was not injured. Instead she was taken hostage by the French captain, who later that night, over a card game after dinner, ransomed her to Cesare for thirty thousand ducats.

Caterina Sforza now belonged to Cesare Borgia, and he could do with her what he wished.

After supper, Cesare took a long, hot bath and then dressed in his black silk robe, retrieved for him from his baggage. The master bedroom of the castle in Forli had remained intact, and now he lay on the bed considering what he would do with Caterina.

She was at this very moment a captive in a small darkened room in the basement of the castle, guarded by two of Cesare's most trusted guards. He had given them explicit instruction not to take their eyes off her for a moment.

At midnight, still clad in his robe, Cesare walked down to

the cellar. He heard her ranting, screaming, and cursing before he ever saw her. He walked into the small damp room, dimly lit with one candle. Caterina lay on her back in an iron bed, each of her wrists and ankles pulled tight to the sides of the bedstead. Tied and chained, the She-Wolf was tossing her head furiously from side to side.

Cesare stood silently before her, and the moment Caterina saw him she stopped shouting. Instead she raised her head as far as she was able, and spit at him with all her might. But he remained just out of reach.

"My dear Countess," Cesare said charmingly. "You could have saved yourself and your people from coming to harm, had you the capacity for reason."

She turned her face and stared into his eyes, her own a startling blue. Then her beautiful face became contorted with rage, and with a venomous voice she challenged him. "What kind of torture do you save for a woman, you cowardly piece of Roman shit?"

"I will show you," he answered, his voice cold.

Cesare shed his robe and climbed upon her, forcing himself into her slowly at first, then thrusting forward and upward as he penetrated her deeply. He waited to hear her screams, her curses, but she was silent. And the only sound in the room was the mumbling of the standing Roman guards.

Cesare continued now as though in a rage, plunging into her with thrust after powerful thrust, until suddenly she began to move along with him. Her full hips lifted, her pelvis pushing toward him, and he began to believe he was bringing her pleasure. Cesare continued to ravish her, for he was certain of his victory over her. And when he finished her cheeks were flushed, and her hair was soaked with sweat.

"You should thank me," he said as he moved off her.

She looked at him with blue eyes blazing. "Is that all you have to give me?" she asked.

Cesare stormed out of the room. But on the next two

nights Cesare visited Caterina at midnight and repeated the same silent act of conquest. The results remained the same. Afterward, her cheeks flushed and her body slick with sweat, she would ask, "Is that all you have for me?"

He determined to continue in the same fashion until she surrendered. But on the third night, some minutes after Cesare entered her and began his thrusts, she commanded, "Untie me, for otherwise there is no contest."

Caterina lay naked; she could conceal no weapons. And his two guards, large and muscular, stood in the room. So what danger could there be? Cesare himself removed her chains, and then gently untied her bands. She nodded in thanks, and for the first time her eyes softened. Then he mounted her. And she wrapped first her legs and then her arms around him, pulling him deeper inside her. She pulled his head back by his hair and ran her tongue around his lips, then she kissed him, and her tongue penetrated him so deeply that his entire body trembled. Moments later Caterina began to make small sounds of pleasure that drove him nearly mad with ecstasy. In minutes they brought each other to a shuddering climax.

The following day, Caterina refused to eat unless she was permitted a fragrant bath. She was taken to the tubs in chains and washed by one of the ladies-in-waiting who had survived the explosion, but that was the only time Caterina left the bed.

Each night for the next two weeks, Cesare came at midnight and mounted Caterina. Halfway through he would untie her, and she would embrace him again. The guards remained, for Cesare could never be certain that in a moment of passion or rage she wouldn't try to gouge his eyes out, but both Cesare and Caterina ignored them. Then one night, the two violent lovers began to speak.

"You must admit that even rape can be pleasurable," Cesare said.

Caterina laughed and said slyly, "You believe you raped

me? You are wrong, you Roman bastard, son of a Pope. Standing on the rampart of the castle, that first moment I saw you, I was determined either to kill you or to rape you. If I had captured you, I would have tied you up, just as you did me. And then I would have mounted you. But no matter; the result is the same."

Caterina had a true gift for strategy. By claiming his will as her own, she had shifted the balance of power. And so, without a weapon, Caterina had effectively disarmed him. For now Cesare felt as much the vanquished as the victor.

The day they were to leave for Rome, Caterina asked Cesare a question. "Will you lead me in heavy chains through the streets of the city like a captured queen, so your citizens can jeer and abuse me as they did in ancient Rome?"

Cesare laughed. Caterina looked quite beautiful on that day, especially for someone who had been kept in a dungeon. "It hadn't occurred to me," he said, "but . . ."

"I know, you will burn me at a stake instead, for my attempt on the Pope's life," Caterina said. "Such fools I chose for messengers."

"The Pope's life is often threatened," Cesare said. "He seldom takes umbrage at that, especially if the plot is foiled. But if that is his intention, to hang you or burn you for heresy, I will assure him that you have been punished by me each day since your capture."

"And he would believe you?" she asked.

"He would consider it rape, and would find that more severe a punishment than death, for he believes that rape causes injury to the soul, and he loves women as I have never," Cesare admitted.

Caterina smiled wryly. "But one would have to believe in a soul to believe in its injury."

"Ah, and that the Pope does," Cesare said, smiling. "In the

meantime, as you are a Sforza, after all, I've made arrangements for you to be held in Belvedere. Without chains. That
castle belongs to me. It has lovely gardens and a wonderful
view of the city. You will be treated as an honored guest—
well guarded, of course."

21

Cesare entered Rome a conquering hero. The grand procession celebrating his victory was the most dramatic the citizens of Rome had ever seen. All Cesare's men-at-arms, his light cavalrymen, and his Swiss pikemen were dressed in stark black; even the wagons of his baggage train were draped with black cloth. And Cesare, wearing jet-black armor, rode at the head of his army accompanied by four cardinals, whose red and purple vestments formed a perfect contrast. To applaud his triumph even the charging bull of the Borgia was emblazoned in red on a banner of black, rather than its customary white. Astride a sleek black stallion, Cesare appeared the regal dark prince.

The procession made its way through the throngs of citizens who lined the streets to the Vatican. There Cesare greeted his father in Spanish as he knelt to kiss the papal ring, and present the Pope with the keys to the cities and castles he had conquered.

Alexander, his face glowing with pride, lifted Cesare to his feet, and embraced his son warmly before the delighted crowd.

Immediately after the procession, Cesare took leave of his father and made his way to his apartments at the Vatican.

Cesare himself had changed dramatically in the time he was away. Once he had grasped that the laughter on the faces of the French was because they thought him a fool, once he had tried to charm Rosetta and failed, and once he discovered that even his happiness with his wife was tainted by his memory of his sister, he vowed to hide his emotions. From that day forward his face rarely broke into a smile, and his eyes gave no hint of his anger.

Alas, his face. Cesare had suffered another severe attack of the French pox of late, and this time the disease dug deep holes in his cheeks and burrowed into his nose and forehead, leaving several round scars that would not fade. On the battlefield, this did not matter, but in the city, at a celebration, or when bedding down with courtesans, it was a curse. At twenty-five years of age, Cesare Borgia was accustomed to being praised and admired for his good looks; now he felt a loss. He covered every mirror in his chambers with black cloth, and warned the servants never to remove it.

The night terrors returned, and so to stave off his fears he slept in the day and worked throughout the night. Again, he spent many hours riding through the countryside enveloped in darkness.

Now he could wait no longer to see Lucrezia. He had been away so long. Her face had been the vision he'd followed into his victories.

Almost two years had passed since they had been together, and he wondered if she had changed. Would she still have the same effect upon him after all this time, after his marriage to Lottie and hers to Alfonso? In his heart Cesare held the hope that Lucrezia would have grown tired of her husband, for now that the papal alliances had changed, Alfonso was in fact a threat to the Borgia family.

Many thoughts filled his mind as he waited to be admitted to Lucrezia's chambers. Though he was reckless to the point of danger in his daily life and seemed concerned about nothing, now he worried. What would his sister think? Would she love him less?

The moment Lucrezia saw her brother she rushed to embrace him, throwing her arms around his neck and hiding her face on his chest. "Good God, I have missed you so," she said, with tears in her eyes.

When she lifted her head to look at him, she felt no shock,

just heartbreak at what had befallen him. She held his face in her hands. "My dear Chez, how life has treated you . . ."

Self-conscious, he looked away. His heart still raced as it had before, and as it had with no one else.

"You look well, Crezia," he said softly, and he could not keep his eyes from showing how he felt. "Are you still as happy?"

She took his hand and led him to the couch. "Only heaven could bring me greater joy," she said. "For with my babies, and Alfonso, I feel such happiness as I have never known, and I live in fear that I will soon wake from this beguiling dream."

He felt himself stiffen. "I have visited with young Giovanni. And I see our son resembles you more than myself," he said. "His blond curls and light eyes give him away."

"But not completely," Lucrezia said, laughing. "He has your lips, he has your smile, and he has your hands, like Papa's." She held his hands up to show him. "Adriana brings him from your quarters each day, and since you have been gone I have had the pleasure of seeing him often. He is an intelligent and reasonable child, though he also has your sudden bursts of temper." She laughed, and he could see the pleasure on her face.

"And your own child?" he asked. "Are you as pleased with him?"

Her face radiant, her blond hair in ringlets on her forehead and cheeks, Lucrezia nodded. "Rodrigo is but an infant; who can tell who he will be. But he is as beautiful as his father, and as sweet."

Cesare looked at his sister warily. "So, you remain content with your husband?"

Lucrezia knew she must be careful in her answer. If she tried to reassure her brother by hinting that she was unhappy, Alfonso would lose her protection and could wind up losing his freedom. But if she said she loved her husband too much, he might lose even more. "Alfonso is a good and virtuous man," she said. "And he is kind to me and the children."

Cesare's tone was measured. "And if Papa would try to annul this marriage, would you consent?"

Lucrezia frowned. "Cesare, if Papa would consider such a thing, tell him I would rather die. I will not live in this world without Alfonso. . . . as I would not want to live without you."

When Cesare left her that day, he was filled with confusion. He found it difficult to accept her love for her husband, yet was comforted that she still professed her love for him.

That night, lying in his bed with only the glow of the moon shining through his window to light his room, he recalled the way she looked, her fragrant smell, and the words she had spoken. It was then that he reflected on her almost imperceptible grimace when she first saw his face. And he heard her voice filled with pity when she said, "My dear Chez, how life has treated you . . ." He knew then that she had seen both the scars on his face, and the deeper scars of his soul.

And so he vowed from that day forward that he would cover his face with a mask, to cover the toll of his life. He swore that he would clothe himself in mystery, and that he would continue to wage war—not *for* his father's God, but *on* his father's God.

One month after Cesare's arrival in Rome, in a solemn ceremony, the Pope stood as Vicar of Christ, clothed in his finest vestments at the magnificently adorned altar of Saint Peter's Basilica.

Cesare Borgia, the French duke of Valentinois, stood before him. The duke's mantle was removed, and the Pope placed the cloak of the *Gonfaloniere* and captain general of the papal army on Cesare's shoulders, while on his head was placed the crimson biretta. Finally, he was handed the commander's baton.

Cesare knelt before Pope Alexander and with his hand on

the Bible swore the oath of obedience, vowing that he would never conspire against the Holy Father to do him or his successors any harm, and that even under torture or fear of death he would not reveal any of the Pope's secrets.

And so it was that Alexander blessed him with the Golden Rose, and intoned, "Receive this rose as a symbol of joy, dear son, for you have shown the virtues of both nobility and courage. May the Heavenly Father bless you and keep you safe from harm!"

Later, in a private meeting in the Pope's chambers, with Duarte Brandao as the only witness, Alexander told his son that he was granting him additional territories and income. "We reward you in this way due to our respect for your victories. And so it follows that we must discuss the resumption of the campaign. It is true that now Imola and Forli are ours, but Faenza, Pesaro, Camerino, and even Urbino are left to be conquered. As captain general you must subdue them, for we must establish the status of the papacy, and create an effective government in order to ensure a united Romagna."

And with that Alexander retired to his quarters, for he had made arrangements with his favorite courtesan.

The jubilee occurred only once every twenty-five years, and so Alexander reasoned that there would be only one grand celebration during his reign as Pope. Because it brought enormous revenue—as pilgrims from all over Europe filled the city of Rome to hear the Easter sermon of the Pope—preparations had to be made to ensure the filling of the coffers of the Holy Catholic Church. The papacy must receive the greatest benefit, for the money would be used to finance the campaign.

Pope Alexander wanted the jubilee to be magnificent, to be so splendid that it would reflect the majesty of God. Therefore, he had much to do. He must build new avenues, broad and clean for carriages to travel upon. The slums must be torn down, and new buildings constructed to harbor the pilgrims in safety and comfort.

Alexander called Cesare into his chambers and asked him to take charge of the project, for it was to his benefit to make this jubilee as financially successful as possible.

Cesare agreed, but then brought his father some unpleasant news. "I have received reliable reports that two men in your service are disloyal to you. The first is the papal master of ceremonies, Johannes Burchard."

"And what have you heard about Herr Burchard?" Alexander asked.

Cesare cleared his throat before he said, "That he is in the pay of Cardinal della Rovere, and that he keeps a diary filled with lies about our family, some quite scandalous."

Alexander smiled slyly. "I've known about that diary for quite a long time, but Burchard is a valuable man."

Cesare asked, "Valuable?"

Alexander explained, "His official duties as social secretary are frivolous. His real value to me is that anything I want della Rovere to know, I tell Burchard. It's a marvelous and efficient system, and so far has served me well."

"Have you read the diary?" Cesare asked.

Alexander laughed out loud. "I have. In secret, for some time now. Portions of it are quite interesting, for were we as depraved as he has made us out to be, we should be having far more enjoyment. Other portions border on the ridiculous, for they show a true lack of intelligence. Some are laughable."

Cesare frowned. "I'm certain that della Rovere plans someday to release it as a true record of your papacy. You're not concerned?"

Alexander's eyes were wise and clear. "Cesare, there are so many scandalmongers in place paid by our enemies, one more won't make a difference."

"Yet you could stop them," Cesare said.

The Pope was thoughtful for several minutes before he

answered. "Rome is a free city, my son," he said. "And I value freedom."

Cesare looked with suspicion at his father. "Slanderers and liars remain free, Father, while those who rule and serve remain unable to defend themselves? For no one believes the truth. If it were me who had to judge the scandalmongers I would punish them severely; they would not get away with such scandalous lies and insults."

Pope Alexander was amused by his son's outrage. As though a Pope could keep people from forming an opinion and recording their thoughts! Better to know what they say than to have it hidden. "Freedom is not a right but a privilege, and one I choose at this time to bestow on Burchard. There may come a time when my mind is changed, but for now the idea of freedom appeals to me."

When Cesare told his father about the next accusation he was disturbed, for he knew what it would mean to his sister. "I have heard from several very trustworthy sources, Father, that someone within our family is plotting with our enemies to destroy us."

Alexander's expression didn't change. "You're not going to tell me it's your poor brother, Jofre?"

"No, Father," Cesare said. "Of course not. But someone close who endangers us. Lucrezia's beloved, Prince Alfonso."

An expression of alertness came over the Pope's face, but for only a fleeting moment before he recovered. "A vicious rumor, Cesare. I'm certain. And we must withhold our judgment, for Crezia loves him very much. Still, I'll look into it."

At that moment they were interrupted by loud and festive music coming from the street below. Alexander reached the window first, pulled back the sash, and laughed. "Come here, Cesare, look at this."

Cesare stood alongside his father and looked out. There, he saw a parade of masked men marching, all dressed in black. There were over fifty of them, and on each mask in place of a nose there grew an enormous raised penis.

"What is this?" Cesare asked, puzzled.

Alexander, quite amused, said, "I expect it's in your honor, my son. I trust you didn't pose for the masks?"

During the months ahead, while he waited to begin the next leg of his campaign, Cesare wrote letters to his wife, Lottie, in France, telling her how much he missed her, and how they would soon be together. But he felt it was not safe for her to come to Rome. He seemed propelled by an unnatural ambition, and tormented by what he feared. Though he was immensely strong, he was thin and muscular; driven by his competitive nature, he toured the villages surrounding Rome in disguise, and challenged the local champions to boxing or wrestling matches which he always won.

Cesare, like many of the royals of the time, believed in astrology, and now he visited the most prominent astrologer of the courts, who by studying the stars and planets concluded that his fate was a troubling one. Yet he did not worry, for Cesare was certain that he could trick even the stars if he were clever enough.

Afterward, at lunch with his sister, he reached across the table to take her hand and revealed what he had learned, with a smile. "I now know that at the age of twenty-six I am in danger of ending my life, in arms and by arms. Therefore you should take advantage of the opportunity to love me while I still live."

Lucrezia chided him. "Don't speak so, Chez. For without you I am helpless. And so are the children. You must be careful, for Father counts on you as much as we do."

But within a week, to test his fate, he ordered a bullfight in which six bulls were to be set free in a specially built enclosure at the Piazza San Pietro.

Cesare rode into the arena mounted on his favorite white stallion and took each bull in turn, driving his light lance, his only weapon, so deeply into them that soon five were killed. The sixth was a large ebony bull, muscular and faster than the others, for it was in its prime. Cesare exchanged his light lance for a double-headed sword, and again rode into the arena. Then, mustering all his strength, with one fierce blow he sliced the head from the body of the bull.

Each day he seemed to have more need to challenge his own skills and courage by performing almost impossible feats of daring. His masked face, his lack of fear, and his mysterious ways began to frighten everyone in Rome.

When Duarte Brandao approached the Pope with his concern, Alexander replied, "It is true he is terrible in revenge, and does not tolerate insults. But other than that, my son Cesare is a good-natured young man."

22

Prince Alfonso of Aragon, the proud son of kings, carried himself regally—even when he had drunk too much wine, as he had on this moonlit evening. The moment he finished dinner at the Vatican with the Pope, Lucrezia, and her brothers, he made excuses to leave. He told them he wanted to return home, for he had something he must attend to. He kissed his wife good-bye with the promise that he would anxiously await the pleasure of her company whenever she chose to return.

The truth was that he found it quite uncomfortable sitting in the company of the Pope and his sons, for he had been meeting in secret with Cardinal della Rovere. On two occasions, della Rovere, driven once again by ambition, had asked for Alfonso's support, and discussed the danger to the young man in the current situation. Della Rovere encouraged the young prince to look toward the future, after the Borgia's fall from power, when he—the cardinal—would become the next Pope. Naples would then have nothing to fear, for the crown would be taken back from the French king and returned to its rightful owners. And someday it would be his.

Now Alfonso was terrified that Alexander would discover the truth about these secret meetings. Since he had returned from the Colonna castle to Rome, he often caught the brothers watching him closely, and he knew they suspected him of treachery.

As Alfonso walked across the empty square in front of Saint Peter's, the sound of his own footsteps seemed suddenly to echo loudly on the pavement. As the moon hid behind some passing clouds, the square suddenly turned black as pitch. Alfonso heard some shuffling, and looked quickly to see if anyone was following him. But he saw nothing. Breathing deeply, he tried to quiet his racing heart. But something was wrong. He felt it.

Suddenly, as the clouds uncovered the moon, he saw several masked men rushing toward him from the shadows of the buildings. They were wielding *scroti,* primitive street weapons made of a leather pouch filled with chunks of iron and fastened to a leather handle. He tried to turn back and run across the square, but three of them grabbed him and threw him to the ground. All three of the men jumped him and with their *scroti* came down hard upon his body. He tried to cover his head with his arms, he tried to turn on his stomach to protect himself, but over and over again the weapon came crashing down unmercifully on his arms and legs, as he tried to stifle his cries of pain. Then one of the men brought his weapon down hard right on the bridge of his nose. He heard the crack of his bones as he felt himself losing consciousness.

Just as the last assailant drew his stiletto and sliced Alfonso from his neck to his navel, there came the shout of a papal guard. The attackers, startled, ran toward one of the streets that led from the square.

The guard standing over the young man judged the severity of his wounds, and knew he must make a choice. He could immediately provide the necessary care to this unfortunate soul, or chase the scum who attacked him. Then, by the pale light of the moon, he recognized Alfonso as the Pope's son-in-law.

Frantically, he called for help. Then he quickly removed his own cape and tried to staunch the bleeding that flowed from the boy's massive chest wound.

Shouting again and again for help, the desperate man carried Alfonso to the nearby headquarters of the papal guard and placed him gently on the iron cot.

The Vatican physician was summoned at once, and rushed to Alfonso's side. Fortunately, the cut was long but not too deep. From what he could see, no major organs had been damaged, and the quick thinking of the guard had stopped the young prince from bleeding to death.

A practical and experienced man, the Vatican physician looked around quickly, then motioned to one of the other guards to hand over a flask of brandy. He poured the alcohol into the open wound, and began to stitch it closed. But there was little he could do for the young man's once-handsome face, except place a compress on his shattered nose and pray it would heal without too much ruin.

Alexander was called from his table by Duarte and informed secretly of the incident.

The Pope ordered Alfonso to be carried to his private chambers and put to bed in one of his own rooms. Sixteen of his finest guards were called to act as sentinels. He then instructed Duarte to send an urgent message to the king of Naples, explaining what had happened to his nephew, and requesting that he send his own physician, as well as Sancia, to Rome to nurse her brother and comfort Lucrezia.

Alexander dreaded telling his daughter what had happened, but he knew he must. Returning to the table, he stood directly before her. "There has been an accident in the square. Your beloved husband, Alfonso, has been attacked by several treacherous scoundrels."

Lucrezia's expression was one of shock. She stood up immediately. "Where is he? Is he harmed badly?"

"The wounds are quite severe," Alexander said. "But with prayer, we hope not fatal."

Lucrezia turned to her brothers. "Chez, Jofre, do something! Find the villains, lock them in a pen, and have the wild dogs rip at their flesh." She began to run then, and cry. "Papa, take me to him."

Alexander quickly led the way, with Lucrezia, Cesare, and Jofre following.

Young Alfonso lay unconscious, his body covered with cotton sheeting, blood streaming in great streaks from each of the wounds on his face.

The moment Lucrezia saw him, she screamed and then collapsed. It was her brother Jofre who caught her and carried her to a waiting chair. Cesare's face was covered with a carnival mask, and yet Jofre noticed that he seemed to betray little of the shock that he himself had felt. "Brother," Jofre asked, "who would have reason to attack?"

Only Cesare's eyes showed, and they glittered like coal. "Baby brother, each of us has more enemies than we can imagine," he said. Then, reluctantly, he offered, "I will see if there is anything I can discover," and he left the room.

The moment Lucrezia came back to herself, she ordered the servants to bring her some clean bandages and warm water. She then carefully lifted the sheet to see what further damage had been done to her beloved, but when she saw the slice from neck to navel she felt sickened and quickly took her seat again.

Jofre stood by, and together they spent the night waiting for Alfonso's eyes to open. But it was two days before he even stirred, and by that time the physician from Naples as well as Sancia had arrived. Sancia, distraught, bent to kiss her brother's forehead but could find no place left uninjured, and so she lifted his hand and placed a kiss upon his bruised and blackened fingers.

She kissed both Lucrezia and her husband, Jofre, who even in these dire circumstances could not hide his pleasure at seeing her. To Jofre, Sancia looked more beautiful than ever; her dark hair lush and curling, her cheeks flushed with fear for her brother, and her eyes shiny with tears made him love her all the more.

She sat next to Lucrezia and held her hand. "My sweet sister," Sancia said. "How dreadful that such terrible villains should harm our prince of grace. I am here now, so you may rest without worry, for I will care for my brother in your place."

Lucrezia was so grateful to see Sancia that she began to cry again. Sancia soothed her. "Where is Cesare? Has he discovered anything of value? Has he captured the attackers?"

Lucrezia was so weary that all she could do was shake her head. "I must rest," she told Sancia, "but only for a brief time. Then I'll return to wait for Alfonso to wake, for I want mine to be the first face he sees when he opens his eyes."

She left them then and walked with Jofre to Santa Maria in Portico, where she greeted her children and Adriana, and then lay exhausted on her bed. But just before she fell into a long dreamless sleep, something struck her and disturbed her.

Her brother Cesare. His expression when he heard the news—or rather, his lack of expression. What went on beneath that mask?

Several days later, Jofre and Sancia were finally alone in their chambers. It had been days since she'd arrived, and he had been longing for time alone with her, yet he understood her concern for her brother as she attended to him.

Now, as she undressed for bed, Jofre came up to her and put his arms around her. "I have truly missed you," he said. "And I am sorry about the tragedy that has befallen your brother."

Standing naked, Sancia placed her arms around Jofre's neck, and in a rare moment of tenderness put her head on his shoulder. "It's *your* brother we must speak about," Sancia said softly.

Jofre moved away so he could see her face. She was strikingly beautiful, and her distress over Alfonso made her look softer than usual. "There is something about Cesare that troubles you?" he asked.

Sancia climbed into bed, and motioned to Jofre to join her. She leaned on her side as he undressed. "There is much about Cesare that troubles me," she said. "Those freakish masks he has taken to wearing make him appear altogether sinister."

"They are to cover the marks of the pox, Sancia," Jofre said. "He is embarrassed by them."

"Jofre, it's not only that," Sancia said. "It is more the mystery that has taken hold of him since he is back from France. He is different, I feel it. Whether he is intoxicated by his own power, or the pox has invaded his brain as well as his face, I feel frightened for us all."

"It is his wish to protect our family, to make Rome strong, to unify the city-states so they may be ruled properly under the Holy Father," Jofre said.

Sancia's voice was strong. "It is no secret that I hold no affection for your father since he sent me away. If it was not for my brother's well-being, I would not step foot in Rome again. If you wish to be with me you will have to return to Naples, for I do not trust this Pope."

Jofre said, "You are still angry with him, and for good reason. But it is possible your hatred for him will pass in time."

Sancia knew better, but she understood that both she and Alfonso were in a dangerous circumstance, and so this time she held her tongue. Yet she wondered just what Jofre thought about his father—what he would even dare to feel.

He had climbed into bed alongside her now, and was leaning on his arm facing her; and again, as before, she was aware of his innocence. "Jofre," she said, touching his cheek, "I have always admitted that when we married I found you young and thought you slow-witted. But since I've begun to understand you, I see the goodness of your soul. I know you are capable of love in ways others in your family are not."

"Crezia loves," Jofre defended. Remembering how loyally his brother had kept his secret, he was tempted to add, *and Cesare loves.* But instead he held his tongue.

"Yes, Crezia does love, and that is unfortunate, for her heart will be torn to pieces by the boundless ambition of both your father and your brother," Sancia said. "Can't you see who they are?"

"Father believes in his mission to the church," Jofre explained. "And Cesare wishes Rome to be as formidable as it was in the time of his namesake, Julius Caesar. He believes his calling is to fight holy wars."

Sancia smiled gently at Jofre. "Have you ever considered what your calling is? Has anyone ever asked, or noticed? And how is it you can keep from hating the brother who steals the admiration of your father, or the father who scarcely acknowledges you?"

Jofre ran his hand over the smooth olive skin of her shoulders. The touch of her flesh gave him great pleasure. "I dreamed, as I was growing up, of becoming a cardinal. Always. The smell of Papa's garments, when he held me as a very young child and I rested on his shoulder, filled me with the love of God and the desire to serve him. But before I was able to choose, Father found a use for me in Naples. In my marriage to you. And so it was that I came to love you with the love I'd saved for God."

His total devotion to her only increased her desire to show him how much had been stolen from him.

"The Holy Father is often ruthless in his aims," Sancia said. "Do you see that ruthlessness, though it's cloaked in reason? And Cesare's ambition approaches madness—do you not see that?"

Jofre closed his eyes. "My love, I see more than you know."

Sancia kissed him passionately, and they made love. He was a kind and careful lover after these years, for she had taught him. And above all, he wished to bring her pleasure.

Afterward, they lay together, and though Jofre was silent, Sancia felt she must warn him in order to protect herself. "Jofre, my love," she said. "If your family tried to kill my brother, or at the very least didn't try to stop it, and they have sent me away for political gain, how much longer do you think we will be safe? How much longer do you think they will allow us to be together?"

Jofre said menacingly, "I will allow nothing to separate us."
It was not so much a statement of love as a promise to avenge.

Cesare had spent the morning riding through the streets of Rome questioning the citizens about Alfonso's attack. Had anyone heard rumors of strangers in the city? Had anyone seen anything that could help in the search? When nothing came of his questioning, he returned to the Vatican, where Alexander reminded him to meet with Cardinal Riario to discuss plans for the jubilee.

They had lunch together on the terrace of the cardinal's palace, and Cesare offered compensation for the many planned festivals, as well as the cleanup of the city.

Afterward, they walked down the narrow alley to the shop of an art dealer who sold antiquities. Cardinal Riario had a fine private collection, and the dealer, who came highly recommended, had an exquisite new sculpture that the cardinal wanted to consider.

After several minutes they stopped in front of a heavy carved wooden door, and the cardinal knocked. An elderly man with crossed eyes, long gray hair, and a sly smile opened the door to let them in.

The cardinal introduced them. "Giovanni Costa, I bring the great Cesare Borgia, captain general, to see your statues."

Gio Costa was effusive in his greeting, and enthusiastically led them through his shop to a courtyard filled with statues. Cesare looked around the cluttered workspace. On tables, and all over the dust-covered ground, there were arms, legs, unfinished busts, and other bits of half-sculpted marble. In the far corner of the courtyard, there was an object draped and covered with a cloth.

Curious, Cesare pointed to it. "What is over there?"

Costa led them to the covered piece. With great drama, and a grand sweeping motion, he whisked away the cover. "This is probably the most magnificent piece I have ever had in my possession."

Cesare involuntarily drew in a breath as his eyes fell upon an exquisitely carved white marble Cupid. Its eyes were half closed, with full lips curved sweetly, its expression at once dreamlike and filled with longing. So translucent it seemed carved of light, with wings so delicate they made one believe that the cherub could take flight at will. The beauty of it, its sheer perfection, took his breath away.

"What is the price?" Cesare asked.

Costa pretended not to want to sell it. "When it becomes known that I have it," he said, "the price will go through the sky."

Cesare laughed and repeated, "How much will you take for it now?" He thought of Lucrezia, how she would love it.

"Today, for Your Eminence, only two thousand ducats," he said.

Before Cesare could say anything, Cardinal Riario began to circle the piece, studying it closely, touching it. Then he turned to Costa and said, "My dear fellow, this is not an object of antiquity. My senses tell me it is something done quite recently."

Costa said, "You have a good eye, Cardinal. I did not proclaim it to be an antique. But it was not finished yesterday, rather, last year. By a very talented young artist from Florence."

The cardinal shook his head. "I have no interest in contemporary works; that is not what I collect. And certainly none at that exorbitant price. Come, Cesare, let's go."

But Cesare stood his ground, fascinated. Then, without further consultation or bickering, he said, "I don't care what it costs or when it was carved; I must have it."

Costa apologized. "The profit does not all belong to me, for I must send the artist and his representative their price. And transportation is costly . . ."

Cesare smiled. "Your job is finished, for I already said I must have it. And so I will give you what you ask. Two thousand it is . . ." he said. Then, as an afterthought, he asked, "What is the name of this young sculptor?"

"Buonarroti, Michelangelo Buonarroti. He shows some talent, yes?"

Rome was wild with rumors. First it was said that Cesare had struck down another brother, but once he denied it publicly that rumor was quickly replaced by another. Now the citizens gossiped that the Orsini, angered at Lucrezia's governing of Nepi, had taken their revenge on her husband, an ally of their enemies, the Colonna.

But in the rooms of the Vatican there were other concerns. The Pope, hit by several bouts of syncope, was becoming weaker, so he had taken to his bed. Lucrezia, who had stayed at her husband's side during his early recovery, now often left Sancia to care for her brother while Lucrezia ministered to her father. He seemed frail, and was comforted by her company.

"Tell me the truth, Papa," she asked him one day. "You had no part in the attack on Alfonso, did you?"

"My sweet child," Alexander said, sitting up in bed. "I would not lay a hand on the one who brought you such happiness. And that is why I have placed such security at his doors."

Lucrezia was comforted knowing her father had not ordered the harm that had befallen her husband. But at the very moment that the Pope was reassuring his daughter, two swarthy Neapolitans familiar to Sancia were led into the Vatican, past the guards of Alfonso's room. Alfonso had been recovering; on that day he was feeling quite well, though it had been only a fortnight since his assault. He could now stand, though he could not yet walk.

Alfonso greeted the men warmly, and then asked his sister to leave them for a few moments so they could converse in the way men do when no women are present, for he explained he hadn't seen these two friends since he had been to Naples several months before.

Pleased to see her brother happy, Sancia left the Vatican to visit Lucrezia's children. She would only be gone a short time. And in the company of these men she was certain he would be safe.

This golden August day in Rome was hotter than most, and the Vatican gardens were in full bloom. Cesare was strolling alone, enjoying the serenity of the tall cedars, the soft murmuring of the fountains and the cheerful chirping of birds. He seldom felt such peace. He was not bothered by the heat; in fact, he enjoyed it—a credit to his Spanish blood, no doubt. He was deep in thought, trying to deliberate on new information he had just received from Don Michelotto, when he saw the beautiful red exotic flower on the path before him. He bent to examine it, and as he did he heard the swift whir of a crossbow bolt pass perilously close to his head. It embedded itself into a nearby cedar.

Instinctively he dropped to the ground as a second bolt sped by. And as he shouted for his guards, he rolled over to see where the arrows were coming from.

There, on the balcony of the Vatican Palace, stood his brother-in-law Alfonso, supported by two Neapolitan guards. One was drawing back his crossbow to shoot again, and Alfonso himself had his own bow aimed straight at Cesare. This bolt landed in the earth only inches from his leg. Cesare called for his guards again, shouting, "Traitor! Traitor! Look to the balcony!" Automatically he reached for his sword, wondering how he could slay his brother-in-law before being hit by Alfonso's crossbow.

By then the Vatican guards were running toward him, shouting, and he watched as Alfonso slipped from the balcony and disappeared. Cesare dug the crossbow bolt out of the dirt beside him, but the one caught in the cedar could not be removed. He immediately brought the bolt he carried to the Vatican assayer, a man highly skilled in the study of metals and other substances. The man confirmed what Cesare suspected: The bolt had been soaked in a lethal poison, and even a scratch would have been fatal.

Next Cesare went to the Vatican apartment, where he found his sister Lucrezia gently bathing her husband's wounds. Alfonso lay motionless, his bare white chest still showing the angry red scar of the attacker's stiletto. The two men who had been with him on the balcony had escaped down some Vatican corridor, but Cesare's guards were in hot pursuit.

Cesare said nothing to his sister. Alfonso looked up at him nervously, not knowing for certain if Cesare had recognized him in the garden attack. Cesare smiled, then leaned down close as though to comfort him, and whispered in his ear. "What was begun at lunch will be finished at supper."

Then he stood tall again, stared at the silent prince, and kissed his sister before leaving.

Hours later, in that same room at the Vatican where Alfonso was recovering, Lucrezia and Sancia were making plans to travel to her palace in Nepi. There they would all spend time together with the children while Alfonso regained his strength, and make up for what they had lost when Sancia was banished to Naples. Lucrezia had developed a deep respect for Sancia's fighting spirit, and they had grown fond of each other.

Alfonso had fallen asleep as the women sat by his bed talking in whispers. But suddenly he was awakened by a hard knock at the door. When Lucrezia opened it, she was surprised to see Don Michelotto.

"Cousin Miguel. What are you doing here?" she said, smiling.

"I've come to see your husband about some Vatican business," he said, thinking fondly of the times he had carried Lucrezia on his shoulders as a child. He bowed and asked, "May I beg your indulgence for a few moments? Your father is calling for you, and I would appreciate the time to speak with your husband privately."

Lucrezia hesitated only a moment before agreeing. "Of

course, I'll go to Papa, and Sancia will stay here, for Alfonso is weak tonight."

Michelotto's face never changed its pleasant expression. He leaned toward Sancia now, and said in apology, "It is very private, this conversation."

Alfonso didn't say a word; he pretended to be sleeping, hoping Michelotto would go away, for he didn't want to try to explain what he had been doing on the balcony that afternoon.

Lucrezia and Sancia left the room, destined for the Pope's chambers, but before they reached the end of the corridor they were summoned back by the urgent call of Michelotto.

They ran back to the room to find Alfonso lying in bed as though asleep, but now his skin was tinged with blue, his body still and dead.

"He must have suffered a hemorrhage," Michelotto explained softly. "For suddenly his breath just stopped." He said nothing about the powerful hands he had placed around Alfonso's neck.

Lucrezia began to sob uncontrollably, as she threw her body over that of her husband. But Sancia began to shriek and scream, throwing herself at Michelotto, her fists swinging and hitting his chest again and again. When Cesare entered the room Sancia immediately fell upon him, scratching and screaming all the more. "You bastard! You godless son of the devil," she screamed.

She began to rip at her hair, tearing shocks of it out of her head, leaving many of her long dark locks lying in heaps on the floor at her feet.

Jofre entered and came toward her, and bore the weight of her fists until she could scream and shout no more. Then he held her, to try to comfort her, until she could stop trembling. Finally, he took her to their quarters.

It was only after Cesare dismissed Michelotto that Lucrezia lifted her head from the chest of her lifeless husband and turned to Cesare. Tears streaming down her face, she said, "I will never forgive you for this, my brother. For you have taken from me a part of my heart that can never love again. It can never be yours, for it is no longer mine. And even our children will suffer for this."

He tried to reach out for her, to explain that Alfonso had shot his weapon first. And yet he found himself speechless in the face of her desolation.

Lucrezia ran from the room then, to her father's chambers. "I shall never feel the same way about you, my father," she threatened. "For you have caused me more misery than you can imagine. If it was on your order that someone did this evil deed, then, out of love you should have considered me. If it was my brother's hand, then you should have stopped him. But I will never love either of you again, for you have broken my trust."

Pope Alexander lifted his head to look at her and his expression was one of surprise. "Crezia, what are you saying? What has happened to you?"

Her light eyes were clouded with grief. "You have ripped the heart from my chest and you have severed a bond that was tied in the heavens."

Alexander stood up and slowly walked toward his daughter, but he kept himself from wrapping his arms around her, for he was certain she would recoil from his touch. "My sweet child, your husband was never meant to be harmed, but he tried to kill your brother Cesare. I ordered your husband's protection," he said, but lowered his head and added, "but I could not stop your brother from protecting himself."

Lucrezia saw the distress on her father's face, and she fell to her knees at his feet. She covered her face with her hands as she wept. "Papa, you must help me understand. What kind of evil comes in this world? What kind of God is this, who would allow such love to be extinguished? This is madness! My husband tried to kill my brother, and my brother kills my husband? Their souls will be lost in hell; they will be damned. I will see neither of them again; with this one tragic deed I have lost them forever."

Alexander put his hand on his daughter's head and tried

to stop her tears. "Shh, shh," he said. "God is merciful. He will forgive them both. Otherwise there is no reason for his being. And one day, when this worldly tragedy is done, we shall all be together again."

"I cannot wait an eternity for happiness," Lucrezia cried, and then she stood and ran from the room.

This time there was no question. Everyone knew Cesare was responsible for the killing. Yet word had spread of the attack on him in the garden, and so most Romans thought his action justified. Within a short time the two Neapolitans were caught, confessed, and were hanged in the public square.

But once the initial shock wore off, Lucrezia was enraged. She entered Cesare's chambers, screaming that he had first killed his brother, and now his brother-in-law. Alexander tried to keep Cesare from becoming angry, for he wanted no breach between his two favorite children. Yet Cesare was stunned and upset by his sister's presumption that he had killed their brother Juan. He had never considered defending himself to her, for he never imagined she suspected him.

After several weeks Alexander and Cesare could no longer bear seeing Lucrezia in tears, or stand to witness her misery. And so they began to avoid her, and finally to ignore her. When Alexander tried to send her and her children back to Santa Maria in Portico, Lucrezia insisted on leaving Rome for Nepi and taking her children and Sancia with her. Her brother Jofre was welcome, she told her father, but no other brother could come. Just before she left, she informed Alexander that she never again wished to speak to Cesare.

Cesare struggled to keep himself from following Lucrezia, for he wanted very much to explain. Yet he knew it would do no good, and so he distracted himself with strategies for his campaign. The first thing he knew he must do was go to Venice in order to reduce any possibility of interference from their quarters, for Rimini, Faenza, and Pesaro were territories all under the protection of the Venetians.

After days of sea travel Cesare finally approached Venice, and the huge shimmering pastel city built on stilts emerged from the vast dark waters like some mythic dragon. He saw Saint Mark's Square before him, then the Doge's Palace.

From the harbor he was taken to an imposing Moorish palace just off the Grand Canal, where several noble Venetians greeted him and helped to make him comfortable. Cesare settled in, and soon requested a meeting with the members of the Great Council. There Cesare explained the Pope's position, and offered an accommodation: papal troops would defend Venice from the Turks in the event of an invasion, and in return Venice would withdraw its protection of Rimini, Faenza, and Pesaro.

In a brilliantly colorful ceremony, the council passed his resolution and draped Cesare in the scarlet coat of an honorary citizen. He was now "a gentleman of Venice."

The two years Lucrezia spent with Alfonso had been the happiest time of her life, a time when the promises her father made her in childhood seemed to come true. But now the grief she felt over Alfonso's death transcended the loss of her husband's sweet smile, bright eyes, and pleasing disposition. It transcended the loss of their laughter, even the loss of her innocence when she first bedded Cesare. For then she'd had faith in her father, trust in her brother's love for her, and in the power of the Holy Father to bind and unbind sin. But since the death of Alfonso, all this was lost to her. Now she felt as abandoned by her father as she did by her God.

She had come to Nepi with Sancia, Jofre, her sons Giovanni and Rodrigo, and only fifty of the most trusted members of her court to accompany her.

There, just a year before, she and Alfonso had spent their

hours together making love, choosing fine furniture and lovely wall hangings to decorate their castle, and walking through the tall dark oak trees and groves in the vibrant countryside.

Nepi itself was a little town, with a small central square, and streets lined with Gothic buildings and a few castles where the nobles lived. There was a church, a lovely church, built upon the temple of Jupiter. She and Alfonso had walked those streets together holding hands and laughing with pleasure at its quaintness. But now everything about Nepi seemed as melancholy as Lucrezia felt.

Whether she looked from her castle window to see the black volcano of Bracciano or turned to look at the blue chain of Sabine mountains, it made her weep. For in everything she saw, she saw Alfonso.

On one bright sunny day, Sancia and she carried the babies as they walked through the countryside. Lucrezia seemed more at peace than she had been, but suddenly the bleating of the sheep and the plaintive notes of the shepherd's flute spun her into melancholy all over again.

There were nights she swore it was a nightmare, that she would turn and find her handsome husband lying right beside her, but then she would reach out and touch the cold empty sheets and find herself alone again. Her body and soul ached for him. She lost her taste for food, and had no appetite for pleasure. Each morning she woke more tired than she was the night before, and the few smiles she managed were brought forth by her children. The only action she took in the first month she was in Nepi was to order some clothes made for her boys, but even to play with them seemed to exhaust her.

Finally, Sancia determined to try to help her sister-in-law recover. She put aside her own pain and devoted herself to Lucrezia and the babies. Jofre was a great help as well, comforting Lucrezia whenever she cried and spending hours at the castle and in the fields playing with the children, reading them stories and singing to them each night as he put them to sleep.

It was during this time that Lucrezia began to explore her feelings about her father, her brother, and God.

Cesare had been in Venice for over a week, and he was ready to return to Rome to resume his campaign. So it was that the night before he was to leave, Cesare dined with several of his old classmates from the University of Pisa, enjoying good wine, engaging in old memories and interesting conversation.

As bright and shimmering as Venice appeared during the day, with its crowds of people, pastel castles and gilded rooftops, grand churches and lovely arched bridges, it was as sinister when darkness fell. The rising moisture from the waters of the canals smothered the city in a thick and misty fog, through which it was difficult to find one's way. Between the buildings and canals the alleys grew like spider legs, providing refuge for the street thieves and other villains who would not come out by day.

As Cesare made his way along the narrow alley that led back to his palazzo, suddenly he was forced to attention by a beam of light that spilled across the canal.

He looked around, for someone had opened a door.

But before Cesare could get his bearings, three men, dressed in drab, worn peasant clothes, rushed toward him. Through the dusky gloom he saw the glint of their knives.

He turned quickly, and saw another man coming at him from the opposite direction, another knife gleaming through the darkness.

Cesare was trapped; there was nowhere to go. Both the entrance and the exit of the alley were blocked by men waiting to attack him.

Instinctively, he dove headfirst deep into the muddy waters of the canal alongside the alley, thick with the garbage and sewage of the city. He swam beneath the surface, holding his breath until he was certain his chest would burst. Finally, he broke through the surface on the other side.

From there he could see two more men running across a narrow arched bridge, from the far side of the canal to the side he was on. They were carrying torches as well as knives.

Cesare took another deep breath; then, submerging himself again, he swam under the bridge itself, where two long gondolas were moored. Sinking low in the water between the two boats, he prayed he wouldn't be seen.

The men ran up and down each of the canals and alleys trying to find him. They searched each nook and cranny with their torches, but each time they came near Cesare he slid beneath the water, and held his breath until he could no longer.

After what seemed like an eternity, when the men turned up nothing, they gathered on the bridge just above his head. He heard one of them grumble, "The Roman is nowhere to be seen. The bastard probably drowned."

"He's better off drowned than swimming in that shit," one of the others said.

"Let's call it a night," came a voice filled with authority. "Nero paid us to cut his throat, not to run around chasing a wild goose till dawn."

He listened to the footsteps of the men as they walked across the bridge above his head, one by one, until he heard nothing more.

Concerned that they had left a guard watching from a window or balcony, Cesare swam quietly along the dark bank of the small canal into the Grand Canal itself, and finally up to the dock of his own palazzo. His night watchman, assigned by the doge, was amazed to see their honored guest pull himself out of the water shivering and foul-smelling.

In his quarters, after a hot bath, Cesare put on a clean robe and drank a mug of hot sherry. He sat for quite a time, deep in thought. Then he gave the orders that he would leave at dawn. When they reached the dry land of the Veneto, he would pick up his carriage.

Cesare didn't sleep that night. As the sun rose over the lagoon, he climbed into a large gondola, manned by three of the doge's men armed with swords and crossbows. They were about to cast off when a burly man in a dark uniform ran out onto the dock.

"Excellency," he said breathlessly. "I must introduce myself before you go. I am the captain of the police overseeing this district of the city. Before you depart I want to apologize for the incident last night. Venice is full of thieves and bandits who will rob any stranger unlucky enough to be caught out at night."

"You must keep more of your men where they can be found," Cesare said sardonically.

The captain said, "You would do us a great favor if you would delay your voyage and accompany me to the area of the attack. Your escort can wait here. Perhaps we can go into one or two of the nearby houses so that you may identify your assailants."

Cesare was torn. He wanted to be on his way, but he also wanted to know who had planned to attack him. Yet investigating the attack could take hours and he had too much to do. Others could bring him information. Now he must return to Rome.

"Captain," Cesare said, "under ordinary circumstances I'd be pleased to help you, but my carriage is waiting. I hope to reach Ferrara by nightfall, for the country roads are as dangerous as your alleys. So you must excuse me."

The big policeman smiled and tipped his helmet. "Will you be returning to Venice soon, Excellency?"

"I hope to," Cesare said, smiling.

"Ah, perhaps you will help us then. You can contact me at police headquarters near the Rialto. My name is Bernardino Nerozzi, but everyone calls me 'Nero.' "

On the long trip back to Rome, Cesare considered who could have hired the police captain to murder him in Venice. But it was a hopeless task, for there were too many possibilities. If he had been killed, he chuckled inwardly, there would have been so many suspects, the crime would never be solved.

Still, he wondered. Could it have been one of Alfonso's Aragonese relatives, seeking revenge for his death? Or Giovanni Sforza, still angry and humiliated over his divorce and the claim of impotence? Or one of the Riario, enraged at the capture of Caterina Sforza? Or Giuliano della Rovere, who hated all the Borgia, no matter how civilized he pretended to be? Surely it could have been one of the vicars of Faenza, Urbino, or some other city who wanted to stop his campaign and prevent his planned attacks. Or any one of the hundreds of men who held a grudge against his father.

As his carriage arrived at the gates of Rome, he was certain of only one thing. He must watch his back, for it was certain now that someone wanted him dead.

If being bedded by Cesare took place in paradise, Alfonso's death was Lucrezia's fall from grace. For now she was forced to see her life, and her family, as it truly was. She felt cast out by her father, by the Holy Father, and by the Heavenly Father as well.

Her fall from innocence was a devastating time. For she had lived and loved in magical, mythical realms, but that had now come to an end. And, oh, how she grieved. She tried to remember how it began, and yet it seemed always to be. There was no beginning.

When she was just a babe, her father, sitting in the living quarters with her upon his lap, had regaled her with exciting myths peopled by Olympian gods and Titans. Was he not Zeus, the greatest Olympian god of all? For his voice was the thunder, his tears were the rain, his smile was the sun that shone on her face. And was she not Athena, the daughter-goddess who sprang full-grown from his head? Or Venus, the goddess of love, herself?

Her father read, with flying hands and eloquent words, of the story of creation. And then she was both the beautiful Eve, tempted by the snake, as well as the chaste Madonna, who gave birth to goodness itself.

In the arms of her father she felt shielded from harm; in the arms of the Holy Father she felt protected from evil; and so it was that she never feared death, for she was certain she would be safe in the arms of the Heavenly Father. For were they not all the same?

It was only now that she wore the black veil of the widow that the dark veil of illusion had been lifted from her eyes.

When she had bent to kiss the cold, stiff lips of her dead husband, she felt the emptiness of mortal man, and knew that life was suffering, and death would someday come. To her father, to Cesare, to her. Until that moment, in her heart they were immortal. And so now she wept for them all.

Some nights she was unable to sleep, and in the day she spent hours pacing her chambers, helpless to rest or find a moment's peace. The shades of fear and shadows of doubt seduced her. Finally, she felt herself losing her last remnant of faith. She questioned all she had believed. And so she had no ground on which to stand.

"What is happening to me?" she asked Sancia, as for days she fell into terror or despair. Then she stayed in bed and grieved for Alfonso, and grew frightened for herself.

Sancia sat on the bed next to her and rubbed her forehead. She kissed her cheeks. "You are becoming aware that you are a pawn in your father's game," her sister-in-law explained. "Not more important than the conquering of your brother's territories for the advancement of the Borgia family. And that is a difficult truth to bear."

"But Papa isn't like that," Lucrezia tried to protest. "He has always been concerned for my happiness."

"Always?" Sancia said, with some sarcasm. "That is a side of your father, and the Holy Father, that I am unable to see. But you must get well, you must stay strong. For your babies need you."

"Is your father kind?" Lucrezia asked Sancia. "And does he treat you with worth?"

Sancia shook her head. "He is neither kind nor cruel to me now, for since the invasion by the French he has become ill—gone mad, some say—and yet I find him kinder than before. In Naples he is kept in a tower in the family palace, with each of us caring for him. Whenever he is frightened, he screams, 'I hear France. The trees and the rocks call France.' Yet for all his madness, I fear he is kinder than your father. For even when he was well I was not his world, and he was not mine. He was only my father, and so my love for him was never great enough to weaken me."

Lucrezia wept even more, for there was truth in Sancia's reasoning that she could no longer deny. Lucrezia swaddled herself in her blankets again. And tried to discern the ways in which her father had changed.

Her father told of a God who was merciful and joyous, but the Holy Father was an agent of a God who was punishing and often even cruel. Her heartbeat quickened when she dared to think, "How could so much evil be for good, and for God?"

It was then that she began at last to question the wisdom of her father. Was all she'd been taught good and right? Was her father truly the Vicar of Christ on earth? And was the Holy Father's judgment also God's? She was certain the gentle God she held in her heart was very different from the punishing God who whispered in her father's ears.

Less than one month after Alfonso's death, Pope Alexander began the search for another husband for Lucrezia. Though it may have been heartless, he was determined to plan for her future, for in the event of his death he did not want her to find herself a helpless widow forced to eat from clay plates rather than silver.

Alexander called Duarte into his chambers to talk about the possibilities. "What do you think about Louis de Ligny?" Alexander asked. "He is, after all, a cousin of the king of France."

Duarte said simply, "I don't believe Lucrezia will find him acceptable."

The Pope sent a message to Lucrezia in Nepi.

And received a message in return, which read, "I will not live in France."

Next Alexander suggested Francisco Orsini, duke of Gravina.

Lucrezia's return message read, "I do not wish to marry."

When the Pope sent another message asking for her reasons, her reply was simple. "All my husbands are unlucky, and I do not wish another on my conscience."

The Pope called again for Duarte. "She is simply impossible," he said. "She is willful and irritating. I will not live forever, and if I die, only Cesare will be left to care for her."

Duarte said, "She seems to get on well with Jofre, and Sancia too. She may need more time to recover from her grief. Call her back to Rome, and then you will have the opportunity to ask her to consider what you suggest. A new husband comes too close to the old, and Nepi is too far from Rome."

The weeks passed slowly as Lucrezia tried to recover from her grief and find a reason to go on living. Finally one night, as she lay in bed reading by the light of her candles, her brother Jofre came to sit beside her bed.

Jofre's thatched blond hair was hidden beneath a cap of green velvet, and his light eyes were bloodshot from lack of sleep. Lucrezia knew he had begged to retire early, and therefore found it peculiar that he was dressed in fresh clothes as though he was going out. But before she had any chance to question him he began to speak, as though his words were being forced from his lips.

"I have done things I am ashamed of," he told her. "And for those I judge myself. No God would judge me so. And I have done things for which our father would judge me, yet I have never judged him so."

Lucrezia sat up straighter in bed, her own eyes swollen from weeping. "What could you have done, little brother, that our father could judge? For, of the four of us, you were the least attended to, and the sweetest of all."

Jofre looked at her, and she was witness to his struggle. He had waited so long to confess, and of anyone he most trusted her. "I cannot bear to carry this sin on my soul any longer," he said. "For I've held it far too long."

Lucrezia reached for his hand, for in his eyes she saw such confusion and guilt it made her own misery seem less. "What is it that so troubles you?" she asked.

"You will despise me for this truth," he said. "If I speak of this to anyone but you, my life will be lost. Yet if I do not unburden myself, I fear I will go mad, or my soul will be lost. And for me that holds an even greater terror."

Lucrezia was puzzled. "What is this sin that is so terrible it causes you to tremble?" she asked. "You can place your trust in me. I vow no danger will befall you, for your truth will never pass my lips."

Jofre looked at his sister, and fell into a stutter. "It was not Cesare who killed our brother Juan."

Lucrezia quickly placed her fingers to his lips. "Do not speak another word, my brother. Do not speak the words I can hear within my heart, for I have known you since you were the babe I held. But I am desperate to ask, what could be so dear that it would call for such an act?"

Jofre put his head on his sister's chest and allowed her to hold him gently as he whispered, "Sancia," he said. "For my soul is bound to hers in ways I do not understand. Without her, my own breath seems to stop."

Lucrezia thought of Alfonso and she understood. Then she thought of Cesare. How tormented he must be. Now she felt a great compassion for all those victimized by love, and in that moment love seemed far more treacherous than war.

Cesare could not continue his campaign for the Romagna without first visiting his sister. He must see her to explain, to ask for forgiveness, to regain her love.

When he arrived in Nepi, Sancia tried to keep him away, but he pushed past her to his sister's chambers and forced himself inside.

There Lucrezia sat, playing a plaintive tune on her lute. When she saw Cesare her fingers froze on the strings, her song stopped in the air.

He ran to her and kneeled before her, placing his head on her knees. "I curse the day I was born to cause you such grief. I curse the day I found I loved you more than life itself, and I wished for just one moment to see you again, before I fought another battle, for without your love no battle is even worth the fight."

Lucrezia placed her hand on her brother's auburn hair, and smoothed it in comfort until he could lift his head to look at her. Yet she said nothing.

"Can you ever forgive me?" he asked.

"How can I not?" she answered.

His eyes filled, though hers did not. "Do you love me still, above all else on earth?" he asked.

She breathed deeply, and found herself hesitating for just a moment. "I love you, my brother. For you too are less a player in this game than a pawn, and for that I pity us both."

Cesare stood before her puzzled, but still he thanked her. "It will be easier to fight to gain more territories for Rome now that I have seen you again."

"Go with care," Lucrezia said. "For in truth, I could not bear another great loss."

Before he left she allowed him to embrace her, and in spite of all that had happened she found herself comforted by him. "I am off to unify the Papal States," he told her. "And when we meet again, I hope to have accomplished all I've promised."

Lucrezia smiled. "With grace, someday soon we will both be back in Rome to stay."

During her last months in Nepi, Lucrezia began to read constantly. She read the lives of saints, explored the lives of heroes and heroines, and studied the great philosophers. She filled her mind with knowledge. And she finally understood that there was only one decision she must make.

Would she live her life or would she take her life?

If she lived, she wondered, how would she find peace? She had already determined that no matter how many times her father traded her in marriage, she would never again love as she had loved Alfonso.

Yet to find peace she knew she must be able to forgive those who had wronged her, for if she could not, the anger she held in her heart and her mind would tether her to hate and rob her of her freedom.

Three months after she had arrived, she began by opening the doors to her palace in Nepi, to see the people, to listen to their complaints, and to construct a system of government that would serve the poor as well as those who carried gold. She determined to devote herself, and her life, to those who were helpless, who had suffered as she had. Those whose fate rested in the hands of rulers more powerful than themselves.

If she took the power her father had allowed her, and used the Borgia name for good as Cesare used his for war, she might find a life worth living. Like the saints who devoted their lives to God, she would from that day forward devote hers to helping others, and do it with such generosity and grace that when she met her death the face of God would smile upon her.

It was then that her father insisted that Lucrezia return to Rome.

23

In Rome again, Cesare readied his army, and this time most of his soldiers were Italian and Spanish. His Italian infantrymen were well disciplined, and wore metal helmets with scarlet and gold doublets on which Cesare's coat of arms had been embroidered. His army was led by talented Spanish captains, as well as veteran *condottieri* including Gian Baglioni and Paolo Orsini. For chief of staff, Cesare chose his captain carefully: Vito Vitelli, who brought with him twenty-one superb cannons. Together there were 2,200 soldiers on horses and 4,300 infantrymen. Dion Naldi, Caterina's old captain, brought his own troops to assist Cesare on his new quest.

The army's first target was Pesaro, still ruled by Lucrezia's ex-husband, Giovanni Sforza. Alexander had excommunicated him when it was discovered that he was in negotiations with the Turks to ward off the papal army.

Here too, as in Imola and Forli, the citizens themselves were not anxious to sacrifice their lives or property for their brutish ruler. Some of the leading citizens arrested Giovanni's brother Galli when they heard Cesare was on his way, but rather than face his terrible ex-brother-in-law, Giovanni quickly fled to Venice to offer them his territory.

Cesare entered Pesaro in the rain, accompanied by his army of 150 men dressed in red and yellow uniforms, and was greeted by happy crowds and great fanfare. The citizens quickly surrendered and handed Cesare the keys to the city. Now he was lord of Pesaro.

With no battle to fight, Cesare went immediately to set up

quarters in Sforza Castle, in the very apartments where his sister Lucrezia had lived. There he slept in her bed for two nights, dreaming of her.

The next morning he and Vitelli managed to confiscate seventy cannons from Pesaro's arsenal before they continued on their campaign. By the time they reached Rimini, Cesare had added ninety cannons to his artillery. The most difficult obstacle to overcome was the heavy rains the army encountered on the long ride up the coastal road. But before Cesare even reached the gates, the citizens—on hearing of his coming—drove out their hated oppressors, the brothers Pan and Carlo Malatesta. And another city surrendered.

Cesare was buoyant about his victories, but his next conquest would prove to be a difficult and overwhelming task. His objective was Faenza, ruled by the beloved Astorre Manfredi. Not only was the city a powerful fortress surrounded by high crenellated walls for defense, but it was peopled by brave and loyal citizens. It was also protected by the best infantry in all of Italy. Faenza would not surrender without a fierce fight.

The battle began badly for Cesare. Vitelli's cannons fired again and again at the walls of the fortress, yet only managed to create a small breach. Unfortunately, when they tried to storm the breach Cesare's men were beaten off by Astorre Manfredi's local Italian infantrymen, and suffered a heavy loss.

In Cesare's camp, quarrels broke out between the Italian mercenary commanders and his Spanish captains, each blaming the other for the defeat.

The weather grew bitterly cold, and everything froze as winter arrived. The troops began to complain; Gian Baglioni, one of Cesare's renowned *condottieri*, became enraged by Spanish criticism and took his men home to Perugia.

Cesare knew that with all these difficulties this battle

could not be won in winter; it would have to wait for spring. And so he left a small force to surround the city and sent the remainder of his soldiers to the local villages that peppered the Rimini road. He told them to plan for a long winter stay, and to prepare to resume the battle in spring.

Cesare himself went to Cesena. This town, formerly ruled by the Malatesta family, who fled at the news of his coming, had a great castle, and citizens who were known throughout Italy to be fierce in battle but fun-loving in life. He took over the Palazzo Malatesta, and found pleasure in inviting the citizens of the town to look around the glamorous and ornate rooms that their former masters had lived in and loved, in order to show them what their hard work and sacrifice had wrought.

In contrast to their former rulers, Cesare played among the people. During the daytime he took part in all the classic tournaments that were held, and even jousted with the nobles who had stayed behind. He found great delight in going to their festivals, dances, and fairs, and the citizens of Cesena enjoyed him and were flattered by his company.

At one such evening fair, Cesare found a large hall set aside for wrestling matches. Straw covered the floor, and in the center they had constructed a wooden ring in which muscular young contestants grappled as they dripped with sweat and cursed each other.

Cesare searched the crowded room for a worthy contestant. There, standing near the ring, he saw a big, bald man, built as solid as a stone wall. He was a head taller than Cesare, and twice as wide. When Cesare asked about him, he was told the man was a farmer named Zappitto, and that he was currently the town champion.

But the townsman who gave Cesare this information was also quick to add, "He will not compete tonight."

Cesare decided to approach Zappitto himself. "My good man," Cesare said, "I have heard of your reputation. Would you consider honoring me with a match on this fine night, as you are the town champion?"

Zappitto grinned, showing his blackened teeth. He would be much admired in the town when he defeated the son of a Pope. And so it was agreed, the match was on.

Cesare and Zappitto removed their jackets, shirts, and boots. Cesare was muscular, but the champion had biceps and forearms twice the size of his. This provided the challenge Cesare needed.

The two men stepped into the ring.

"Two falls out of three," the referee called aloud, and suddenly the crowd was silent.

The two men circled each other several times; then, suddenly, the huge man rushed Cesare. But Cesare ducked, and threw his weight at the legs of Zappitto. Using the weight and force of his opponent, Cesare threw him up and over his body, and Zappitto slammed to the floor on his back. As the champion lay stunned, Cesare dropped on his chest, scoring an immediate fall.

"One fall for the challenger!" the referee shouted.

The surprised crowd sat in silence for a moment, then began to shout and applaud.

Cesare and Zappitto went back to opposite sides of the ring. The referee cried, "Go!"

Again the two men circled each other. But Zappitto was not a fool. This time there was no blind rush. He took his time and continued to circle.

Cesare made the first move. He whipped his leg against the knees of his rival, in an attempt to knock the farmer's legs out from under him. But it was like kicking a tree trunk. Nothing happened.

Now Zappitto, who moved more quickly than Cesare expected, caught hold of Cesare's foot and began whirling him around in circles, until Cesare's head was spinning. The huge man then moved his grip to Cesare's thigh and lifted him onto his own shoulders, spinning him around twice more. Finally he slammed Cesare facedown onto the straw and pounced on his groggy opponent, flipping him over and pressing his back to the floor.

The crowd roared as the referee called, "One fall for the champion!"

It took Cesare a minute or two to clear his head.

Then he was ready.

As the referee cried, "Go!" Cesare came out quickly.

He planned to grab Zappitto's hand and fingers in a grip he had learned in Genoa. Then he would force the fingers back, and when the big man tried to step backward to avoid the pressure he would throw his own leg quickly behind Zappitto's knees and push him over his own leg onto his back.

With this in mind, Cesare managed to grasp the farmer's huge hand. With all his strength, he began to push Zappitto's fingers backward. But to his surprise they were stiff as iron pipes.

Then slowly, sweating with the effort, Zappitto closed his fingers around Cesare's hand, crushing his knuckles together. Cesare kept himself from crying out, and tried to use his free arm to get a headlock on Zappitto, but the big man caught that arm as well. Now, with a frown and a look of grave intensity on his face, Zappitto began to crush the knuckles of both Cesare's hands.

The pain was so intense it took Cesare's breath away, but in a strong last effort Cesare swung both his legs up and wrapped them around his rival's gigantic waist. His legs were muscular and strong, and with all his might Cesare tried to squeeze the breath out of Zappitto. The farmer, with a loud growl, simply threw his entire weight forward, easily driving Cesare onto the floor on his back.

Zappitto quickly lay on top of him.

"Fall and the match!" cried the referee.

When he lifted Zappitto's arm in victory, the crowd applauded happily. Their champion had won.

Cesare shook Zappitto's hand and congratulated him. "A worthy contest," he said. Cesare then grabbed for his jacket, which he had placed alongside the ring, and there he found his purse.

With a deep bow, and a charming smile, he handed it to Zappitto.

Now, the crowd went wild with enthusiasm. They shouted and cheered. Not only did the new *grande signore* treat them well, he shared their pleasures. He danced, wrestled, and more important was even gracious in defeat.

Cesare engaged in these festivals and tournaments not for his pleasurè alone, though he did enjoy them, but because winning the hearts of the people was part of his plan to unify the area and bring peace to all his subjects. Yet goodwill was not enough. Cesare also ordered his troops not to rape, loot, or harm the townspeople of the territories he conquered in any way.

Therefore Cesare was angry when, on a cold winter morning, only a week after his wrestling match with Zappitto, one of his guards brought three infantrymen to him in chains.

The sergeant of the guard, one Ramiro da Lorca, was a tough Roman veteran, and he announced that the three had been drinking all day. "But more important, Captain General," Ramiro said. "They broke into a butcher shop, stole two chickens and a leg of mutton, and beat the son of the butcher bloody when he tried to stop them."

Cesare approached the three men, who now huddled miserably on the steps of his palazzo. "Are you guilty, as the sergeant claims?"

The oldest man, almost thirty, spoke up in a false and pleading tone. "Your Worship, all we did was fetch us some meager food. We was hungry, Your Worship; we just . . ."

Sergeant da Lorca interrupted. "That's nonsense, sir. These men were paid regular, like everyone else. They'd no need to steal."

Alexander had always told Cesare that choices had to be made when one was a leader of men. Difficult choices. Now he looked at the three men, and at the crowd of townspeople who had gathered in the square. "Hang them," Cesare said.

The prisoner spoke as though he had not heard Cesare. "It

was just some chickens and a bit of meat, Your Worship. Nothing serious."

Cesare walked toward him. "You misunderstand, my man. It is not just some chickens. At the command of the Holy Father, every man in this army has been well paid. Why? So they won't steal from or brutalize the people of the towns we conquer. My soldiers have been given enough food, and comfortable quarters, in order to prevent any harm to the locals. I have done all of this so that the citizens of the towns we conquer will not hate the papal forces. They don't have to love us, but my hope is that they will, at least, not despise us. What you fools have done is spoil my plan, and violate a command of the Holy Father himself."

That evening at sunset the three prisoners, soldiers of the papal army, were hanged in the square as an example to all the other papal troops, and as an apology to every citizen of Cesena.

Afterward, in taverns and houses throughout the town and along the country roads, people celebrated, and all agreed better times were coming. For the new ruler, Cesare Borgia, was just.

As spring approached, Cesare's force was strengthened by a French contingent sent by King Louis. A Milanese friend also highly recommended the artist, engineer, and inventor Leonardo da Vinci, who was claimed to be an expert in modern warfare.

When da Vinci arrived at the Malatesta Palace, he found Cesare poring over a map of the fortifications at Faenza. "These walls seem to shake off our bombardment like a dog shaking off water. How can we ever create a breach wide enough to allow a successful attack by cavalry and infantry?"

Da Vinci smiled, his curly brown hair hanging in long limp strands that almost covered his face. "Not difficult. Not difficult at all, Captain General."

"Please explain, Maestro," Cesare said with interest.

Da Vinci began, "You simply use my movable ramp-tower. I know, you are thinking that siege towers have been used for centuries and that they don't work. But my tower is different from the others. It is made in three separate parts, and can be wheeled to the walls of the fortress at the last moment of attack. Inside, the ladders lead to a covered staging area large enough to hold thirty men. They are protected in the front by a hinged wooden barrier that can be lowered like a drawbridge to the top of the wall, creating a ramp up which the thirty men race. Then they can hurl themselves into the battlements with their weapons in hand, while thirty more men quickly replace them in the staging area. Within three minutes, ninety men can be inside the walls hacking away at the enemy. In ten minutes more there can be three hundred, which is what my tower holds." Da Vinci stopped, breathless.

"Maestro, that's brilliant!" Cesare said, with a loud and boisterous laugh.

"But truly, the most brilliant feature of my tower," da Vinci said, "is that you will never have to use it."

"I don't understand," Cesare said, puzzled.

Da Vinci's stern face relaxed. "Your diagram shows that the walls of Faenza are thirty-five feet high. Several days before the battle, you must circulate the word to the enemy that you are about to use my new tower. And that it can blow a hole in any wall up to forty feet high. Can you do that?"

Cesare said, "Of course. Every tavern on the Rimini road is filled with men who'll race back to Faenza with that news."

"Then you begin construction of the tower, and make certain it's within sight of the enemy." Da Vinci unfolded a sheet of parchment on which the massive three-part tower was beautifully sketched. "I have the design right here," he said. But alongside the drawing, each part was described in a language that Cesare could not read.

Noting Cesare's puzzled expression, da Vinci gave a small laugh. "It is a special trick of mine to deceive spies and plagiarists, for one never knows who will try to steal from you.

In most of my designs, I write so that the only way to read it is to hold it before a mirror. Then the writing becomes perfectly clear."

Cesare smiled, for he admired cautious men.

Da Vinci continued. "Now, Captain General, the enemy has heard about the fearsome tower. They watch it as it is constructed. And they know they've not much time. The tower will come, and with thirty-five-foot walls they'll be overrun. What do they do? They build up the walls, they pile stone upon stone around the fortress until the walls are ten feet higher. But they have made a terrible error. What did they forget? Those walls are no longer stable, for the base must be fortified to hold that extra weight. But by the time they reason that out . . . your artillery fires."

Cesare collected his army from all the neighboring towns, and his men told anyone who would listen in every local tavern about Cesare Borgia's stupendous new tower.

As da Vinci suggested, Cesare had his men start construction within sight of Faenza. When Cesare's forces took their positions around the city and his cannons were brought forward, Cesare could see the frantic effort beginning. Men raced around the ramparts carrying and placing huge stones one atop another, on the fortress walls. Amused, Cesare delayed the attack to give them more time.

Now Cesare sent for Captain Vito Vitelli. They stood in his tent overlooking the unfortunate city.

"Here's what I wish, Vito," Cesare said. "Direct all your fire at the very base of the wall between those two towers." He pointed at an area more than wide enough for his army to pass through.

"At the base, Captain?" Vitelli asked, incredulously. "That's where we aimed last winter and failed miserably. We should fire at the ramparts now. At least that way we can kill their men a few at a time."

Cesare wanted no one to know the secret of da Vinci's tower, for later there might be other towns on which he'd wish to use it.

"Vito, just do as I say," Cesare instructed. "Fire every shot at the base."

The artillery commander looked puzzled, but consented. "As you wish, Cesare. But it will be a waste of shot." He bowed slightly and left.

Cesare could see Vitelli giving orders to his artillerymen, who then moved the cannons toward the area Cesare had marked. The men cranked the guns to lower the angle of their fire.

Cesare commanded the infantry and light cavalry to gather just behind the guns. He had put on his own armor hours before. Now he directed his men-at-arms to ready themselves and their horses, for they were to remain mounted. They grumbled. The siege could last for months. Were they to remain in the saddle until summer?

When Cesare was certain his forces were ready, he gave Vitelli the signal to begin the bombardment.

The *condottieri* in turn shouted, "Fire!"

The cannons roared once, reloaded, and roared again. Cesare saw the balls smash into the walls just three or four feet above the ground. On and on the relentless cannonade continued. Twice, Vitelli looked back at Cesare as if he were insane. Twice, Cesare signaled to continue firing as he had ordered.

Suddenly, they heard a low rumble. And it grew louder and louder as the entire fifty-foot section of the wall fell in on itself, crumbling to the ground and raising a huge cloud of dust. They could hear the screams of the soldiers who had been defending that part of the wall—those few who still lived.

Immediately, Cesare called for his troops to charge forward.

With a great cheer the light cavalry flew into the breach, followed by the infantry. All of them would fan out inside the walls, to attack again from the rear.

Cesare waited just four minutes. Then he gave the signal for the charge of his men-at-arms.

The reserve forces of the town raced to the area of the breach and prepared to defend the opening. But they were trampled to dust by the onrushing of Cesare's men.

The dismayed Faenzans on the sections of the wall that were still standing found themselves attacked from the rear. The crossbows, swords, and lances of Cesare's soldiers quickly felled them. Within minutes, a Faenzan officer shouted, "We surrender! *Surrender!*"

Cesare saw the local soldiers lay down their arms and raise their hands. He nodded, then signaled his commanders to stop the slaughter. And so it was that Faenza passed into papal control.

Their ruler, Prince Astorre Manfredi, was given safe conduct by Cesare, and permission to leave for Rome. Instead, impressed by Cesare and his army, craving adventure, he asked if he might stay for a time, perhaps to serve on Cesare's staff. Cesare was surprised, but agreed. Manfredi was sixteen years old, but he was a young man of intelligence and good judgment. Cesare liked him.

After a few days' rest, Cesare was ready to push his men forward once again.

He gave da Vinci a substantial quantity of ducats, crammed into a leather pouch, and now asked him to accompany the army on its march. But da Vinci shook his head. "I must return to the arts. For the sweaty young stonecutter Michelangelo Buonarroti is getting good commissions, while I am wasting my time on a battlefield. He has talent, I'll admit, but no depth, no subtlety. I must return."

Now, as Cesare mounted his white charger and prepared to ride north, he bid da Vinci good-bye. The maestro reached up, handing Cesare a sheet of parchment. "It's a list of the various skills I practice, Principe . . . painting, frescoes, plumbing systems . . . many things. Payment is something we can discuss." He smiled, and then had a thought. "Excellency, I've done a fresco of the Last Supper in Milan. I'd love the Holy Father to see it. Do you think he would?"

Cesare nodded. "I have seen it, when I was in Milan. Truly wonderful. The Holy Father has a great love of all things beautiful. I'm certain he will be interested." He folded the parchment carefully and slid it into a pocket of his cape. Then, with a salute to da Vinci, he turned his spirited mount into the road leading north.

24

As Cesare moved his army northward up the Rimini-Bologna road toward Bologna itself, Astorre Manfredi rode beside him. Astorre had a pleasant disposition and a willingness to work hard. Each night he dined with Cesare and his commanders, entertaining them with ribald songs of the Faenzan peasants. After the evening meal, he listened to Cesare analyze their situation, and make plans for the following days.

At this point, Cesare faced serious strategic problems. He had almost completed the campaign to establish papal control over the Romagna, but he could not hope to take Bologna, for it was under French protection. Even if he could, he did not wish to antagonize King Louis, and he was certain that the Pope would not approve of such an attack.

The truth was, Cesare's real objective was not the city of Bologna itself, but Castel Bolognese, a powerful fortress outside the city. And Cesare had a hidden card: the Bentivoglio, who ruled Bologna, knew only that the estimable Cesare Borgia and his troops were headed their way. Even Cesare's commanders were unaware of his aims, and were worried about his plan to attack Bologna.

After much thought, and with great cunning, Cesare marched his men to within a few miles of the city gates. The ruler of Bologna, Giovanni Bentivoglio, a large man, rode out on a gigantic horse to meet with him. Behind him rode a standard bearer carrying his banner—a red saw on a field of white.

Bentivoglio, a strong leader but a reasonable man, approached Cesare. "Cesare, my friend. Must we battle? It is not likely that you will win—and even if you do, your French friends will destroy you. Is there no way I can induce you to abandon this foolish pursuit?"

After twenty minutes of intense bargaining Cesare agreed not to attack Bologna, and Bentivoglio agreed that in return Castel Bolognese would be given to Cesare. At Cesare's request, to show good faith, Bologna would also provide troops for future papal campaigns.

The following day, Cesare's men occupied Castel Bolognese. The powerful walls would help them ward off their enemies, the large underground storage rooms held vast munitions, and the officers' quarters were unusually comfortable for a military fortress. Cesare and his commanders were pleased.

That night, Cesare entertained them with a sumptuous feast of roast kid swimming in a sauce of figs and peppers, along with dark red radicchio sautéed in olive oil and local herbs. They talked and sang and drank a great deal of red Frascati wine.

All his troops and infantrymen celebrated as well, as Cesare walked among them, thanking them and congratulating them on their victory. His army felt a great affection for him, and was as loyal to him as were the citizens of the towns he conquered.

After the meal, Cesare and his officers undressed and jumped into the castle's steaming sulfur baths, which were fed from an underground spring. Finally, relaxed, they splashed around in the hot, muddy water, which smelled slightly of rotten eggs.

Later, one by one, Cesare's commanders left the baths and washed themselves with buckets of clean cool water from a nearby well. Finally only Cesare and Astorre Manfredi remained, floating lazily in the warm sludgy waters.

After a moment or two, Cesare felt a hand on his inner thigh. Quite drunk, he reacted slowly as the fingers moved lightly upward to stroke and arouse him.

Suddenly alert, Cesare gently pushed Astorre's hand aside. "I'm not that way, Astorre. It's not you. It's just not my preference."

"Cesare, you don't understand. This isn't lust I feel for you," Astorre said, sincerely. "I am truly in love with you and have been for quite some time."

Cesare sat straight up in the muddy water, trying to collect his thoughts. "Astorre," Cesare said, "I think of you as my friend. I like and admire you. But that is not all you hope for, is it?"

"No," Astorre said, with some sadness. "It is not. I am in love with you in the same way Alexander the Great loved his Persian boy. In the way the English King Edward the Second loved Piers Gaveston. I am certain, at the risk of sounding foolish, that it is a true love."

"Astorre," Cesare said, softly but with certainty, "I can't be that for you. I know many good men who are soldiers, athletes, even cardinals, who have such relationships and enjoy them. But that is not who I am, Astorre. That I cannot give. I can be your loyal friend, but not more."

"I understand, Cesare," Astorre said, but now he stood, embarrassed and distraught. "I will leave for Rome tomorrow."

"You don't have to do that," Cesare said. "I think no less of you that you have claimed a love for me."

"No, Cesare," Astorre said. "I can no longer stay. I must either accept what you have said, and then it becomes too painful to be with you each day, or I must trick myself into believing there is hope. In that case I would keep trying for your attention until finally you became angry or, even worse, disgusted with me. No, I must go."

At dawn the next day, Astorre shook the hand of each of the commanders. He turned to Cesare and embraced him, whispering in his ear, "Good-bye, my friend. My dreams will always be filled with what might have been." Then, with a smile of affection, Astorre Manfredi swung into his saddle and rode south toward Rome.

That night, Cesare sat in his tent considering his next military target. When he realized that he had accom-

plished every goal his father had set for him, he knew the
time had come for him to return to Rome.

Yet Cesare still had an appetite for conquest, as did his
commanders, Vito Vitelli and Paolo Orsini. Now they urged
him to attack Florence. Vitelli despised the Florentines, and
Orsini wanted to restore the Medici, who had been longtime
allies of his family. Cesare had a fondness for both Florence
and the Medici—as well as loyalties from long ago. Still, he
hesitated.

As the golden rays of morning sun filtered into his tent,
Cesare considered his decision. Possibly Vitelli and Orsini
were right; possibly they could take the city, and restore his
Medici friends. But young and aggressive as he was, Cesare
knew that an attack on Florence was an attack on France.
Such an adventure would be foolhardy, for many lives
would be lost; and even if he could take the city, the French
would never let him keep it. Finally, he decided: rather than
attacking the city, he would employ a strategy similar to the
one he had used with the Bolognese.

He led his army southward into the Arno valley, bringing
them, as at Bologna, to within a few miles of the city walls.

There the Florentine commander rode out to parley, accompanied by a small envoy of troops, with flags flying and
the sun glinting off of their armor. Cesare saw them looking
nervously at Vitelli's cannons. He was certain they would
want to avoid a battle. There was no castle or fort that Cesare sought, so this time he settled for a promise of a sizable
annual payment, plus a continuing alliance against enemies
of the Pope.

It was not a great victory. It had not restored the Medici.
But still it was the right decision. And there were other lands
to conquer.

Cesare now marched his army southwest to the coastal city
of Piombino. Unable to defend itself against the powerful
force of the papal army, another city quickly surrendered.

Afterward, still restless, Cesare walked along the docks of
Piombino. There, off the coast, he could see the island of

Elba, with its famous and richly fed iron mines. Here was a target he might take! What a splendid conquest the island would make! What a prize for his father! But it seemed an impossible task, for Cesare had no naval experience.

He was about to abandon his latest dream when he sighted three men riding toward him from the direction of Rome. With astonishment, at last he discerned who it was: his brother, Jofre, along with Michelotto and Duarte Brandao.

Jofre strode forward to greet him. To Cesare he seemed broader, and somehow older. He wore a green velvet doublet with green and gold particolored hose. His blond hair flowed out from under a green velvet biretta. But his message was short and clear, though it was delivered with affection. "Father congratulates you on your brilliant campaign. And he is anxious for your return. He wishes me to tell you that you are sorely missed. And he directs you to return to Rome without delay, for your deceptive tactics with the military near Bologna and Florence have brought resentment from the French king. Cesare, Father warns that nothing of that sort must occur again. Nothing."

Cesare resented the use of his younger brother to deliver this message and he realized that Brandao and Michelotto were there in case he proved stubborn or resistant.

Cesare asked to speak privately with Duarte Brandao. As they walked along the docks, Cesare pointed out Elba lying offshore in the distant haze. "Do you know how rich those iron mines are, Duarte?" he asked. "Enough to finance a campaign against the entire world. I would like to conquer it for Father. It would make a fine gift for his coming birthday, and I've seldom had such a chance to surprise him. What else can one give the Holy Father? He's been so serious of late, that I would enjoy seeing him roll with laughter. And by next year it may fall under French protection if nothing else is done. Yet no matter how much I want it for him, at the moment the challenge lies beyond my skills."

Brandao remained silent, gazing out into the haze. Cesare appeared so filled with excitement at the prospect of such a grand gift for the Pope that Duarte was moved to help him. He turned and looked at eight Genoese galleons tied up at the wharf. "I think I can accomplish what you wish, Cesare, if your men are willing. At one time, long ago, I commanded ships and fought battles at sea."

For the first time in Cesare's life, Duarte was speaking of the past with longing. Cesare hesitated a moment. Then, quietly, he asked, "England?"

Duarte stiffened, and Cesare knew he had been presumptuous. He put his arm around the older man. "Forgive me," he said. "It's not my affair. Just help me take that island."

He felt Duarte relax. For another moment they stood quietly looking across the bay to Elba. Then Duarte pointed to the Genoese ships. "Those ancient, clumsy vessels, if sailed competently, are reliable, Cesare. And I am confident the defenders of the island worry more about pirates than invading armies. Their defenses—cannons, iron nets, and fire ships— will be concentrated in the harbor, where pirates are expected to attack. We will find a quiet beach on the other side of the island. There we will land enough of your army to take the place."

"How will the horses and cannons fare on such a trip?"

"Not well, I'm afraid," Duarte said. "The horses would create havoc and even carnage in their terror; and the cannons would roll and smash through the sides of our own ships, sinking them rather quickly. We will not take either. Infantry will be enough."

After studying Genoese maps and planning for two days, the invasion force was ready. The eight galleons set sail crammed with infantrymen and their captains. They set sail waving gaily to their cavalry and artillery comrades left on the docks.

Their gaiety was short-lived. On the slow, rolling voyage across the bay and around the island, many of the men became violently ill, vomiting everywhere. Cesare himself was nauseated, but bit his lip trying fiercely to hide it. Michelotto and, surprisingly, Jofre, seemed unaffected.

Duarte, at perfect ease, ordered the ships into a quiet bay, its sandy beach white and shimmering. Behind the beach were scattered gray-green bushes and a few gnarled olive trees, with a path cutting through the hills. There was not a soul in sight.

The eight galleons pulled close to the shore, yet not close enough. With water five feet deep, the infantrymen were reluctant to wade to shore. Aware of their fear, Duarte ordered the men from each ship to fasten the long, heavy rope to its bow and heave the rope into the sea. Then one sailor who could swim well was chosen from each galleon and ordered to grab the rope and swim to the beach to tie it to one of the gnarled olive trees that lined the shore.

Next, Duarte asked Cesare to order half the men to strap their weapons to their backs. The other half were to remain on the ships until they saw the signal that the town had been taken.

They did as they were told, but not without grumbling. Duarte slipped over the side first; then, gripping his ship's rope and holding it high so all could see, he waded hand over hand along the rope to the beach.

Cesare went over the side next, following Duarte along the rope to the shore. Reassured, one soldier after another went over the side clutching the taut line as he made his way to land, for anything was better than remaining on the swaying, rolling ships.

Once the troops landed and dried themselves in the sun, Cesare led them off the beach and up a steep and winding path through the hills. In an hour, they had reached the crest. From there they could look down on the town and the harbor.

As Duarte predicted, huge cast-iron cannons were aimed in fixed positions at the entrance to the harbor. An hour later, they could still see no movable artillery from the crest, and no more than one small defense unit of militia marching in the main square.

Silently, Cesare led his forces down the mountain path until they reached the edge of town.

"Charge! *Charge!*" Cesare shouted, and they ran screaming and brandishing their weapons down the principal street and into the central square. The militia, vastly outnumbered, was taken by surprise and quickly surrendered.

The terrified townspeople scurried to their homes. Cesare sent a force to secure the massive cannons, and another to take possession of the iron mines, while Duarte led a contingent to seize the docks. Finally, Cesare ordered his standard bearer to raise the charging bull of the Borgia, and his own flame flag, on the empty flagpole in the town square.

When the nervous delegation of citizens arrived in the square, Cesare identified himself and advised them that the island was now under papal control, but he reassured them that they had nothing to fear.

By this time, his eight Genoan ships rounded the headland.

The troopers then built a fire on the beach to signal that the town had been taken, and that it was safe for the galleons to enter the harbor. As they sailed in flying the Borgia flag and tied up at the docks, the remaining soldiers disembarked.

After inspecting the iron mines and selecting a contingent of men to hold the island, the troops were ready to return to the mainland. Cesare loaded his men back onto the ships.

And so it was that, just four hours after their first landing on the beach, Cesare Borgia and Duarte Brandao had captured the island of Elba. Now Michelotto, Jofre, Cesare, and Duarte rode side by side on the long journey back to Rome.

25

Cardinal della Rovere and Cardinal Ascanio Sforza met in secret over a lunch of pink salted prosciutto ham, roasted red peppers dripping with green olive oil dotted with several shiny cloves of garlic, and crusty loaves of freshly baked semolina bread. The fine red wine was plentiful, and helped to loosen their tongues.

Ascanio spoke first. "It was a mistake, placing my vote for Alexander in the last conclave. It is an impossible task being his vice-chancellor, for though his administrative skills are above reproach, he is too fond a father. And he indulges his children to such an extent that he will bankrupt the church by the time a new Pope takes the throne. Cesare Borgia's desire to conquer and unite the territories in the Romagna has almost emptied the papal coffers through his endless payments to his troops. And no queen or duchess has as fine a wardrobe as this young son of the Pope."

Cardinal della Rovere smiled knowingly. "But my dear Ascanio, you did not come all this way to discuss the sins of the Pope now, for there is nothing new here. There must be another reason that remains invisible to me."

Ascanio shrugged. "What is there to say? My nephew Giovanni has been humiliated by the Borgia, and Pesaro now belongs to Cesare. My niece Caterina, a true virago, is being held in one of the Borgia castles and her territories have been conquered as well. My own brother, Ludovico, has been captured and relegated to a dungeon by the French, for they have Milan. Now I hear Alexander has made a se-

cret pact with France and Spain to divide Naples, in order
that Cesare may wear the crown. It is an abomination!"

"And your solution?" della Rovere asked. He had expected Ascanio to come to him sooner, but now he felt the
need for extra vigilance, for in a time of such treachery one
could never be too cautious. Though the servants were
sworn to have no eyes or ears, della Rovere and Ascanio
alike knew that a few ducats could bring the deaf the gift of
hearing and the blind the gift of sight. For those who suffered poverty, gold could always work more miracles than
prayer.

And so when Ascanio spoke, he whispered. "When
Alexander no longer sits on the throne as Pope, there is the
hope our problems can be resolved. And there is no doubt
that in a new conclave it is you who will be chosen."

Della Rovere's dark eyes looked like slits of black on his
pale and puffy face. "I have seen no indication that Alexander is willing to step down. I hear that his health is quite
good, and as for any other possibility, it is known that his
son is a madman. Who would chance bringing him harm?"

Ascanio Sforza placed his hand on his chest and spoke
with sincerity. "Cardinal, don't misunderstand. This Pope
has enemies who would be grateful for our help. And a
younger son—one who has truly prayed for the hat of a cardinal. I am not suggesting that we take a hand in any deed
that will stain our souls. I am suggesting nothing that would
cause us danger," he said. "I am only asking that we consider
an alternative to this papacy—no more, no less."

"Are you suggesting that this Pope might suddenly fall
ill? A drink of wine, perhaps, a spoiled clam?" della Rovere
asked.

Ascanio spoke loud enough for the servants to hear. "No
one can attest to when the Heavenly Father will call one of
his children home."

Della Rovere digested what Ascanio said, making a mental list of the Borgia enemies. "Is it true that Alexander is
planning a meeting with the duke of Ferrara to suggest a

new marriage alliance for his daughter with the duke's son, Alfonso?"

"I have heard little about that," Ascanio said. "But if it is true my nephew, Giovanni, is sure to get wind of it, for he has taken himself to Ferrara of late. And no matter how hard anyone tries, he cannot be convinced to hold his tongue. I have no doubt that Ferrara will refuse any alliance that involves the infamous Lucrezia. For she is used goods."

Della Rovere stood up. "Cesare Borgia will capture the territories of the Romagna, and bring them under the control of the Pope. Ferrara is the last remaining territory, and once an alliance is formed the Borgia will own us all. I am certain Alexander would prefer to win by love rather than war. Therefore, he will push hard for this alliance. We must push as hard against it. For he must be stopped."

Now, with his family back in Rome, Alexander hastened the critical negotiations for the match of his daughter, Lucrezia, with the twenty-four-year-old Alfonso d'Este, the future duke of Ferrara.

The d'Este family was the oldest and most respected of Italian nobility, and everyone thought Alexander's latest attempt would surely fail. Yet he knew it must not.

The duchy of Ferrara was located in an area of great strategic importance. It formed a buffer between the Romagna and the Venetians, who were often hostile and not to be trusted. Moreover, Ferrara was well armed and well defended, and would make a highly desirable ally.

Yet most Romans found it hard to believe that the aristocratic and powerful d'Este would ever commit the much-adored heir of their proud duchy to a Borgia—a family of Spanish newcomers—despite Alexander's prestige as Pope and Cesare's wealth and excellence as a warrior.

But Ercole d'Este, Alfonso's father and the present duke of Ferrara, was a hardheaded realist. He was quite aware of Cesare's military skill and aggressiveness. With all its defenses, Ferrara would have a difficult time if Cesare's powerful army attacked. And Ercole had no guarantee that, in the coming year, Cesare would not attack.

He knew that a Borgia match could change a potentially dangerous enemy into a powerful ally against the Venetians. And, he reasoned, a Pope was, after all, Christ's Vicar on Earth and supreme head of the Holy Mother Church. If that were taken into consideration, it made up, at least in part, for the lack of family background and culture in the Borgia.

The d'Este, who were dependent on the French, were anxious to please King Louis. Ercole knew that the king was determined to maintain the goodwill of the Pope, and that he favored the match between Alfonso and Lucrezia—a fact he had impressed upon Ercole forcefully in recent weeks.

And so the difficult and complex negotiations continued for days. In the end, as in so many situations of this kind, there was the question of money.

On the final day Duarte Brandao joined Alexander and Ercole d'Este for a session that each hoped would, at last, result in an agreement. The three sat in Alexander's library.

"Holy Father," Ercole began, "I have noticed that throughout your splendid apartments you have only the works of Pinturicchio. No Botticelli? No Bellini or Giotto? And what a shame to have none of the works of such artists as Perugino or Fra Lippo Lippi."

Alexander was unfazed. He had his own unshakable views on art. "I like Pinturicchio. Someday he will be recognized as the greatest of them all."

Ercole smiled patronizingly. "I think not, Holiness. I suspect that you may be the only man in Italy to hold that view."

Duarte recognized Ercole's remarks as a thinly disguised negotiating tactic—a way of emphasizing the greatness and cultural richness of the d'Este, and then by comparison, the pedestrian tastes and cultural ignorance of the Borgia.

"Perhaps you are correct, Don Ercole," Duarte replied slyly. "The cities we conquered this year contained many works by the fine artists you mention. Cesare offered to send them here, but His Holiness refused. I still hope to persuade him of the value of such artworks, and how they would enhance the Vatican. Indeed, we have only recently discussed that your own city, Ferrara, has the largest and most valuable collection of all—in addition to its wealth in silver and gold."

Ercole momentarily paled, grasping at once the point Duarte was none too subtly making. "Well," he said, changing the subject. "Perhaps we should discuss the matter of a dowry."

"What were your hopes, Don Ercole?" asked Alexander with some apprehension.

"I was thinking of three hundred thousand ducats, Holiness," Ercole d'Este said smugly.

Alexander, who had planned to begin his offering at thirty thousand, choked on his wine. "Three hundred thousand ducats is an outrage," he said.

"Yet, that's the least I could accept without insult," Ercole replied. "For my son, Alfonso, is a fine young man with an extraordinary future, and in much demand."

For over an hour they bargained, each side making every imaginable argument about the largesse of its offer. When Alexander refused to budge, Ercole threatened to leave.

Alexander reconsidered, and proposed a compromise.

Ercole refused, and Alexander threatened to leave, until he noticed the startled expression on the duke's face and allowed himself to be talked into remaining.

Finally Ercole accepted two hundred thousand ducats, which Alexander still considered a huge dowry, for Ercole also insisted on the elimination of the annual tax paid by Ferrara to the Holy Church.

And so it was on that day the match of the decade was made.

One of the first things Cesare did when he returned to Rome was to meet with his father privately to inquire about his prisoner, Caterina Sforza. He was told that she had tried to escape from the Belvedere, and, as punishment, had been held captive in the Castel Sant' Angelo—a far less pleasant and healthy place.

Cesare went to see her at once.

The Castel Sant' Angelo was a massive round fortress with richly decorated apartments upstairs, but the massive cellar that comprised much of the fortress housed several large dungeons. Cesare had Caterina brought upstairs by his guards and ushered into a grand reception room. She peered at the world through squinted eyes, for she had not seen the sun for quite some time. She was still beautiful, though somewhat disheveled from her time in the dungeons.

Cesare greeted her warmly, and bowed to kiss her hand. "So, my dear friend," he said, smiling. "Are you more foolish than I imagined? I place you in the finest quarters in Rome and you repay my generosity by attempting to escape? You are not quite so clever as I imagined."

"You must have known," she said, without emotion.

Cesare sat on a brocade couch and offered Caterina a seat, but she refused. "I suppose your attempt to escape crossed my mind," Cesare explained, "but I counted on your self-interest, and believed you would prefer to be imprisoned in comfort, rather than in misery."

"Imprisonment in the finest quarters is nonetheless miserable," she said coldly.

Cesare was amused, for though she spoke with obvious resentment, still he found her charming. "But what is your plan now?" he asked. "For I am certain you cannot spend the rest of your days in Castel Sant' Angelo."

"What do you offer as a choice?" she asked defiantly.

"Sign over your territories of Imola and Forli on official papers," Cesare said. "And agree not to attempt to retake them. I will then give orders to release you, and you may retire freely to any place you choose."

Caterina smiled at him slyly. "I can sign any paper you present, but how will that prevent me from trying to recapture my lands?"

"Another ruler, less worthy, might do that," he said, "but I find it difficult to believe that you would betray yourself by signing if you could not in good conscience agree. Of course it is always possible that you might break your word, even after it is given, but in that case we will prove in the courts of Rome that we are the legitimate rulers. And our case will be strengthened by your dishonesty."

"You count on this?" she asked, laughing good-naturedly. "I find that difficult to believe. There is something else you are withholding from me."

Cesare gave her a charming smile. "It is far too sentimental to be clever, but in truth, I dislike the thought of a beautiful creature rotting in a dungeon forever. It seems such a waste."

Caterina was surprised to find she was enjoying him, but she refused to let that distortion of her heart cause her too big a compromise. She had a secret she could tell, but would she? For that decision she needed time. "Come back tomorrow, Cesare," she said pleasantly. "Allow me to consider it."

When Cesare arrived the following day, he had Caterina brought upstairs once more. She had made use of the maids he had sent, to help bathe her and wash her hair. Now, though her clothes were still dingy and torn, he could see that she had attempted to make herself more attractive.

He walked toward her, and instead of stepping back she moved forward. He reached for her and pulled her down onto the couch with him, kissing her passionately. But when she pulled away, he did not force himself upon her.

She spoke before Cesare, as she ran her fingers through his auburn curls. "I will do as you suggest. But others will say you are mad to trust me."

Cesare looked at her fondly. "They already do. If my commanders had their way, you'd be floating in the Tiber," he said. "Where have you decided to go?"

They sat up on the couch together, and he held her hand. "To Florence. Imola and Forli are out of the question, and my relatives in Milan are such bores. Florence, at least, is an interesting place. Perhaps I'll even find another husband there—God help him."

"He will be a lucky man," Cesare said with a smile. "The papers will be here tonight, and you can be on your way to-morrow . . . with a reliable guard, of course."

He began to leave, but stopped at the door and turned to her. "Care for yourself, Caterina."

"And you as well," she said.

When Cesare had gone, she felt a surprising sadness. For in that moment she was certain they would not meet again, and so he might never know that those papers could not make any difference. For she held within her womb the part of him she had already claimed. And as the mother of his heir, those territories would in the end once again belong to her.

Filofila was the finest verse scandalmonger of Rome. Secretly in the pay of the Orsini family, he was under the personal protection of Cardinal Antonio Orsini himself. Filofila invented the grossest crimes for the most saintly men. He had an even better time with people of villainous deeds, as long as they were ranked in high place. He could vilify cities as a whole: Florence was the big-breasted, wide-hipped harlot, a city full of riches and great artists but lacking in fighting men. The citizens of Florence were moneylenders, cronies to the Turks, versed in sodomy. And like a whore she went to all kinds of foreign powers for protection, instead of coupling herself with her fellow Italian cities.

Venice was, of course, the secretive unforgiving city of the doges, who would sell its citizens' blood for trade, who executed its own people if they as much as told a foreigner how many ducats it cost to buy silk in the Far East. Venice was a huge snake, waiting in its great canal to snap up any morsel of the civilized world that could help it profit. A city without art or artisans, without great books or a great library, a city forever closed to the humanities. But a city expert in treachery, executing both small and great alike for their crimes.

Naples was the city of the syphilitic pox, the French disease—just as Milan was the French sycophant, fellow to the sodomitic traitor Florence.

But it was the Borgia clan that Filofila made the target for his most scabrous verses.

He sang out in rhyme about their orgies in the Vatican, their murders in Rome and in all the city-states of Italy. His verse was eloquent, his prose exquisite, when he took up his pen to claim that Pope Alexander had used simony to purchase the papacy, or that he had twenty natural children. He had betrayed the Crusades, stealing money from Peter's Pence to pay Cesare Borgia's soldiers, making his son master of Romagna and forcing the Papal States to heel. And for what? To support his family, his bastard children, his mistresses, his orgies. And even more: as if committing incest with his natural daughter were not enough, he had taught her to poison his rich enemies in the college of cardinals and then traded her off in marriage more than once to cement his alliances with other powerful families of Italy. One marriage was annulled; the other ended in widowhood—that condition brought about by her own natural brother, Cesare Borgia.

Yet it was when Filofila wrote his poems about Cesare Borgia that he surpassed himself. With loving detail he described how Cesare always wore a mask to hide a face disfigured by the suppurating sores of the French pox; how he had deceived both the Spanish and French kings, and betrayed Italy with both of them at the same time; how Cesare too committed incest, with both his sister and his sister-in-law. He had made one brother a cuckold and the other a corpse. Rape was his special pleasure, murder his most subtle diplomacy.

But now, with the fabulous d'Este marriage soon to take place, Filofila turned his venomous pen to Lucrezia. She had lain with her father and her brother—separately at first, then all together in the same bed. She had sex with dogs, monkeys, and mules; and when her footman caught her at these vile perversions, she poisoned him. Now unable to bear the shame of her lustful conduct, her father was trading her off to Ferrara to cement a relationship with an illustrious Italian family. Yes, Filofila thought, he had outdone himself with his work on Lucrezia.

All this made Filofila famous. The verses had been copied and posted on the walls of Rome, circulated through Florence, and especially requested by rich Venetians. Not that Filofila dared to sign his name, but the two sketched ravens cawing at each other beneath each poem had become his trademark. And so the people knew.

One sunny afternoon the poet dressed and perfumed himself, preparing to join the court of his patron, Cardinal Orsini. The cardinal had given him the use of a small house on the grounds of the Palazzo Orsini. Like all great lords, the cardinal wanted his supporters and blood relatives nearby to protect him. And Filofila was as expert with a dagger as a quill.

Hearing the clatter of horses and the metallic clanking of armor, he looked out his bedroom window. A dozen mounted horsemen were riding up to his house and surrounding it. They were all in light armor, except for the leader, who was clothed completely in black—black doublet, black hose, black gloves, and, on his head, a black biretta. With a faint sickening in his throat, Filofila recognized the black-masked Cesare Borgia—and noted the sword and dagger he wore.

With relief, Filofila then saw a band of Orsini soldiers approach on foot. But Cesare ignored them and came straight up to the house. Filofila went out to meet him for the first time.

To the poet, Cesare looked as tall and muscular as a Ger-

man. On his face he wore a cheerful smile. He addressed
Filofila directly, with an exaggerated politeness. "Why,
Master Poet," he said, "I have come to help you rhyme. But
it is impossible in this place. You must come with me."

Filofila bowed low. "My Lord, I must decline. My cardinal has summoned me. I will come when you are free
again." He felt resentment that the Borgia had come to his
house, but he dared not put his hand on his sword or dagger.

Cesare did not hesitate. Lifting the man as though he were
made of rags, he threw him over his horse. When he
mounted he hit Filofila just once, but the blow left him unconscious.

When the poet opened his eyes, he saw rough-hewn
beams and walls covered with the stuffed heads of
animals—boars, bears, and oxen. He seemed to be in some
kind of hunting lodge.

Then he looked across the room and saw a man he recognized. Only shock stopped the cry in his throat as his bowels churned with fear: it was the notorious strangler Don
Michelotto. He was sharpening a long knife.

After a moment Filofila found the courage to speak. "You
must know that Cardinal Orsini and his guard will find me
here, and will severely punish anyone who harms me."

Michelotto said nothing, just continued sharpening the
long blade.

"I suppose you plan to strangle me," Filofila said, his
voice trembling.

Now Michelotto seemed to pay attention. "No, Signor
Poet. Not at all. That would be too fast, too easy for a man
of your vast cruelty. What I intend to do," he said smiling,
"is to cut out your tongue, then your ears and nose, then your
genitals, then your fingers, one at a time. Then I may cut off
other things. Or, if I am moved to pity, maybe then I will do
you the favor of killing you."

The following afternoon, a large blood-soaked sack was

hurled over the wall of the Palazzo Orsini. The contents sickened the cardinal's guards who opened it. Inside was a headless, fingerless corpse. Its severed genitals, tongue, fingers, nose, and ears were inside as well, neatly wrapped in one of Filofila's poems.

Nothing was said of the incident. No further poems by Filofila appeared. The rumor was that he had gone to Germany for the health-giving mineral baths.

26

Silverlake was beautiful that spring. Cesare and Lucrezia made a handsome couple as they walked along the shore, she in her jeweled cape and hood and he in his black velvet, his beret studded with feathers and precious stones. They had returned to the place where they had spent their happiest moments, for their time together would be scarce now that her marriage to Alfonso d'Este was close at hand.

Cesare's auburn hair shone bright in the sunlight, and despite his usual black mask the smile on his face was evidence of his joy at being with his sister.

"So next week you will be a d'Este," Cesare said teasingly. "You will then have the responsibility as well as the good fortune of being a member of a *distinguished* family."

"I'll always be a Borgia, Chez," Lucrezia said. "And there is no reason for jealousy in the case of this alliance, for I have not fooled myself into believing that this marriage is for love. This Alfonso is as reluctant to have me as a wife as I am to have him as a husband. But, as I am my father's daughter, he is his father's son."

Cesare smiled fondly at her. "You have grown more beautiful through your misfortunes. And this marriage will allow you to do many of the things you enjoy. The d'Este love the arts, the gathering of poets and sculptors. Ferrara is steeped in culture and humanities, the very subjects that breathe life into you. It is also fortunate for me that it rests alongside my territories in the Romagna, and that King Louis directs the duke with a strong hand."

"Will you see that Giovanni and Rodrigo are well whenever you are in Rome? For I despise having to be without them for even a short time in Ferrara. Will you care for them and let them feel your strong arms around them, and treat one as important as the other—for me?" she asked.

"There is no question. For one child is more of me, the other more of you—so both have my everlasting love," Cesare reassured her. "Crezia, if Father had not allied you with the d'Este, would you have passed your life in widow's weeds, living and governing Nepi?"

"I considered this decision carefully before I agreed," Lucrezia told him. "And though I know Father could have forced my hand, he would have discovered I had hidden away in a convent, even become a nun, if I were violently opposed to this alliance. But I have learned to govern, and believe that in this place, I may find my own. There is also the matter of you and the children to consider. A convent is not the best place for children, and I cannot imagine living my life without them."

Cesare stopped and faced his sister with admiration. "Is there nothing you have failed to consider? Nothing you cannot adapt to with grace and intelligence?"

A look of sadness, like a shadow, passed across her face. "One small problem I have not managed to find a solution for. And though it is tiny compared to all the other issues, it seems to cause me some unhappiness."

"Must I torture you to pull this truth from you," he joked, "or will you confess it voluntarily, to see if I might help?"

Lucrezia shook her head. "I cannot call this new husband Alfonso without my heart recoiling when I compare him to my last. And yet I know no other way to modify his name."

Cesare's eyes glistened with amusement. "There is no problem too large for me to solve, and so I may have the answer to your prayers. You say he is his father's son; why not call him Sonny? Say it the first time on your marriage bed, with great affection, and he will believe it is a term of endearment."

Lucrezia wrinkled her fine nose, and laughed aloud. "An aristocratic d'Este? Sonny?" But the more she thought of it, the more comfortable she became.

They walked to the end of the old dock from which they had fished and dived as children, splashing in the water with complete freedom. Then their father sat close, watching them, protecting them, and making them feel safe. Now, this many years later, they sat on that same dock and looked out at the rippling water, which sparkled like a million tiny diamonds reflecting the afternoon sun. Lucrezia leaned against her brother, and he wrapped his arms around her.

Her voice was soft and serious. "Chez, I've heard about the ill-fated poet Filofila."

"Oh?" Cesare said without emotion. "Did his death disturb you? For he felt no such affection for you, or he would not have been able to write such evil rhyme and verse."

Lucrezia turned and touched his face. "I know that, Chez," she said. "And I suppose I should thank you for all you do to defend me—in spite of Alfonso's death, for even that I have long understood. It is your well-being that concerns me. For you seem to kill so readily of late. Are you not concerned for your own soul?"

Cesare explained. "If there is a God, as the Holy Father describes him, he does not mean we must never kill—for otherwise there could be no holy wars. What is meant by 'Thou shalt not kill' is that killing without good and honorable cause becomes a sin. We know that it is not a sin to hang a murderer."

"Chez, *do* we know that?" she asked. Lucrezia shifted to face him as she spoke, for this subject was important to her. "Is it not an arrogance to decide what is a good and honorable cause? To the Infidel it is good and honorable to slay the Christian, but to the Christian the opposite is true."

Again Cesare paused, amazed as he often was by his sister.

"Crezia," he said. "I try never to kill for personal satisfaction, only for the good of us all."

Lucrezia's eyes filled, but she tried to keep her voice steady. "Will there be that many more killings, then?"

"Certainly in war there will be, Crezia. But aside from war, we sometimes must take lives for a greater good as well as for our own protection," he said. Then he described his own decision to hang the chicken thieves on his last campaign in Cesena.

Lucrezia hesitated before responding, for she was not convinced. "It worries me, Cesare, that you may find yourself using 'the greater good' as an excuse to eliminate troublesome men. And life is full of troublesome men."

Cesare stood gazing out at the lake. "It is lucky for all of us that you are not a man, for you tether yourself with doubt, Crezia, and it could stop you from acting."

"I'm certain you are right, Chez," Lucrezia said thoughtfully. "But I'm not sure *that's* bad . . ." She was no longer so certain that she understood evil, especially once it was hidden in the shadows of the hearts of those she loved.

As the pink dusk fell over the silvery lake, Lucrezia took her brother's hand and led him back along the path to the cottage. Inside they lay naked together on the white fur rug in front of the warm fire which crackled and blazed in the stone fireplace. Cesare marveled at the fullness of his sister's breasts, the softness of her belly, transfixed by how much of a woman she had become and how drawn to her he was by an even greater passion.

Lucrezia spoke in a tender, affectionate voice. "Chez, remove that mask before you kiss me? For with it on you could be anyone."

The smile fell from his lips, and his eyes lowered self-consciously. "I will be unable to make love to you if I see your eyes fill with pity for my pockmarked face," he said. "It will keep me from enjoying what may be our last time together."

"I swear I will not look upon your face with pity," she said. And then she tickled him as she said, "I may even laugh, and then you will stop this senseless drivel. For I have loved you from the time my eyes first opened, and you stood above me smiling. I have played with you and bathed with you as we were growing up. I have seen you look so handsome that I had to turn away, or give myself away, and I have seen you when your heart has broken and the sadness in your eyes has forced my own eyes to fill with tears. But I have never once thought you less, or loved you less, for some small marks on your face."

She bent over him then, her lips covering his, her body already trembling. When she lifted her head again, she looked into his eyes and said, "I just wish to touch you, to see your eyelids closed in ecstasy, to run my fingers gently down your nose, to feel your sweet full lips. I wish no barrier between us, my brother, my lover, my friend. For, from this night on, all that is left of my passion will rest with you."

Cesare sat up and slowly removed his mask.

Lucrezia married Alfonso d'Este by proxy in Rome the following week. With the contract of their marriage he had sent a small portrait, which showed a tall, rather stern-looking man, not unattractive, who held himself with strict reserve. He was dressed in the dark uniform of state, with many medals and ribbons to decorate it; just beneath his long fine nose a mustache tickled his top lip, though it did not make him smile. His curly dark hair neatly capped his head, with no stray strands let loose. She could not imagine this Alfonso loving or making love with wild abandon.

She was to join him in Ferrara, where they would live. Yet in Rome wedding festivities were being celebrated—festivals far more lavish and costly than her wedding to Giovanni, and many times what they had been in her marriage to her beloved Alfonso. In fact, it was more extravagant than any celebration the citizens had ever seen.

The palaces of noble families were numerous and opulent. Still, they were all given stipends to offset the costs of these feasts and festivals. The Pope seemed prepared to empty the Vatican treasury in celebration of his daughter's brilliant match. He decreed a holiday for all Roman workers, and throughout the following week there were new pageants, processions, and festivals. Bonfires were lit in front of the Vatican, as well as before all the large castles—the one in front of Santa Maria of Portico the largest of all.

On the day the wedding contract was signed and the Pope gave his blessings, Lucrezia wore a gown of gold covered with precious jewels, which she then threw from the balcony to the crowd below as soon as the ceremony was over. It landed on a court jester, who ran through the streets crying, "Long live the duchess of Ferrara! Long live Pope Alexander!"

Cesare himself played a great part in this wedding of his sister's, and showed his skill as a horseman by leading a street march in his sister's honor.

That night, at the wedding celebration for all the family and their closest friends, Lucrezia performed several of her Spanish dances for the pleasure of her father.

Alexander, his face radiant, sat on the throne clapping his hands with enjoyment. Cesare, his eyes shining through his carnival mask of gold and pearl, stood behind the Pope to his right. Jofre stood to his left.

Now Alexander, clad in his finest papal vestments, stood up and slowly descended the stairs to walk across the ballroom floor toward his daughter. A hush fell over the crowd and all laughter ceased.

"Will you honor your father with this dance?" Alexander asked. "For soon you will be too far away."

Lucrezia curtsied and took his hand. Turning to the musicians, Alexander instructed them to play, and then he took his daughter in his arms. She marveled that he was still so strong, his smile so radiant, his step so light and smooth. She felt as though she were a child again, remembering how she had placed her own tiny feet in her pink satin slippers upon her father's, and riding his steps, how she glided along. Then, she loved her father more than life itself. It was a magical time for her when all things were possible, long before she realized that life required sacrifice.

Suddenly she raised her head and looked over her father's shoulder, to see her brother Cesare standing just behind him. "May I, Father?" he asked.

Alexander turned and looked at Cesare with slight surprise, but he quickly recovered, and said, "Of course, my son." Still, rather than letting go of Lucrezia's hand and handing her to Cesare, Alexander instructed the musicians to play on . . . a light and happy tune.

The Pope stood between his children, one hand holding his daughter's, the other holding his son's, and with a great smile and a boisterous laugh he began to dance with both of them. With incredible energy, he began to whirl and spin, taking them with him. And his face was aglow with ecstasy.

The crowd began to laugh until their breath came short. They cheered and clapped and finally joined in, until the entire room was filled with people dancing in a frenzy.

There was only one who stood aside, one who did not dance. Behind the Pope's throne, Alexander's younger son, Jofre, tall and brooding, stood silent and unsmiling as he watched.

Shortly before Lucrezia was to leave for Ferrara, the Pope hosted a stag banquet to which all of Roman male society was invited. He had summoned dancing girls to entertain, and he filled the hall with card and gaming tables in celebration of his new alliance.

Alexander, Cesare, and Jofre sat at the head table with the aging duke of Ferrara, Ercole d'Este, and his two young nephews. Alfonso d'Este, the bridegroom, had stayed in Ferrara to rule in his father's place.

The dinner was a sumptuous feast with all manner of delicacies, and an array of large carafes of wine added to the gaiety and good humor of the guests.

When the plates had been cleared by the servants, Alexander's son Jofre suddenly rose unsteadily and raised his goblet in a toast. "As a gift from my family in Naples, and in honor of my new family, the d'Este, a very special entertainment has been arranged . . . something not seen in Rome for many years."

Alexander and Cesare were surprised at this announcement, and embarrassed at Jofre's crude presumption in referring to his "new family." They wondered, with great anxiety, what he had in store for them, as the guests looked around in anticipation.

The great carved wooden doors swung open, and four footmen entered the room. Without a word, they scattered golden chestnuts across the floor in the center of the room. "My God," Cesare thought, looking toward his father. In a sudden flash of horror, he realized what was about to happen. He called to his brother, "Jofre! Don't do this," but it was already too late.

To the sound of trumpets, Jofre opened another door and let in a procession of twenty naked courtesans, their dark hair loose, their soft skin oiled and perfumed. Each had a small silk purse dangling from a thong around her waist.

Jofre was loud, giddy with wine, as he continued. "What you see on the floor before you are chestnuts of pure gold. And these lovely ladies will be pleased to bend over so that you may see them from a different angle. This will be a new treat . . . at least for some of you."

The guests roared with laughter. But both Cesare and Alexander tried to stop the lewd display before too much damage had been done.

Jofre, ignoring the signals being given by his father and brother, continued, "You gentlemen may mount these mares any time you like. Mind you, you must mount standing up from the rear. And for each successful mount, your lady may pick one golden chestnut from the floor and place it in her purse. It goes without saying that the ladies may keep the chestnuts they gather as gifts for the entertainment they have provided."

The courtesans began to bend over and wiggle their naked asses sensuously at the male diners.

Ercole d'Este, shocked by the vulgar display, grew pale in astonishment.

Yet, one by one, the noblemen of Rome began to stand and drift away from the tables, moving toward the beckoning, bending courtesans. Some, though they didn't mount, grabbed lustily at the mounds of courtesan flesh.

In his youth Alexander had enjoyed such events, but now he was mortified, aware that on this occasion it was grotesquely out of place. And he was certain that it was meant to be, for he understood the ill reflection on his family's sophistication—and judgment—this represented.

The Pope approached Ercole d'Este and tried vainly to apologize. But Ercole, shaking his head, told himself that if the proxy wedding had not already taken place, he would cancel the match and take his chances with the French and with Cesare's armies—ducats or no ducats. Since he had already banked the gold, now he simply left the room, muttering "Borgia peasants."

Later that night, Cesare received news that disturbed him even more. The body of Astorre Manfredi had been found floating in the Tiber. Cesare had promised him safe conduct after the fall of Faenza, and this news would make it seem to many as if he had broken his word. Cesare knew that once again he would be suspected. There were those who would believe that he had killed once more: with Michelotto, Cesare certainly had the means. But who would do this? And why?

Two days later, upstairs in the room called the Pappagallo, the Pope bid his daughter good-bye. She was sad to be leaving her father, despite all the trouble he'd caused.

The Pope himself attempted to appear more jovial than he felt, for he would sorely miss this daughter. "If you are ever unhappy," he told her, "send a message, for I will employ my greatest influence to see it made right. And do not worry about the children, for Adriana is well suited to caring for them, as you well know."

"But Papa," Lucrezia said. "I have learned so much about entertaining and governing, and yet I am frightened to go to this new place, where I know no one favors me."

"In no time they will be as much in love with you as we are," Alexander said. "You need only think of me, and I will know it," he said. "And each time I think of you, you will know it." He kissed her on the forehead then. "Go. It is unseemly for a Pope to shed tears over the loss of one of his children."

Alexander watched from the window. As Lucrezia prepared to leave, he waved and shouted from the window. "Be of good cheer! For anything you wish for is already granted."

Lucrezia set out for Ferrara, accompanied by a thousand richly attired nobles, servants, musicians, and entertainers. The nobles rode on fine horses or in splendid coaches. Lucrezia herself rode a small Spanish horse, richly caparisoned and fitted with a gold-studded saddle and bridle. The rest rode on donkeys or in crude wagons. Some walked.

They stopped at each of the territories Cesare had conquered, so that Lucrezia could wash her hair and bathe. In each city the children ran excitedly to meet her party, dressed in the red and yellow that were Cesare's colors. All along the journey, the entire entourage stopped for fantastic and hugely expensive balls and other celebrations.

The spectacular journey took more than a month to travel from Rome to Ferrara, and on the way it emptied the purses of many a local host.

Ercole d'Este, duke of Ferrara, was a man known for his stinginess, and within days he had sent most of Lucrezia's expensive entourage back to Rome. She was forced to fight for every attendant and aide she wanted to keep in her new Ferrara household.

When most of the disappointed Romans and Spanish who had accompanied Lucrezia left on the duke's orders, Ercole gave Lucrezia a dramatic lesson on how things were done in Ferrara. He led Lucrezia up a narrow spiral staircase to a room near the top of the castle. There he pointed to a dark brown stain on the stone floor and told her, "An earlier duke beheaded his wife and his stepson, for he discovered they were lovers. Look, my dear," he cackled. "You can still see their blood."

Lucrezia shuddered at the stains on the floor.

Only a few months after living with Alfonso d'Este, Lucrezia was pregnant. The people of Ferrara were overcome with happiness, for they had prayed for a male heir. But in an unfortunate circumstance, that summer was humid in Ferrara, and it became a breeding ground for the mosquitoes which carried malaria. Lucrezia fell ill.

Alfonso d'Este sent a message to the Pope, explaining that the duchess of Ferrara, Alexander's daughter, was suffering from the fever, shaking chills, and sweats. He explained that she had recently fallen into a serious delirium, and that Alexander might wish to send his own physicians from Rome.

Alexander and Cesare were terrified at the thought of losing Lucrezia. Both feared she might have been poisoned. And so the Pope sent instructions, written in his own hand, that only the physician he was sending was to treat her.

On that very night, Cesare, disguised as a Moorish peasant, with darkened skin and a hooded gown, accompanied this physician to Lucrezia's bedside.

Not knowing who these men were when they arrived in Ferrara—just that they were sent from Rome—both Alfonso and Ercole d'Este stayed in their own quarters while a manservant led Cesare and the physician up the stairs to Lucrezia's room.

Though she was lethargic and delirious, Lucrezia recognized Cesare at once. Her skin was white and pale, her pasty lips cracked with fever and her stomach too tender to touch from the constant vomiting that had plagued her for more than two weeks now. She tried to greet Cesare, but her voice was so hoarse and weak that no sound escaped her lips.

Once the manservant had gone, Cesare bent to kiss her. "My princess looks a little pale tonight," he whispered to her. "The glow of rosy cheeks does not grace your face. Could it be that love eludes you in this place?"

Lucrezia tried to smile back, to acknowledge his humor, but she could not even lift her arm to touch his face.

It was apparent that her condition was critical; still, Cesare became more upset when the physician confirmed it.

Cesare strode to the washstand, shed his hooded robe, and scrubbed the stain from his face. Then he ordered a servant to fetch the duke.

Moments later Ercole arrived, plainly alarmed at being summoned to Lucrezia's room. He saw Cesare at once.

"Cesare Borgia!" Ercole gasped. "Why are you here?"

Cesare's voice harbored no warmth. "I have come to visit my sister. Am I not welcome? Is there something in the shadows I should not see?"

"No, of course not," Ercole said, stammering with nervousness. "I . . . I am just surprised to see you."

"I will not stay long, dear Duke," Cesare said. "Only long enough to deliver a message from my father—and from me as well."

"Yes?" Ercole said, his eyes narrowed now with suspicion and dread.

Cesare put his hand on his sword as if ready to fight all of Ferrara. Yet his voice was cold and reasonable as he moved close to Ercole and spoke. "The Holy Father and I are most desirous that my sister be restored to health. If she should die, we will surely blame her hosts and their city. Am I clear?"

"Am I to assume this is a threat?" Ercole asked.

"I believe you understand me," Cesare said, his voice more steady than he felt. "My sister must not die. For if she does, she will not die alone!"

Cesare and the physician stayed for several days. Finally, it was decided that for a cure, Lucrezia must be bled. But she refused it.

"I will not be drained white," she cried, shaking her head and kicking her legs with what little energy she had.

Cesare sat beside her, holding and soothing her, imploring her to be brave. "You must live for me," he whispered. "For what other reason should I live?"

Lucrezia finally stopped struggling and hid her face in Cesare's chest so as not to see what was being done. As Cesare held her foot the doctor made several small cuts in her ankle and on the tops of her feet, until enough blood was let that the physician felt she could recover.

Before he left, Cesare kissed Lucrezia and promised to visit her again shortly, for now he was living in Cesena, only hours from Ferrara.

Lucrezia did not die. Over the following weeks, she began to heal. She began to feel warm again, her soaking sweats ceased, and she remained awake more of the time, without falling into the deep and dreamless sleep of her darkest nights. Although her child was stillborn, she gradually regained her health and vitality.

It was only in the quiet moments of the dark night that she grieved for this small child, for she had come to understand that time spent in grief was time wasted—that there had been too much grief in her life. And if she were to make the most of what she had been given, and do the greatest good, she must focus on what could be done, not on what she was powerless to change. And so it was that she began to live a life of virtue.

By her first anniversary in Ferrara, she had begun, gradually, to win the love and respect of her subjects, as well as

the love of the strange and powerful d'Este family with
whom she now lived.

The old duke, Ercole himself, was the first to appreciate
her shining intelligence. As the months passed he began to
value her counsel even more than that of his sons, and to as-
sign critical government decisions and duties to her care.

27

Jofre and Sancia lay sound asleep in their apartments in the Vatican when, without warning or explanation, several papal guards entered and pulled her from their bed. As Sancia kicked and screamed, Jofre shouted his resistance.

"This is an outrage!" Jofre said to one of the young lieutenants. "Have you spoken to my father about this?"

"It was the Holy Father himself who gave the order," the soldier confessed.

Jofre rushed to the Pope's quarters, where he found Alexander sitting at his desk in his study. "What is the meaning of this, Father?" he asked.

The Pope looked up and answered crossly. "I could say it was due to the looseness of your wife's morals—for she is a spicy little clove—or your inability to help her keep her temper," Alexander said. "But it is far less personal this time. I seem to be unable to impress upon the good king of Naples, who is aligned with Ferdinand of Spain, the importance of French interest in Naples. Louis has requested that I do something, and so to prove my allegiance I have."

"What has this to do with Sancia?" Jofre asked. "She is but a girl, and she has done nothing in regard to France."

"Jofre. Please! Don't be a hairless eunuch!" Alexander said impatiently. "Your brother's welfare is at stake; the papacy rests on its ability to support its alliances. And at this moment, our strongest alliance is with France."

"Father," Jofre said, his eyes lit with fire. "I cannot allow this, for Sancia can never love a man who cannot, at the very least, protect her from the dungeons."

"She may send a message to her uncle, the king, and explain her need for assistance," the Pope said.

In that moment Jofre had to look away from his father, for he feared the Pope would see the hatred written on his face. "Father," Jofre said, "I will ask this one more time, as your son. You must free my wife, for otherwise you will cause the end of my marriage. And I cannot allow that."

Alexander seemed puzzled for a moment. What was this son saying? His wife, Sancia, had been trouble from the day she had arrived, and he had done nothing to harness her or even rein her in. What insolence now made him dare to tell his father—and the Holy Father as well—how to run the Holy Mother Church?

But the Pope's voice held to reason, devoid of all emotion, when he answered this son. "Because you are my son, I will forgive you this trespass," he said. "But if ever you speak in this way again, for any reason, I will have your head upon a pike, and I myself will swear to your heresy. Do you understand?"

Jofre took a deep breath. "How long will my wife be imprisoned?"

"Ask the king of Naples," Alexander said. "For it is all up to him. The moment he agrees that Louis shall wear the crown is the moment your wife goes free." As Jofre turned to go, the Pope added, "From this day forward, you will be guarded day and night to keep you from temptation."

All Jofre asked was, "May I see her?"

Alexander looked surprised. "What kind of father would I be if I would keep my son from his wife?" he asked. "Do you think me a monster?"

Jofre could not keep the tears from streaming down his face, for on this night he had lost not only his wife, but his father as well.

Sancia was taken to the cellar of the fortress at Sant' Angelo, and placed in a dungeon alone. From the cells around her she could hear the cries and screams of the others, who moaned and shouted obscenities to the papal guards.

Those who recognized her taunted her, and those who didn't wondered how such a fine-fashioned young woman could have placed herself in such a situation.

Sancia herself was livid, and raging mad. This time he had done it. The Pope who had once before sent her away had now sealed his fate; for she would make certain, even from this place, that she helped take him down. He would sit on the throne of the Holy Father no longer, she vowed; if she had to give her life to that one mission, it would be worth more than all the ducats in the world.

When Jofre came, Sancia had already overturned the cot and dumped its straw onto the dungeon floor. She had taken the water and food she had been brought, and even the wine, and tossed it against the small wooden door, leaving pieces of her dinner stuck to it.

Jofre was surprised to find that when he greeted her, she came to him and embraced him. "Husband, you must help me," she told him. "If you love me, you must get a message to my family. You must let my uncle know what has become of me."

"I will do that," Jofre said, holding her and smoothing her hair. "I will do more than that. And in the meantime, I will spend as many hours in this dungeon as you wish me to."

Jofre lifted the cot then and both of them sat upon it, his arm around her shoulders, comforting her. "Will you bring me paper at once, and make certain the message goes quickly?" she asked.

"I will," Jofre said, "for I cannot bear being without you."

Sancia smiled then, and he felt hopeful.

"We are as one," he said. "And therefore what they do to you, they do to me as well."

"I know it is a sin to hate another," Sancia said. "But for the hate I hold against your father, I am willing to stain my soul with sin. No matter that he is the Holy Father: he is as evil in my eyes as the greatest of the fallen angels."

Jofre had no desire to defend him. "I will write to my brother, Cesare," he said. "For I have no doubt he will help us as soon as he returns."

"Why? I have not seen this side of him that makes him so endearing," Sancia said.

"I have my reasons," Jofre said. "My brother Cesare will understand, and I trust he will release you from this hell."

When he kissed her good-bye, he held her longer than usual. And she allowed it.

But that night, once he had gone, one guard after another entered her cell and ravished her. They stripped her of her clothes, they kissed her lips and breathed their ugly breath into her face, and they pushed themselves inside her without any regard for her resistance. For once she had been placed among the prostitutes and thieves she was no longer under the protection of the Borgia Pope, and so they feared no punishment.

By the time her husband came to visit in the morning Sancia was dressed and washed again, but she had ceased to speak. And no matter what Jofre said to her she did not notice, for the light that had once shone so brightly in her sparkling green eyes had been extinguished, and now they were merely a muddy gray.

Cesare Borgia controlled the Romagna now, at last. But there were other cities still to be conquered before he could accomplish his vision to unify all of Italy. There was Camerino, run by the Varano family, and Senigallia, where the della Rovere ruled. And there was Urbino, where Guido Feltra ruled as duke. Urbino seemed too powerful for Cesare's army to attack; still, it blocked his route to the Adriatic, and could cut off communication with Pesaro and Rimini, if nothing were done to alter the situation in the Borgia's favor.

And so Cesare's campaign continued . . .

His first objective was the small city-state Camerino. Cesare assembled an army to strike north from Rome. There they would link up with one of Cesare's Spanish captains and his troops that remained in the Romagna.

In order to accomplish his goal, however, he was forced to request that Guido Feltra allow the passage of his captain, Vito Vitelli, and his artillery through Feltra's Urbino. Now, it was known throughout Italy that Feltra had little affection for the Borgia. Feltra, whose reputation as a *condottiere* was greater than his skill and intelligence, was eager to avoid an immediate confrontation, and so he granted Cesare permission—in order to disguise his true intention, which was to help Alessio Varano defend Camerino.

Unfortunately for the duke, Cesare's spies discovered his plan, and Vitelli's powerful artillery moved on Urbino. Without warning, both Cesare's force from Rome and his army from the north arrived at the gates of the city.

That view of the entire papal force, with Cesare in his black battle armor riding his spirited charger back and forth before them, was enough to persuade Guido Feltra to flee.

The city quickly surrendered to Cesare—to the amazement not only of Italy but of all Europe, since the powerful duke of Urbino had before this day been considered invincible.

And so, as he had planned, Cesare moved on to Camerino. Without the help of Guido Feltra, that city also surrendered with little resistance.

Once Urbino and Camerino had been conquered, it appeared that nothing could stop Cesare from imposing his will—and papal rule—on any town or city in Italy.

In Florence that summer the afternoon sun hung high in the sky, a steaming red disk that burned hot on the city below. The windows of the Palazzo della Signoria opened wide to the square outside inviting flies, but no breeze cooled the stifling room. There the men of the Signoria sweated and fidgeted, anxious for the difficult session to be completed, so that they could rush home to a cool bath and a glass of chilled wine.

The most important matter to consider was the report of Niccolò Machiavelli, special emissary to the Vatican. That could foretell the future of their city.

The situation in the Papal States was a matter of growing concern. Cesare Borgia had threatened Florence itself on his last campaign, and they feared that the next time he might not be bought off so easily.

Machiavelli rose to address the Signoria. Despite the heat he wore a doublet of pearl-gray satin, and his gleaming white blouse remained dry and crisp.

"Excellencies," he said, in a dramatic and eloquent voice, "you all know that Urbino has fallen, that the duke was taken by surprise. Some say by treachery, but if so it was not undeserved. Guido Feltra was clearly plotting against the Borgia, and they duped him in return. It would seem to be a case of *frodi onorevoli*—honorable fraud." Machiavelli paced in front of them as he continued.

"Where does Cesare Borgia stand? Well, his army is large and well organized, and his men are loyal. It is known throughout all the cities and towns he has conquered that Cesare's soldiers adore him. He has subdued the Romagna, and now Urbino. He terrified the Bolognese—and, if the truth be known, he has terrified us as well." He placed his hand over his eyes in a theatrical gesture, to impress upon the members the severity of what he was about to say. "We cannot rely on the French to interfere with Cesare's plans. It's true, the French were suspicious of the Borgia in the revolt of Arezzo, and they were quite displeased by Cesare's threatening Bologna and our own great city. But remember, Louis still needs the Pope's support in dealing with Spain and Naples—and given the strength and skill of Cesare's army, their position seems quite sensible."

Machiavelli lowered his voice. "Now, I will share with you a confidence. Cesare has paid Louis a secret visit, traveling in disguise without guards. By placing himself totally in the power of the French king, and begging his forgiveness for Vitelli's erroneous adventure in Arezzo, Cesare has healed whatever breach may have existed between France and the papacy. Therefore, this time, if Cesare attacks Bologna, I predict that the king will support him. If he attacks Florence, the French may or may not interfere."

A perspiring signor rose, mopping his forehead with a white linen handkerchief, his brow furrowed with worry. "What you seem to be telling us, Machiavelli, is that Cesare Borgia is unstoppable, and that those of us lucky enough to have villas in the mountains should flee."

"I doubt it's that bad, Excellency," Machiavelli reassured. "So far our relationship with Cesare is amicable, and he has a genuine fondness for our city.

"But there is something else to consider, which may shift the balance of this equation. Cesare Borgia has defeated and humiliated a number of dangerous men by driving them from their territories, and though it is true that his army is loyal and his soldiers adore him, I am far less certain of his *condottieri*—for they are violent and unpredictable men, capable of jealousy and worse. I fear they will someday turn and seek to overthrow him. You see, while becoming the most powerful man in Italy, Cesare Borgia has built up a list of formidable enemies . . . a list not one of us would wish to share."

In Magioni, at a castle in Orsini territory, the conspiracy began to take shape. Giovanni Bentivoglio of Bologna was determined to lead the conspiracy. A large, athletic man with crinkly peppered hair and coarse features, he smiled readily, and spoke in a voice rich with persuasion. But he had a dark side as well. Before he reached full manhood he had killed a hundred men, as part of a group of bandits. He had reformed to become a good ruler of Bologna, and all his fierce and bloodthirsty urges seemed to have fallen aside— that is, until he was threatened and humiliated by Cesare.

Bentivoglio held a meeting at his castle in Bologna and invited the short, stocky Guido Feltra, the displaced and outraged duke of Urbino. Feltra spoke so softly that one had to listen carefully to each word he said—unless one knew, of course, that with Guido Feltra each sentence held a threat.

Joining the conspiracy were key *condottieri* from Cesare's army: Paolo and Franco Orsini, one a madman and the other the aging prefect of Rome and duke of Gravina, who had made his reputation as a ruthless soldier by displaying the head of one of his victims on the tip of his spear for days after a conquest. The Orsini were always eager to conspire against the Borgia.

It was no surprise that those men were enemies of Cesare's; of greater note was the participation of commanders who had once served Cesare well. Oliver da Fermo—and, even more shocking, Vito Vitelli himself—rode up to the castle. Vitelli was enraged that he had been forced to return Arezzo. These men, who were close enough to Cesare to know that his military strategies had put him in serious danger, still commanded a great part of his army.

Together, now, they formulated a plan. First they agreed they would need other allies. Once that was accomplished, they would meet again to organize their troops, and more important to decide where and when they would attack Cesare. And so it appeared that Cesare Borgia's days were numbered.

Unaware of the dangers he faced, Cesare sat by the fire in his new Urbino headquarters, enjoying a fine port wine from Guido Feltra's cellar, when his aide announced a gentleman from Florence had ridden out to see him: Signore Niccolò Machiavelli.

Machiavelli was ushered into the room. As he threw off his long gray cloak, Cesare noticed his pale and tired countenance, offered him a comfortable chair, and poured him a cup of port. "So what brings the brilliant star of Florentine diplomacy to Urbino in the dark of night?" the gracious host asked with a smile.

Machiavelli's face showed his concern. "Critical business, Cesare. I'll be blunt. Florence has been asked to join a massive conspiracy against you. Some of your own best commanders are involved. Many whom you would suspect, but one that you would not, Excellency: your commander, Captain Vito Vitelli." Machiavelli also named the others who had met at Magioni.

Cesare was stunned, but did not show it.

"Why have you told me this, Niccolò?" Cesare asked. "Wouldn't it be in the best interest of Florence if my campaign were stopped?"

"Cesare," Machiavelli said, "we have debated that very question. Are the conspirators a less dangerous devil than the Borgia? It was not an easy decision, and it was made not by the Signoria, but in an emergency session of the Council of Ten.

"I told them you are quite rational, and at least your objectives, the ones that you have confessed, are reasonably sound. And I believe that you would abide by the preference of France that Florence not be attacked.

"The conspirators, on the other hand, are not altogether rational men. Paolo Orsini is half mad. The whole Orsini family despises the government of Florence, and your friend Vito Vitelli simply despises the city itself. Who knows why? We do know, for example, that Orsini and Vitelli were the ones who urged you to attack Florence on your last campaign, and that you refused. That show of loyalty was an important consideration for us.

"If these men succeed in destroying you, they will depose your father, and we will have a militant Pope of *their* choosing. In that instance, their power would be catastrophic. They, unlike you, would not hesitate to attack—and even sack—Florence.

"Besides, I told the council that you would learn of the conspiracy—these men cannot keep a secret—and that, knowing of their treachery with your superior tactical skill, you would defeat the conspirators." A look of amusement crossed Machiavelli's face. "So I simply said, 'Let's warn him ourselves. We may buy some goodwill.' "

Cesare laughed, and clapped the Florentine on the back. "By God, Machiavelli, you are matchless—simply matchless. Your candor is breathtaking, and your cynicism a delight," he said.

Although in an almost impossible position, Cesare moved with great speed. He pulled his loyal forces out of Urbino and Camerino, concentrating them farther north in the well-protected fortresses of the Romagna.

Moreover, he sent delegates riding in all directions throughout the day and night, to search for replacements for the *condottieri* who had betrayed him. He wanted skilled new captains, and veteran mercenary troops, hopefully with cannons, and he also wanted to mobilize the vaunted Val di Lamone infantry—the best infantrymen in the whole of Italy—from the area near Faenza, a place that had been well treated and governed since his occupation. He even contacted Louis seeking French troops.

Within a week Machiavelli sent a report to the Council of Ten. "There is a firm conviction held here," he wrote, "that the king of France will help Borgia with men, and the Pope will provide him with money. The delay of his enemies in closing in on him has given Cesare an advantage. Now I judge that it is too late to do Cesare Borgia much harm, for he has provided all the important cities with garrisons and has adequately stocked all the fortresses."

The conspirators soon saw the same thing Machiavelli had. And so the conspiracy began to unravel.

Bentivoglio was the first to approach Cesare, to ask forgiveness and swear his allegiance. Then the Orsini expressed a willingness to establish peace—or, if the other conspirators were unwilling, to betray them. Only Guido Feltra stayed away.

Finally, Cesare met with and offered all his enemies generous terms: First, he assured them there would be no punishment. But on Camerino and Urbino, which had been occupied by the conspirators, unfortunately, he could not budge. They must be returned to him. Yet he reassured Bentivoglio that he could keep Bologna, for the Pope had signed a treaty with Bentivoglio at the urging of the king of France.

In exchange, Bentivoglio agreed to provide both lances and horses, with soldiers for the next campaign.

The *condottieri*—Orsini, Vitelli, Gravina, and da Fermo—would resume their positions as commanders in Cesare's armies.

For six weeks, peace reigned. When the French army arrived, Cesare sent them back to Louis with his thanks.

The conspiracy had ended.

In Rome, however, without Cesare's knowledge, Alexander had also taken it upon himself to help his son. He knew that Franco and Paolo Orsini could not be punished as long as Cardinal Antonio Orsini remained alive—for as the patriarch of the family the cardinal would see to it that there was brutal retaliation, and the Pope was unwilling to risk the loss of another son.

And so, in a friendly manner, Alexander invited the cardinal to the Vatican, telling Antonio that he was considering another of his nephews for a position in the church.

Antonio Orsini accepted the invitation to the Vatican not without misgivings, though feigning humility and gratitude.

Once seated in the Pope's quarters, the cardinal was served a sumptuous dinner, with countless delicacies, and several varieties of wine. They disputed each other good-naturedly on political issues, and joked with each other about certain courtesans they had both known. To all appearances they seemed to enjoy each other's company, and an onlooker could not have guessed what lay in the heart of either holy man.

But the cardinal, always alert and wary of the Borgia, refused to drink the wine for fear it had been poisoned. Still, noting that the Pope ate with gusto, he also ate heartily, only requesting fresh water in the place of wine, for water was clear and any cloudiness of intention could not be hidden from him.

After the dinner was finished, just as the Pope was inviting the cardinal to join him in his study, Cardinal Antonio Orsini grabbed for his stomach, crumpled over in his chair, and fell straight to the floor, his eyes rolling around in his head like the martyrs in the frescoes on the walls of the Pope's apartments.

"I drank no wine," the cardinal whispered hoarsely.

"Yet you ate the inky black squid," the Pope said.

That very night Cardinal Orsini was carried away by papal guards from the Vatican to be buried. During a Mass in the chapel the following day, the Pope himself offered prayers for the soul of the cardinal, and sent him off to heaven with his blessings.

Alexander then sent the papal guards to confiscate Cardinal Orsini's possessions—including his palace, for Cesare's expanding campaign needed increased funds. But when the guards arrived they found Orsini's gray-haired crone of a mother living there, and so they put her out into the streets of Rome.

"I must have my servants," she cried, frightened, as she stumbled along, steadying herself with her cane. And so they sent her servants with her.

It was snowing that night in Rome, and the wind was cutting and brutally cold. But no one would give the old woman shelter, for they feared the Pope would be displeased.

Two days later, in the Vatican chapel, the Pope offered another Mass—this time for Cardinal Orsini's mother, who had suffered misfortune and been found dead, curled in a doorway, her cane frozen to her withered hand.

In December, on the way to Senigallia, Cesare stopped in Cesena to inquire about its governor, Ramiro da Lorca. He had been placed in charge, but now word had reached Cesare of a certain discontent among his citizens.

The latest rumors of da Lorca's brutality forced Cesare to call a hearing in the town square, before the townspeople, in order that da Lorca might defend himself. "I hear you have used extreme cruelty to punish the townspeople. Is this true?" Cesare asked.

His wild red hair a ring of fur around his head, his thick lips pursed tight, da Lorca spoke in a voice so high it was almost a shriek. "I hardly think I have been unduly cruel, Excellency," he said. "For no one listens, and fewer behave as I order."

Cesare asked, "I am told that one young page was thrown into a raging fire in the square on your orders, and that you held your foot upon him as he burned alive?"

Da Lorca hesitated. "But of course it was with reason . . ."

Cesare stood stiffly, his hand on his sword. "Then I must hear it . . ."

"The boy was insolent . . . and clumsy," da Lorca said.

"Governor, I find your defense inadequate," Cesare responded sternly.

Cesare had also heard that Ramiro had plotted with the conspirators to trap him. But the goodwill of the people of Cesena was of greater import to him. Any undue cruelty would undermine the Borgia control in the areas of the Romagna Cesare ruled, and so da Lorca must be punished.

On Cesare's orders, da Lorca was immediately thrown into the dungeon of the fortress. Afterward, Cesare sent for his loyal friend Zappitto, made him the new governor of Cesena, and gave him a purse full of ducats, along with detailed instructions.

To the surprise of the citizens, once Cesare left the town Zappitto released the ruthless and brutal Ramiro da Lorca from the dungeons. And though the townspeople were displeased that he had been set free, they felt fortunate—for they realized Zappitto was a governor with the ability for mercy.

But the morning after Christmas, Ramiro da Lorca was discovered speeding headless through the marketplace, still dressed in his bright red and gold Christmas cape and finery, tethered to his horse.

Then everyone agreed it was a great misfortune for da Lorca that he had been set free from the dungeons.

Cesare prepared for the attack on Senigallia, ruled by the della Rovere family. He had long planned to occupy this port city on the Adriatic, and so he gave the order to move his loyal troops to the coast, where he would be joined by the former conspirators and their own forces. The loyal *condottieri* and those who had conspired were pleased to be working in harmony again, and both groups moved toward the coast as directed.

As these forces approached Senigallia, the town quickly surrendered. But Andrea Doria, commander of the fortress, insisted on surrendering only to Cesare.

As Cesare waited for the time of this meeting, he ordered his most loyal troops placed nearest to the city, while those of the other commanders occupied an area farther from the city gates.

At Cesare's order, his loyal commanders met with a small group of infantrymen outside the gates of Senigallia in preparation for accepting the surrender of the citadel. This group also included Paolo and Franco Orsini, Oliver da Fermo, and Vito Vitelli.

At Cesare's direction, the party entered the gates to meet Commander Andrea Doria in a local palace, where the terms of surrender were to be worked out.

As they passed into the city and the massive gates closed behind them, Cesare laughingly remarked that the suspicious citizens were taking no chances on the papal army sacking the city while the talks went on.

Entering the small palace, they were led by Cesare to an octagonal, peach-colored reception room with four interior doors, a large conference table, and peach-colored velvet chairs.

The conversation was relaxed while they drank from goblets of local wine the servants had poured. There would be no fighting here, and Paolo and Franco Orsini, Oliver da Fermo, and Vito Vitelli, the former conspirators, were glad to be accepted again, especially to be a part of a campaign that was already successful.

Cesare walked to the center of the room. Removing his sword, he suggested to his commanders that, this being a peace parley, they join him in disarming before the arrival of

Commander Doria. They readily followed his lead, handing their weapons to one of Cesare's aides. Only Vito Vitelli looked concerned—for the city gates were closed and their own troops were hundreds of yards outside the city walls.

"Gentlemen, please be seated," Cesare commanded. "Senigallia has always been a significant port, but it will, I believe, be far more significant after today. You have all richly deserved your rewards and you shall have them. Now!"

On the word, "Now," two dozen heavily armed men burst into the room from all sides. And in less than a minute Paolo and Franco Orsini, Oliver da Fermo, and Vito Vitelli were tied securely to their chairs.

Cesare, his eyes black with intensity, said, "So, gentlemen. For your reward allow me to introduce my good friend Don Michelotto."

Michelotto bowed and smiled. He detested treachery. Taking his garrote from an aide, he moved from one disloyal commander to the next, strangling each one in turn as the others watched in horror.

Upon his return to Rome Cesare was greeted warmly by both the citizens and the Pope, who was waiting with his envoy at the gates for his arrival. Since his conquest of the Romagna, Cesare smiled more readily; he seemed as pleased with himself as his father was, and had no doubt that all of Italy would soon be under his rule.

Secretly, the Pope and he had even spoken of turning over the tiara to him, or at the very least crowning him as king of the Romagna. But first he must take Tuscany, which until now his father had refused to allow.

In his apartments that night, as Cesare relaxed and enjoyed the memory of his victories, he was brought a box with a note from Isabella d'Este, the sister of the duke of Urbino, whom he had deposed.

When Cesare was staying at her brother's palace in

Urbino, he had received a message from her, begging him to return to her two precious statues he had confiscated with the castle—one of Cupid, the other Venus. They held sentimental value for her, she had explained, and mentioned nothing of her penchant for collecting antiquities.

But now that she was Lucrezia's sister-in-law, he had been taken by her pleading, and immediately had some of his men carry the statues to her. In this note she thanked him for his kindness, and sent a little something in return.

It was a large box, wrapped with silken ribbons and tied with golden bows. As he opened it, he found himself as excited as he had been as a child whenever he had opened an unexpected gift. Lifting the cover carefully, he slowly lifted the parchment that covered it, and discovered within one hundred masks—of all kinds. Carnival masks of gold and jewels, satin masks of red and yellow, mysterious masks of black and silver, and others formed like faces of dragons and demons and saints.

Cesare laughed aloud as he examined each and every one, taking the time to look in the mirror as he placed them on his face, enjoying the many different images that appeared before his eyes.

A month later Cesare and Alexander met in the Borgia apartments, awaiting Duarte, who had just returned from Florence and Venice.

Alexander enthusiastically told Cesare of his new plans for beautifying the Vatican. "With much difficulty I have persuaded the artist Michelangelo to draw up plans for a completely new Basilica of St. Peter. I wish to create something magnificent, a glory to the Christian world."

"I don't know about his skill as an architect, but the Cupid I purchased tells me this Michelangelo is a great artist."

At that point Duarte entered the room and greeted Alexander, kissing the papal ring.

Cesare asked, "So Duarte, did you find the villains in

Venice? And do the good people of Florence again consider me an ogre, a devious strangler of the innocent, because of the events at Senigallia?"

"No, Cesare, they tend to believe that you did what you had to, and did it with cleverness and skill. It was, as they put it, *scelleratezzi glorioso,* glorious trickery. The people love revenge—the more dramatic the better."

Now Duarte's expression became serious, and he turned to Alexander. "Your Worthiness," he said, "in the present circumstance, I believe true danger remains."

"What is it that concerns you, Duarte? Serious gossip, or some fateful truth you have discovered?" asked Alexander.

Duarte said, "The conspirators may be dead—but their families are not. Now they are more angry, and will no doubt seek vengeance." He looked at Cesare. "They cannot match your strength, Cesare, but they will never forgive you. And because the papacy supports you, the Pope too is in danger."

28

Cardinal Giuliano della Rovere paced around his apartments in Ostia, raging like a madman. He had just received word that Cesare Borgia had conquered Senigallia, and now the Borgia rule was law even in the place that had belonged to his family. But that was not the worst of it.

Once Cesare left to return to Rome, the troops he left behind within the gates of Senigallia had raped, looted, and pillaged the entire town. Not one of the women escaped—not even his sweet niece, Anna. And she was but a child of twelve.

The cardinal's fury rose to such a fever that he was beyond even prayer. Instead he picked up his quill, and as he stood at his desk, his feet and legs trembling uncontrollably, he penned a message to Ascanio Sforza. "If the good in us holds to virtue," he wrote, "evil will reign. For the greater good of God and the Holy Mother Church, we must now right the wrongs that have been done." Then he gave the time and the place they should meet.

With his hands shaking, he held the sealing wax over his candle and watched the red drops fall slowly on the folded parchment. Then he took his stamp and impressed the warm wax with the head of the martyred Christ.

Cardinal della Rovere was about to call for a messenger when a sharp bolt of pain struck his head with such intensity as to force him to his knees. He covered his face with his hands, his head bowed. He tried to call out, but was rendered speechless by what he saw before him.

The vision, in slow motion, was of the standard bearer of

the Pope, his white flag with the red Borgia bull embroidered upon it flying free in the wind. But as he watched the flag was dropped, and a thousand horses rode upon it, leaving it torn and tattered in the muddy earth. When he lifted his head and looked around, there was nothing in its wake. And he understood at once: the Borgia bull was slain.

He stood then, shaken by his vision, and leaned against his desk. When his legs felt steady, he again picked up his quill. He penned more messages. And as the red wax sealed them, over each he said a prayer. One was sent to the king of Naples, another to Fortunato Orsini, who was now the patriarch of the Orsini family since the death of Cardinal Antonio. One was sent to Cardinal Coroneto in Rome, another to Cardinal Malavoglia in Venice, still another to Caterina Sforza in Florence, and the last to Queen Isabella in Spain.

Now he must begin to end it . . .

A s he had for the last several weeks, Jofre walked down the long spiral staircase in the cellar of the Castel Sant' Angelo, to the dungeons. There he moved past the sleeping guards, who noticed him less each day, and made his way into the small squalid dungeon in the corner.

There on a simple cot covered with straw, her dark hair wild and gnarled with knots, Sancia sat silent as a statue. Tears filled his eyes as he watched her, but she did not seem to see him.

The guard unlocked the gate, and Jofre walked inside. When he sat down next to her and reached for her hand, she did not pull away, but her hand was limp and cold.

"Sancia, Sancia," he pleaded. "Please don't do this. Please don't let yourself leave me without a fight. I have sent a message to your uncle, and I am certain he will come to claim you shortly. But I fear to leave myself, for fear some harm will come to you."

Sancia began to hum softly, but said nothing.

Jofre knew what he must do. But how?

Since the day his father had thrown Sancia in the dungeon

Jofre had been guarded constantly, his every movement watched. Except when he walked down the stairs at the Castel Sant' Angelo, he had spent not one moment alone.

Cesare had just returned, and had reassured his brother that after a small period of time he could see to it that the Pope would set Sancia free.

Now Jofre looked over at his wife, and tears filled his eyes. She would free herself forever if he did not hurry. And he would not be able to bear it.

It was then that a guard came toward him, and called him by name. But Jofre did not recognize him, though his voice was reminiscent of someone he had heard before. He had clear blue eyes and a cap of dark hair, and though his features were heavy, they were definite enough to give him the appearance of strength.

"Do I know you?" Jofre asked.

The young man nodded, but only when he held out his hand in greeting, did Jofre remember.

"Vanni," he said, embracing him. "Vanni, how did you appear without being caught?"

The guard smiled. "It is an effective disguise, don't you agree? Now, come, we must speak for a time—before we have no time at all."

A few days later, as the orange sun set over the dusky countryside, two men stood in front of a large stable. Dressed in cardinal's robes, the taller one was giving instructions to four mounted riders. They were masked and wore black, hooded cloaks.

"Do exactly as I direct," the more imposing cardinal said. "There must be no trace. No trace. It must be finished . . . finally."

The four masked riders swept over the sand dunes to the farm of the old woman called Noni. She shuffled slowly forward to meet them, her wicker basket on her arm.

One rider leaned far down from his saddle to speak to her,

quietly, as if he were whispering an important secret. She nodded, looked from side to side, then shuffled back to her garden. In a moment she returned, carrying a handful of dark berries. She walked into her cottage, slid the berries into a small leather bag, and handed them to the rider, who was now waiting inside.

"*Grazie,*" he said politely. Then he drew his sword, and with one swift stroke split her skull in two.

Within minutes Noni's cottage was in flames, her body inside.

The riders mounted again and rode off over the hills.

The morning of the banquet in celebration of Cesare's victories and Alexander's eleventh anniversary on the papal throne, Alexander awoke with a feeling of uneasiness. He had tossed and turned all night, unable to sleep. And so as he sat on the side of his bed to steady himself before standing, he reached up as he always did, to rub his amulet and say his prayers. At first, when he felt his neck and it was bare, he didn't understand. Then he laughed to himself. It must have turned itself around. It could not be lost, for it had been soldered on the chain those many years before, and not once since then had it fallen from his neck. Yet on this morning it was nowhere to be found, and Alexander was concerned. He shouted for his servants, all of them. He called for Duarte, for Cesare, and for Jofre. But though his chambers were diligently searched, the amulet had disappeared.

"I will not leave my chambers," he told them, his arms folded before him.

But they reassured him that they would search the grounds, and the cathedral, and even the woods, never stopping until it was found.

When the amulet still had not been recovered by evening, and Cardinal Coroneto sent word that everyone was waiting to celebrate, the Pope agreed to go. "But if it is not brought back to me by morning, all church business will cease," Alexander warned.

At the luxurious country castle of Cardinal Coroneto, the tables had been moved into the fabulous garden beside the lake, with fountains spraying crystal-clear water onto gaily colored floating rose petals. The rain had stopped, and the food was delicious. There were large platters of tiny Genoan shrimp in an herb lemon dressing, venison in a sauce of juniper berries, and a magnificent pancake of fruit and honey. The splendid entertainment included a Neapolitan folksinger and a group of dancers from Sicily.

The wine was plentiful, and it was poured by the servants into large shining silver goblets. Coroneto, the immensely fat Roman cardinal, raised his cup to toast the Borgia, as did the thirty rich and influential Romans in attendance.

Alexander had for the time put aside his concerns and was in a splendid mood, jovial and joking with his sons. Cesare sat on one side of him, Jofre on the other, and during the meal the Pope put one arm around each of his sons and held them in a warm embrace. It was then that Jofre reached over to say something to Cesare, and by some strange accident or design dislodged Cesare's cup from his hand, spilling the wine, bright as blood, all over Cesare's gold silk shirt.

A manservant came to wipe the spill, but Cesare shoved him away impatiently.

As the evening wore on, however, Alexander began to feel extremely tired and very hot. Soon he asked to be excused. Cesare felt odd as well, but was more concerned about his father, who looked ghostly pale and had begun to sweat.

Alexander was helped back to the Vatican to his apartments. By now he was burning with fever, and was barely able to speak.

His physician, Michele Maruzza, was summoned at once.

He shook his head after he had examined the Pope. Then, turning to Cesare, he said, "I suspect malaria." Looking more closely, he added, "Cesare, you yourself do not look well. Take to your bed, and I will return in the morning to see both of you."

The following morning, it was plain that father and son were seriously ill. Both were burning with fever.

Dr. Maruzza, not certain whether he was dealing with malaria or poison, prescribed immediate bleeding with leeches he had brought along. From an apothecary jar which Maruzza held, Cesare could see the dark thin leeches crawling around the bottom of the jar, like long brown threads come alive.

His thick black brows knit together in concentration, Dr. Maruzza gently reached inside the jar with small metal tongs and carefully pulled one of the leeches out. The doctor held the leech out toward Cesare on a small tin plate, and with great pride explained: "These are the finest leeches in all of Rome. They were purchased at great cost from the Monastery of Saint Mark, where they are nurtured and grown with care."

Cesare winced as he watched the doctor place one of the leeches on his father's neck, then another. The first leech fast grew dark with blood, its thready body now growing shorter and stubbier as it filled. By the time the fourth leech was placed the first was filled to bursting; round and purple as a berry, it dropped off and fell onto the clean silk sheets.

Cesare grew sicker as Dr. Maruzza, fascinated by both his leeches and his own skill, continued. "We must give them time to feed. They will suck the bad blood from your father's body, and help him to recover."

When Dr. Maruzza felt sufficient blood had been let, he removed the leeches, declaring, "I believe His Holiness is already better."

Indeed Alexander's fever seemed lower, but now he was cold, clammy, and deathly pale.

Maruzza then turned to Cesare. "And now for you, my son," he said, holding forth more leeches. But Cesare found the process disgusting, and so he refused. But what did he know of modern medicine? Besides, he felt so sick he was beyond caring.

By evening, despite the doctor's optimism, it was plain that Alexander was becoming sicker; some feared he must be nearing death.

Upstairs, in his own apartments, Cesare was informed by Duarte that his mother, Vanozza, had visited the Pope and was seen leaving his room weeping. She had stopped by to see Cesare, but did not want to wake him.

Now Cesare insisted that he be brought to his father's bedside. Unable to walk, he was carried on a litter down to the musty sickroom, where he slumped weakly into a chair beside Alexander's bed. He reached out and took his father's hand, kissing it.

Pope Alexander, lying on his back, his belly fermenting with toxins, his lungs filled with thick fluid, found it difficult to breathe. He fell in and out of a dreamlike sleep, his mind often cloudy, but occasionally clear as a bell.

He looked up to see his son Cesare sitting beside his bed, his face drawn and pale, his auburn hair dull and lifeless. He was touched by the concern he saw on Cesare's face.

He thought about his children. Had he taught his sons well enough? Or had he corrupted and disarmed them by exercising too much power, both as their father and as the Holy Father?

No sooner had he asked the question than the sins he had visited upon his children seemed to pass before his eyes, in separate images of such clarity, dimension, and emotion as he had never seen before. And suddenly he understood. All his questions had been answered.

Now Alexander looked up at Cesare. "My son, I have wronged you and I beg your forgiveness."

Cesare watched his father with a mixture of compassion and wariness. "What is it, Papa?" he said, with such tenderness that he almost brought the Pope to tears.

"I spoke of power as evil," Alexander said, struggling to breathe. "But I fear I never explained it fully. I warned you of it, rather than encouraging you to examine it more closely. I never explained that the only good reason to exercise power is in the service of love." His breath made a hissing sound.

"How does that follow, Papa?" Cesare asked.

Suddenly Alexander was light-headed. He felt young again—a cardinal sitting in his quarters, discoursing with his two sons and daughter while the baby played. He felt his breath come easier. "If you love nothing, then power is an aberration, and more important still a threat. For power is dangerous, and can turn at any moment."

He slipped back into a dream, it seemed, and now imagined his son as papal general, imagined the battles fought and won, saw the bloody woundings, the brutal killings, and the devastation of the people he had conquered.

He heard Cesare call to him. He heard his son ask, as though from long ago and far away, "Is power not a virtue? Does it not help save the souls of many?"

"My son," Alexander mumbled. "Power for itself proves nothing. It is an empty exercise of one man's will over another's. Not something of virtue."

Cesare reached for his father's hand and held it tight. "Father, speak later, for it seems to draw strength from you."

Alexander smiled, and in his mind it was a brilliant smile, but Cesare saw only a grimace. Sucking in as much air as his sick lungs could bear, he spoke again. "Without love, power places man closer to the animals than to the angels." The Pope's skin was turning gray, and he was becoming paler by the moment, but when Dr. Maruzza was called again Alexander waved him away. "Your work here is finished," he told the doctor. "Know your place." Then he turned to his son again, struggling to keep his eyes open, for they seemed very heavy. "Cesare, my son, have you ever loved anyone in greater measure than yourself?" he asked.

"Yes, Papa," Cesare said. "I have."

Alexander asked, "And who would that be?"

"My sister," Cesare admitted, his head lowered, his eyes shiny with tears. It seemed to him a confession.

"Lucrezia," Alexander said softly, and again he smiled, for in his ears it sounded like a song. "Yes," he said, "that was *my* sin. Your curse. And her virtue."

Cesare said, "I will tell her you love her, for her grief at not being with you at this time will be immeasurable."

His face naked of pretense, Alexander continued. "Tell her she has always been the most precious flower in my life. And a life without flowers is no life at all. For beauty is more necessary than we can imagine."

Cesare looked at his father, and for the first time saw him as the man he was: uncertain and flawed. They had never before spoken freely, and now there was so much he wished to know about this man who was his father. "Papa, have *you* ever loved anyone more than yourself?"

With great effort, Alexander forced himself to speak again. "Yes, my son, oh yes . . ." and he said it with such longing.

"And who would that be?" Cesare asked, as his father had.

Alexander said, "My children. All my children. Yet I fear that too was a fault. In one who was blessed to be the Holy Father, it was excessive. I should have loved God more."

"Papa," Cesare said, reassurance in his voice, "when you raised the golden chalice on the altar, when you raised your eyes to heaven, you filled the hearts of the devoted, for your own eyes were filled with love of the divine."

Alexander's whole body began to tremble and he began to cough and choke. His voice filled with irony. "When I held up the chalice of red wine, when I blessed the bread and drank the wine—that symbol of the body and blood of the Christ—in my own mind, I imagined the body and blood of my children. I, like God, had created them. And, like him, I sacrificed them. Hubris, to be sure. It was never so clear to me as it is in this moment." He chuckled at the irony, but he began to cough again.

Cesare tried to comfort his father, but he himself was feeling weak and faint. "Father, if you have need for forgiveness, I can give that now. And if you have need of my love, you must know that you have always had it . . ."

For a moment the Pope had a thought, and seemed to

rally. "Where is your brother, Jofre?" he asked, a small frown on his brow.

Duarte went to find him.

When Jofre arrived, he stood behind his brother, away from his father. His eyes were cold and hard, with no hint of grief.

"Come close, my son," Alexander said. "Take my hand for just a moment."

Someone helped move Cesare away, and reluctantly Jofre took his father's hand. "Bend closer, my son. Come near," he said. "There are some things I must say . . ."

Jofre hesitated but then bent near. "I have wronged you, my son, and I do not doubt you are my son. But until this night, my eyes were fixed on foolishness."

Jofre looked through the clouds that covered the eyes of his father and said, "I cannot forgive you, Father. For because of you, I cannot forgive myself."

Alexander looked at his youngest son. "This comes late, I know, but before I die it is important that you hear it from me. You should have been the cardinal, for it was you who was the best of us."

Jofre's head shook almost imperceptibly. "Father, you do not even know me."

At that Alexander smiled slyly, for when things were so clear there could be no mistake. "Without Judas, Jesus himself would have stayed a carpenter, lived a life of preaching that few would have listened to, and died an old man," he said, chuckling. For suddenly, life seemed so absurd.

But Jofre rushed from the room.

Cesare took his place again at his father's bedside. And held his father's hand until he felt it grow icy cold.

Alexander, then comatose, did not hear the soft knock on the door. He did not see Julia Farnese, in her black hooded cloak and veil, enter the room. Removing these things, she turned to Cesare.

"I could not bear to have the Holy Father go without seeing him one last time," she explained as she bent to kiss Alexander on his forehead.

"Have you been well?" Cesare asked her. But she did not answer.

"You know," she said instead, "this man was my life, the foundation of my existence. I have known many lovers, over many years. Most are boys—callow, bullying, glory-seeking boys. But with all his faults," she said, turning again to Alexander, "he was a man."

As tears began to well up in her eyes, she whispered, "Good-bye, my love." She gathered her cloak and veil and quickly left the room.

An hour later Alexander's confessor was summoned, and the last rites administered.

Cesare moved close to his father again.

Alexander felt a great peace encompass him as Cesare's face faded from his sight . . .

And his gaze fell upon the resplendent face of death. He found himself bathed in light, walking through the citrus groves at Silverlake, his golden rosary beads threading through his hands. It was such a glorious life. He had never felt so well . . .

Outside, his body grew black quickly, and swelled until it was so large it had to be forced into his coffin, for it seemed to spill over the sides. The top of the casket had to be nailed down, for no matter how many men tried to secure it, it would not stay closed.

And so it was that in the end Pope Alexander VI seemed not only larger than life, but larger than death as well.

29

The very night of Alexander's death, armed mobs surged through the streets of Rome, beating and killing anyone of Spanish descent—*Catalans,* as they were called—and looting all their homes.

At his own castle in Rome, Cesare, younger and stronger than the Pope, still struggled, and remained dangerously ill. He had been in bed for weeks, trying with all his might to recover, to resist the call of Death. Yet it seemed he was not getting any stronger. And so, despite his refusal, on the advice of Duarte, Dr. Maruzza was forced to apply the leeches.

In the following days Cesare was too weak to stand, and so he was unable to take the necessary steps to protect his properties. While the families of the rulers whose territories he had conquered held meetings and formed new alliances, he could barely keep awake. As his enemies gathered their troops to retake the towns of Urbino, Camerino, and Senigallia, and other rulers quickly returned to their cities to take up residence again in their own castles, Cesare could put up no fight. Even as the Colonna and Orsini families united and sent troops to Rome, in the hope of influencing the election of the new Pope, Cesare could not leave his bed.

Over the years, Cesare and his father had developed strategies to be put in place when Alexander died in order to safeguard his family, their riches, titles, and territories. But now, the Pope's son remained too sick to execute those plans.

A healthy Cesare could have concentrated his own loyal

troops in and near Rome at a moment's notice. He could have seen that his fortresses in the Romagna were defended and provided for, and would have cemented his alliances. But now he could do none of it. He asked his brother, Jofre, but Jofre refused, for he was deep in mourning—not for his father, but for his wife.

Sancia had died in the dungeons before she was released.

Now Cesare called Duarte to him and attempted to assemble an army nearby, but the college of cardinals, no longer in his power, demanded that all troops be withdrawn from Rome at once.

The election of a new Pope was of the highest priority; any foreign troops would be a distraction, he was told, and could cause undue influence upon those who must vote. So strictly was this dictum enforced by the cardinals that even the Colonna and Orsini families obeyed. Soon all troops were exiled from Rome.

The college of cardinals was a powerful force. And so Cesare sent messengers to seek French and Spanish aid. But the situation had changed dramatically, and those powers were no longer willing to intervene on his behalf. Instead they would await the verdict of the cardinals.

Duarte Brandao visited Cesare often, bringing the offerings of new terms by his enemies. "They are not so severe as they might have been," Duarte explained. "You may retain all of your personal wealth, but the cities and territories you have claimed must be restored to their former rulers."

The rulers of the conquered cities were being not generous but cautious. Cesare was still alive, and the vicars who had been stripped of their lands still feared him. They even worried that he might just be pretending weakness to lead them into another trap—as he had at Senigallia.

Moreover, the citizens of the cities of the Romagna were satisfied with Cesare's rule. He was fairer and more generous than their old masters had been, and he had improved their lives dramatically. If Cesare accepted the offer of these rulers, there would be little chance of revolution among the people.

Cesare delayed his response, but he knew that, barring a miracle, he would have to accept. He could see no way out.

That night, he forced himself to sit at his desk. The first thing he did was write a letter to Caterina Sforza in Florence. If he must give back the conquered castles, at least hers should be first. He wrote out an order for the immediate return of Imola and Forli to Caterina and her son, Otto Riario. But in the morning, feeling slightly better, he decided to put both the letter and the order in a drawer. He too would wait to see what happened.

"*The Pope is dead! The Pope is dead!*" came the sound of the criers as they rode through the streets of Ferrara. Lucrezia got out of bed sleepily and looked outside her windows. But before she could come fully awake—for it seemed like a dream—Michelotto stood cold and shaking before her. He had ridden his horse without stopping from Rome, and arrived just behind the news.

"Miguel?" Lucrezia said. "Is it true about Papa? Is it true he has died?"

Michelotto could not speak, for his head was bowed with grief.

Lucrezia felt as though her screams could be heard throughout Ferrara, and yet she had not made a sound.

"Who did this?" she asked, and even to herself her voice was strangely calm.

"It was malaria, it seems," Michelotto answered.

"And you believe this is true?" she asked. "Does Chez believe it too?"

"Your brother has fallen ill as well," he said. "He has barely escaped dying."

Lucrezia's breath came short and hard. "I must go to him," Lucrezia said, calling for her lady-in-waiting. Her father was dead; her brother had need of her. "I must have clothes and shoes and something black," she told the girl.

But Michelotto objected, stiff as stone. "Your brother asks that I keep you from Rome—far from danger. The citizens in the streets are rioting, pillaging, and looting. It is not safe for you there."

"Miguel, you can't keep me from him, from my children, from seeing Papa one more time before he is put beneath the ground . . ." Now her eyes filled with frustration and tears.

"Your children have been taken to safety in Nepi," he said. "Adriana still cares for them, and Vanozza will arrive shortly. Once Cesare is well, he will meet you there."

"But Papa?" she said. "What of Papa?"

Michelotto could not imagine how Lucrezia would feel had she seen the blackened remains of her father's mortal body. That picture had carved deep sadness and revulsion in his own brain; what could it do to this tender woman's?

"You may pray for your papa from Ferrara," Michelotto told her. "For God knows where you are, and he is listening."

Both Ercole d'Este and Alfonso entered the room now, and each approached Lucrezia to try to comfort her. And yet there was no comfort. She spoke to Michelotto and told him to rest, that he could return to Cesare the following day. She assured him she would be at Nepi whenever her brother called for her.

Ercole and Michelotto left the room, but Lucrezia was surprised that her husband stayed. For the entire time they had been married, Alfonso had spent his time not in marital bliss, or even communion, but rather toying with his gun collection and spending time with courtesans. She, in turn, had spent her evenings opening her home to artists, poets, and musicians, and her days listening to the troubles of ordinary citizens. But now Alfonso stood before her, his face a palette of compassion. "May I be of comfort, Duchess?" he asked. "Or does it cause you more grief to have me with you?"

Lucrezia could not think, could decide nothing. She

couldn't even sit or walk. Finally she collapsed, and darkness obliterated all thought.

Alfonso quickly lifted her in his arms. Then he sat on the bed, and instead of laying her down he held his wife in his arms, rocking her gently.

"Speak to me, Sonny," she said, when her eyes opened. "Fill my head with any thoughts but those that fill it now." She could not yet cry, for her tears were far too deep to reach.

Alfonso stayed with her throughout the night, and for all the days and nights that followed while she was torn apart with grief.

The election of a new Pope could not be postponed any longer. Yet Cesare was determined to defeat Giuliano della Rovere, the ever-present enemy of the Borgia.

Cesare's choice was Cardinal Georges d'Amboise, who was, of course, supported by the other French cardinals. The majority of Italian cardinals would hear none of what Cesare had to say, and they supported della Rovere. Cesare tried to convince the Spanish cardinals to back d'Amboise, but they had their own candidate. Those who remained loyal to Cesare at least opposed his enemy.

Florentines loved gambling, and their favorite form was betting on the election of a Pope. Aside from personal bets between individuals, the bulk of the wagering on papal elections was through the Florentine banks. And the amount bet was enormous.

The odds on d'Amboise were five to one; della Rovere was given a better chance at three to one. It seemed as though no one else was in the running, for the odds on every other candidate were greater than twenty to one. But elections were unpredictable. Many times the favorite when the conclave began remained just a cardinal when it ended.

This conclave was no exception. After the first few scrutinies—as the votes were called—it became apparent that neither d'Amboise nor della Rovere would gain sufficient votes.

After two more scrutinies, the white smoke finally appeared from the Vatican chimney. In a surprise occurrence, the college had chosen the aged and infirm Cardinal Francesco Piccolomini. And Cesare was relieved, if not completely happy.

Piccolomini, at his coronation, took the name Pope Pius III. He had not always agreed with Alexander, but he was a fair and gentle man. Cesare knew he would treat the Borgia honestly and protect them as best he could, so long as such protection was not contrary to the interests of the Holy Mother Church. By some miracle, the danger of a hostile Pope had been averted.

In the weeks following Pius's election Cesare gradually recovered his strength, first walking up and down the length of his apartment, then strolling through his garden, finally riding his white charger through the countryside. Now he began preparing a strategy to keep his conquests in the Romagna, and to vanquish his enemies.

Then one day, when Cesare returned home from a long, vigorous ride, he dismounted to find Duarte Brandao waiting for him.

Duarte's expression reflected his distress. "The news is not good, Cesare. Pius the Third is dead."

He had been Pope for only twenty-seven days.

Now Cesare's prospects were bleak. With the death of Pius, the possibility of papal protection—or even papal fairness—was a distant hope. Cesare's enemies saw this as he did, and moved quickly. The Orsini persuaded the Colonna to join them against Cesare.

With few loyal troops in the city, Cesare retired to Castel Sant' Angelo, still thought to be an impregnable fortress. He sent Vanozza to safety in Nepi, thinking her life more important than her inns and her vineyards.

Cardinal Giuliano della Rovere could not be stopped. Since the last conclave, he had become the overwhelming favorite. No serious rival was even discussed. As the day of the election approached, the banks immediately made della Rovere an even-money bet. Soon the odds shifted more dramatically, making him an even heavier favorite at one to two. Cesare knew he must accept this defeat and marshal all his forces if he was to withstand this staggering blow.

And so it was that Cesare Borgia met with Giuliano della Rovere and struck a bargain, using the threat of his influence over the Spanish and French cardinals and the strength of Castel Sant' Angelo to extract the compromise he desired.

Cesare offered to support della Rovere in the elections, on the condition that he be allowed to keep his castles and towns in the Romagna. He also insisted on being designated as *gonfaloniere* of the church, and captain general of the papal army.

To be certain that the cardinal would honor his promises, Cesare insisted that a public announcement be made. Della Rovere agreed, for he wanted nothing to stop this election.

Now, with Cesare's support, della Rovere was chosen in the fastest election anyone could remember—on the first scrutiny, the moment the doors of the conclave were closed.

Cardinal della Rovere, like Cesare, idolized Julius Caesar. Therefore, as a name he chose Pope Julius II. Good Lord, how long he had waited for this miracle to happen; how many visions he'd had for the reform of the Holy Mother Church.

Though Pope Julius was not a young man he was still physically strong, and now that he was in the position he felt he should be, he seemed less sullen and angry. Ironically, his plan for the Papal States was very much like Alexander's and Cesare's, which was to unify all the territories and bring them under a centralized government. The only difference, of course, was that his plan made no provision for a Borgia rule.

When Julius took the throne, he was undecided as to how he would deal with Cesare. It was not that he was concerned about keeping his word, for that was of little consequence to him. But Julius understood that he needed to concentrate his power and position, and ward off his enemies.

At this time he feared the Venetians as much as he feared Borgia power, and he knew that Cesare could be a strong ally against Venetian expansion in the Romagna. Since he knew that he might need Cesare, Julius ensured that relations between the two men—who had spent their lives as enemies—appeared friendly.

Meanwhile, Cesare was seeking to strengthen his own position. He stayed in close touch with all the captains of his remaining castles and towns, assuring them that his position was a strong one, despite the longtime malice of the new Pope. To strengthen his position, Cesare contacted his friend Machiavelli, seeking aid from Florence.

The two men met on a brisk December day in the gardens of the Belvedere, overlooking the spires and towers of Rome. They walked through the rows of tall cedars and sat on a worn stone bench, the vast view of the city spread out below them. The wind had swept away the smoke and dust, and the terra-cotta and marble buildings seemed to have been cut and placed against the clear blue sky.

Machiavelli noticed that Cesare was agitated as he spoke, his cheeks red and his lips tight. He was gesturing broadly, and as he spoke his laughter came a bit too often and too loudly. Machiavelli wondered if he might still be feverish.

"You see all that out there, Nicco?" Cesare said, waving his arm. "That was the city of the Borgia once. And it will be again, I promise you. Reclaiming fallen fortresses will be no more difficult than claiming them in the first place. Defending the ones I have kept will be no problem at all. My commanders are strong now, and loyal. The people support them, and I am raising a new force, including both foreign mercenaries and Val di Lamone infantry.

"Once my position in the Romagna has been made solid in Rome, all that you see out there will fall into my hands. Yes, Pope Julius has been my enemy in the past, but that is behind us now. He has made public promises on his holy oath. He swore to the citizens, and to government and church officials, that he would support me. I am still *gonfaloniere*. We have even discussed a match uniting our two families—possibly my daughter, Louise, and his nephew, Francesco. This is a new day, Nicco. A new day!"

Where was the brilliant, hardheaded commander he had once idolized? Machiavelli wondered. Yes, he had to admit it, the man he had *idolized*. Machiavelli considered himself a friend of Cesare's. But when it came to his official report, he had only one friend: Florence. That evening he rode as hard as he was able, in order to reach his city before it was too late. And this time the views he expressed to the Signoria were quite different from any that came before.

Now he rose, his clothes not as fresh as usual, his voice not as dramatic; in fact, he himself was not in his usual form. In the smaller private chamber used by the key ruling council, his expression was grim. He disliked what he had to say, but he knew he must.

"Excellencies, it would be the height of folly to provide any support to Cesare Borgia. Yes, the Holy Father, Pope Julius the Second, has publicly promised to confirm Cesare in his conquests and to make him *gonfaloniere*. But, Excellencies, I am convinced this Pope considers himself no more bound to carry out that promise than I feel bound to leave this chamber by the north rather than the south door. He still despises the Borgia. He will betray Cesare; he has already decided privately to do so.

"As for Cesare himself, I see a fearsome change. This man, who would never even hint at what he intended to do, now regales men with things he plans but can never accomplish. Inch by inch, Excellencies, Cesare Borgia is slipping into the grave. Florence must not slip with him."

Machiavelli was correct. Pope Julius, convinced at last that both the Venetian threat and Cesare's power were exaggerated, made haste to dissolve his agreement. He demanded that Cesare surrender all of his castles at once. That accomplished, Pope Julius II placed Cesare Borgia under arrest, and sent him to Ostia accompanied by an elderly cardinal and an armed guard to be certain his orders were carried out.

Cesare Borgia turned over the first two fortresses, and wrote to the commanders of others telling them he had been ordered to return them to their former owners. He hoped these messages would be disregarded, at least for a time.

He then asked the elderly cardinal for permission to travel to Naples, now under Spanish control. Believing that Cesare had complied in substance with the Pope's orders, and that he could cause no trouble as long as he stayed out of the Romagna, the cardinal accompanied Cesare to the port at Ostia and put him on a galleon bound for Naples.

In Naples, Cesare had one more card to play: Gonsalvo de Córdoba.

The Spanish were now the sole masters of Naples, allowing them to wield greater influence than ever before throughout Italy. Cesare immediately sought help from Ferdinand and Isabella, for he believed them to be Borgia allies. With their support, he told de Córdoba, he and his loyal men could hold out in his fortresses indefinitely, raise additional troops, and force Julius to make and keep favorable terms.

De Córdoba agreed to present his case to the Spanish monarchs. In what was now Spanish territory, Cesare finally felt safe from the reach of Pope Julius. While he waited for a reply from Ferdinand and Isabella, Cesare sent messages to his remaining commanders urging them not to surrender their fortresses. He also began to assemble mercenaries who could fight side by side with the Spanish under de Córdoba.

For three weeks Cesare waited, and still there was no reply from the Catholic majesties in Spain. Cesare grew restless, filled with apprehension. He could sit still no longer; he must do something!

And so Cesare rode through the coastal hills near Naples, to the Spanish military encampment. There he was escorted to the commander's quarters and shown inside.

Gonsalvo de Córdoba rose from a map-strewn desk to embrace him with a smile. "You look worried, *amigo*."

"*Si, Gonsalvo, claro,*" Cesare said. "I am fighting to hold my fortresses and to raise additional men. But I need your king's support, and then I need you and your men."

"No answer yet, Cesare," de Córdoba said. "But there is a galleon arriving from Valencia at noon tomorrow. If we are lucky, the reply should be on it."

"You say 'no answer.' There is doubt in your mind they will help me?" Cesare asked, puzzled.

"This is not a simple matter, Cesare. You know that very well," de Córdoba told him. "My monarchs have many things to consider. The Pope is your sworn enemy, and he is a hard and vindictive man."

"Of that there is no question," Cesare said. "But Gonsalvo, Ferdinand and Isabella are lifelong friends. It was my father who interceded and made their marriage possible. He was godfather to their first child. And you know I have always supported them . . ."

De Córdoba placed his hand on Cesare's arm. "Be calm, be calm, Cesare," he said. "I know all this. My Catholic majesties know it too. And they do consider you a friend, a loyal one. Tomorrow afternoon we should have their reply, and God willing it will instruct me to throw the full weight of my forces behind your efforts."

Cesare was somewhat comforted by de Córdoba's reassurances. "I'm sure that will be the message, Gonsalvo; and then we must act quickly."

"Absolutely," de Córdoba said. "And without attracting attention before we are ready. There are spies everywhere—even among the workers here in our camp. We must find a meeting place less public. Do you know the old lighthouse on the beach north of here?"

"No," Cesare said, "but I'll find it."

"Good," the captain said. "I'll meet you there at sundown tomorrow. It is then we will plan our strategy."

The following evening, just as the golden sun was sinking below the horizon, Cesare walked along the beach north of the port, alongside water pale as bones, until he saw the old stone lighthouse.

As he got closer, he saw de Córdoba step out from the lighthouse entrance.

In his eagerness, Cesare shouted, "Gonsalvo, what is the news?"

The Spanish commander put his finger to his lips, and spoke in hushed tones. "Quiet, Cesare," he said. "Come inside. We cannot be too careful."

He followed Cesare through the lighthouse door. As Cesare stepped into the darkness inside, he was seized at once by four men. He was quickly disarmed, and just as quickly his hands and feet were bound tight with heavy rope. Then they ripped off his mask.

"What treachery is this, Gonsalvo?" Cesare asked.

De Córdoba lit a candle, and Cesare could see that he was surrounded by a dozen heavily armed Spanish troopers.

"No treachery, Cesare," he said. "I am just obeying the orders of my king and queen. They do recognize you as an old friend, but they also remember your alliance with France, and recognize that the power of the Borgia is ended. It now lies with Pope Julius. And the Holy Father does not consider you a friend."

"Dios mío!" Cesare said. "They forget that Spanish blood flows in my veins!"

"On the contrary, Cesare," de Córdoba said. "They still consider you their subject. And for that reason my orders are to return you to Spain. They will give you sanctuary—in a Valencian prison. I'm sorry, my friend, but you know that my Catholic majesties are extremely devout. They are convinced that both God and the Holy Father will be pleased with their decision." De Córdoba began to move away, but then he turned back to Cesare. "You must also know that your brother Juan's widow, Maria Enriquez, has formally accused you of his murder. And she is a cousin of the king."

Cesare felt so betrayed, he could say nothing.

De Córdoba gave a curt order, and without ceremony Cesare was carried outside and thrown over the back of a mule, struggling ferociously. Then, accompanied by de Córdoba and his troopers, he was transported across the dark beach and taken up into the foothills to the Spanish encampment.

At dawn the next morning, still bound hand and foot, Cesare was gagged, wrapped in a shroud, and placed in a wooden coffin. The coffin was closed and driven by wagon to the port, where it was loaded aboard a Spanish galleon bound for Valencia.

Cesare could not breathe; there was too little room in the small box even to struggle. He tried with all his might to resist his own panic, for he was certain that if he gave in, it could make a madman of him.

De Córdoba had chosen this method of transport, for he had no intention of allowing any Neapolitans still loyal to Cesare to learn that he had been arrested. He felt he had more than sufficient men to repel any rescue attempt. But, as he put it to his lieutenant, "Why take a chance? This way any waterfront spy will see only the coffin of a poor dead Spaniard being carried home for burial."

When the galleon was an hour out at sea, the captain finally gave the order to free Cesare from the coffin and remove his shroud and gag.

Pale and shaking, still bound, he was thrown into a storage locker near the stern of the ship.

The locker was cramped, but filthy as it was, at least it had a vent in its door, better than the stifling coffin in which Cesare had spent his last hours.

Once each day during his journey across the sea, Cesare was fed wormy biscuits and water by one of the crew. Kind and obviously experienced in sea voyaging, the man pounded each biscuit on the deck to knock the worms loose before breaking off pieces to push into Cesare's mouth.

"Sorry about the bonds," he told Cesare. "But the captain ordered it. You stay trussed up until we arrive in Valencia."

After a miserable voyage marked by rough seas, disgusting food, and cramped, foul-smelling quarters, the galleon finally docked at Villanueva del Grao. Ironically this was the same Valencian port from which Cesare's great-uncle Alonso Borgia—later Pope Calixtus—had left Spain for Italy more than sixty years before.

The bustling port was filled with the soldiers of Ferdinand and Isabella, and so there was no further need to disguise or conceal the prisoner.

Once again, Cesare was thrown over the back of a mule and carried down a cobblestone street alongside the harbor to a tall castle which was now a prison. This time he did not fight.

Cesare was pushed into a tiny cell near the top of the castle and there, with four armed guards present, his bonds were finally removed.

Cesare stood, rubbing his sore wrists. He looked around the cell, taking in the stained mattress on the floor, the rusted food bowl, and the foul-smelling slop bucket. Would this be his home for the rest of his life? If so, that would in great likelihood not be long, for his devout friends Ferdinand and Isabella, anxious to please both the new Pope and Juan's widow, would almost certainly decide to torture and kill him.

Days passed, then weeks. And Cesare sat on the floor of his cell trying to keep his mind alert by counting things—roaches on the wall, flyspecks on the ceiling, the number of times each day the tiny slot in his door would open. Once a week, he was allowed an hour of fresh air in the small prison courtyard. On Sundays, he was brought a basin of rancid water with which to cleanse himself.

Was this better than death? he wondered. He could not be certain, but he knew he would find out before too long.

Still, the weeks turned into months and his situation remained the same. There were times he was certain he had gone mad, when he forgot where he was, when he imagined himself walking along the shores of Silverlake, or arguing good-naturedly with his father. He tried not to think of Lucrezia, and yet there were times she seemed to be standing in the same cell, stroking his hair, kissing his lips, talking to him in sweet comforting words.

He had the time now to think about and understand his father, to see what he had tried to do, not fault him for his errors. Was his father as great as he appeared to Cesare? Though he knew it had been a brilliant strategy to secure the bond between himself and Lucrezia, it was also the one thing he felt unforgivable, for it had cost them both too much. Yet would he rather have lived his life without loving her in this way? He could not imagine it, though it had kept him from truly loving any other. And poor Alfonso—how much of his death was due to his own jealousy? He cried that night, tears for himself as well as for his sister's husband. And that naturally led him to the memories of his dear wife, Lottie. She loved him so . . .

That night he was determined to rid himself of his passion for Lucrezia and to live an honorable life with Lottie and his daughter, Louise. If he ever escaped his present fate—if he was granted grace by the Heavenly Father.

Cesare remembered then what his father had said years ago, when Cesare told him he didn't believe in God, the Virgin Mary, or the saints. He could hear his father's voice. "Many sinners say they don't believe in God, because they fear punishment after death. So they try to renounce truth." The Pope had taken Cesare's hands in his own and continued fervently. "Listen, my son, men lose their faith. The cruelties of this world are too much for them, and so they question an everlasting and loving God; they question his infinite mercy. They question the Holy Mother Church. But a man must keep faith alive with action. Even the saints themselves were men of action. I think nothing of those holy men who scourge themselves and ponder the mysterious ways of mankind while hidden away in their monasteries. They do nothing for the living church; they will not help it endure in this temporal world. It is men like you and myself who must do our own particular duty. Even though," and here Alexander raised a commanding papal finger, "our souls may rest for a time in purgatory. When I say my prayers, when I confess my sins, that is my consolation for some of the terrible things I must do. It does not matter what our humanists say, those believers in the Greek philosophies who think that mankind is all that exists. There *is* an Almighty God and he is merciful and he is understanding. That is our faith. And you must believe. Live with your sins, confess them or not, but never lose faith."

At the time the Pope's speech had meant nothing to Cesare. Now, though he struggled with faith, he had confessed to whatever God could hear. But back then the only words he heard were these: "Remember, my son, you are my brightest hope for the future of the Borgia."

One night, after midnight, Cesare saw his cell door swing quietly open. Expecting a guard on some late mission, he saw instead Duarte Brandao carrying a coil of rope.

"Duarte, what in heaven's name are you doing here?" Cesare asked, his heart beating wildly.

"Rescuing you, my friend," Duarte answered. "But hurry. We must leave at once."

"What about the guards?" Cesare asked.

"They have been handsomely bribed—a skill I mastered long ago," Duarte said as he uncoiled the rope.

"We're going to climb down that?" Cesare asked, frowning. "It looks too short."

"It is," Duarte said, smiling. "I have it here only for show, to protect the guards. Their commander will believe that is how you escaped." Duarte tied the rope to an iron bracket in the wall and threw it out the window, then turned to Cesare. "We will take a much easier route."

Cesare followed Duarte down the circular staircase of the castle, and out a small door in the rear of the building. No guard was in sight. Duarte ran to the spot where the rope he had thrown was dangling from the window, far short of the ground. He reached in the pocket of his cloak and pulled out what looked like a terra-cotta flask.

He said, "Chicken blood. I'll spread some on the ground below the rope, then in a trail leading south. They'll think you were hurt jumping from the rope and limped off in that direction. But in truth you are going north."

Cesare and Duarte made their way across a field and climbed to a hilltop where two horses were waiting, held by a small boy.

"Where are we going, Duarte?" Cesare asked. "Very few places are safe for either of us."

"You are correct, Cesare—very few," Duarte said. "But there are some still. You will ride to the castle of your brother-in-law, the king of Navarre. He's expecting you. You'll be welcome there and safe."

"And you, Duarte?" Cesare asked. "Where will you go? Italy would be deadly. Spain, after tonight, will be fatal as well. You never trusted the French. Nor they you, for that matter. So where?"

"I have a small boat waiting on the beach not too far from here," Duarte said. "I'll sail it to England."

"To England, Sir Edward?" Cesare said, with a small smile.

Duarte looked up, surprised. "So you knew? All along?"

"Father suspected for years," Cesare said. "But won't you encounter a hostile king—perhaps a deadly one?"

"Possibly. But Henry Tudor is a shrewd, practical man, one who tries to gather able men to advise and assist him. In fact, I have lately heard rumored that he has inquired after my whereabouts, which have been unknown to him. He has given a strong indication that, if I return to serve him, I might find amnesty and perhaps even the restoration of my former status. Which, I must admit, was quite a handsome one. This may, of course, be a trap. But, realistically, what choice do I have?"

"None, I suppose. But, Duarte, can you sail that far alone?"

"Oh, I've sailed farther than that, Cesare. And over the years I've come to enjoy solitude."

Duarte paused. "Well, my friend, it's growing late," he said. "We must go our separate ways."

They embraced there on the hilltop, lit by the bright Spanish moon. Then Cesare backed away. "Duarte, I shall never forget you. Godspeed and fair sailing!"

He turned, leapt on his horse, and rode off in the direction of Navarre before Duarte could see the tears streaming down his cheeks.

30

Alert to the danger of being recaptured by Spanish militia combing the countryside, Cesare avoided all towns and rode only at night, sleeping in the woods during the day. Filthy and exhausted, he finally reached Navarre, in the north tip of the Iberian peninsula.

Cesare was expected by his brother-in-law, for Duarte had told the king of his coming. He was quickly passed through the gate and escorted to a spacious room overlooking the river.

By the time Cesare had bathed and dressed in the clothes provided for him, a soldier arrived to lead him to the royal apartments.

There, King Jean of Navarre, a large man with tanned skin and a trim beard, embraced him warmly.

"My dear brother, how good to see you!" Jean said. "I have heard all about you from Charlotte, of course, and you are welcome here. Oh, we have minor skirmishes with disorderly barons from time to time, but nothing that would threaten your safety or peace of mind. So rest, relax, and enjoy yourself. Stay as long as you like. And, for God's sake, we must have the royal tailor make you some clothes!"

Cesare was immensely grateful to this man, whom he had never before met, and who was saving his life. He had no intention of leaving that debt unpaid, especially after leaving his dear Lottie in France so long ago.

"I thank you, Your Majesty, for your gracious hospitality," Cesare said. "But I would like to assist you in these 'minor skirmishes' about which you have spoken. For I have experience in war, and would be pleased to put that experience at your service."

King Jean smiled. "Well, of course you may. I know of your exploits." He drew his sword and playfully touched it to Cesare's shoulder. "I make thee commander of the royal army. I should tell you, however, that the previous commander was blown to bits last week." The king laughed now, showing dazzling white teeth.

For two days Cesare rested, for he was completely exhausted. He slept around the clock, but as soon as he woke, after dressing himself in his new clothing—complete with armor and weapons—he went to inspect the army he was to command. Beginning with the cavalry, he saw that they were experienced professionals, well trained and well led. They would carry themselves well in battle.

Next Cesare inspected the artillery. There were twenty-four guns, clean and in fair shape. The gunners, like the cavalry, seemed to be battle-hardened veterans. They might not be the equal of Vito Vitelli's unit, but they would serve.

The infantry was another story. Comprised mostly of local peasants reporting periodically for military service, they were willing enough, but ill equipped and apparently ill trained. When trouble came, he would have to count on the cavalry and artillery to do the job.

The next few weeks passed peacefully. Strangely, they were the happiest times Cesare could remember, other than perhaps his time with Charlotte and the days at Silverlake. For once, his life was not in danger. There was no need to scheme against anyone, and no one was scheming against him.

King Jean was a charming companion, who seemed grateful for Cesare's company. He was kind, and Cesare had no fear of betrayal. They spent virtually every day together, riding and hunting, and he felt about Jean as he would have liked to about his brothers. Evenings, after supper, they sat by the fire discussing books they had read, the methods of good government, and the responsibilities of leadership. They even had a wrestling match. But though Cesare won, it wasn't a true victory, for he was certain that the muscular, chivalrous king had surrendered out of fondness for him.

Cesare felt secure for the first time in years. And so he told the king, "I believe it is finally time to send for my wife and child. For since we have parted I have written Lottie, and sent gifts for her and the child; but more than once I have planned to send for them, only to face some new crisis, some new peril that would put them at too great a risk."

Jean, Charlotte's brother and now Cesare's as well, agreed with great enthusiasm. They toasted the time when she would arrive.

At midnight, in his quarters, Cesare picked up a quill and wrote to his wife at the Château de la Motte Feuilly in the Dauphine.

> *My dearest Lottie,*
>
> *At last the news I've wanted to send you for so long. I believe that it is time for you to join me here in Navarre—with la petite Louise. Of course Jean has been a staunch friend, and the situation here permits all of us to be together—finally. I know the trip will be long and arduous, but once you are here we will never be parted again.*
>
> *Yours in Love,*
> *C.*

Cesare sent the letter by royal courier the following day. He knew it would be months before Charlotte and the child could join him, but his heart filled with joy at the thought.

A few days later, as Cesare joined the king at supper, Jean's mood was sullen and he was quiet with rage. "What is it that troubles you, brother?" Cesare asked. The king was so angry he could barely speak, but when he began he could hardly stop. "Count Louis de Beaumonte has been causing me trouble for months. His men steal the cattle and grain from our villages, which is a disaster for the people. His bishop pretends to be on a mission for the church but instead contacts my officers, offering them lands and money to betray me. Now he has gone further still. And now it is too far. Today his soldiers burned a village to the ground, slaughtered every man, and of course raped every woman. This was not some random escapade by an unknown drunk, Cesare. Beaumonte has designs on a significant portion of my lands. And his tactic is terror. He will terrorize the villagers until they desert me and support him, in order to save their own lives and homes."

Again treachery, like a dragon from the depths, had reared its head. Cesare recognized it, and was afraid for Jean.

The king slammed his fist on the table, spilling his wine. "I will stop him! At once! As ruler of Navarre, I owe my subjects protection. They should not have to live in fear. Tomorrow I will lead a raid on his castle at Viana. There, I will drive him out or kill him."

Cesare said, "You are a true king. You should order such a raid, Jean. But you must not lead it yourself. For it is too dangerous a battle, and you are much too important to your people to risk your person. I am truly grateful for all you have done for me, when I had no chance at life except for you. I beg that you allow me to lead the attack. For I have led many, and we will succeed."

The king finally agreed, swayed by Cesare's logic. That night the two men spent hours studying a map of Viana's fortifications, and planning strategies for the following day.

It was before dawn when Cesare awoke. The king's army had arrived, and was waiting. His mount, a spirited bay stallion, was impatiently stomping his foot at the gate. The army wound its way out of the castle, and with Cesare leading they crossed fields, climbed hills and streams, and finally arrived before the walls of Louis de Beaumonte's castle.

Cesare studied the fortress. The walls were high and well

designed. But Cesare had seen higher, better walls. Compared to Forli and Faenza, this should be no difficult task.

Cesare deployed his men as he had so many times before, then donned light armor and prepared himself to fight once again. He himself would lead the charge of the cavalry; given the infantry's condition, Cesare knew that charge would be critical—it could carry the day.

Recalling the lessons he had learned from Vito Vitelli, Cesare began by spreading his cannons around the perimeter of the walls and protecting them with units of cavalry and infantry. Once that was accomplished, he ordered them to fire initially at the ramparts. This behavior would kill or disable many of the defenders and reduce the ultimate risk to Cesare's own forces. The artillery officers passed on his orders, and the bombardment began.

It went well. Time after time, as the guns fired, portions of the upper walls crumbled and fell on all sides of the castle. As the cannons continued their fire, Cesare could hear the screams of the defenders who had been mutilated or blown off the ramparts by the ceaseless attack.

But now, after more than an hour, it was time to change his tactics. Cesare instructed that all cannons be wheeled to one side of the castle. Then he ordered their fire directed to a single section of the wall no more than fifty feet wide. There, thought Cesare, is where my cavalry charge will strike.

This castle was not as well built as those Cesare had attacked in Italy. The walls began to sway with each barrage, and Cesare knew the end was near.

It was then he gave the command for the cavalry to prepare to charge. The cavalry officers passed on his command, and each of the mounted men placed a deadly-looking lance under his arm in the attack position. Each was wearing a sword as well, and even if dismounted would be a formidable foe.

Cesare himself mounted his bay charger, placing his own lance at the ready. He checked his sword and the spike-

studded mace that hung from his saddle, ready for use if he
were dismounted and lost his sword.

Cesare's fighting spirit was aroused. But it was more than
that. This was not just another battle for conquest. This king
had been kind to him, had saved his life, had become a friend.

Moreover, Cesare knew all too well what a vicious baron
like Beaumonte could do if left unchecked. He owed it to the
king to put an end to Louis de Beaumonte.

Now Cesare heard the familiar cry: "A breach, a breach!"
A huge, jagged hole had been opened in the wall, through
which his cavalrymen could pass unimpeded and take the
castle.

His heart beating mightily, Cesare turned and shouted at
his troops to charge the wall. Pulling down the visor of his
helmet, he spurred his charger straight ahead directly at the
breach.

But as he raced toward the wall, he knew suddenly that
something was terribly wrong. There was no sound of
hooves beside him.

Without stopping, he turned in the saddle.

Behind him, where he had left them, the entire cavalry
troop was standing motionless. With horror, he realized that
not a man had followed him.

Any moment the castle reserve would rush to the breach,
and without a cavalry charge, they would be difficult to
dislodge.

Cesare slowed his charger. He turned again toward his
cavalry unit, raised his visor, and bellowed, "Charge, you
cowards!"

But once again the entire cavalry unit stood unmoving.

Now Cesare understood. These dastardly men had been
bought and paid for. They were betraying their king . . . his
friend, his savior, Jean of Navarre.

Well, he would not!

Cesare hesitated no more. He lowered his visor, secured
his lance, and raced into the breach . . . alone.

There was dust and confusion everywhere. Immediately,

hordes of reservists with pikes, spears, and swords rushed toward him. He rode into the pack, and they scattered. But he had slain only two with his lance. Now the enemy regrouped and swarmed around him again.

Instinctively Cesare fought, his sword in one hand, his mace in the other. One enemy after another fell, cut down by his sword or smashed to the ground by his mace.

Then, suddenly, Cesare's horse went down, and he was on the ground, rolling to one side to avoid the sharp thrusts of the enemy pikes. He leapt to his feet, his mace gone now, but still he slashed out with his sword in all directions.

Yet there were too many of them—just too many. And suddenly they were all around him, stabbing and hacking at him. He felt the sharp pain of a spear thrust into his armpit. He felt weak; he was losing blood now. Then he heard a voice, a comforting sound: *"In arms and by arms . . ."* He thought of Lucrezia. Then he slipped to the ground, and all thought ceased.

Cesare Borgia was dead.

EPILOGUE

Cesare Borgia, who had been a cardinal, a duke, and a *gonfaloniere*, was honored in an elaborate ceremony in Rome conducted by his brother, Cardinal Jofre Borgia, and Pope Julius himself. Afterward, his ashes were placed beneath a huge monument in the Church of Santa Maria Maggiore. It was said that Pope Julius wanted Cesare where he could keep an eye on him even after death.

But Lucrezia Borgia had arranged for her brother's ashes to be stolen by Michelotto and placed in a golden urn. Michelotto, who had by some miracle stayed alive, then rode through the night to bring them to her in Ferrara.

The following day, Lucrezia set off with a retinue of three hundred nobles and men at arms, and led the funeral cortege on the long journey to Silverlake.

Tents were pitched along the shore. There were the usual penitents from the Tolfa mines only ten miles away and mistresses of some of the high-ranking clergymen shedding their repentant tears into the waters. Lucrezia's men cleared them away.

From the hilly ground above, she could see the spires of Rome. And it brought back memories of when she had been a carnal sinner, when she had suffered pangs of fear for her brother and her father because of what she knew of them. Like many other sinners, she had come to this lake to be cleansed of her sinful desires, truly believing that the magical waters would wash away her temptations, for the lake had a reputation for providing solace, for reforming evildoers.

But her father, the Pope, with his sly yet good-humored smile, reminded her that there was nothing as treacherous as the evildoer seeking redemption. After all, such a person was a proven example of weakness of character, prone to shifting winds.

Now, Lucrezia sat by the lake in her golden tent and felt those silvery waters bring her a peace she had never really known before. Her father and her brother were dead. And her destiny was settled. She would give birth to more children; she would help rule Ferrara; she would be just, and above all merciful, for the remainder of her life.

She would never rival her father and brother in worldly achievement, but that was of no consequence, for she would be what they never were. Sadly, she acknowledged in her heart that they were never truly merciful. She remembered how Cesare had punished the Roman satirist Filofila, who had composed the scurrilous verses about the Borgia clan. What did all that matter now? What was the harm in words? Would anyone ever truly believe them?

And so she had brought Cesare's ashes to Silverlake, as if his mortal remains could be tempted to sin even yet. Or as some sort of pilgrimage to atone for her own sins of the flesh, the only sins of which she was guilty and of which she would be guilty no more. Finally, she would be redeemed.

And that brought her back with fondness to the memory of her father. A cardinal of the Holy Church when she was born, a loving and dutiful father when he was Pope and the Vicar of Christ. Did his soul roast in hell forevermore for his sins? If she could feel mercy, how could not an all-powerful God? She remembered then what her father had said when she wept over Cesare's murder of her husband.

"God will forgive them both," he had told her. "Otherwise there is no reason for His being. And one day, when our worldly tragedy is done, we will all be together again."

Near nightfall, the lake had taken on a silvery glow. Lucrezia walked slowly out onto the small dock from which they had swum and dived as children. And in her mind, she could hear her brother Cesare's voice as it sounded when she was a child. "No, Crezia, it's too shallow." "Don't worry, Crezia, I'll save you." And later, when they were older, with more of their lives lived and some dreams destroyed, his voice again, promising, "If that is what you want, Crezia, I'll try to help." Then, when she had seen him for the very last time, his plea: "If I'm ever killed, Crezia, you must live for me." And she had promised she would.

As she walked to the end of the dock the night began to envelop her in its shimmering darkness, and she saw the pale moon rise just over the cedars. It was then Lucrezia removed the cover from the urn, and slowly scattered Cesare's ashes into Silverlake.

Later, as she reached the shore again, several of the penitents walking back through the hills after their day of prayer and penance noticed her.

One beautiful young woman turned to the young man she was with and pointed to Lucrezia. "Who is that lovely woman?" she asked him.

"Lucrezia d'Este, the good and merciful duchess of Ferrara," he said. "Have you never heard of her?"

AFTERWORD

Carol Gino

The biggest surprise for me when I first met Mario Puzo was that he was nothing like his characters. The Mario I came to know was a husband, a father, a lover, a mentor, and a true friend. He was kind and generous, authentic as any human being could be, true and funny and smart. From him came the loyalty, the fairness, the compassion that he wrote about in his books, but not the villainy. That aspect came from his nightmares, not from his dreams. He was a shy, soft-spoken, generous man who held very few judgments about others. We spent twenty years together, playing, brainstorming, and working.

Mario was fascinated with Renaissance Italy, and especially with the Borgia family. He swore that they were the original crime family, and that their adventures were much more treacherous than any of the stories he told about the Mafia. He believed the Popes were the first Dons—Pope Alexander the greatest Don of all.

For most of the years we spent together, Mario told Borgia stories. Their escapades both shocked and amused him, and he even rewrote some of the incidents to make them contemporary enough to put in his Mafia books.

One of Mario's greatest pleasures was traveling, and we did it often. After we visited the Vatican in 1983, he was so enchanted by the look, feel, and food of Italy, so taken by its

history, that he wanted to write a novel about it. It was that
many years ago that he began to write the Borgia book,
though even then he referred to it as "just another family
story." Although he would write several other novels in the
years between, each time he had difficulty writing, each
time his creativity felt blocked or he felt discouraged, he
went back to the Borgia book for inspiration or refuge.

"I wish I could write a book with this material and have it
make a lot of money," he told me one day as he was lying on
the couch in his study, staring at the ceiling as he always did.

"Why don't you?" I asked.

"I was a struggling writer until I was forty-eight years old,
honey," he said. "I wrote two books the reviewers called
classics, and only made five thousand dollars. It was only
after I wrote *The Godfather* that I could feed my family. I
was poor for too long to take a chance on something different this late in life."

After his heart attack in 1992, I asked him again, "Have
you thought about the Borgia book?"

"I have to write two more Mafia books first, and then I'll
be set," he said. "Besides, I still enjoy hanging out with
those characters. I'm not sure I'm ready to let them go just
yet."

During the time we spent in Malibu while he was recovering from his heart surgery, whenever he was uncomfortable or wanted a diversion, he read books on the Italian
Renaissance and scribbled Borgia pages for me to read and
us to discuss.

Mario was a very funny man with a unique way of looking at things.

"Lucrezia was a good girl," he said one day while we
were working in his study. And I laughed.

"And the rest of the family?" I asked. "They were the villains?"

"Cesare was a patriot who desired to be a hero. Alexander was a doting father, a true family man," he said. "Like most people, they did some bad things, but that didn't make them bad people." That day we talked and laughed about them for hours, and later that night he completed the scene of Cesare and the Pope fighting over whether he wanted to be a cardinal.

During this time he was only willing to leave his house and go out to dinner when Bert Fields was coming into town. Bert is not only a distinguished historian and lawyer, but was also one of Mario's dearest friends. Each time we met, whether it was on the east coast or the west, the dinner conversation somehow always came back to the Borgias. Bert was as excited and amused about the power and treachery of the Renaissance as Mario. "When are you going to get the Borgia book together?" Bert always asked.

"I'm working on it," Mario would say.

"He's got a bunch of it done," I told Bert.

And Bert seemed pleased.

As time went on, Mario called Bert frequently to trade stories, asking questions and sharing observations. Each time he finished a conversation with Bert, Mario and I would talk about the Borgias, and he was excited again about writing the stories of the Family.

I'll help you finish the Borgia book," I offered one day in 1995, after we'd spent a particularly interesting day talking about the nature of love, relationships, and betrayal.

"I don't collaborate until after I'm dead," he said, smiling at me.

"Okay," I said. "But then what do I do with an unfinished book?" I sounded calmer than I felt.

He laughed at me. "Finish it," he said.

"I can't finish it. I don't remember what you taught me," I said, unable even to imagine living in a world without him.

He patted me on the shoulder and said, "You can do it. You know the story. I've written so much of it and we've

MARIO PUZO

talked about it for years. You can fill in the missing pieces."
Then he touched my cheek, and said, "I really have taught
you all I know."

Two weeks before he died, though his heart was failing,
Mario was still completely lucid. And one day, as I was sitting in his study across from his desk, he reached down and
pulled a bunch of pages, handwritten in red felt marker on
yellow lined paper, from the bottom drawer of his desk. I
thought it was something from *Omerta*, but it wasn't. "Read
it," he said, and handed it to me.

And as I read I began to cry. It was the last chapter of the
Borgia book.

"Finish it," he said. "Promise me."

And so I did.